A LOVE THROUGH TIME

"Are you thinking of going back again?"

Sarah whirled to find herself facing Damien. He stood across from her, all in black, staring at her with beautiful, anguished dark eyes. Her heart sang with joy that he had come to her. "Oh, Damien! Have you forgiven me at last?"

Sarah seemed to fly across the room into his arms. She kissed him feverishly, trembling as he clutched her close. Excitement raced along her nerve endings as he groaned and kissed her back with a vehemence to match her own.

He drew back and brushed a tear from her eyelash with his thumb. "Are you thinking of going back again?" he repeated anxiously.

Sarah blinked at him. In her joy at seeing him, she hadn't really heard his question the first time. "You knew!" she whispered as realization dawned. "You knew I came from another time!"

A TRYST IN TIME

EUGENIA RILEY

LOVE SPELL **NEW YORK CITY**

*With love to my daughters Lienna and Noelle—
because the only thing they ever agreed on
was this book.*

A LOVE SPELL BOOK®

January 2001

Published by

Dorchester Publishing Co., Inc.
276 Fifth Avenue
New York, NY 10001

ISBN 0-505-52419-8

Printed in the United States of America.

Visit us on the web at www.dorchesterpub.com.

Faith is to believe what we do not see; and the reward of this faith is to see what we believe.

—*St. Augustine*

Prologue

Atlanta, Georgia—September, 1967

For the third night, the dream came to Sarah Jennings, with its strange, haunting message: *Elissa . . . The three gifts . . . The answer is Elissa. . . .* Endlessly, the words replayed themselves through the caverns of her mind, like a litany, a prophecy, a dirge. *The three gifts . . . Elissa . . . The answer is Elissa.* A voice was calling her, bidding her to follow it. From whence it came, she did not know. There was smoke there and mists and a peace deep, dark and beckoning.

And still the message came. *The answer is Elissa. . . .*

Sarah awakened to the coolness of an early September morning and the chirping of a mockingbird outside the window of her downstairs apartment. At first she smiled and stretched. Then pain washed over her, as it had every morning for the past four months.

Brian was dead. His light was gone from her life forever. The only time she didn't hurt was in those brief, slumberous moments between sleep and awakening. When she first stirred in the morning, she would know a momentary wholeness and peace; then awareness would dawn, and pain would shatter her anew.

Sarah got out of bed, putting on her quilted satin robe and terry scuffs. At least she was feeling the pain of her brother's death now; her psychiatrist, Dr. Hogan, had said this was a good sign, following her breakdown. She was well on the way to recovery, he'd said.

Recovery in a world where she felt out of sync.

Sarah headed down the hallway toward the kitchen, passing her own oil paintings on the walls—soft, impressionistic splashes of color, mostly landscapes of the hills surrounding Atlanta and paintings of old homes in the historic districts of town. Sarah's art was very much in demand these days, which was odd, since her romantic style was definitely out-of-vogue, anachronistic. She'd often thought of her own work as a single voice of old-fashioned grace and elegance in a sea of abstract expressionism.

Yet even that wellspring of creativity had dried up in her with Brian's passing. She hadn't touched a paintbrush ever since the day she had learned of his death.

Now the odd dream had come for three nights in a row. What on earth had that strange, cryptic message meant? *Elissa . . . The three gifts . . . The answer is Elissa . . .* As an artist, Sarah was heavily into symbols. What could the three gifts represent? Light, dark and shadow? The sun, the moon and the earth? The Trinity?

She smiled ruefully. Dr. Hogan would doubtless have a Jungian field day with this particular dream.

She wondered if the dream could somehow be a message from Brian. She sighed. At least this dream was more bearable than the nightmares she'd had for so long—agonizing episodes where she would hear Brian screaming out for help. Each time, the harrowing vision was so real; each time, Sarah would find herself tied to a chair, locked in a dark room, powerless to go to his aid. At last she'd awaken, drenched in sweat, gasping for breath, the pain like a vise on her heart. Those very dreams had precipitated her breakdown, and she shuddered at the memory.

Out in the kitchen, Sarah placed coffee grounds and water in the percolator and turned it on. Answers. The dream had mentioned answers, and Sarah Jennings was a young woman desperately in need of answers right now. She was living in a world where she felt displaced—the twentieth century, with its technology and wars, its riots and unrest. Even before the turmoil of the sixties, Sarah had never quite felt comfortable in the age in which she lived. She disliked much of the art, literature and music of the later twentieth century; her paintings, her tastes and mind-set were all fixed in an earlier, more romantic age. And ever since Brian's death, her feeling of displacement had grown stronger than ever.

Idly, she flipped on the black and white TV on the countertop. A few seconds later, the morning news showed a picture of dying soldiers being carried to a helicopter in Vietnam.

Reeling, Sarah turned off the set, gripping the countertop for support. *Oh, Brian. You dear, sweet fool. I loved you so. Why did you do this to me? Why did you have to be such a free spirit? Why couldn't you have listened? Now you're gone, and the world has lost your beautiful talent forever.*

Sarah poured herself a cup of coffee, lifted the cup with a trembling hand and took a long sip. Let yourself feel it, Dr. Hogan had urged. Grief is a process you can't short-circuit. Sarah knew that she had anesthetized herself with her breakdown, that she had totally withdrawn from life. Now she had to learn to feel the pain again, just as she had to feel the scalding sting of the coffee on her tongue. At least the pain proved she was alive.

Only it hurt so much. Hurt to know her beloved brother Brian, a violinist with world-class potential, had been senselessly killed in a rice paddie in Vietnam, all because he'd rashly gone bicycling through Europe with some friends, instead of going on to college as he was supposed to. He'd been only 18 years old when he'd been drafted. Such a waste.

The doorbell rang, drawing Sarah out of her painful thoughts. She drew a hand through her shoulder-length blond hair and headed for the front of her apartment. She opened the door to find the elderly postman standing on the porch of the old, converted mansion; the cool morning breeze, with its scent of jasmine, swept over her.

"Good morning, Mr. McAllister," she said.

"Good morning, Sarah." Smiling, he held out a letter. "Registered mail."

Sarah reached out for the letter, unaware that her life was about to change forever.

12

Chapter One

New Orleans, Louisiana—September, 1967

On a balmy afternoon two and a half weeks later, Sarah Jennings drove her '67 Mustang convertible down St. Charles Avenue in New Orleans, gliding past stately Greek Revival mansions and graceful oaks lining the famous old thoroughfare. She'd put the top down, and she loved the feel of the Gulf breeze caressing her face. She wore a sleeveless blouse, a wraparound skirt, and sandals; her long blond hair was blowing free. The air smelled marvelous, scented with nectar and morning dew. The radio was playing, "Cast Your Fate to the Wind."

Sarah had just spent a day and a half at the Garden District home of Brenda Birmingham, her old roommate from college. Now, she was on her way to Meridian, a small burg about 30 miles north of the city. In the trunk, she'd packed enough clothing for an extensive stay in Louisiana, and she'd optimistically included her oils, canvases and brushes.

Sarah thought of how radically her life had changed in the last two weeks, ever since that fateful morning when Mr. MacAllister had delivered the letter from Louisiana. The correspondence had been from a lawyer, Jefferson Baldwin of Meridian. Baldwin had written to inform Sarah that she had inherited the entire estate of a distant cousin, Erica Davis, whom Sarah had never even met. Sarah had been flabbergasted, and her own family back in Atlanta had been able to shed little light on her cousin's astonishing bequest. When Sarah had phoned Baldwin in Meridian, he'd informed her that the estate was sizable, that there was a large amount of real estate involved, and that she would need to come to Louisiana to take charge of her new holdings and to decide what she wanted to do with her inheritance.

The prospect had appealed to Sarah. She'd been in a mood for a major change in her life, anyway. Indeed, the very night after Baldwin's letter had arrived, she'd broken up with her fiancé of three years, Bill Bartley.

Sarah's eyes gleamed with bitterness at the memory. She and Bill had grown up together, and she'd always known that he hadn't wanted children, but not until that night had she realized how deep his aversion went. They'd been sitting in Sarah's apartment, sipping coffee and listening to the Beatles, when Bill had abruptly announced that he'd recently had a vasectomy, because he "didn't want to bring children into this troubled world." Sarah had been stunned and crushed to learn that Bill had made this decision without even consulting her, and she had suspected that Bill had had himself steri-

14

lized mainly because he was too self-absorbed to ever become a good father.

They'd argued heatedly about his rash action. To Bill, the entire matter was "no big deal;" he'd even smugly pointed out that now they wouldn't have to worry about birth control. Sarah had lashed out at him bitterly, and ultimately she had shown him the door.

She'd discussed her breakup with Bill and her decision to go to Louisiana with her psychiatrist the next day. Dr. Hogan had been understandably concerned about the drastic turns Sarah was taking with her life. She remembered him frowning at her from behind his desk.

"Sarah, didn't I warn you not to make any major life changes in the first few months after your release from the hospital? Now you've broken up with Bill, and you say you want to run off and live in some obscure little burg in Louisiana?"

"I told you that I have to take charge of my inheritance," Sarah had argued. "As for Bill, can you blame me for feeling betrayed? Good Lord, I didn't even know what a vasectomy was until he told me last night."

Hogan had sighed. "I realize how shocked and hurt you were, but Bill has also been a big part of your life for many years. Don't you think that cutting yourself off from him totally is a bit drastic at this point?"

"And what he did to me wasn't?" Sarah asked indignantly.

"The vasectomy was extreme, of course. But would you really have wanted Bill to become a father if his heart wasn't in it?"

"No," she admitted readily. "And that's one major reason we can't make it together. I want children

15

someday." She shook her head. "Anyway, sometimes I think Bill and I only got engaged because our families have always wanted the marriage. The truth is, he barely tolerates my sensibilities. As far as he's concerned, I ruined myself by going off to Sarah Lawrence to study art. He likes my family's standing in the social register, all right, but he doesn't approve of my liberal attitudes, my tastes in music, or my Flower Child clothing."

Dr. Hogan had chuckled. "Are you certain you're not rejecting Bill simply because he's a conservative establishment lawyer?"

"Our differences go much deeper than that," Sarah had assured him. "Even our sex life has always been more mechanical than truly satisfying. Still," she added, hoping to sway him, "it's something I could think about while I'm away."

Dr. Hogan leaned toward Sarah, lacing his fingers together on the desktop. "Sarah, I just hope you've thought this through. So often, when people break contact with their loved ones this way, then go off by themselves—"

"I'm not contemplating suicide, if that's what you're hinting," Sarah had cut in. Then, almost dreamily, she had added, "I'm searching for something."

He looked intrigued. "What?"

For a moment, she thought of telling him about her dream of Elissa and the three gifts, but somehow, the experience seemed too profound and personal to share as yet. She shrugged and said, "I don't know. Something."

"And you think you'll find what you're looking for in Louisiana?"

"I hope to find something simpler, something healing." She looked him square in the eye and continued earnestly, "Dr. Hogan, I'd like to start fresh somewhere. I might even be able to get back into my painting. Here there are just too many memories. Brian's grave is here. And even at my apartment, every time I look at the phone, and remember getting that call . . ."

Dr. Hogan nodded. "Okay, Sarah, I see your point. Maybe a change in environment will help you. As long as you realize that you can't really run away from your problems."

"Believe me, I do," she'd said ruefully.

"All right, then. I'll support you in this—with two conditions. First, you're to stay in touch with me and your parents, phone us at least once or twice a month."

"Okay. And second?"

"I want you to take instruction in transcendental meditation before you leave Atlanta. In fact, I'm sure I can get you signed up with a new group that's beginning early next week."

Sarah had rolled her eyes. For weeks, Dr. Hogan had been trying to get her interested in TM. "You never give up, do you?"

"Sarah, the lessons only take a few days, and we can postpone your checking session until you return. TM could help you get through your artistic block and could also aid with the healing process. It's wonderful for alleviating stress."

Sarah had sighed. "Okay, you've got me convinced. I guess if it's good enough for the Beatles, it's good enough for me."

Dr. Hogan had raised an eyebrow at that. "Just remember that I endorse TM—but not the drugs some people have associated with it. And Sarah . . ."

"Yes?"

Smiling, Hogan said, "I think you're doing quite well, but don't be surprised if more of your pain over Brian spills to the surface in the coming weeks or months. It's only natural. Try not to fight it."

Sarah had nodded with painful resignation. "I know. I've got to move through it, right?"

In the following days, as she prepared to leave town, Sarah had dutifully taken her instruction in TM from a local disciple of the Maharishi Mahesh Yogi. She had found the lessons enjoyable and enlightening, and she had even begun daily meditation on her own.

Sarah's parents had not been pleased by her plans to leave Georgia, especially since she'd also had to tell them of breaking up with Bill. But when she'd told them of Dr. Hogan's support, they at last had quit fighting the idea.

Then, just as Sarah was feeling comfortable about her decision to depart, Bill had called. He'd learned from her mother that she was planning to go to Louisiana. He'd seemed convinced that her breaking up with him had been just an angry whim and had urged her to stay and work on their relationship.

Sarah sighed at the memory. She had a feeling she hadn't heard the last of Bill Bartley.

On the outskirts of New Orleans, Sarah pulled into a sleepy-looking gas station. A hound was dozing near the front door, and a blond attendant in overalls came out to greet her. "Hello, ma'am. Fill 'er up?"

Sarah smiled at the man. He looked to be in his early twenties and was husky, blue-eyed and very attractive. He reminded her of Troy Donahue, one of her favorite movie stars. "Yes, thank you. Better check the tires and under the hood, too."

"Yes, ma'am." He had started pumping the gas and was now washing the windshield. "Georgia plates, I see. You're quite a long way from home, aren't you, miss?"

"That's true."

"Just passing through?"

"Yes. I'm on my way to Meridian."

The man grinned. "Aw, shucks. I was hoping a pretty thing like you might be sticking around New Orleans."

Sarah smiled. She knew the attendant was flirting with her, but she didn't mind. She glanced at the gloss of sweat on his tanned arms and shoulders and watched his muscles ripple as he worked. She surprisingly found that he stirred something in her, something she had assumed was long-dead.

As he cleaned the side view mirror with a chamois, she caught a brief glimpse of her own face—a long, attractive oval with large blue eyes, a straight nose and full mouth. Sarah was 25 now, but with her youthful attire and straight long hair, she looked younger. Her eyes appeared fresher and more alert than they had in a long time, she noted. Something was springing back to life in her. Of course, her pain over Brian's death was still there—perhaps it would always be there—but she was beginning to feel more free than she had in months.

The man was now peering under the hood. "Everything looks fine here," he said as he checked the oil. He whistled. "289 V-8. Hey, ma'am, this car is out of sight."

"Thanks," she called as the hood slammed down.

After he checked the tires, Sarah handed him some bills. "You be careful now," he said. "You're

some brave lady, going through the South all alone
—after everything that's been happening, all them
riots."

"I know, but things seem calmer now."

He frowned as he stuffed the bills in a pocket of
his overalls. "It sure was a shock to me when I got
home from 'Nam to see everything going on in this
country, all the demonstrations against the war."

At once, Sarah's interest was piqued. "You were
in Vietnam?"

"Yes, ma'am. Army First Division, the Big Red
One. Just got home in May."

"My brother was with the Twenty-Fifth Infantry.
He was killed in May," Sarah added tightly.

He shook his head, giving her a look of warm
sympathy. "Hey, ma'am, I'm sorry. But you know it
was rough on those of us that made it back, too.
When I returned, there were members of my own
family that turned their backs on me. Hell, I didn't
want to go to 'Nam in the first place. I was drafted.
But the way some folks carry on about it—I don't
know what this country's coming to."

"I know what you mean," Sarah murmured.
"Take care, will you?"

"Yes, ma'am. You, too."

As Sarah pulled out of the station, she glanced at
the attendant in her rearview mirror. He stood
watching her drive away, his stance casually masculine, the chamois hanging out of one pocket. She
smiled to herself. Too bad she wasn't the type for a
one-night stand. He had stirred something in her, all
right. He'd proven she was alive.

And he'd also been the first stranger she'd told of
Brian's death. She wondered at the ease of her
disclosure. Kindred spirits were often found in odd
places, she mused.

For the first time in months, things were looking a little brighter.

Moments later, Sarah's car emerged out on River Road, which followed the contour of the Mississippi River from New Orleans to Baton Rouge.

Sarah was entranced as she drove slowly down the moss-laden road, past spectacular Greek Revival mansions, recessed from the roadway at the end of alleys of sweeping, magnificent live oaks. Some of the houses were meticulously kept, while others had fallen to ruin; yet even the decaying mansions cast their own majestic, ghostly spell. Sarah poignantly wished that Brian could be here with her to see the "Grand Parade." She and Brian had shared an interest in old houses, and they had even made a few trips together to Savannah and Charleston to tour antebellum mansions.

Lagoons snaked off from the roadway, and Sarah caught glimpses of swamps teeming with cypress and tupelo trees, of waters near choked by thick vegetation—duckweed, yellow pond lilies, giant blue irises and water hyacinth. Large blue and white shorebirds floated past, and a thick haze hanging above the waters completed the image of subtropical splendor.

It was after four by the time Sarah arrived in Meridian, a sleepy little burg just east of River Road. Sarah found the town to be like many she had driven through in the South, arranged around a central square with a colonial courthouse and a Confederate war memorial. A few old-timers with straw hats and newspapers lolled about on the benches, chewing tobacco and whiling away the afternoon. Shoppers moved indolently about the stores, while a black man was busily shining shoes outside the apothecary. The movie marquee announced a showing of "The Fantastic Voyage."

Finding Jefferson Baldwin's office was every bit as easy as he'd told her; it was just off the square. She remembered his friendly voice on the phone, the cultured southern drawl. "Just drop on by as soon as you get to town," he'd said.

Sarah parked her car. She smoothed wrinkles from her skirt and blouse as she approached the old-fashioned storefront with its large, etched glass panels. A bell jangled on the door as she swept inside.

The inside was quaint with high tin ceilings and whirring ceiling fans. A thin middle-aged woman sat pecking away at a typewriter. She looked up at Sarah, adjusting her steel-rimmed glasses. "May I help you, miss?"

"I'm Sarah Jennings," she replied with a smile. "Mr. Baldwin wrote me about the Davis estate."

The woman smiled. "Oh, yes, Miss Jennings, we've been expecting you. Just have a seat and I'll buzz Mr. Baldwin."

Sarah sat down on a vinyl-covered sofa. As the secretary spoke in muffled tones through her intercom, Sarah idly picked up an old issue of Time Magazine, whose enormous headline posed the question, "Is God Dead?" Frowning, she tossed the magazine aside.

"You can go on in, miss," the secretary piped up.

Sarah stepped into the inner office. An older gentleman in a blue and white seersucker suit sprang up from a massive desk to greet her. "Miss Jennings. What a pleasure," he said.

Jefferson Baldwin seemed the epitome of a southern gentleman. He was white-haired, smiling and had shrewd eyes. Sarah extended her hand and found his handshake firm and warm. "Pleased to meet you, Mr. Baldwin."

"Well, have a seat, dear," he continued. "I'm glad you were able to come so soon." As they both sat down, he added, "Any problems getting here?"

She shook her head. "My trip was quite pleasant."

"May I offer you a refreshment?"

"Well, actually, a soft drink would be great, if you have one."

Mr. Baldwin buzzed his secretary to bring them two Coca-Colas, and they continued their small talk about Sarah's trip until the woman came in.

Afterward, Sarah took a long sip of her ice-cold drink, then smiled at Mr. Baldwin. "So, tell me about my Cousin Erica's estate."

"Well, dear, the situation is pretty much as I outlined to you over the phone. Basically, aside from an annuity left to Erica's maid, you get it all—all the money in Miss Erica's accounts, plus two houses and almost three thousand acres of prime bottomland. Most of the land is let out to tenants, and the income is substantial. There are some technicalities to settle, of course, getting the will through probate and all. But essentially, you're going to have to decide what you want to do with everything—whether you want to stay here and manage the plantation yourself, hire an overseer, or sell out."

"I see," Sarah murmured. "Do you have any idea why my cousin left everything to me? I mean, my mother shed a little light on the situation."

"What did your mother tell you?"

"Well, she said that Miss Davis was her second cousin, and that Erica never did have much contact with our family. But a few years ago, while I was on vacation in the Virgin Islands with some friends,

Erica passed through town and stayed with my family. It seems she really admired my work. In fact, when I called home, my mother mentioned that Erica was very taken with one of my paintings. I insisted Mom give it to her."

Baldwin snapped his fingers. "So, you're the one—the artist! You know, I think I saw that painting out at Erica's house. She spoke quite highly of you."

Sarah smiled. "I'm pleased to hear it. Still, the gift of one painting seems a rather flimsy reason for Cousin Erica to leave me her entire estate."

Baldwin gave her an open-handed gesture. "I suspect Miss Erica left everything to you because she didn't have any kin hereabouts. Still, Erica was an odd one, very much to herself. She was mighty religious, though, very active in the Methodist Church here. Maybe some of her friends in the Women's Society might be able to tell you a little more about her."

Sarah frowned. "How much business is involved in the actual running of the estate?"

"Mainly keeping all the accounts up-to-date. Erica employed a part-time bookkeeper, Maudie Wilson. Very honest and reliable. I've kept her on since Erica's death. I'm the executor of the estate, you see. And, of course, I've always handled the legal work for all the properties," he added meaningfully.

"I'll certainly want you to continue handling everything," Sarah hastily assured him. "And I'll need Miss Wilson, too."

He grinned. "Fine. There is one thing."

"Yes?"

"Well, if you want my advice on managing the estate—"

"Of course."

Jefferson Baldwin hooked his thumbs in his lapels and leaned back in his chair. "There's a drilling company that's been wanting to drill oil wells on Miss Erica's property for years now. The income off leases could be quite lucrative. I advised Erica long ago to let 'um drill, but for some reason she always resisted the idea."

Sarah smiled. "And I'm afraid I'll resist, too. I haven't seen my cousin's estate yet, but I did see some breathtaking ones on the road out from New Orleans. It would be a shame to mar their loveliness with oil wells."

He sighed, managing a disappointed smile. "Whatever you say, Miss Jennings. But I can tell right now that you have a lot of Erica in you."

Sarah smiled. "Perhaps so."

"Now, you will have to keep in mind that it may be some months before the will passes probate. In the meantime—"

"In the meantime, I'd like to stay on at the plantation."

He raised an eyebrow at that. "Well, that would be fine. I know Erica would want you to make yourself right at home until everything's settled. But I am surprised, a young thing like you wanting to stay out there all alone. We could certainly find accommodations for you here in town."

Sarah shook her head. "Actually, I'd like the solitude. For my art, you see."

"Of course."

"Didn't you mention that there were two houses?" Sarah continued. "I'm assuming I can set up housekeeping in one of them."

"Indeed you can. Erica lived in the new house. She had it built nine years ago and added central air

25

conditioning only last summer. That house is all set for you now. I've kept the maid on."

"Good, I'll be needing her, too. And the other house?"

He grinned. "That'd be the old plantation house near the Mississippi. You know, that picture of yours reminds me of it somewhat."

Sarah was at once charmed. "What's the old house like?"

He leaned back in his swivel chair. "Well, ma'am, it's quite a legend hereabouts. Built in 1860, right before the war broke out. Steamboat gothic, like that famous one over in St. John the Baptist Parish. Built of cedar, and I reckon it'll be standing forever."

"And no one's living there?"

"Oh, no, ma'am. It was abandoned many years past. Actually, it's rumored to be haunted."

Far from chilled, Sarah felt intrigued and excited. "Just think—my very own haunted house. I can't wait!"

Chapter Two

Half an hour later, Sarah left Mr. Baldwin's office and headed out of Meridian. It was almost 6:00 p.m., and shopkeepers were locking their stores. In her purse were the keys to Cousin Erica's house that Mr. Baldwin had given her; he'd also jotted down simple instructions for driving out to the plantation.

On her way out of town, Sarah stopped at a restaurant run by a friendly Cajun and his wife. There, she ate her fill of turtle soup and crawfish *étouffée*.

Later, as she drove past the outskirts of town, she was intrigued by a cottage she passed—a white and yellow Victorian bungalow with neat shutters and a long, homey gallery with rockers. Out in the yard, a sign read, "Madame Tuchet. Reader and Advisor." Sarah smiled at the sight.

The sun was setting by the time she turned back onto River Road. To the west, the mighty Mississippi was capped with gold. With the top of her convertible down, she was acutely attuned to the sights and sounds and smells surrounding her. There was the earthy smell of the river, the restrained power of it slapping against the jetties, the hum of barges that occasionally floated past. There was the ghostly splendor of the Spanish moss cascading from the old oaks entwined over the roadway, the sprays of smoky light sifting down through the tree limbs. There was the majesty of the old plantation homes she passed—some of them ancient West Indian style cottages, others looming mansions of Greek or Classical Revival design. Over all was a sense of isolation, of being cut off from time and space and civilization. When she listened to the soothing sawing of cicadas, the comforting cooing of mourning doves, when she watched an alligator move indolently to the edge of a mudflat to catch the sun's last rays, it was hard to believe that the war and technology and turmoil of the twentieth century even existed. How she loved it here!

In due course, she spotted the mailbox with Erica Davis's name and turned down the narrow lane entering her cousin's property. The thick, tangled forest surrounding her was beginning to throb with night sounds—frogs, crickets and owls. In the dusky light, she emerged in a clearing where a modern, one-story colonial brick house stood, surrounded by oleander and azalea bushes. This would be her cousin's home, she thought—the "new house" Mr. Baldwin had mentioned. He'd also told her that the old "steamboat gothic" plantation house was farther north, just off River Road.

As Sarah parked under the carport and got out, a wave of fatigue swept over her. Her day had been long and exciting, and the heavy supper she'd eaten was beginning to weigh her down, making her feel sleepy.

She opened the trunk and took out her overnight case. She decided to leave the heavier unpacking for tomorrow. In the deepening dusk, she climbed the steps to the unlit porch, inhaling the heavy perfume of oleander blossoms. For a moment, she fumbled with the keys, then the heavy door creaked open.

A musty closeness greeted her. She flipped on a light switch and blinked at the sudden brightness. She stood in a long foyer with a terrazo tile floor partially covered by a blue and gold Oriental runner. To her right was a marble-topped table with a gold filigree mirror above it. To her left was an archway leading to a large, living-dining room combination.

Closing the door, Sarah set down the keys, her overnight case and purse. She went into the carpeted living room, switching on the lamps. The pleasant room looked recently vacuumed and dusted, and the antique furniture was lovely. Along the far wall stood a Duncan Phyfe sofa with elegantly curved back and rose silk damask upholstery; it was flanked by Chippendale wing chairs done in mint green and Queen Anne tea tables.

Over the sofa was hung Sarah's painting of the old house in Atlanta. She studied it with a gasp of pleasure. The ghostly, time-washed Greek Revival home appeared suspended in morning mists; pink honeysuckle and yellow jasmine curled about its weathered columns. The old door stood slightly ajar, as if in welcome.

Sarah could well understand why Cousin Erica had loved this painting so much. Softly impressionistic, it was a fine example of Sarah Jennings working at her prime. Then the thought that her artistic prime may have passed washed over her with sudden sadness, and she turned away from the painting with a sigh.

In the dining room, she studied the gleaming Hepplewhite table and chairs and matching, carved sideboard. Laid out on the sideboard were pieces Sarah was sure were of museum quality—an Old English china tea set, a Sèvres Old Paris dinner set and Sheffield silver pieces. She proceeded through an archway and flipped on a light, revealing a modern, impeccably clean kitchen with yards of counter space and every modern convenience imaginable, even a countertop TV. Attached to the kitchen was a dining nook with colonial table and chairs.

A mewling sound now drew Sarah's attention, and she looked down to see a beautiful white Persian cat at her feet. She leaned over and picked him up, and he stared up at her with large amber eyes. "Why, hello, fella. What's your name? You're such a pretty thing."

The cat purred in response, rubbing his jaw against Sarah's hand. She wondered if he was hungry. Then she spotted filled feeding dishes on the floor nearby. The maid must have fed the cat earlier today, she mused.

Putting the cat down, Sarah passed through another archway, entered a shadowy den and flipped on a lamp.

Sarah at once felt at home in the large room. Cozy colonial furniture lined the walls, and a braided rug added warmth to the terrazo floor. In one corner stood a large console color TV set. Near the window was a ladies writing desk with neat stacks of bills and correspondence. Sarah walked over to the desk and ran her fingertips over the polished oak. Opening the middle drawer, she saw a ledger, a journal and some old letters tied with a rubber band. Obviously, no one had gone through Cousin Erica's effects as yet, she thought, closing the drawer with a sigh.

In the hallway, Sarah found a thermostat for the central air system. She flipped a switch and smiled contentedly as she heard the system *whoosh* on. She then explored a modern bathroom and two guest rooms with comfortable colonial furnishings. At the end of the hallway she found the master suite and gasped in delight.

The bed itself was a marvel, heavily carved out of rosewood. It looked like a large box, with rounded corners and scoops on the sides; the high head-board and elaborate footboard were sculpted into the structure of the bed itself. Sarah idly touched one of the oiled, grapeleaf carvings; she'd never before seen such a magnificent bed. The dressers and armoire were also elegant and looked to be Chippendale. A pale gold rug with soft pastel flowers completed the classical ambiance of the room.

Sarah opened the mahogany armoire and was inundated with the fragrance of violet sachet. A poignant sadness swept over her as she studied Cousin Erica's dresses, mostly flowered prints, which were hung neatly in the interior. Erica's sturdy shoes were arranged in a row beneath the dresses, and a collection of hats was stacked on the shelf above.

Sarah shut the armoire doors, feeling like an intruder. She recalled how, when she'd first phoned Mr. Baldwin, he'd told her that her cousin had lived a long life and had died in her sleep. Dear Erica—to think that she'd left all of this to a stranger.

Continuing her exploration of the suite, Sarah

found a large closet filled with more clothes, baskets for sewing and knitting, and numerous stacks of clean linens. There was also a private bath, with a large tub that looked distinctly beckoning to Sarah now. She knew that she would make Cousin Erica's suite her own. In some uncanny way, she sensed her cousin would have wanted this.

Sarah fetched her purse and overnight case from the front hallway, checked all the doors to make sure they were locked, and turned off the lights at the front of the house. Then she had a long soak in the tub, washing off the grime of the road and relaxing muscles stiff from sitting in the car.

Before retiring, Sarah picked up the bedroom phone and called her parents' home in Atlanta. The maid answered, informing Sarah that her folks were out at a dinner party. Sarah had a brief, pleasant conversation with her ten-year-old brother, Teddy. She asked Teddy to let their parents know that she had arrived safely in Meridian and was doing fine.

Afterward, sitting on Cousin Erica's magnificent bed, Sarah flipped off the lamp and did her daily meditation. Then, at last, she crawled between the cool, starched sheets. The bed seemed strangly short, but since Sarah was only five-foot-four, it was more than adequate. People were shorter in the last century—she recalled reading that somewhere.

Cradled in the rosewood bed, she fell deeply asleep.

The next morning, Sarah awakened early to a banging at the front door. Since she didn't have a robe in her overnight case, she went to the closet and grabbed an old chenille robe of Erica's. A moment later, she opened the front door and stared confusedly at a withered black woman who stood on the porch. Beyond the woman, at the end of the walkway, was parked a black '53 Chevy.

"Good morning," Sarah murmured.

"I be Ebbie," the old woman mumbled back.

"Ebbie?" Sarah repeated.

"I be the maid."

"Oh," Sarah said, smiling. "Yes, Mr. Baldwin told me all about you. I'm—"

"You Miz Jennings." Ebbie stared at the porch as she spoke.

"That's right. But how did you know who I am?"

"Mr. Baldwin, he call me this morning."

"Well, how efficient of him. Won't you come in?"

The little old woman followed Sarah into the front hallway. Sarah studied Ebbie with interest. She wore a dark gray dress and a ragged shawl. Her face was small and wrinkled; her mouth and chin seemed shrunken in. She wore steel-rimmed glasses, and her fuzzy gray hair was caught in a bun. Her posture was stooped; she wore opaque gray hose and well-worn, granny-type shoes.

"You've kept the house so nicely," Sarah murmured.

Ebbie had already turned through the living room and was lumbering on toward the kitchen. "Yes'um. I get started now."

"Oh—wonderful," Sarah said, following her.

In the kitchen, Ebbie opened the refrigerator and took out a can of food for the cat. As if on cue, the white Persian bounded into the room, meowing and rubbing against Ebbie's leg.

"What's the cat's name?" Sarah asked.

"Casper cat," she replied, leaning over to place a dish of tuna before the cat.

Ebbie proceeded to make Sarah a marvelous breakfast—grits, hominy, and poached eggs on toast—but the little old maid was obviously a woman of few words. When Sarah asked Ebbie to join her for the meal, Ebbie simply looked at her as if she had lost her mind. Sarah had to smile to herself ruefully, recalling how Bill, too, had found her liberal attitudes perplexing.

Afterward, Sarah brought in her things from her car. She dressed in Miss Erica's room, putting on white slacks, tennis shoes and an aqua "poor boy" sweater. She made up the bed, so Ebbie wouldn't have to, then went hunting for the maid. She found the stooped little woman vacuuming the den, and she could already hear the dishwasher running in the kitchen beyond. Ebbie was a marvel, she realized. If only she weren't so very taciturn.

"I'm going to go find the old plantation house," Sarah called out over the roar of the Electrolux.

Ebbie shut off the vacuum and looked up. She appeared strangely startled, even a little fearful. "Missy, they haints up at that old house."

Sarah fought a smile. "Haints? You mean ghosts? Even in the light of day?"

Frowning fiercely, Ebbie did not appear the least bit amused.

"Don't worry, I'll be careful," Sarah assured her. "Besides, I don't really hold with that sort of thing."

Ebbie looked highly skeptical for a moment. Then she shrugged and turned back to her vacuum.

Sarah went out the rear door of the den, emerging on a wonderful porch. The long veranda was screened in with chaise longues and wicker rockers. She couldn't wait to curl up with a book out here, but now, a more pressing purpose called her.

She left the porch, shutting the screen door behind her. The morning air was sweet and cool, heavily infused with the perfume of the honeysuck-

le growing behind the house. At the edge of the
neatly mowed lawn she spotted a swath of wild
indigo, with palmlike fronds and pink and white
blossoms. Beyond was a lovely grove of trees, stately
oaks, sycamores and cottonwoods fluttering in the
morning light. She watched a brilliant cardinal flit
about.

Rather than walk out to River Road, Sarah decided to proceed north through the forest in search
of the old plantation house. Of course, she might get
lost, but this was a civilized area, with much of the
plantation let out to tenants, and surely there would
be someone around to give her directions.

She went down a narrow path through the grove
of trees and soon emerged in a field of waving cane.
The plants were six feet tall, the tassels almost
purple. She assumed that the cane would be cut
soon. She followed a path along the field, beyond
which was a cedar cottage with a high, pitched roof.
Smoke curled from its flagstone chimney. Sarah
was sure the cottage must be the home of one of the
tenants. Well-weathered, with a broad gallery spanning its front, the cabin looked as if it dated to
another century. On the porch, a black man in
overalls sat smoking a pipe; out in the yard, two
small children were playing with a rambunctious,
mixed-breed dog and a mangy black cat. Sarah
smiled at the sight.

From the field, she entered another wooded area.
She walked across a footbridge spanning a lagoon
and paused in the center. This was her first, close-up
view of a Louisiana swamp, and it captivated her.
The twisting bayou was lined by towering cypress
and tupelo trees; cascading Spanish moss added a
haunting beauty to the scene. Duckweed and vibrant giant water lilies covered the waters. Sarah

watched a black catfish and a large bass float by, while ducks, colored in various shades of green and brown, paddled about and quacked to one another. Sarah stared in wonder at a white osprey swooping down from a tree, catching a fish in its talons then soaring off again. In the distance she could hear the eerie scream of yet another bird. How this area throbbed with life!

Standing there, Sarah suddenly realized that today was the first morning in recent memory that she had awakened without being torn apart with grief over Brian. This thought brought both guilt and a strange sense of wonder. She knew it would be a long, long time before the pain really went away, and that she would never, of course, forget her beloved brother. But maybe she was starting to heal that first, tiny bit.

As she continued on, Sarah was intrigued to watch a bent, white-haired woman move through the trees about 20 yards to the east of her. Like Ebbie, this woman wore a shawl. Her hair was snow-white and caught in a bun. Yet oddly, the woman wore a severe black dress that dragged the ground. She appeared as if she belonged to another time—like the Amish people Sarah had once seen on a trip to Pennsylvania. Sarah called out to her, but the woman didn't seem to hear. Moments later, she disappeared in the maze of trees, making Sarah wonder if she had seen the woman at all.

The incident soon slipped to the back of her mind as she emerged in a large clearing. She gasped as she at last spotted the old plantation house. "Oh, my God," she murmured, riveted to the spot. She drank in the structure with her artist's eye.

Before her stood the gray, timeworn specter of an enchanting antebellum mansion. Surrounded by mature oak trees, the house was raised high off the ground, with two flights of steps laid back to back in a pyramid shape leading to the first story. Both stories had long railed galleries and thin circular columns topped by jaunty bric-a-brac. Steamboat Gothic, Mr. Baldwin had told her. And the house did, indeed, appear like a grounded steamer. Just to the east, across River Road, the mighty Mississippi rolled on, as if waiting for the old house to return home to the river.

Oh, how Brian would have loved this house, she thought with sudden sadness. If only he could be with her to share this moment.

Swallowing the lump in her throat, Sarah climbed one of the old staircases. The steps felt surprisingly sturdy beneath her feet. She paused on the gallery, studying the windows with their missing or broken panes, the shutters standing askew. The front door was slightly open—just like the door on her painting. With a building sense of wonder, she walked past the portal into a long central corridor.

Flanking her were two enormous rooms. The one on her left had a bay window at its side, and she assumed it had once been the dining room. The one on her right had an enormous fireplace; she supposed it must have been the parlor. Both rooms showed visible evidence of their abandonment; the plaster on the walls and ceilings was gray and water-marked, the floors scarred.

Sarah walked into the parlor. The wind rattled the broken windowpanes, creating a creepy cacophony as she strolled about. The room was barren, but there was a stunning plaster medallion centered on the ceiling, a sculpture of cupids intertwined with grapevines. Sarah was sure that in the past, a dazzling chandelier must have hung from the medallion. She shivered slightly as she imagined the grandeur that this parlor once must have known. She could almost see the floorboards well-polished with a Savonaire rug spread out. She could almost feel the texture of velvet portieres at the windows, the silk brocade of French Revival furniture lining the walls. She could almost hear the laughter of guests at a harvest ball—beautifully dressed men and women swirling about to a lilting Strauss waltz. She could almost taste the sweetness of rum punch on her lips.

Then the lovely images receded, and the emptiness that remained twisted Sarah's heart.

She walked over to the fireplace on the far wall. The tiles surrounding it were hand-painted, although a few were missing. The mantel was of white marble. She ran her fingertips over the dusty, cool stone, feeling the smooth texture beneath. She wondered how many cold nights had been warmed by fires blazing in this hearth.

Going to the back of the room, Sarah opened a door to a small anteroom. This must have been used as an office, she mused. A door on the far side of the little room led to the large, open back porch, which Sarah decided she would explore later.

Going back through the parlor, Sarah crossed over to the dining room. Studying the carved wood cornices atop the archway and windows, the handsome wainscotting, she wondered why Miss Erica hadn't chosen to live in this house. The edifice appeared structurally sound, and some refurbishing could have restored the house to its former grandeur. And she could just see her cousin's wonderful antiques ensconced in these rooms.

At the back of the dining room were two doors. On the left was a small anteroom Sarah assumed had once been a butler's pantry; on the right was a medium-sized, sunny room Sarah was certain had been a study or library. A built-in bookcase still remained along one wall. Sarah stood at the center of the room for a long moment, and a strange, eerie feeling crept over her, a feeling of *déjà vu*. It was almost as if she had been in this room before, yet she knew this was impossible. Still, she seemed to sense a presence here and felt drawn into an emotion she couldn't even name.

At last Sarah shook herself from the odd, hypnotic spell the room had cast about her. Leaving the study, she returned to the central corridor and proceeded to the stairs at the back. The old steps creaked slightly beneath her feet, but like the rest of the house, the staircase appeared basically sound.

Upstairs, she explored four bedrooms, two on each side of a central hallway. One of the front rooms enchanted her. Large, airy and lined with windows, it seemed more like an upstairs salon than a bedroom. What a wonderful artist's studio this room would have made!

Behind the salon, Sarah found a sunny bedroom with an anteroom off it. Stepping down into the tiny adjacent room, Sarah tried to imagine its function 100 years ago. She decided it must have been a sewing room or nursery.

As Sarah stood in the anteroom, she was again gripped by the eerie feeling she had felt in the study downstairs. She suddenly felt as if she were touching the very heart of this house. The room was cool, yet a strange warmth crept over her. This tiny room had known much love; somehow she knew this.

At last, Sarah left the bedroom suite and went to stand on the upstairs veranda. She looked out at the surrounding trees with their Spanish moss, the gleaming Mississippi in the distance. How she yearned to have lived in this house during its heyday!

Returning downstairs, Sarah went out the back-door. She emerged on the covered back gallery and stared out at the courtyard with its high brick walls lined with lushly blooming crepe myrtle. The walls were attached to the structure of the house itself, and their height gave the garden a cool, dappled feel. The smell of nectar and greenery filled the air.

The garden itself was a snarled maze of bougainvillaea, honeysuckle, weeds and small, shrublike plants. In the center was a tall, stately fountain, its Grecian goddess choked by vines. In the far left corner was a small brick building Sarah assumed was the kitchen.

Sarah went down the back steps and crossed the tangled yard, taking care to look out for snakes. She tried to open the door to the small brick building, but the entire structure was so encrusted with vines, the door wouldn't budge. After struggling valiantly, she turned, breathless, almost dizzy, and looked back at the porch.

For an electrifying moment, Sarah thought she saw the shadowy image of a man standing on the back veranda. He seemed to be smiling at her, yet he radiated an inexplicable sadness that at once tugged at her heart. She shook her head to clear her senses, and then he was gone.

Sarah's first thought was that the specter might have been Brian. Then she realized this couldn't be true. Whoever the phantom was, he had been dark and dressed in strange, black clothing. Brian had been light, like her, and he had normally worn light clothing, as well.

So she'd seen the ghost that haunted the aban-doned house! Sarah knew she should feel frightened, but she didn't. Instead, she felt intrigued, energized—and determined to find out more about this fascinating old house.

Sarah went back to Miss Erica's house feeling consumed with excitement. She knew now that she wanted to paint the old house, but she also realized that first, she would have to break through the artistic block that had strangled her creative abilities ever since Brian's death. Dr. Hogan had told her that daily meditation should help her break through the block, and that it would also help ease her suffering over Brian. Already she felt filled with hope, for she knew that if Brian were here, he would insist that she paint the old house.

Back at Miss Erica's house, Sarah discovered that Ebbie had prepared a wonderful rich gumbo for her lunch. After eating, Sarah got a pencil and pad and sat down on the couch in the den. She picked up the phone and dialed Jefferson Baldwin's number. The secretary answered and promptly put Sarah's call through.

"Mr. Baldwin, I hope I'm not catching you at a bad time," Sarah began.

"No, not at all. Just going through my mail."

"I was wondering if you'd tell me more about the old plantation house. You see, I found it this morning."

She heard him chuckle. "So that old house has already cast it's spell on you, has it?"

"I guess you could say that."

"Well, dear, it's hypnotized many before you."

"What I'm wondering is why Miss Erica didn't live there, instead of living here in this modern house. Many of her antiques would have fit beautifully in the old house."

"Well, of course, there are the local superstitions about the place being haunted."

Sarah fought a shiver as she remembered the image of a man that she'd seen this morning. "Did Miss Erica hold with that sort of thing?"

She heard Mr. Baldwin sigh. "I'm not sure just what Erica's thinking was there. But you know, Miss Jennings, restoring these old homes can cost a fortune."

"I realize that, but the house itself seems so sound."

"It is, I'll grant you that. I do know the anchoring peers and much of the woodwork are cedar. Such structures are practically impervious to time—and to termites."

Sarah's excitement was building. "Please, Mr. Baldwin, tell me anything you know about the old house."

"Well, as I said yesterday, it was built right before the war—civil, that is. I don't recollect the name of the family that built it—perhaps the parish courthouse might help you there. I do know that around the turn of the century, Miss Davis's family bought the plantation. They fixed up the old place and put on a new slate roof, which, as I'm sure you know, is the best roof there is. That roof is no doubt the reason the interior isn't a complete shambles today. But sometime around 1910, the Davis family moved to a more modern house. Then about nine years ago, Miss Erica had that house torn down—bad foundations problems, as I recall—and built the house you're staying in now."

"So no one has lived in the old house since the early 1900's?"

"Well, there have been a few transients caught there, and the house has no doubt served as a rendezvous for lovers over the years. If you want my opinion, I think that's where the rumors started—you know, about the place being haunted. Folks probably just saw lanterns that were lit by transients or lovers meeting there."

"That could be," Sarah murmured. Then, thinking aloud, she added, "I want to restore the house and go live there."

She heard Mr. Baldwin whistle. "Young lady, do you have any idea of the magnitude of the task you're contemplating? Do you realize it would cost a small fortune just to get the parish to run electricity and water out to the old place?"

"Cousin Erica left me a substantial sum, and I can't think of a better use for it."

"Well, I suppose the choice is yours," Baldwin said, but his voice was heavily laced with skepticism.

"Don't worry, I'm not planning to start renovations immediately," Sarah assured him. "For now, I'd just like to get the place cleaned up a bit, so I can go there to paint. The courtyard at the back is truly a shambles. Do you know of anyone I could hire to begin work on the yard?"

"Well, most of the blacks around here have a healthy fear of that place. But I'll tell you someone who might help, and that's Reuben Voisin, one of your tenants. He's been keeping Miss Erica's yard for years now. Reuben has a very strong back and he's a pretty fearless sort. He's always needing money for his children."

"You know, I think I saw his cabin this morning."

"Yes, that would have been Reuben. He's the tenant living closest to you."

"And you think he'd help me start cleaning up the old house?"

"Yes. But catch Reuben now, while his cane is

still laid by. Once it's fully ripened and he starts cutting, you won't get any extra work out of him till winter.''

"Thanks, Mr. Baldwin. I'll get in touch with him right away.''

That night when Sarah went to bed, Casper, the cat, hopped onto the bed and curled up with her. Sarah felt pleased that the Persian had so quickly warmed up to her. With Casper purring in her lap, Sarah closed her eyes and chanted the mantra her TM teacher had given her back in Atlanta. Soon, she was deep into meditation. Fanciful images of another age danced in her mind, much like the visions she'd seen in the house today.

Later, as she slept, the shadowy image of a man standing on the steps of a steamboat gothic house haunted her dreams.

Chapter Three

Sarah, help me! Please, help me!

Toward morning, the nightmare came again—
Brian, screaming out for help. His voice was real,
terrifying. Sarah wanted desperately to go to him,
but she was locked in the dark room, tied to the
chair. She couldn't even cry out, for her mouth was
gagged. She struggled against her own agonizing
powerlessness, her heart pounding until she was
sure it would burst.

Sarah awakened to the sound of her own scream.
The room was flooded with sunshine, and the first
thing she saw was Casper bolting off the bed. She
glanced about the room wildly, her heart pumping
furiously, her breath coming in ragged gasps.

At last, she gained her bearings. Then she hung
her head in her hands and sobbed.

Once she calmed a bit, she glanced at the clock.

7:15. It would be almost 8:30 in Atlanta. All at once, Sarah felt desperate to speak with Dr. Hogan. He should arrive at his office soon, and with luck, she could catch him before his first appointment.

As she waited the few minutes before she could call, Sarah remembered the first time she'd met Hogan. Following her breakdown, she'd been in the psychiatric hospital for several weeks, and no one had been able to break through the walls of her withdrawal. She'd fought medication or treatment of any kind. Finally, in desperation, her parents had called in Hogan, who was considered something of a maverick, a nonconformist in his field. Yet Hogan had also established a reputation in Atlanta for successfully treating depression and nervous breakdowns.

Hogan had simply walked into her room that day and had taken a seat across from her bed. She remembered him sitting there in his Nehru jacket, quietly smoking his pipe, until at last she turned to look at him.

He had smiled then. "Sarah, I hear you're a lost cause," he'd said. "And I don't believe in lost causes."

Later, Sarah would wonder what special quality it was that drew her to him. Perhaps it had been his laid-back demeanor, his longish hair or his antiestablishment clothing. But for the first time in many weeks, she had smiled.

Over the next six weeks, Dr. Hogan had helped Sarah deal with her own terrible guilt and grief. He'd helped her face her nightmares and accept the fact that she was not responsible for Brian's death, that her brother had made his own choices.

The day she'd left the hospital, she'd confessed to him that she still wasn't whole. "That's okay,

Sarah," he'd said. "Don't expect too much of yourself too soon. The healing process takes time, but you've taken charge of your life again. Now you can start to cope."

Cope, Sarah thought to herself ruefully. Coping seemed to be about the best she could do here in this world.

At last, with trembling fingers, Sarah picked up the receiver and asked the operator to put through her person-to-person call.

Within seconds, she heard Hogan's comforting voice on the other end. "Sarah! What a pleasure to hear from you. How was your trip to Louisiana?"

"Just fine." Briefly, she told him about her drive and also described the estate she had inherited. "It looks like I'll be staying here for some time," she finished.

"Sarah, are you sure you're all right?"

She sighed. "I never can fool you, can I?" As he waited patiently, she added, "Dr. Hogan, I had the dream again—the nightmare about Brian."

"I see."

Her hand clenched the receiver. "And I thought I was so much better. I thought I was safe from the nightmare now. During the trip and my first night here, everything was fine. Now this."

He was quiet a moment. "Sarah, didn't I warn you to expect this sort of thing? You see, transcending grief is so often a two-steps-forward, one-step-backward process. Over the past few days, you've had the trip and your new surroundings to distract you. I find it only natural that your feelings would catch up with you this way."

She spoke haltingly, through tears. "Only . . . it's so damned painful!"

"I know. But you must face up to what you're

feeling. After all, your refusal to face the loss of your brother is what led to your breakdown in the first place. As far as the nightmare itself is concerned, the fact that you are bound, gagged and powerless to me symbolizes all the feelings you are trying to repress and deny."

Sarah nodded miserably. "It's just that when I hear Brian screaming for help and know I can't do anything . . ."

"Let's talk about that for a moment. Didn't Brian's company commander write your parents that he was killed instantly? I'm sure he didn't suffer."

"Then why do I hear him screaming?"

"Again, it's just your own grief, fighting to be acknowledged and dealt with." He paused. "Sarah, don't try to force away your thoughts of Brian, and try to think of the good times, as well—the legacy of pleasant memories your brother left you. That should help."

"Okay. I'll try."

"And have you been practicing your meditation?"

"Yes. Every day."

"I think that within a few weeks, you'll see some results there. Beyond that, if the nightmare should continue to disturb you this way, perhaps you should return to Atlanta fairly soon—"

"Oh, no," Sarah quickly cut in. "I really love it here. You see, I've become fascinated by an old abandoned house that's on my property. There's something—I don't know—very healing about that old house. I think I may be able to paint there, and this could be a real breakthrough for me."

"I see. Okay, then, I'll not try to talk you into coming home right away. But if you should need me—anytime—please don't hesitate to call."

"Believe me, I won't. Thanks, Dr. Hogan."

After she hung up the phone, Sarah felt a little better. Nevertheless, a feeling of melancholy dogged her as she went about her morning routine. First, she went hunting up Casper, feeling badly that she had scared him. She found the cat sitting on a footstool in the den, eyeing her warily. She petted him and spoke to him softly, apologizing for frightening him earlier. By the time she fed Casper a dish of tuna in the kitchen, he was again ready to eat out of her hand.

Sarah took a shower and dressed in a calico granny gown and sandals. As she drew the brush through her long hair, she ruefully recalled how often Bill had criticized her "Flower Child" attire and unsophisticated hairstyle. What a relief not to be subject to his disapproval any more!

When Sarah walked into the den a few minutes later, she was surprised to see a stranger sitting at Miss Erica's desk. The woman was plump and middle-aged, with blunt features; she wore her hair in short, tight curls. She was pouring over an account book as Ebbie ran the vacuum nearby. Sarah noted that Ebbie's wrinkled little face was screwed up in a pout, and she was intrigued to watch the two women exchange a look of barely veiled hostility as Ebbie passed near the desk.

"Good morning," Sarah called out over the roar.

The plump woman turned to smile at Sarah. "Why, good morning. You must be Miss Jennings."

"Yes. And you're . . . ?" Sarah was still half-shouting, but mercifully, Ebbie turned off the vacuum, unplugged it and began dragging it off toward the living room.

The newcomer rose. "I'm Maudie Wilson, Miss Erica's bookkeeper."

"Oh, yes." Sarah smiled, shaking the hand the woman extended. "Mr. Baldwin told me about you."

"Welcome to Meridian, dear."

"Thank you."

"Well." Maudie cleared her throat. "I'm sure Mr. Baldwin told you that I come each Wednesday to do the books and pay the bills. And I assume you'll be wanting to go over the accounts with me now that you've taken over for Miss Erica?"

Sarah bit her lip. She knew little about such matters, beyond how to balance her own checkbook. Bill would know, she thought, then shoved the idea aside. She'd ask Mr. Baldwin about the accounts. To Maudie, she said, "Oh, one day soon we'll go over the books, but I'm sure you're doing a fine job."

Maudie rolled her eyes. "Then you're a lot more trusting than Miss Erica was." As Sarah stared at her, bemused, she went on. "Are you finding everything you need here in town?"

Sarah laughed. "Actually, I've only just arrived."

"Be sure to come see us at the Methodist Church on Sunday," Maudie went on, returning to her desk. "Just off the square in town—you can't miss it."

"Thanks, I'll remember that." The vacuum had gone off in the living room now, and Sarah could hear Ebbie banging pots in the kitchen, presumably making breakfast. What a dynamo the little woman was, she thought ruefully. To Maudie, she added, "Guess I'll go have some coffee and leave you to your work."

Out in the kitchen, Sarah drank coffee and ate the delicious eggs and sausage Ebbie prepared for her. She wondered about the antagonism between Ebbie and Maudie. And what had Maudie meant when she'd said that Miss Erica hadn't trusted her? She must ask Jefferson Baldwin about these things.

After finishing a second cup of Ebbie's delicious *café au lait,* Sarah decided she'd walk to the old house again. She had an almost overpowering urge to do her morning meditation there. And maybe she'd run across Reuben Voisin on the way, and she could ask him about cleaning up the tangle of brush around the house.

Moments later, as Sarah started toward the rear door of the den, Maudie Wilson turned to raise an eyebrow at her. "I know this is none of my business, honey, but you're not going out in your nightie, are you?"

Sarah laughed. "No, this is a grannie gown. They're all the rage in Atlanta, where I live."

Maudie harrumphed. "I hear those Atlantians still haven't recovered from Sherman's march to the sea."

"Perhaps not," Sarah said dryly. She was beginning to understand why Maudie had so obviously rubbed Miss Erica the wrong way.

As Sarah reached for the doorknob, Casper rushed up, meowing plaintively. "Is the cat allowed out?" she asked Maudie.

"Oh, yes. Miss Erica liked him to keep the field mice away from the house." Watching Sarah grimace, she added, "Don't worry, the cat's had all his shots. No reason not to let him out."

"Okay, then. See you later. Come along, Casper," Sarah said.

Sarah went out, crossed the porch, then entered the yard. The morning was crisp and cool, and the smell of fall greenery was very enticing.

As she walked away from the house, she was surprised to observe the cat following her. Every cat

Sarah had ever known had been fiercely indepen-
dent, and she found it odd that this tomcat had so
quickly adopted her. She thought of how the Hindus
believed in transmigration and wondered if the cat
could somehow be Brian. With Brian's free-spirited
nature, she could almost see him wishing to be
reincarnated as a cat. Then she chided herself for
her silliness. Brian was gone, she thought achingly,
really gone. There was nothing to be gained from
clinging to illusions.

Feeling sobered and saddened by this realization,
Sarah continued through the grove of trees and
emerged at the edge of the first cane field. She
spotted a familiar cedar cottage in the distance. The
black man she'd seen yesterday was again sitting out
on the porch. She figured he must be Reuben
Voisin. As she drew even closer to the cabin, Casper
abruptly took off into the field.

Sarah paused before the steps of the house; the
black man set down his pipe and quickly came
down the steps to greet her. "Yes, ma'am?" he asked
respectfully.

Sarah smiled at him. He looked to be in his early
twenties, was handsome and appeared very strong
and muscular. He had a sincere, honest-looking
face, and from the appearance of his patched overalls, he very much needed money. "Are you Reuben
Voisin?" she asked.

"Yes, ma'am," he replied in his soft, deep voice.

"I'm Sarah Jennings," she said. "I inherited the
plantation from Miss Erica."

"Yes, ma'am," he repeated, shifting from foot to
foot. "When I done the lawn last week, Miss Maudie,
she told me Miss Erica's kin was coming from
Georgia to keep house here."

"Yes, that's right. And I was wondering—are you

familiar with the old house, north of here near the river?''

A guarded look flashed across his chocolate-brown eyes. ''Was that where you was going yesterday, miss?''

Sarah was not at all put off by his curiosity. ''Yes. I've looked over the old house, and I think it's really a shame the way it's been neglected. And I was wondering—would you be willing to do some work around the place, if I pay you? I mean, I've noticed what a fine job you've done on Miss Erica's yard.''

He grinned with a flash of white teeth. ''Thank you, miss. What sort of work do you need done at the old place?''

''Mainly just clearing away the garden in the back and getting all the vines and weeds pulled away from the front of the house.''

He shifted again. ''They's some folks around these parts say that old house is haunted.''

''What do you say?'' Sarah asked.

He hesitated, and as Sarah waited for his reply, a black girl who looked no more than 17 came out on the porch, an infant in her arms. Two toddlers, a boy and a girl, followed along, clinging to her skirts. The smells of woodsmoke and hot pork wafted toward Sarah as the girl and her charges eyed the newcomer suspiciously.

Reuben scowled at the girl, then turned back to Sarah. ''Miss Sarah, this here be my wife and children.'' To the young woman, he added, ''This here be Miss Sarah. She come to stay at Miss Erica's place.'' With a curt nod, he added, ''Now git back in the house, girl.''

Reuben's wife flashed Sarah another suspicious glance, then fled into the house with the baby. The two toddlers followed close on her heels.

"I'm sorry," Sarah said to Reuben. "I hope I haven't come at a bad time."

He shrugged. "I reckon I can do your work, Miss Sarah."

She smiled. "Well, great, then. But could you come in the afternoons? You see, I'm an artist, and I'll be doing some painting at the house in the mornings."

"I come in the evenings," he said.

"It'll be hard work," Sarah added. "I'm willing to pay you whatever you think is fair."

He shifted his weight again. "Miss Maudie, she pay me two dollars a week to keep the yard."

Sarah was shocked at this low pay for what she was sure was several hours' hard work. She made a mental note to tell Maudie to triple Reuben's pay for the yard work. "How does two dollars an hour sound?" she asked him.

He smiled broadly. "That be fine, miss."

Sarah left Reuben and continued on toward the old house. She felt sorry for the Voisin family, especially the lovely young girl with three small children to raise. They seemed a proud young family. Maybe she could find some work for the wife up at the new house even though Ebbie already kept things immaculate.

Soon, Sarah arrived at the old place. Again, the time-washed splendor of the house captivated her; the weathered mansion sat sweetly dappled in the morning light, the leaves of the grand old oak trees fluttering above it.

Sarah went inside and again roamed the rooms, memorizing every nook and cranny. She wanted to paint here, yet she sensed she still wasn't quite ready. Her nightmare this morning was certainly proof of this. For now, she would try to meditate in the house.

Sarah went into the old parlor, sat down on the floor against a wall and tried to concentrate on her mantra, but trying to mediate in the house today proved difficult. She soon became distracted by the haunting sound of a swamp bird's cry, the humming of cicadas. And the memory of her nightmare earlier this morning continued to haunt her. Indeed, now that she was still and quiet, there was no escaping its onslaught. She realized that Dr. Hogan had been right when he'd said that her pain had caught up with her. Rage and meditation simply did not mix, and she knew her TM teacher back in Atlanta wouldn't want her to force things right now.

So, instead, she leaned back against the wall, closed her eyes, and let the tears come as she remembered Brian. At 16, he'd made his debut as a virtuoso with the Atlanta Symphony. His performance of the Brahms Concerto had brought a standing ovation. Sarah, her parents and Bill had occupied front row seats. It had been the proudest moment of their lives—Brian, blond and beautiful, and so masterfully handsome in his formal clothes, taking his bows on the stage above them, smiling down at them.

Two brief years later, Brian had graduated from high school and had taken off with some friends to bicycle through Europe. Like a true romantic, he'd thumbed his nose at the full scholarship to Juilliard. School could wait, he'd told his sister. Life was for living—now.

When he'd returned home, the draft notice had awaited him. Sarah had begged him to go off to Canada, but he'd refused, laughing at her fears. "I took my chances, Sarah, and now it looks like the Army has me."

Then, he'd been inducted into the service, and then . . .

Sarah's fist pounded the floor, and bitter tears stung. "Why . . . Oh, why?"

Then a voice answered, *Don't ask why.*

Sarah opened her eyes, amazed and moved. She stared around the room, but saw only emptiness. She listened, but heard only the low, haunting dirge of the wind.

Where had the voice come from? Had it truly existed, or was it simply a message from her own mind, trying to offer her some comfort?

She didn't know. But in that one moment, Sarah experienced a feeling of peace she hadn't known in many months.

Sarah went back to Miss Erica's house feeling strangely euphoric. She had a feeling that tomorrow, she'd be able to meditate in the old house. She thought of the haunting voice she was sure she had heard—the voice that had said, "Don't ask why." Could the words have been uttered by the dark, mesmerizing ghost she was sure she had seen yesterday? Oh, how she yearned to see and hear more! She sensed that the answers she was seeking were contained somewhere within the old house.

Casper rejoined Sarah not far from the new house. She picked him up and carried him the rest of the way. "Where you been, fella?" she asked, petting him. "Did you find a nice juicy mouse in that field?"

Casper purred and stared up at his mistress with his inscrutable gold eyes.

When Sarah entered the den, she found Maudie

Wilson still at her desk. Setting down the cat, she flashed Maudie a brittle smile, struggling to contain a feeling of annoyance that the woman was still there.

"Did you have a nice walk?" Maudie asked.

"Yes, I did. And by the way, I've hired Reuben Voisin to do some extra yard work at the old plantation house."

Maudie raised an eyebrow. "That old place? Haven't you heard the rumors that it's haunted?"

Sarah shrugged. "Every old, abandoned house spawns such rumors, I'm sure. Anyway, I wanted to let you know that we'll be paying Reuben for the additional work at the rate of two dollars an hour."

"Two dollars an hour?" Maudie looked stunned.

Sarah's chin came up slightly. "Yes. It will be very hard work. In addition, I want you to start paying Reuben six dollars a week for doing the yard."

Maudie's mouth fell open.

"Is there some problem?" Sarah asked.

"Well . . . no, miss," Maudie sputtered. "But you should know that most blacks in these parts will work for much less."

"That doesn't mean we should take advantage of them, does it?" Sarah interjected crisply.

Maudie's broad face tightened with resentment. "Very well, then, miss. I'm sure you know what's best."

"Thank you."

As Sarah started out of the room, Maudie added, "By the way, miss, have you thought of what you'll do about Miss Erica's things?"

Sarah turned, biting her lip. "Frankly, I haven't. But I suppose I will have to go through her personal effects. Do you have any suggestions there?"

Maudie smiled slyly. "Well, it may not be my place

to say, but I did always fancy Miss Erica's beaver coat. And she didn't leave me anything at all in her will—not that I was expecting anything, of course."

Sarah stiffened her spine, annoyed by the woman's presumptuousness. "I'll give it some thought."

"Of course, her other clothes wouldn't fit me," Maudie went on rather irritably. "Miss Erica was such a frail little thing."

"Perhaps I could give some of her clothing to Ebbie or to Reuben Voisin's wife. Both of them are quite small."

Maudie's eyes grew enormous. "You'd give Miss Erica's clothing to those—colored women?"

"I have a feeling it would please Miss Erica," Sarah said coolly. "Well, I'll leave you to your duties, then."

Maudie was frowning fiercely as she turned back to her ledger.

Later that day, after Maudie and Ebbie had left, Sarah phoned Jefferson Baldwin. She told him all about her conversations with Maudie and the obvious antagonism between Maudie and Ebbie. She also told him of how Maudie had complained because Erica had failed to mention her in her will.

Afterward, Mr. Baldwin chuckled. "You must understand that there was a feud between Maudie and Erica for many years. They both competed for the presidency of the Women's Society at the Methodist Church, and Erica won time and time again. As for Ebbie, she always was fiercely protective of Erica, so it's easy to understand her hostility toward Maudie."

"But if Miss Erica didn't like Maudie, why did she keep her on as bookkeeper for all these years?"

"Because she's the only decent bookkeeper in these parts. And Maudie is scrupulously honest."

"Ah, yes. She mentioned that I'd want to go over the accounts with her."

"I think you should. But don't worry there. Miss Erica had me audit the accounts annually, and of course, there will be another thorough audit as we settle the estate."

"I see. Mr. Baldwin, what should I do about Miss Erica's things?"

"You mean her clothing and such?"

"Yes."

He sighed. "Well, dear, there are no specific instructions regarding personal effects in her will. If you have time to start packing up her things and giving them to charity or whatever, I certainly have no objection."

"I'll see what I can do, then, Mr. Baldwin. Thanks."

As Sarah hung up the phone, she frowned. She realized that along with Erica Davis's estate, she had inherited a host of new responsibilities— employees, tenants, as well as personal effects of Miss Erica's to deal with.

Yet at the same time, Sarah could sense a strong bond building between her and the old house—and somehow her new responsibilities threatened that bond.

Chapter Four

The next morning, Sarah awakened with a feeling of relief. She'd been granted a reprieve; her nightmare about Brian had not recurred. She wiped a tear of mingled gratitude and guilt, then hopped out of bed. She could barely wait to leave for the old house; she still believed that the answers she sought —indeed, the cure for her own grief and suffering —dwelled somewhere within its walls.

Sarah dressed in another of her grannie gowns, this one a pale yellow cotton sprigged with tiny violet flowers. Right after breakfast, she went out the backdoor with Casper following her. Since Ebbie had mentioned that she would leave at noon today, Sarah slipped her keys under the back mat.

On her way to the old house, Sarah spotted some white wildflowers growing at the edge of a cane field. She plucked several blossoms and stuck them in her hair, inhaling their sweetness as she walked along. The breeze was crisp, and the fresh essence of the morning dew filled her lungs.

As she crossed a footbridge spanning the swamp, she again saw the strange, white-haired woman in the distance. Again, Sarah called out to her, but once more the woman didn't seem to hear and simply slipped off into the trees.

Sarah shook her head at the bizarre incident. After the woman had disappeared the first time, she had wondered rather whimsically if she could be the ghost haunting the old house. But the woman had appeared real enough today. Sarah started to remark about the old woman to Casper, but when she looked down at her feet, she observed that the cat, too, had vanished.

When Sarah arrived at the old place, she noted that many of the vines had been pulled away from the front. Good, she thought, Reuben had already started his work. Sarah went inside and sat down on the parlor floor. She shut her eyes and listened to the familiar ghostly cry of a swamp bird, the creaking of a loose shutter. She chanted her mantra and tried to get into meditation, but again she found she felt too tense. Her pain always seemed to catch up with her at these moments of stillness and reflection. Even now, poignant memories of Brian again flooded her mind—Brian smiling as he created magic with his violin, Brian laughing as he thumbed his nose at fate . . .

Brian being buried on a lonely hillside in Atlanta. Sarah realized that her anger and grief were blocking her once more, that her pain was keeping her from seeking the very healing she so desperately needed. She clenched her fists in silent frustration.

Then she felt something furry crawling into her lap. She gasped and opened her eyes, looking down to see Casper there. He was purring and gazing up at her with his magnificent golden eyes.

And suddenly, Sarah was at peace. Closing her eyes and petting Casper, she found herself mouthing her mantra and drifting deep into relaxation. She heard the voice again, a man's voice, whispering to her soothingly: *Don't ask why*. She drifted deeper still, abandoning thought. Fanciful images swirled in her mind—a trailing of lace at the window, footsteps on the stairs, the ghostly plink of a piano. "Beautiful Dreamer," wasn't it?

Wake unto me, the voice said. *Wake unto me*.

Every day for a week thereafter, Sarah meditated in the old house. At first, she couldn't relax unless Casper was with her, purring in her lap. But after a few sessions with the cat there, she was able to get deeply into meditation whether Casper was with her or not.

Often Sarah fell asleep as she meditated. Fanciful images again danced through her mind. Sometimes, she saw fleeting visions of the house as it used to be—with flocked wallpapers on the walls, heavy velvet draperies on the windows, beautiful French Revival furnishings lining the rooms. She heard the voice—and sometimes more than one voice. Sometimes she heard Brian's violin, playing "Beautiful Dreamer," with the dissonant clink of the old piano accompanying him. There was laughter there and pain and poignance and tears. Sometimes Sarah would awaken with tears streaming down her face, yet she instinctively knew that there was healing in her anguish.

Sometimes, she saw the man again, and she began to realize that it was his voice she heard. His image was blurred, hazy, yet he drew her—a dark, mesmerizing presence. She sensed a pain in him that touched an answering chord in herself. She suspected that she was becoming fascinated by a ghost, and she wondered why this realization brought no fear.

Twice more, as Sarah left the house, she saw the old woman walking near the swamp. Sarah called out to her, but as always, she disappeared into the trees.

As the days passed, Reuben cleared away the tangle of vines and weeds from both the front of the house and from the garden at the rear. Soon, Sarah was able to explore the old stone kitchen at the back of the courtyard. She marveled at its huge oven and open hearth. She toyed with the idea of restoring the house and turning the kitchen into a guest bungalow.

Yet curiously, as the days passed, the idea of renovating the house interested her less and less, and Sarah made no definite plans. It was almost as if forcing the old house to enter this modern age would be an intrusion, a desecration.

One evening, Sarah stood on the back veranda at sunset. She stared at the fountain with its gleaming statue of a Grecian goddess, now cleaned of its vines and lichen. She gazed at the high, brick courtyard walls with their lining of still-blooming crepe myrtle. Then she looked up at the sky, and it occurred to her that this same sky was here the day the house was built.

The wind whipped up then, fluttering the trees above her, sending brilliant light showers dancing across the yard. The Greek goddess seemed to shift with the whims of the wind and the fading light. For a fleeting instant, time also ceased to exist; only the moment itself was real.

The man haunted her now, every time she meditated. She called him her "dark cavalier." He spoke to her often, and in his voice was both pain and healing. Always, there was music there—sad, beautiful music. And images of the house—sometimes beautiful and whole again, sometimes old and abandoned. She sensed she was becoming a part of the house, that she was being drawn into its very soul. Pain dwelled in that soul along with need and grief. She wanted to understand the house, to embrace its very aura. She knew it was becoming her obsession.

And on the eighth morning of meditation, Sarah awoke consumed with a desire to paint the house.

She awoke that day in the parlor with Casper in her arms. For the first time in a number of months, she knew she was ready to take up her brushes once more. Like one possessed, she rushed back to Miss Erica's house to gather her paintbox, a canvas and easel. Ebbie, spotting her about to leave again, insisted on packing her a lunch.

Sarah went back to the old house and set up her easel on the bare ground before it. The late September morning was lovely, an envigorating coolness lacing the air. The light was perfect as it hit the time-washed house. Sarah knew she would paint it just as it was, in its gray, abandoned majesty.

Sarah was normally a very controlled, precise painter, drawing many sketches before she ever put brush to canvas. But in painting the house, everything was different. She mixed vivid hues on her palette—cerulean blue, viridian green, yellow ocher and raw umber—and splashed them on the canvas boldly with her sable brushes and palette knife. Her strokes were powerful, unrestrained, more expressionistic than they'd ever been before.

She worked all day, praying the light would not fail her. She captured the house awash in light and shadow, the vivid curtain of green branches entwined above it, mixed in with the ghostly splendor of Spanish moss, the silvery Mississippi off in the distance.

Casper hovered nearby as she worked. At noon, she stopped to nibble on the lunch Ebbie had made her and fed the cat half her tuna sandwich.

By sundown, the painting was finished. Sarah marveled at her own speed as she gathered up her supplies. Most of her paintings took several weeks.

She went home in the scant light, holding the wet painting carefully so as not to smear it. When she arrived back at the house, it was darkened and locked, so she let herself in with the keys she now kept under the mat.

In the den, she set the painting on an easel to dry and turned on all the lights so she could get a better look at it.

Studying her work, Sarah was stunned. Never before had she done anything so energetic and passionate. The painting literally vibrated with bright colors and vivid contrasts. The boldness of her brush strokes amazed her. The house itself was so real, it seemed to jump out at her from the canvas.

Sarah backed off to take in the effect as a whole, and that's when she saw the face—its lines superimposed on the lines of the house itself, a perfect study in counterpoint. Sarah gasped, for she had no conscious memory of putting the face there.

It was a man's face, a poignantly smiling face. Yet the eyes were dark, haunted, filled with pain.

"Damien," she whispered.

Then Sarah fell to her knees on the rug, staring at the face as if hypnotized.

When Sarah went to bed that night, she was still trying to make sense of things. She had stared at the painting with its amazing superimposed face for hours. Clearly, the old house was haunted, and she was being drawn toward ghosts who'd lived there a hundred years ago.

One, in particular—Damien, her dark cavalier. The very thought of him made her shiver with fear and excitement.

Sarah knew she shouldn't go back to the house again. To do so would be insane. If there were a presence dwelling in the house, there was no guarantee that it was benign. Indeed, what if it were malevolent, seducing her for its own dark purpose?

Yet Sarah knew she couldn't resist the house's magnetism, any more than she could get the man's ghostly, smiling face out of her mind.

The next morning dawned brisk and cool. Sarah arose early, again feeling consumed with energy. Before Ebbie even arrived, she made coffee and sat drinking it in the den as she stared once again at the vivid painting. She studied the face of the man, so hauntingly superimposed there, and recalled the name she had uttered last night—Damien. Had a Damien lived at the house once? Was he indeed the ghost who haunted it now?

Sarah realized that she would have to find out more about the family that originally built the old house. She'd have to ask Jefferson Baldwin for suggestions on finding old records. But for now, she couldn't wait to go to the old house and do her morning meditation. Despite some fear, Sarah realized that the only peace and healing she had known had occurred at the old house. Each day, she reached toward the house irresistibly, like a drooping flower stretching toward the sun.

Sarah dressed in a blue and gold calico grannie gown, donned her sandals and styled her hair loosely about her shoulders. She left Ebbie a note that she'd return later, then left the house with Casper, placing her keys under the mat. Strolling toward the old place in the sweet coolness of morning, she plucked wildflowers and stuck them in her hair. Casper followed at a discreet distance, pausing occasionally to bat at a passing butterfly or bird.

Soon, Sarah left a curtain of trees and approached the old house. Then she stopped in her tracks, mesmerized.

The old, white-haired woman stood on the porch. Seen at close range, she was a hunched little figure with almost unnaturally white hair and a deeply wrinkled face. Again, she wore the strange clothing—a gray shawl and a long, severe black dress.

At last Sarah gathered her wits. She stepped forward eagerly. "Good morning," she called.

But before Sarah could get close enough to detain her, the woman descended the steps and disappeared into the trees at the side of the house. Following, Sarah could see no trace of her in the forest beyond. She shivered. It was as if the old woman were, indeed, a phantom—a ghost that had just vanished into thin air.

Who was she? Sarah wondered for the dozenth

time. And why was she interested in the old house? She resolved to ask Ebbie if she knew anything about the woman.

Sarah went inside and sat down in her familiar spot against the parlor wall. A moment later, Casper came bounding in and settled in her lap. Sarah chanted her mantra and soon settled into deep, relaxing meditation. She felt as if cradled by loving arms, profoundly at rest. She was enchanted by images that swept her through the house, up and down the old staircase, into the past and back into the present again. Again, the music delighted her, "Beautiful Dreamer" played by Brian's violin, with the haunting accompaniment of the piano. Then the violin faded away, but the piano played on, slightly discordant yet irresistibly hypnotic.

Wake unto me, the voice said. *Wake unto me.*

And Sarah awakened.

Chapter Five

The music stopped.

The first thing Sarah felt was a cool autumn breeze caressing her face. The first thing she heard was a melodic clinking, as if two crystal glasses were being raised in a toast.

She blinked and glanced down at her lap. Casper was gone. Then she gasped as she gazed around the room in which she sat.

It was the same, yet radically different. At first Sarah was sure she must be hallucinating, but as she blinked again and shook her head, her surroundings remained in focus.

The room was vintage nineteenth century. She sat at the edge of a pink and gold Persian rug, in a parlor filled with tufted rosewood furniture upholstered in pale rose and gold silk damask. The windows were draped in mauve-colored velvet with

Brussels lace panels fluttering to the floor. The front two windows were slightly raised with the merest of breezes drifting in. Sarah smelled honeysuckle and the crisp scent of fall vegetation.

She glanced around in deepening amazement. The walls were covered with cream and gold flocked wallpaper. A fire was snapping in the grate. The missing tiles on the fireplace had been replaced, and handsome brass and irons stood before the hearth. On the fireplace mantel were European court figurines Sarah was sure must be Dresden porcelain; between the figurines, a girandole clock ticked away.

Hearing the clinking sound again, Sarah glanced overhead at a fabulous crystal chandelier which glittered in the light and rang mellifluously. The chandelier was hung from the familiar cast plaster medallion of cupids and grapevines. Sarah's heart lurched into a frantic beat as she realized that the room had been restored precisely as she had imagined it.

She struggled to her feet, still half-believing she was in the middle of a dream. She moved toward the center of the room, her sandals soundless on the soft old rug. On the coffee table was a book, *Little Women*, by Louisa May Alcott. She picked it up. The book looked and felt real enough with its leather binding and gold lettering. Then she flipped it open. The paper appeared no more than a few years old, and yet the publishing date was 1868!

Sarah set the book down hastily, as if touching it had burned her. She glanced around in deepening shock. If this were a dream, she certainly wasn't awakening.

"Oh, my God, where am I?" she gasped.

Then Sarah was even more stunned to watch a

gray-haired woman walk briskly into the room. She was short and plump and wore her hair in a tight bun; she reminded Sarah vaguely of Maudie Wilson. But it was her clothing that flabbergasted Sarah.

The woman wore a floor-length gray wool gown with voluminous skirts. Black braid sculpted the hem, waist and wrists. At least two dozen tiny mother-of-pearl buttons traveled up the high bodice toward a demure white linen collar. A cameo brooch was pinned at the throat. All in all, the woman looked as if she had just walked out of the nineteenth-century novel on the coffee table.

She was staring at Sarah in consternation. "My, you do give a body a start, girl," she said at last.

Sarah was too dumbfounded to reply.

"Was it Baptista who showed you in?" the woman went on irritably. "You'd think that gal would condescend to mention your presence to me, but these darkies have had no respect for their superiors ever since the war."

Still, Sarah was astounded. She could only muse crazily how much this woman reminded her of Maudie Wilson. Even the attitudes matched.

"Well, then." The woman drew herself up huffily. "I take it you're the artist they sent out from the museum in New Orleans?"

At last Sarah found her voice. "I beg your pardon?"

"And what might your name be, miss?" the woman went on archly, stepping forward slightly. As Sarah stared back blankly, she added with strained patience, "The curator wrote that he'd find someone for us, but he didn't send us your name."

"Oh," Sarah stammered, "I'm Sarah Jennings."

"Sarah Jennings, is it?" The woman stared with obvious distaste at Sarah's straight-lined calico grannie gown. "Well, then, Miss Jennings, a body would think they'd teach you to dress better than that. I can't present you to my nephew in that scandalous attire—not even a petticoat underneath, by the looks of it." She glanced downward, then sucked in her breath in deepening horror. "And what in the name of all that's holy do you have on your feet, child?"

"S-sandals," Sarah sputtered.

"How queer," the woman said. "Don't tell me these immodest slippers are the new style in New Orleans these days?"

Not knowing what else to say, Sarah stammered, "Well . . . actually they are."

The woman threw up a hand. "Good heavens, what is this world coming to? I'm sure I don't know. Nothing's been the same since the war, I must tell you." She fixed a fierce frown on Sarah. "Have you brought along anything more suitable?"

"Well, actually, no, I—"

"Where is your trunk, miss?"

"My . . . my trunk? I—er—suppose it's coming later."

"You suppose?" the woman repeated incredulously.

Sarah struggled not to wring her hands. "I traveled here in something of a hurry," she muttered with a touch of irony.

The woman rolled her eyes. "Doubtless, your other garments are as indecent as those you're wearing." She stepped closer and gripped Sarah by the arm. The odor of some pungent, spicy sachet swept over Sarah as the woman added briskly, "Come along, then. We must get you upstairs and changed into more fitting garments. Perhaps something of Lucy's will suffice."

"Lucy?" Sarah repeated weakly as the woman tugged her out of the room.

"My nephew's deceased wife. I still have a few of her things packed away upstairs in a trunk."

Sarah remained stunned as the imperious little woman led her into the central hallway. Her eyes grew huge as she took in the polished wooden floors, the Oriental runners, the marble-topped tables with freshly cut flowers in crystal bowls. She caught her image and that of the strange woman in a gold filigree mirror and lurched to a halt, shuddering.

"My kingdom, girl," the woman was saying, her hands on her hips as she studied Sarah's wide-eyed countenance. "A body would think you'd never seen the insides of a proper house before. Now come along. You must change and my nephew must meet you at once, else we'll have to hold luncheon. Damien won't like that."

Sarah almost collapsed. "Damien?" she repeated, turning to the woman in amazement.

Her hostess expelled an exasperated sigh. "I've heard you artists are eccentric types, but really! If Mr. Rillieux has sent us a simpleton, it won't do at all, but I suppose we must let Damien decide on your suitability. Now step lively, miss."

After this scathing lecture, Sarah could only fall into step behind the strange little woman. Numbly, she followed her up the stairs, which were carpeted with a floral-printed wool runner. Pale rose flocked wallpaper graced the walls, with handsome brass sconces positioned every few feet. Staring at the woman's sweeping skirts ahead of her, Sarah gripped the polished banister and prayed her trembling limbs wouldn't fail her.

Had she lost her mind? She seemed to be in the

middle of a dream or a nightmare, yet it all seemed so real. She had pinched herself several times already, and she simply couldn't wake up.

What if it was real? she thought. What if someone had played a gigantic joke upon her while she meditated—moving in antique furnishings, as well as actors in historical costumes.

No, she told herself quickly. That was impossible. She knew of no one who would perpetrate such a cruel hoax. Besides, she knew this house. No one could have replaced the missing tiles on the fireplace or the broken spindles on the stairs, while she meditated briefly. No one could have repapered all the walls and moved in a truckload of period furnishings, rugs, draperies and gewgaws, all in a scant 20 minutes!

Merciful heavens, what was happening?

Even as these frantic thoughts splintered Sarah's mind, the two women arrived at the second story. The upstairs hallway was also luxuriously carpeted, papered and furnished. An elegant rosewood settee rested against one wall, with two Chippendale side chairs and an Empire pier table flanking it on the opposite side. At the end of the hallway, a lush green fern spilled from its stand.

"Come along, now," the woman called.

In a deepening state of shock, Sarah followed the woman into the front bedroom on the right. "This will be your room while you're here," her hostess said with a sweeping gesture. "That is, if Damien decides to retain you."

Sarah stared at the magnificent room. The walls were a soft yellow, the ceiling and curtains stark white. An Aubusson rug was spread out on the floor. The furniture was of carved rosewood—an armoire, a dresser, and a delicate ladies dressing table with a beveled mirror. The bed was a masterpiece with beautifully carved headboard and footboard and a half-tester, lined in pale yellow, on top. Indeed, the bed looked just like an antique Sarah had once seen in a museum in Savannah; that bed had been designed by the famous New Orleans furniture craftsman, Prudent Mallard.

As Sarah continued to gaze, captivated, at the room, the woman walked briskly over to a cedar chest sitting beneath the west window. "There should be something suitable in here," she mumbled, opening the chest. "Ah, yes, this navy wool looks serviceable enough."

As Sarah watched, the woman tossed the long, dark gown on the bed. Other strange garments followed it—a corset, camisole and bloomers, several long petticoats, and gray silk stockings. Shutting the chest, the woman turned and handed Sarah an odd-looking pair of shoes; they were black with short heels, and they buttoned up to the ankles. Sarah had seen such shoes in museums before.

"Well, I'll leave you to dress, then," the woman said. "And please do something about that hair. It looks quite risque, trailing down about your shoulders so wildly. And those flowers! You look as if you've been rolling about in a field, miss."

Sarah's hand automatically flew to her hair as she watched the woman turn to leave. "B-but, what is your name?" she gasped.

The woman turned frowned at Sarah in consternation. "Why, I'm Olympia Fontaine, of course. Surely Mr. Rillieux told you? However could you have gotten here, child, if you don't know our names?"

However, indeed? Sarah wondered, staring at the woman in stupefaction.

Olympia shook her head in disgust. "Again, Miss Jennings, I must urge you to hurry. Let's just hope you're more nimble with your paintbrush than you are with your wits."

And the strange little woman tossed her head and swept out of the room.

Sarah walked numbly about the room. She approached the front window and stared through the lacy curtains. Outside was the upper gallery of the house; it appeared much newer and recently whitewashed. To the west was the wide Mississippi, right where it should be.

Yet straight ahead was a weedy, fallow field where the forest should have been. Sarah rushed forward, then paused a foot away from the window. She could feel an eerie vibration, an almost electric heavyness in the air next to the window. Instinctively, she backed away from the charged area. She sensed that some danger lurked near the outer walls of the house.

Feeling more bemused than ever, Sarah went to sit down on the bed. The tick appeared to be feather; she sank deeply into it. She fingered one of the strange, lacy undergarments laid out next to her. She had read enough historical fiction to know that these articles of clothing dated from the later nineteenth century. Yet the garments showed no signs of being almost a hundred years old. What on earth was happening to her? Was this real, or was she being entertained by lunatics?

Either she had lost her mind, she was dreaming, or she had gone back in time almost a hundred years—

To meet Damien. The answer hit Sarah with stunning clarity. She was about to be introduced to the very phantom who had haunted her so sweetly for so long. Whether this was insanity, a dream, or reality, she knew now that she must meet Damien.

Sarah undressed quickly and placed her garments in the cedar chest. She then went back to the bed, staring skeptically at the old-fashioned clothing. Deciding that the corset looked like a torture device, she returned it to the cedar chest and donned the bloomers and camisole. The undergarments were of starched linen and chafed against her skin. She put on the stockings and petticoats, then donned the button-down shoes, which were tight and pinched her toes. Then she put on the voluminous navy blue gown and buttoned the many tiny buttons on the bodice. Though the room was cool, the wool felt oppressive and scratchy. The bodice was tight, the skirt barely long enough, just reaching the tops of her quaint little shoes.

Sarah walked awkwardly over to the dressing table and sat down, staring at her transformed visage. The close-fitting lines of the dress highlighted her upthrust breasts and tiny waist. She looked as if she had, indeed, stepped back into another century—except for her hair, which, as the strange little woman had said, looked quite unseemly, her locks trailing down over her shoulders with wildflowers interspersed. Sarah plucked out the blooms Olympia Fontaine had objected to and placed them in a pale pink satin ware dish on the dressing table. Then she picked up a silver-plated hairbrush and vigorously brushed her hair.

Sarah found hairpins in a porcelain jar and used them to pin up her heavy tresses. She found the styling process quite awkward, since she seldom wore her hair in a bun. As she worked, she recalled Olympia Fontaine's last, odd remark: Let's just hope you're more nimble with your paintbrush than you are with your wits.

Had she been brought here to paint something? The very thought sent a shiver down her spine. Then she recalled Olympia's earlier remark about her being the artist sent out from a museum in New Orleans.

Good Lord, was she *supposed* to be here?

Sarah's musings were interrupted by a sharp rap at her door. Without waiting for permission, Olympia Fontaine opened the door and lumbered back inside. "Well, miss, I must say that's quite an improvement. Shall we go?"

Sarah gazed into the mirror at her amateurish yet presentable bun, at the glow in her blue eyes and the high color on her cheeks. Mercy! She was clearly out of her mind to be going along with this mad charade. She was no doubt demented to even feel excitement at the prospect of meeting Damien. Yet at the moment, it appeared she had little choice but to play her assigned role in this bizarre masquerade.

Catching Olympia Fontaine's frowning, impatient countenance in the mirror above her, Sarah nodded and stood. "Yes, I'm ready," she said bravely, turning to face Olympia.

She followed the older woman out of the room. As they headed toward the stairwell, Olympia called over her shoulder, "Now when you meet my nephew, miss, be mindful of what you say about Vincy. You'll be repairing Vincy's paintings, so of course some discussion will be in order. But bear in mind that Damien still hasn't recovered from his brother's death. Indeed, he's spent these past six years working on Vincy's memoirs."

Sarah listened in intense curiosity as they started down the stairway. She lifted her heavy, cumbersome skirts so she wouldn't stumble. "How did this—Vincy—die?" she asked.

"Why in the war, of course, child," came Olympia's forbearing reply. "Have you been asleep for the last decade? As if New Orleans hasn't been crawling with carpetbaggers for ages now! One would think you hailed from the netherworld."

Feeling the sting of this sharp rebuke, Sarah clamped her mouth shut. She did feel amazed to learn that the man she was about to meet had also lost a brother at war.

Downstairs, Olympia rapped on the middle door on the west side of the hallway. A muffled, rather preoccupied male voice called out, "Come in."

Sarah's heart hammered as Olympia opened the door; she followed her into the small but airy room.

The furnishings were minimal—built-in bookcases along one wall, a couple of side chairs opposite them, and, along the far wall beneath the narrow windows, a massive mahogany rolltop desk. It was the man at the desk who captivated Sarah. Even though he sat with his back to her, she at once felt mesmerized by his powerful presence.

Like Olympia, he was dressed in old-fashioned, dark clothing. Even seated, he appeared quite tall. His hair was jet-black and thick, gleaming with silken highlights. She couldn't see his face, yet she could tell by the motion of his arm and shoulder that he was writing furiously. Paper was everywhere —in piles on the desk, even spilling onto the floor.

Those must be the memoirs of his brother that Olympia had spoken of, she thought.

Olympia broke the silence. "Damien," she said in a surprisingly gentle tone, "this is the young woman, Miss Sarah Jennings, who has come from New Orleans to repair Vincy's paintings." As he turned in his chair, she added stiffly to Sarah, "Miss Jennings, this is my nephew, Mr. Fontaine."

And Olympia left the room, leaving Sarah alone with the man named Damien.

By now, he was on his feet, nodding to her stiffly. "Miss Jennings," he said in a deep baritone voice.

Sarah stared back at him as if hypnotized. Damien Fontaine was a tall, magnificently proportioned man, with broad shoulders tapering to a trim waist and long, muscular legs. He wore a black frock coat and matching trousers, a silver moire waistcoat, a pleated linen shirt and black cravat. All these details Sarah drank in within seconds. Then she glanced up at his face and barely managed to stifle a gasp. For the face on her portrait was now staring back at her!

Damien's face was the most handsome Sarah had ever seen on a man. His visage was long and well-sculpted, with a high-bridged, straight nose, a full mouth and firm chin. His cheekbones were aristocratically high, his brow straight and broad. But it was his eyes that slayed her; they were dark brown, deep-set, intense and brilliant, filled with a haunted pain—a pain that at once touched a response in herself.

My God, I've found him, she thought.

As the charged silence stretched out between them, she spotted a spark of curiosity in his gaze as he, in turn, looked her over. A half-smile tugged at his handsome mouth, a smile which told her he was pleased by what he saw. An unaccountable thrill swept over her.

"So you came," he said at last.

"Yes," she managed breathlessly.

"You're the artist."

"Yes."

He moved slightly closer, his eyes impaling her,

making her heart thunder in her ears. She noticed how long and thick his eyelashes were, how beautifully curved his brows were. His temples and sideburns were slightly streaked with gray, lending him an exciting, distinguished air. He looked to be in his early thirties. His presence and intensity stirred her so that she momentarily forgot to breathe. When she did, his scent—a potent mixture of bay rum and shaving soap—filled her lungs, thrilling her senses.

"You're the one we sent for?" he now asked.

"Yes," she answered without hesitation.

"Good," he said with that same devastating, half-smile. "Come along, then. I'll show you Vincy's paintings."

And even as Sarah oddly ached to reach out and touch him, he swept past her through the still-open door, leaving her awash in his essence. She felt like a sleepwalker as she followed him out of the small room and up the staircase. When they arrived on the upper story, he extracted a key from his pocket, and unlocked the door opposite hers. He swung it open and gestured for her to proceed inside.

Sarah walked into a large salon. At first she could see little beyond the indistinct boundaries of the room, for the heavy velvet draperies were drawn, giving the room the closed in feel of a tomb.

Then Damien flung open the draperies, flooding the room with light.

And Sarah looked around, captivated.

The room was filled with oil paintings. They sat on easels, rested against the wainscoting and were hung on the walls. There were literally dozens of them. They were all brilliantly expressionistic, seething with energy yet throbbing with pain. Their colors ranged from dark and morose to vibrant and bright. There were landscapes, portraits and still lifes, all done with the same bold, emotional strokes.

Sarah noted at once that almost all the paintings were damaged in some way—scratched or torn or chipped. Yet even the blemishes could not really mar their magnificence.

"My God," she gasped, staring at a brilliant painting of a starlit sky, with a blazing comet streaking across the dark heavens. "Are these by van Gogh?"

Damien had been watching her reactions closely. "Who is this van Gogh?" he asked with a scowl.

"He's . . ." All at once, Sarah clamped her mouth shut. Obviously, this man knew nothing about Vincent van Gogh. She hurriedly remembered the copyright date on the book downstairs, and Olympia's remarks about the war and carpetbaggers. If she truly had gone back in time, then she'd clearly landed in a period before van Gogh's heyday. "He's a Dutch artist whose work I once saw," she finished lamely. "His style is much like these paintings."

"These are the work of my brother, Vincy Fontaine," Damien announced sternly, with a slow, sweeping gesture at the room. "And I presume that you have been thoroughly instructed as to your duties here, Miss Jennings."

"Oh, yes, of course," Sarah assured him hastily. She realized that, even if she and the occupants of the house were all quite mad, she was so fascinated with Damien and his brother's paintings that she had to see this bizarre melodrama through.

"Well then, Miss Jennings," Damien continued, "have a look around. Tell me what you think."

Sarah walked slowly about the room, studying the paintings in greater detail. She scrutinized a landscape of a swamp scene cloaked with mists. She marveled at the trees—dark, twisted shapes dripping with moss. She studied the artist's bold signature. She then paused before a blazing landscape of wildflowers, their rainbow hues delighting her eyes. Next, she studied a portrait of the steamboat gothic house itself. The painting was much like her own, except that this time the house was whitewashed with every shutter in place—as it would have been a hundred years ago. She shivered at the thought.

Sarah noted that even in the brightest paintings, there was an underlying torment in the artist's powerful, exaggerated strokes. All of the paintings were magnificent, incredibly compelling. At last she paused before a portrait of a man with haunted, pain-filled eyes. He was dark and masterfully handsome, yet his countenance was tortured, almost crazed. Dark shadows rimmed his eyes; a haze of red supplied the background around his head.

Sarah realized that she was staring straight into the face of a soul in purgatory. Everything about the visage was familiar. With an expression of wonderment, she turned to Damien. "This is you?"

He drew closer, shaking his head. A look of haunted pain crossed his eyes, a pain that matched the dark suffering in the portrait. "That is Vincy's self-portrait."

Sarah gasped. "You look enough alike to be twins."

"Vincy was a year younger," Damien said. A muscle jumped in his jaw as he added, "We lost him eight years ago."

"I'm so sorry," Sarah said.

But Damien didn't seem to hear her as he continued to stare at the portrait. She knew he was off somewhere else right now, locked up in his own private hell. Then, in a voice so low that Sarah wasn't sure she heard him, he murmured, "It should have been me."

Staring at Damien's anguished countenance, Sarah felt a keen surge of empathy for him. Yet she strongly sensed that he hadn't meant for her to hear his last words. Not knowing how to respond, she turned awkwardly to finger a tear near the center of the self-portrait. "I've noticed that almost all of the paintings are damaged in some way," she remarked.

At last, Damien tore his gaze from the self-portrait and nodded to her. "Which is why you're here, of course," he remarked grimly. "When the Yankees occupied New Orleans, they ransacked many of the plantations outside the city. Aunt Olympia heard that they were headed toward Belle Fontaine and had the servants hide Vincy's paintings and many of our other valuables in an old cedar cottage out in the swamp. However, in the rushed atmosphere, most of Vincy's paintings were torn or chipped." He stepped closer and stared at her intently. "Can the paintings be repaired?"

Sarah's pulse pounded in her ears at Damien's closeness. The air between them seemed literally to vibrate with electricity, and he was staring at her as if his whole world depended on her reply. She bit her lip, then managed a nod. "Yes, I think the paintings can be repaired, although matching the colors is always quite challenging."

A hint of a smile played at his mouth and a glimmer of joy lit his eyes. "But it can be done?"

"Yes." Sarah knew a sudden pleasure herself, at giving this obviously tormented man a small moment of happiness.

"Good." His look of pleasure vanished as quickly as it had come, and a mask closed over his features. He gestured at a work table which rested against one wall. "I think you'll find everything you'll need here in the salon."

Sarah glanced at the table, which was cluttered with jars of paints, bottles of solvents, brushes and rags. "I'm sure I will."

"And I presume Mr. Rillieux explained the financial arrangements to you?"

"Er—yes," Sarah stammered, glancing away to cover her lie.

"Then you can start this afternoon. Shall we go?"

Though startled by Damien's abrupt dismissal of her, Sarah nodded and stepped forward. They left the room and Damien locked the door. "I'm sure you'll want to rest from your journey, Miss Jennings," he continued with the same remote courtesy as he pocketed the key. "My aunt will call you when luncheon is ready."

And Sarah's first meeting with Damien Fontaine was concluded.

Watching him turn and stride off toward the stairs, Sarah almost called after him. Then she wisely clamped her mouth shut. She definitely needed some time to sort everything out.

Sarah crossed the hallway and entered the relative safety of her room. She shut the door behind her and leaned against it, drawing a deep, steadying breath. She'd met Damien now, and a strange yet captivating man he was.

She thought over the events of the last hour. She had meditated in the old house, then she had awakened to what was clearly another time. Though the house was radically different and the landscape outside her windows was different, she knew to her soul that she was still in the same place.

Had she truly lost her mind? By all the evidence, she was very much alive and living in the nineteenth century. There was even a bizarre logic in her being here; she was the artist, come to repair Vincy Fontaine's brilliant, turbulent paintings. A chill gripped her heart as she remembered Damien asking, "You're the one we sent for?" She had a strong conviction that no other artist would come out from New Orleans, that she was somehow meant to be here at this moment in time.

Should she tell Damien and his aunt where she had truly come from? No, she decided. If she told them she was from the twentieth century, they'd surely think she was mad. She didn't know if they were real as yet; she didn't even know if *she* was real. And if she told them where she had truly come from, the spell might break, propelling her back to a world where she always had felt displaced.

One truth loomed central in her mind. No matter how she had gotten here, she felt fascinated by this world, by Vincy's paintings—and most of all by Damien Fontaine.

Chapter Six

Luncheon was a quiet meal held in the large, sunny dining room. Sarah sat toward the middle of the Queen Anne table, with Olympia Fontaine flanking her on one end and Damien on the other. Still feeling like an alien in this new yet fascinating world, Sarah took in every sight and sound surrounding her as they waited to be served.

The room, like the rest of the house, was beautifully decorated. Lavish silver pieces rested on the sideboard, and a gleaming brass chandelier hung over the table. On the northern wall of the room, just beyond Damien's chair, sat a handsome cabinet grand piano; sheet music was laid out on the music stand, and Sarah found herself wondering if perhaps Olympia had been playing that very piano when she awakened in the parlor.

She studied the table itself. The linen was starched and snowy white, the china blue and white

Staffordshire with a floral border. A blue and gold oriental bowl filled with yellow marigolds provided a stunning centerpiece; candles in silver holders flanked it on either side. The flatware was sterling, as were the water goblets. Sarah ran her fingertips over the smooth silver handles of her knife and spoon, as if to reassure herself that they were, indeed, real. Fingering her china cup with its vibrant painting of a bluebird, Sarah was astonished to see the signature of John James Audubon.

As Sarah replaced her hand in her lap, she caught Damien Fontaine staring at her with his intense, dark eyes. His expression was unsmiling, almost grim. As their gazes locked briefly, a shiver coursed through her. She wasn't used to the very presence of a man exciting her this way. Indeed, just being in the same room with him, she felt shaken, thrown off balance. She swallowed hard and turned away from his unsettling scrutiny.

When she'd entered the room moments earlier, Damien had nodded to her stiffly, holding out her chair for her. Yet beyond this brief show of courtesy, he'd said nothing to her. By comparison, he'd seemed almost loquacious earlier, when they'd been upstairs in the salon. Then she recalled that as soon as he'd explained her duties to her, he'd abruptly ended the interview. He was obviously a man of few words, a man very much locked up in himself. Yet she realized that his aloofness now fascinated her every bit as much as his earlier deference had, just as his intensity and brooding masculinity stirred her in every way. Again, she marveled at how drawn she felt toward him.

Damien's aunt, meanwhile, was becoming impatient. "Oh, where is that lazy Baptista with our luncheon?" she asked.

As if on cue, an attractive black woman moved indolently into the room, carrying a silver tray with a china soup tureen and a loaf of hot sliced bread. The woman was tall and statuesque; she wore a black dress, a white apron and a white lace housecap. She had chocolate-colored eyes and smooth, honey-brown skin.

"Well, it's about time, Baptista," Olympia said sharply. "Our guest, Miss Jennings, is bound to think we have no sense of hospitality here at Belle Fontaine."

If Baptista was affected by this rebuke, she did not show it, beyond a slight tightening of her features as she glanced coolly at Sarah. The negress moved slowly, soundlessly, on the Persian rug, serving them their first course, a rich turtle soup. Baptista was guardedly grim around the women; only around Damien did she smile. As he accepted a slice of French bread to go with his soup, he smiled back at her, and Sarah wondered if there were something going on between the two of them. It was the first time she had actually seen Damien smile, and she had to admit that the slight softening of his features made her senses quiver and made her long to become the object of his pleasure.

Sarah found the soup rich and succulent and subtley seasoned; actually having food in her mouth deepened her sense of verisimilitude, of actually being here.

As they were finishing their soup, Olympia remarked to Sarah, "Well, my nephew has mentioned that you will be staying on to repair Vincy's paintings."

Sarah glanced at Damien, and found his expression dark and inscrutable. "That's true," she said to Olympia.

Olympia glanced toward Damien. "I take it, then, that you're satisfied with Miss Jennings' qualifications?"

Damien shrugged. "If Mr. Rillieux is satisfied with Miss Jennings' qualifications, then I'm sure that I am, as well."

Olympia raised an eyebrow at what she obviously felt was a cavalier attitude on the part of her nephew, but she didn't comment, turning again to Sarah. "How are things in New Orleans these days, Miss Jennings?"

Sarah nearly dropped her spoon, quite taken aback by the question. "Oh—fine," she stammered.

"Fine?" Olympia gasped. "With the scalawags and carpetbaggers robbing everyone blind? Of course, I haven't even been to the city since '61, when we went to hear Adelina Patti sing at the French Opera. But my friend Mary Broussard tells me there's so much hardship there these days. All the fine mansions are just crumbling away, and everyone is going wild over the lottery, as if they want to recapture—well, as we all know, nothing's been the same since the war."

"I'm sure that's true," Sarah said cautiously.

"And yet you can say everything is fine there?" Olympia went on.

"Well, actually, I've only come to the city recently from Atlanta," Sarah put in lamely.

"Atlanta!" Olympia was aghast. "However did you survive the siege, child, not to mention Sherman's burning the city to its very foundations?"

"I—er—" Sarah thought fiercely. "Actually, my family stayed with some friends in the country during the siege. We moved back after the war, and now most everything has been rebuilt."

"Well, I'm sure you would know, living there,"

Olympia put in, yet she looked highly skeptical.

"Aunt, pray allow Miss Jennings to finish her luncheon," Damien put in rather tiredly. He paused to watch Baptista step back into the room with their main course of baked fish and rice pilaf. "I'm sure our guest dislikes talking about the war as much as any of us."

At Damien's words, Olympia looked properly rebuked. "Yes, nephew," she murmured, and the rest of the meal passed in strained silence. Sarah would almost have preferred Olympia's nosy inquisitiveness, especially as several more times she caught Damien's intense, unnerving perusal.

At the end of the meal, Damien was the first to excuse himself. He paused by Sarah's chair on his way out of the room, laying the key to the salon next to her plate. "I presume you'll be needing this, Miss Jennings," he said stiffly, and then he was gone.

Sarah glanced at Olympia, but the older woman was sipping her tea as she stared off toward a window. Muttering her own excuse, Sarah took the key and left, her movements awkward due to her heavy skirts and painfully tight shoes.

Out in the central hallway, Sarah approached the front door of the house, anxious to take a look at the outside from a different perspective. Yet again, as she drew closer to the outer walls of the house, she felt the same subtle, almost mystical vibrations she had encountered earlier, upstairs. Some primal instinct warned her to go no further.

Feeling bemused, Sarah turned and went back upstairs. What did the strange, invisible barrier mean? she wondered. Why did she feel she couldn't proceed beyond it? She sighed heavily. In a way, she had to concede that the existence of the odd vibrations was no more bizarre than the fact that she had apparently awakened in another century. Again, her insticts urged her not to question, but to play out the role assigned her. She couldn't deny that since she had arrived here, a feeling of purpose, of rightness, had consumed her. Now, she could no more leave than she could understand the strange forces that had brought her here.

Sarah went back to the salon where Vincy's paintings were housed. She decided to spend the afternoon studying them, assessing the damage to each canvas and planning her repairs. She was again awed by the raw brilliance of the paintings. She mused that it was such a tragedy that Vincy Fontaine's talent was lost to this world, just as Brian's talent was lost to the twentieth century. She recalled Damien saying, "It should have been me." Obviously, he felt great guilt over his brother's death. That guilt was something Sarah could certainly relate to, since she, too, had felt enormous responsibility for Brian's death. She remembered how she'd agonized at the time, telling herself endlessly that she should have done more, that she should have somehow prevented Brian from going off to Europe. She had literally driven herself over the edge with recriminations, and then, ultimately, she'd had to be hospitalized. Finally, after weeks of therapy, Dr. Hogan had convinced her that self-flagellation was futile and that it was the last thing Brian would have wanted. Still, the guilt crept back to haunt her at times.

Sarah tried to put aside her painful feelings and concentrate on the task before her. Already, she felt a bond with Vincy Fontaine, just as she felt a bond with his tormented, reclusive brother. If she had indeed been brought here to repair Vincy's paintings, she would certainly do her best, preserving his brilliance for the world.

Sarah picked up a sketch pad and pencil and took notes on the planned repairs. Some of the paintings had small tears or holes that she would repair with canvas patches. Touching up the numerous chips and scratches on the panels would be more difficult, but luckily, Sarah had done some volunteer work at the High Museum of Art in Atlanta, cleaning and repairing old paintings, so she was at least moderately skilled in the techniques she would need.

She knew that the first step in any touching-up process was to become intimately acquainted with the unique style and brush strokes of the artist. She found Vincy's paintbox and a blank canvas and tried duplicating some of his bold, exaggerated strokes. She also tried blending some of the hues she would need to touch up the scratches. This was an arduous process at best, since the colors tended to change somewhat as they dried. She would have to touch up large areas of some of the paintings in order to keep the various hues uniform.

As Sarah continued to work, she heard piano music drifting up from downstairs. The songs were sad, poignant Stephen Foster melodies—"Beautiful Dreamer," "My Old Kentucky Home," and "Under the Willow She's Sleeping." Sarah smiled as she realized that the piano music she'd heard before *had* been real. And surely Olympia was the pianist.

At one point, Sarah took a break from her labors and walked toward the front windows. Again she felt the eerie vibrations; again her instincts warned her not to proceed. She realized that she felt instinctively afraid of the world outside those windows.

Once her inventory was completed, Sarah de-

cided she would begin the actual restoration process the next morning, when the light was best—
assuming she was still even here then! At any rate,
she knew she wanted to repair Vincy's self-portrait
first; of all the paintings, it compelled her the most.

Late in the afternoon, Olympia came into the
salon. Glancing about, she raised an ·eyebrow at
Sarah. "I assume you've found everything you'll
need to repair the paintings, Miss Jennings?"

Sarah was seated on a stool before an easel, still
staring at Vincy's self-portrait, her sketch pad in her
lap. "Yes, I've found everything I need."

"Good. I just wanted to let you know that we
won't be dining formally tonight. Damien has decided to work through the dinner hour."

"Work?" Sarah repeated confusedly.

"On Vincy's memoirs, of course."

"Ah, yes."

"Anyway, I'm sending Damien a tray. Would you
like me to have Baptista bring you something, as
well?"

"Yes, that would be nice," Sarah said.

"Very well."

As Olympia turned to leave, Sarah called out,
"Miss Fontaine?"

Olympia turned sharply. "Yes?"

"Was that you playing the piano downstairs?"

For once, Olympia smiled. "Why, yes."

"Your music is so lovely."

"Thank you. The piano does help to relieve the
monotony of my days here." As Sarah continued to
stare at her, Olympia added, "Was there something
else, Miss Jennings?"

Sarah hesitated. There were a million questions
she wanted to ask Olympia—about the house,

about Damien, about the strange age in which she had astoundingly awakened. Yet she sensed Olympia was already suspicious of her and that this wasn't the moment to press her. "I just wanted to say thank you," Sarah said at last.

"You're quite welcome, I'm sure," Olympia replied stiffly.

Sarah sighed as Olympia left the room. Soon thereafter, Baptista, as taciturn as before, brought up her tray. Sitting at the work table in the fading light, Sarah ate her modest repast of oyster stew and biscuits. Then she stayed on in the salon late into the evening, studying Vincy's paintings awash in moonlight. She could literally feel Vincy's energy, his torment, the demons driving him as he had painted. And she knew now that she understood the paintings well enough to begin the repairs in the morning.

Late that evening, she left the salon. As she started across the hallway, she glimpsed Baptista knocking on a door on the other side of the stairwell. A low masculine voice called out, "Come in." Baptista turned to give Sarah a look of sultry triumph before she slipped into the room.

Sarah barely restrained a gasp. She returned to her room and leaned against the shut door for support, feeling highly unsettled. So Baptista was evidently Damien's mistress. She supposed that shouldn't bother her—and yet it did. It bothered her more than she cared to admit.

Suddenly, Sarah gripped the doorknob as a wave of fatigue swept over her. She realized she felt exhausted, too drained to try to solve any more mysteries tonight. Her feet felt nearly numb from being constricted in the old-fashioned shoes all day, and her body felt abused from carrying around so many layers of oppressive, scratchy clothing. She wondered how women of past centuries had managed to endure beneath the heavy impediments of their own clothing.

It seems she was finding out! Again, she wondered if she'd gone quite mad, yet it seemed that no hallucination could come complete with feet that ached this badly.

Sarah undressed and saw to her needs with the chamber pot. She donned a handkerchief linen gown she had found in the old chest. The gown felt soft and cool against her hot, chafed skin. She crawled into the magnificent bed and sank deeply into the feather tick. She slept, not knowing when—or where—she might awaken.

That night the prophetic dream came again, and with it the haunting message: *The three gifts . . . The answer is Elissa. . . .*

Late that night, Olympia Fontaine sat at the writing desk in her bedroom, the kerosene lamp casting a sinister glow over her features. She was not at all pleased by the strange young woman, Sarah Jennings, who had arrived at Belle Fontaine today. Sarah's abrupt appearance had shocked Olympia; her scandalous attire had aroused her suspicions.

Olympia found it difficult to believe that Mr. Rillieux had chosen such a highly unsuitable young woman to repair Vincy's paintings. Yet who else could the young woman be? They were certainly expecting no one else to arrive here at Belle Fontaine.

Still, Olympia was not at all pleased with Mr. Rillieux's choice. Moreover, she didn't like the way Damien stared at Miss Jennings. It was bad enough that her nephew sought his ease with Baptista; at least that liaison was purely physical in nature. Yet Damien obviously would risk much emotionally should he become involved with the strange and unconventional Miss Jennings. And the poor man had already endured enough suffering to last a lifetime.

To make matters worse, Damien had expressed no curiosity whatsoever regarding Miss Jennings' background or qualifications. It appeared that she must take the reins in hand, then, and write to Mr. Rillieux to express her displeasure and misgivings.

Nodding to herself firmly, Olympia took writing paper from the desk drawer and plucked her pen from the inkwell.

Chapter Seven

Sarah awakened to her fantastical new world. She heard the sound of a rooster crowing and stretched and yawned to find herself in the same bed, the same room, the same century. A rosy glow bathed the room, outlining the high ceiling and antique furnishings. Any doubts she might have harbored about being in the middle of a hallucination were beginning to recede.

Sarah remembered having the strange dream again last night, the dream where she kept hearing the words, *The three gifts . . . the answer is Elissa.* The cryptic message continued to baffle her, but at least it had been a peaceful dream, unlike the terrifying nightmare of Brian, which mercifully hadn't recurred last night.

Sarah arose and walked toward the window, venturing close, but not too close. She could still feel the eerie vibrations every time she ventured near the front walls of the house. Standing back slightly, she glanced at the fallow field in the distance. Fascinated, she watched a huge, three-decked steamboat glide down the Mississippi River to the west of her. The steamer was magnificent, its decks edged with gleaming railings, its stacks billowing smoke into the morning skies. A couple stood on the high promenade, their figures awash in sunshine. The man wore a frock coat, top hat and dark trousers, the woman a long traveling cloak and a bonnet. Sarah gazed at them in wonder. She was in another century, all right.

Then a flurry of motion directly beneath her caught her eye, and she glanced downward to watch Damien Fontaine ride up to the house on a handsome black stallion. He handled the spirited, prancing beast with ease. Watching the motions of his muscular arms and long legs, Sarah again marveled at what a fine figure of a man he cut.

As Damien stopped the horse before the steps, a black lad hurried forward, taking the reins from him. She watched Damien climb the steps with hat in hand, his hair tousled, his features flushed from his ride. Then he glanced upward and she backed away, her heart tripping with sudden excitement. Had he seen her?

A rap at her door distracted her. Turning, Sarah called out, "Come in." She watched Baptista enter with a breakfast tray.

"Why, good morning, Baptista," Sarah said with a smile. "How kind of you to bring my breakfast."

Baptista merely nodded sullenly as she set the tray down on the dressing table. She turned away and began making the bed.

With a sigh, Sarah went to sit at the dressing table. As she ate her breakfast of poached eggs and toast and drank the rich *café au lait,* she decided to make another stab at starting a conversation with the black woman. "Have you been at the plantation long, Baptista?"

Baptista glanced at Sarah. "All my life, mam'zelle."

"You didn't want to leave after the war?"

Baptista shrugged as she plumped the pillows. "I got nowheres to go, mam'zelle." Meaningfully, she added, "And Master Damien, he got no one to care for him."

Something about the woman's stance, her eyes, communicated a certain territorial possessiveness to Sarah. So something *was* going on between Baptista and the master of Belle Fontaine. Again, she found the thought unsettling.

By now, Baptista had finished with the bed. As she picked up the clothing Sarah had folded across a chair the previous night, she added, "Mam'zelle, I send in the day maids with your bath."

"Day maids?"

"Girls from town. Mistress Fontaine, she hire them to help with the heavy cleaning. They come four days a week."

"I see."

At the portal, Baptista turned to stare at Sarah. "Is there anything else, mam'zelle?"

"No, thank you."

It was not until after Baptista left that Sarah realized her fingers were tightly clenched on her coffee cup. Something about Baptista definitely bothered her; she seemed as mysterious, taciturn and unreachable as the mercurial master of Belle Fontaine. Sarah had to admit that she felt threatened by the possibility that Baptista was Damien's mistress, and this made her realize anew how quickly Damien had come to fascinate her.

A few minutes later, the day maids, two shy black girls wearing blue cottonades, brought up Sarah's bath. Sarah marveled at the arduous process as the two girls first hauled in a tin tub and then made numerous trips to fetch hot water. When the older girl offered to assist Sarah with the actual bathing, she politely declined. After the maids left, Sarah found it awkward sitting in the cramped tub, but the hot water did feel marvelous against her skin, and she felt quite feminine and invigorated after cleansing herself with the lilac-scented soap one of the girls had brought in.

After drying off, Sarah put on a new set of scratchy underwear, then donned another of Lucy's old gowns, this one a gold muslin. As she pinned up her hair, she wondered if it had caused Damien pain to see her wearing his deceased wife's old clothing yesterday. He'd certainly displayed no reaction to the navy blue gown she'd worn. Did he even remember that these clothes had once belonged to his wife?

Sarah didn't see Damien or Olympia that morning. She spent her time working on Vincy's self-portrait. The painting had several bad chips and a tear near the center. Fortunately, the tear was in an area painted black, right in the center of Vincy's cravat. Sarah began by using alcohol to remove the outer layer of varnish on the entire painting. This was a delicate, difficult process that took many hours. Indeed, when Olympia stopped by to tell Sarah luncheon was ready, she begged for a tray. It was sent up, but remained untouched all afternoon as Sarah worked on. After removing the last of the

101

varnish, she patched the hole from the back. Only then did she begin touching up the brush strokes themselves.

Luckily, there was no damage on Vincy's face, so Sarah had only to touch up the patch and the chipped paint in the red background. She had just corrected two chips and had painted over the patch and was standing back scrutinizing her work, when abruptly Damien Fontaine burst into the salon.

Startled, Sarah whirled to stare at him. Like yesterday, Damien was dressed all in black. He seemed even taller and more handsome than she had remembered. He was an awesome, masterful presence, even in the large room. His stride was quick and assured as he proceeded toward her; his eyes were alive with feeling as he stared at the painting on the easel, studying Sarah's brush strokes that so precisely imitated Vincy's.

"Yes!" he cried. "Yes!"

Sarah was stunned by Damien's sudden ebullience. She barely had time to put down her paintbrush before he arrived at her side and grabbed her around the waist, swinging her about. He was laughing—actually laughing—and his eyes gleamed with a near-fanatical joy as he whirled her about. Sarah found his delight infectious, and her heart hammered wildly at his exciting nearness.

Just as abruptly, he set her on her feet and turned back to the painting. "Oh, yes, you've got it, Sarah! You have just the right touch. That's just how Vincy would have repaired the damage."

"Well, thank you," she said, very pleased but equally taken aback.

His gaze was still riveted to the painting. "Already the entire portrait looks brighter. What did you do?"

"I removed the outer layer of varnish," Sarah

said. "You see, some nineteenth-century painters—"

As Damien glanced at her sharply, Sarah bit her
lip, realizing her *faux pas*. "Some painters of this
century," she hastily amended, "apply the varnish
with a rather heavy hand. It's called the 'museum
look'. In Vincy's case," she glanced about the room,
"it rather mutes the brilliance of his work. Don't
you agree?"

Damien grinned. "Ah, yes, I do agree."

"Once the repairs are complete, I'll reapply the
varnish, of course," Sarah went on. "But my finishing coat will be a little lighter—that is, if you have
no objection."

"Certainly not," Damien said excitedly. "That's
precisely what you must do. You're good, Sarah,
really good. You must stay. Now, work—work!"

And he turned to leave.

Sarah rushed forward, calling, "Please don't leave
yet! There's so much I want to ask—"

But her words fell on deaf ears. As abruptly as he
had appeared, Damien Fontaine was gone.

Afterward, Sarah could not get Damien
Fontaine's astounding visit out of her mind. He was
certainly a mercurial, unpredictable man. Her
heart quickened as she remembered the electrifying moment when he'd appeared; she felt half-dizzy
as she recalled him swinging her around and laughing. She still tingled everywhere his wonderful,
strong hands had touched her. She knew they'd
shared something very special in that moment—a
feeling of intense communication, of shared exultation.

Yesterday, Sarah would have sworn Damien
Fontaine was incapable of such a moment of una-
bashed joy. The thought that her efforts might have

brought such delight to this haunted man filled her heart with gladness. And after seeing this new side to him, she felt even more fascinated by him.

Soon after Damien's visit, the light became too weak for Sarah to continue working successfully. She carefully cleaned her brushes in turpentine and put away her supplies. Feeling exhausted from standing on her feet all day, she took a brief nap in her room, then freshened up for dinner. When she went downstairs, she discovered to her dismay that she and Olympia were the sole occupants of the dining room. Baptista served them a rich gumbo, French bread and white wine.

After a while, Sarah asked Olympia casually, "Is Mr. Fontaine working through dinner again?"

"Ah, yes," Olympia replied, dabbing at her mouth with her napkin. "After Damien checked on your progress, he returned to the study to continue his writings. He told me he won't be joining us tonight." With a stiff, fleeting smile, Olympia added, "I must say that Damien seems inspired by your accomplishments, Miss Jennings. Indeed, he insisted that I stop by the salon to see for myself what you've done. I saw your repairs on Vincy's self-portrait, and I do agree that you've made an impressive beginning."

"Thank you," Sarah said. She was pleased to receive this compliment from Olympia, although she still wasn't sure whether the spinster really approved of her presence here.

And from the dark look Baptista now shot her as she cleared away the dishes, she could tell the black woman most definitely disapproved.

* * *

The next morning, Sarah decided it was high time she pressed Olympia regarding Vincy, Damien and the Fontaine family in general. She felt somewhat encouraged by Olympia's compliments the previous night, and it was important to her to try to win the older woman over to her side. After all, Olympia had alluded to being lonely here, and she did seem to enjoy having someone to converse with; Sarah intended to provide a sympathetic ear.

After breakfast in her room, Sarah dressed in yet another of Lucy's old gowns, a rose-colored wool, and went downstairs to look for the spinster. The dining room was deserted, as was the parlor. Damien was nowhere in sight, but the door to his study was closed, so Sarah assumed he was already busy writing away.

Sarah was standing in the hallway, wearing a puzzled frown, when Baptista came in with a tray. "Baptista, have you seen Miss Fontaine this morning?"

"Yes'um," Baptista replied, eyeing Sarah with petulant brown eyes. "She out back having her tea in the garden."

Sarah swallowed hard at this revelation. "Thank you."

Baptista nodded and went off toward the dining room. Sarah started down the hallway, cautiously proceeding toward the backdoor. Should she risk going outside?

Since she'd come here two days ago, she'd felt safe inside the confines of the house. She'd felt as if she were a part of this house, as if embraced by its aura and its soul. Yet she still instinctively feared the world beyond the house, and she still encountered the strange yet palpable barrier every time she drew too close to the front walls.

Yet the courtyard was surrounded by high walls which were anchored to the house itself, she recalled. Would the aura of the house extend there? Would she be safe?

Cautiously, she moved closer to the door. Its glass panels were veiled by a gauzy white curtain. As she reached for the doorknob, she felt no electricity, no sense of forboding. Cautiously, she opened the door.

A sweet, cool breeze swept in. Sarah inched her way out onto the back gallery. So far, so good. She stared at the courtyard, surrounded by its high brick walls. It was the same, yet different. The courtyard she'd seen back in the twentieth century was crumbling away across the top, with bricks broken or missing. The walls of this courtyard were perfectly sound and regular. The tall crepe myrtles were absent, as well, and in their place were climbing pyracantha dripping with red berries.

The kitchen was in the same place, in the western corner. Smoke curled from its chimney, and its roof looked much newer. The planting area was vastly different, not barren as she had left it, but covered in neat rows of flowers and spices flaring outward from the fountain. The area resembled an authentic English formal garden, Sarah mused. Its colors were dazzling—the pinks and reds of roses, the whites and yellows of carnations and marigolds, the blues and violets of petunias. The sweet perfume of the flowers mingled with the pungent, minty and tart essences of the spices.

The fountain, too, looked much newer, its Grecian goddess spurting cascades of gleaming water. Near the fountain sat Olympia, drinking tea at a wrought-iron table. The spinster was watching a ruby-throated hummingbird dart at a blue morning glory, and she seemed oblivious to Sarah's presence.

"Good morning," Sarah called out, starting cautiously down the steps.

Olympia set down her tea and turned. "Good morning."

"What a lovely garden."

"Thank you, I do try my best." Olympia ventured a smile.

"You did all this?" Sarah asked incredulously as she approached the table. "What an accomplished horticulturist you are. Why, the courtyard is enchanting."

"Thanks again, dear." Now Olympia looked genuinely pleased. "Actually, as a girl, I took my schooling in England, and I so admired the formal gardens there." She nodded toward the chair across from her. "Will you join me for tea?"

"I'd love to." Sarah seated herself and accepted the cup of tea Olympia handed her.

"Well, Miss Jennings, is there something I can do for you?"

"Actually, there is." Sarah took a long sip of the excellent, strong tea, then set down her cup with a smile. "Miss Fontaine, I was wondering—could you tell me a little about your family, their history and so forth?" Watching Olympia's round face tighten in suspicion, she added, "You see, when I do this type of restoration, it's important to me to understand fully the background of the artist."

"Ah," Olympia said, nodding as realization dawned on her. "I suppose it would be."

"Really, I'd appreciate anything you can tell me —how the family came to live here, whatever comes to mind."

Olympia nodded. "Of course, the Fontaine family

107

has been in this country for many decades. Damien's great-grandfather emigrated from France in the early part of this century. With his family, Philippe Fontaine settled in New Orleans. He became a highly successful commission merchant there. It was one of his grandsons, Damien's father, who bought the plantation and brought his family here to live. Louis was my brother, and when he and Lenore settled here in Meridian in the early fifties, I came along to help with the children. You see, there were six of them back then—like little stairsteps. Damien was the eldest, then Vincy, then four sisters."

"I see," Sarah murmured. "Where are Damien's four sisters now?"

Olympia sighed. "I must backtrack a bit there. When the family first came here, we lived in the old house near the river. It was little more than a Greek Revival cottage, and of course it was quite crowded with all nine of us living there. So Louis decided to build the big house." She smiled. "My brother always had a whimsical streak, and he also was friends with Valsin Marmillion who had built San Francisco over in St. John the Baptist Parish. Thus, Louis had the architect pattern Belle Fontaine after Valsin's steamboat gothic style."

"It's quite magnificent," Sarah murmured.

"Thank you." Olympia's expression grew poignant. "At any rate, even as the big house was nearing completion, there was a yellow fever epidemic in the parish, and I'm afraid all four of Louis's young daughters, as well as his beloved Lenore, succumbed."

"How awful!"

"Yes, it was all so tragic," Olympia concurred. She took a lacy handkerchief from her pocket and twisted it in her fingers, appearing genuinely pleased to have gained a sympathetic ear. "Louis was never the same afterward. He burned down the old cottage near the river. I'll never forget the sight of him, standing there watching the blaze, with tears streaming down his face. We all moved into the new house, but a sad day it was. Louis was a broken and haunted man by then. On a night two years later, he quietly expired in his sleep."

"I'm so sorry," Sarah murmured. "And Damien and Vincy?"

"The boys were in their teens by then. I tried my best to raise them, to help them overcome the tragedy of their past. For a while it seemed to be working. I'll never forget the sight of them as young men—carefree and full of life, courting all the fair belles of the parish. They were very close, those two, back then."

"Of course they would have been—after what happened."

"When Damien was twenty-one, he married Lucy St. Pierre," Olympia continued. "Actually, the wedding had to be rushed somewhat, due to the outbreak of war. Nevertheless, it was a most happy day. They married right here in my garden, with Vincy standing up as Damien's best man. Let's see, Vincy would have been—yes, twenty then. How handsome my boys looked, standing by the fountain with the minister, watching Lucy, so beautiful, as she came down the back steps on her father's arm. Within a couple of months, Lucy was expecting Damien's child. We were all so happy—and then, that wretched war ruined everything!"

"Please, go on," Sarah urged, her fingers tensely gripping the tabletop.

Olympia dabbed at a tear. "In that first year after

the boys went off, Lucy lost Damien's child. I'm convinced that it was the war and all the worrying that brought on the stillbirth. We thought she was going to be all right, but the day after she miscarried, she contracted childbed fever. She died the following night."

"How terrible!"

Olympia expelled a painful sigh. "Indeed. That was still fairly early in the war, and the boys managed to get leave to come home and bury Lucy and the child. Even then, my poor boys were so grim and defeated. Something seemed dreadfully changed between them, something that went beyond the tragedy here at Belle Fontaine. They they went off again, and sometimes half a year passed with no word from either of them. Finally, I received word that Vincy had been killed at Gettysburg."

"Oh, Miss Fontaine," Sarah said, instinctively touching Olympia's hand, "I'm so very sorry."

Olympia dabbed at tears again. "Somehow, Damien managed to bring Vincy's body home. I think he just walked off from his regiment. At any rate, I'll never forget the tortured look in his eyes, and how he spent almost his whole time here at his brother's grave. Then Damien was off again. He came home for good in '65, but by then, he was a haunted shell of a man, just like Louis had been after he lost Lenore and the girls. My nephew has been a veritable recluse ever since. To this day, no guests have been received at Belle Fontaine, and he leaves the house only for his daily ride or to take care of our business in town."

"What about the plantation itself?" Sarah asked. "I mean, I've seen no real activity since I've arrived here."

Olympia nodded. "The cane fields have lain fallow ever since the war, I'm afraid. Damien has refused to start up the crops again. Most of the slaves left, of course, but my nephew could easily have hired on help if he wanted to."

"But—forgive me if I'm prying, Miss Fontaine—but how can you manage?"

Olympia smiled. "Fortunately, my brother anticipated the war many years ago. You see, talk of secession began here back in the early 50's. Louis knew that war would come eventually, and he made provision by depositing a substantial amount in gold in a bank in England. So we'll never lack for anything material here at Belle Fontaine. I only wish I could say as much for the fortunes of our friends."

Sarah frowned. "So Damien has no compelling reason to get the plantation going again?"

"None whatsoever. To this day, he just sits in his study, endlessly working on Vincy's memoirs."

"Has he ever shown them to you?"

She shook her head adamantly. "Never."

"And how many years has Damien been this way?" Sarah continued.

"Well, as I said, ever since the war ended in '65. Six years."

So it was 1871, Sarah thought with wonder. She was living in the autumn of the year 1871.

Chapter Eight

That day as Sarah worked, she thought over her conversation with Olympia. She thought of the tragedies that had plagued the Fontaine family for so many years.

No wonder Damien Fontaine was a recluse. Here, she thought she had suffered in losing Brian—and, of course, she had suffered grievously. But to lose one's entire family—both parents, four sisters and a beloved brother, not to mention a wife and child! It was beyond comprehension. Sarah was certain she could not even begin to know the depth of Damien's torment, and when she thought of the transitory joy she'd brought him through her work on Vincy's paintings, her heart welled with happiness and her eyes filled with tears. She wanted to know Damien better; she sensed that they could share so much, that they could seek true healing together.

Was that the real reason she had been brought

here? Had their anguish drawn them together across time? This thought was such a revelation to her that her hand began to tremble and she had to stop her work momentarily.

That afternoon, Sarah finished touching up Vincy's self-portrait. Standing back and studying her work critically, she was quite pleased. Her brush strokes fit in beautifully with Vincy's strokes, his anguish and his brilliance shone through. For now, she would let the wet areas of the painting dry; then in a few weeks, assuming she was still here, she would apply a new, light coating of varnish to the entire portrait.

Sarah was still admiring her work when Damien walked into the salon. Somehow, she felt his presence even before she heard the floorboards creak. She turned to him, smiling and radiant, awash in her own pleasurable satisfaction at having done the job well. As she studied him standing near her, her heart tripped into a faster rhythm. He looked so handsome in his black suit and white ruffled shirt, his dark eyes gleaming as he stared back at her.

"Good afternoon, Sarah," he said.

"Good afternoon, Damien," she whispered back. It was amazing, she thought, how they'd already established this familiarity, how they'd so quickly dispensed with formalities and had gone to a first-name basis.

He stepped closer, studying the portrait intently; she watched a muscle twitch in his strong jaw. "You've done a splendid job," he said with a catch in his voice.

"Thank you. I'm pleased myself, I must say."

He glanced about the room. "I can't wait to see how you touch up the other paintings."

"I hope they'll all go as well."

"I'm sure they will," he said with a kind smile. "You definitely are gifted, Sarah."

"Thanks, again."

"Well, then . . ." Awkwardly, he turned to leave.

"Damien?" she called after him.

He turned to her. "Yes?"

Sarah drew a deep, steadying breath at the look of tense expectation in his eyes. "I spoke with your aunt this morning, and she told me—well, a little of your family history. I just wanted you to know how sorry I am about everything."

"Thank you," he replied stiffly, and she could tell by his strained expression that he was feeling pressed. "Is there anything else?"

She stepped forward, swallowing hard. "Please don't go as yet," she said in a small voice. "Stay and tell me about Vincy."

At her words, a look of terrible pain crossed his eyes, and his features tightened into an implacable mask. "That's impossible," he said gruffly, turning away.

"Please," she repeated, forcing herself to step even closer and touch his sleeve. She could feel the sinew of his arm tensing beneath her touch, and his eyes were raw with feeling as he turned to stare back at her. Oh, he was so real, she thought, and in so much pain.

She glanced about the room in anguish and awe. "I just want to understand him," she said quietly.

Damien's eyes were equally tormented as he followed Sarah's gaze about the room. Then his vision settled on the completed self-portrait, and his smile, his voice, were surprisingly kind as he whispered back, "Ah, but you already do."

* * *

That night, Sarah felt restless, unable to sleep. Finally, she donned a wrapper and went back into the salon, studying Vincy's paintings awash in moonlight.

All evening, her thoughts had been consumed by Damien and their brief meeting again today. How she yearned to reach him, to reach Vincy through him! Every time she looked at Vincy's work, she saw a soul in torment—and oh, how she recognized that pain! She saw it in herself; she saw it in Damien. Every time she was in Damien's presence, he increased her belief that she was meant to be here. If only the two of them could share more.

Yet he seemed impossibly locked up in his own grief. The thought of the terrible isolation he was suffering brought tears to her eyes.

Then a soft voice said, "Good evening, Sarah," and she whirled to find herself facing him again.

He was standing in the archway, a beam of moonlight outlining his tall, striking figure. Silver washed his thick, wavy hair, the quicksilver light glinting off his satin vest and flashing off his deep-set eyes. The very sight of him was a sweet feast for her senses.

Sarah felt no shame standing before Damien in her gown and wrapper. It was as if he were an old friend, someone she'd known all her life. "Good evening, Damien," she whispered back eagerly.

He stared at her for a long moment, his expression rather bemused. Then he asked, "What are you doing in here so late?"

She sighed, glancing about the room. "I'm studying Vincy's paintings," she admitted. "It's strange how I can't seem to take my eyes off them. I guess you could say I've become . . ." She dared to glance back at him and finished in a whisper, "Fascinated."

Again, Damien stared at her, and a feeling of electricity hung thickly in the air between them. "Ah, yes, I understand."

"Do you?" she asked with a smile.

To Sarah's surprise, Damien came forward and took her hand; his flesh felt warm, strong and electric on hers. A thrill shot through her at his trusting gesture of intimacy, even as his crisp male scent filled her lungs, deepening her excitement.

He nodded toward the front window. "Come sit with me by the window, Sarah."

Sarah smiled, touched and warmed by his invitation. She knew that his words represented an important first step he was making in her direction. And the window seat did look so cozy and beckoning, its cushion bathed in a warm beam of moonlight.

Yet Sarah also feared the mysterious barrier that hovered near the front windows of the house. Would she be safe sitting there with him?

Even as this anxiety flitted to mind, Damien squeezed her hand and smiled at her, and she was lost. Somehow, she sensed a safety in his touch, and her instincts urged her to trust him and take the risk. She walked with him to the window seat and sat down, breathing a sigh of relief as no calamity befell them. She could still feel the edge of the ominous border hovering near the glass, yet Damien's presence seemed to hold the strange electricity at bay.

Beyond them, a tree rustled in the night breeze, sending a shifting, silvery light across their bodies, washing them with a haunting beauty. Looking out, Sarah watched a barred owl glide across the glittering dark river.

For a long moment, Damien simply held Sarah's

hand, and she could literally feel the strength and healing flowing from his touch alone. Just sitting there touching, they shared their pain, and she knew that in that first mere breath of sharing lay the beginning of affirmation and recovery.

Studying Damien, Sarah found his handsome brow was furrowed; he appeared immersed in thought. Would he tell her about Vincy tonight? Would he even make a beginning? Oh, how she yearned to learn more about both brothers! She knew that Damien needed to share his feelings, his pain, with someone, yet she also sensed that sharing would not come easily to this haunted man.

At last he spoke. "Are you happy here, Sarah?"

She smiled, rather taken aback by his question. "Why, yes."

"I had wondered how you were getting on," he continued awkwardly. "You must feel isolated here. I'm busy with my writing much of the time, and my aunt has her regimen established, as well."

Sarah glanced about the room. "I've all of Vincy's paintings to repair. That is enough. You see, as an artist, I'm used to a fairly solitary existence."

He smiled. "Ah, yes, I suppose you would be. Then you don't mind working alone?"

She shook her head. "On the contrary," she said in a low voice, "sometimes the time alone can be quite healing."

He nodded, and she knew he empathized. "What of your family? Do you miss them?"

His question set off a warning along her nerves. She decided to try to answer him as honestly as possible, without actually giving anything away. "Yes, I miss them."

"You're from Atlanta, are you not?"

She nodded, pleased that he had remembered.

117

"Tell me about your family."

Sarah bit her lip, considered her words for a moment, then began cautiously. "My family is quite prominent in Atlanta and also quite wealthy. Most of our money came from the railroads."

"And your people weathered the war all right?"

Her jaw tightened, and she stared off at the cold pane of glass as she remembered another war, another anguish.

"Sarah?" he prodded gently.

She turned, smiling at the look of concern in his eyes. "We weathered the war all right."

"I'm glad."

An awkward silence stretched between them; Sarah sensed that Damien had spoken of everything but the things that truly mattered to him. At last, he stood and said, "I suppose I'd best be going."

"So soon?" she asked in disappointment.

He was silent for a long moment, gazing down at her. Then he offered her an open-handed gesture and said ironically, "Actually, I'm not used to this sort of thing. Sharing with someone this way."

"You seem to have made a pretty good start to me."

"Have I?" Again, he fixed his intense gaze on her. "You know, Sarah, I sense we have a great deal in common. I guess I'm trying to say that I'd like to be your friend."

His words delighted her, and her eyes gleamed with happiness. "Oh, yes, Damien, I would love to be your friend, too." Wistfully, she added, "Will you come visit me again?"

He smiled. "Would you like that?"

"Oh, yes."

Damien continued to stare at her for a long moment, the searching intensity in his eyes seeming to reach into her very soul. Sarah felt herself melting beneath his scrutiny. She longed to touch him, to draw them closer still. For a breathless, exhilarating moment, she was sure he was going to kiss her.

But then, he merely nodded. "Good night, Sarah."

As he turned to leave, she caught his hand, gazing up at him with her heart in her eyes. "Please, won't you stay and tell me about Vincy?"

At once she could sense the change in him. His hand stiffened in hers and then was pulled away. His features tightened, and his eyes darkened with emotion.

"Perhaps in time," he said.

And Damien was gone.

After Damien left, Sarah almost wondered if she had imagined the entire encounter, but no— Damien had been there. Damien had held her hand. Damien had made a beginning with her.

How touched she had felt when this reclusive man had said that he wanted to be her friend. How transported she had felt by his smile.

After so many years of isolation, Damien Fontaine was at last reaching out to another human being and learning to trust again. She sensed that he hungered to talk about Vincy, but she had learned her lesson tonight. She wouldn't again press him regarding his brother. She would stick with safe subjects as long as necessary. She would become Damien's friend and wait patiently for him to become willing to share his pain with her.

Several days passed, and Sarah continued her work on Vincy's paintings. Occasionally, she would have tea with Olympia in the back courtyard, but she remained quite fearful of the world outside the front windows of the house.

Sarah did become better acquainted with the routine at Belle Fontaine. While Olympia left the house several times a week to go to Mass or attend social activities, Damien left only for his daily ride or to conduct occasional business in town. No one else ever came to Belle Fontaine, with the exception of the town girls, Hattie and Jane, who came four days a week to help Baptista with the heavy cleaning. Hattie, the older girl, seemed involved in a romance with Ben, the stableboy. The two spent every free moment sitting outside together on a weathered log. Sometimes, Sarah would stand near an upstairs window and watch the two of them laughing and talking, even as the breeze fluttered the leaves of the old oak shading their visiting place. At those moments, Sarah would often catch a whisper of autumn fragrance drifting in through the lace panels, and she hungered to go outside. But her fear of the menacing border held her back.

While Sarah's existence was very isolated, she didn't really mind that much. For nighttime was her salvation now. Nighttime found her with Damien, sitting on the window seat with him, talking, their huddled figures washed in moonlight. Often, Olympia's lovely piano music would drift up to them from downstairs, enchancing the poignancy of their mood.

Without ever actually arranging it, they'd set up a nightly rendezvous. Physically, they were chaste, holding hands and exchanging occasional, longing glances. Still, emotionally, they drew closer each day; indeed, there was an attraction and electricity that hovered, ever-present, between them.

For several nights, they spoke of everything but the reality of Damien's loss. They discussed Vincy's paintings and reviewed Sarah's progress each day. They talked about Sarah's life back in Georgia, and somehow she managed to supply details without actually giving anything away. Damien spoke little of his own life and experiences, but still, their visits grew longer each day. The words they exchanged were largely meaningless, but with each touch, each yearning glance, the bond between them deepened.

Then at last came the fateful night when they were sitting together on the window seat, and Damien said, "You wanted to know about Vincy."

It was a moment Sarah would never forget. The room was cool and strewn with silvery shadows; ghostly images danced across Vincy's dark, masterful paintings. A owl hooted in the distance, and a branch scraped against the side of the house. The beautifully sad strains of "The Last Rose of Summer" drifted up from downstairs.

And Sarah's heart seemed to cease beating when Damien said his words. A split second later, her pulses thundered into a frantic rhythm. She glanced at Damien quickly and saw the pain and need in his eyes—and the uncertainty, too. How thrilled she was that he was at last willing to share with her, to make himself vulnerable to her.

"Oh, yes," she said joyously. "Do tell me all about Vincy."

Damien glanced off at the window, his expression half-wistful, half-anguished. "Vincy was my brother," he began haltingly. "He was my friend. He was all I had."

"I know," Sarah whispered back, squeezing his hand. "I mean, your aunt told me how you lost your sisters and your parents."

Damien nodded. "We were so alike, Vincy and I. We thought alike. There were times when we were miles apart, yet our thinking would be identical." He smiled. "One time, when I was only twelve, I got in trouble. Defying our father's wishes, I rode a horse I had no business riding. He was a stallion, spirited and ungovernable, and he threw me out in the field. Yet Vincy knew just where I'd landed. He came after me."

"I understand." Indeed, she and Brian had shared that same, special sort of bond.

"It was always that way with us," Damien continued. "We didn't even need to talk, we just understood. We were such splendid friends. We knew such good times. . . ."

Words seemed to fail him then. He swallowed hard and glanced off at some unseen point in space, blinking rapidly. Sarah touched his arm. "Please. Tell me more. Tell me about the good times."

"Before the war," he said hoarsely. For a moment, a fleeting joy crossed his dark gaze, and Sarah knew that emotionally he was in another place. "Those were the glory days at Belle Fontaine. The picnics, the parties, the endless rounds of calling, especially in the summers when the cane was laid by. Vincy and I went to New Orleans frequently. To the opera, the *bals de société*." Whimsically, he added, "We courted fair maidens and took excursions to the lake. We chartered gambling parties on the Mississippi, and we even fought a duel or two beneath the Oaks." His hand tightened on hers. "And then the war came. I married Lucy St. Pierre right before Vincy and I left. And then my bride . . . then Lucy . . ."

Sarah's heart twisted at Damien's tortured expression. "I know. Your aunt told me about how she

122

and your son died. I'm so sorry, Damien."

"When I lost Vincy," he went on in a choked voice, "I lost an entire way of life."

She nodded, her heart swelling with empathy for him. "Your aunt told me he was killed at Gettysburg. Do you want to talk about it?"

He shook his head and said tightly, "I can't, Sarah."

"But you're writing his memoirs?" she prodded gently.

"Yes."

"I would love to see them sometime."

He glanced up at her, his expression miserably torn. "Yes, perhaps at some point, but not now—not yet."

She nodded. "I understand." Taking a deep breath, she added, "You see, I, too, lost a brother."

He stared at her in mingled compassion and fascination. "You did? Poor darling."

Damien reached out and touched the curve of her jaw with his fingertips, and Sarah shivered in pleasure. In an emotional voice, she confided, "I lost him—well, my brother was also killed in battle. Brian was only eighteen. He was destined to become a world-class violinist, and then he was taken from us so quickly, so cruelly. He left no legacy of his work as Vincy has. All I have now are a few . . ." About to say, "tape recordings," Sarah caught herself in time and finished, "memories."

"I'm so sorry," Damien whispered. He squeezed her hand, and she felt a special bond with him in that moment.

They sat quietly for a long time, communing in the silence. Then Damien asked, "Sarah, why did you come here?"

She understood his question at once and was not

the least bit afraid or put off. "I think to help you," she answered honestly, staring deeply into his eyes. "And perhaps to help myself."

"Oh, Sarah."

Damien leaned over and kissed her—a kiss of warmth and power, laced with tenderness and need. Sarah reeled with emotion, kissing him back eagerly, her eyes welling with tears of joy. The feel of Damien's mouth on hers was heavenly, exciting her in both a spiritual and a physical way. When his arms slipped about her, her ecstasy was complete. She whimpered and clung to him, feeling deliciously aroused, as he whispered soothing words against her wet cheek. In that moment, she could feel the huge rent in her heart beginning to heal.

He drew back and smiled down at her, feasting his eyes on her face and hair. "You're so lovely. I'm glad you're here."

"So am I," she whispered back.

"We must talk again," he added.

"Oh, yes, Damien," she said radiantly. "We must talk again."

They left the room holding hands and parted reluctantly in the hallway. Sarah went off to bed, hugging her pillow dreamily, recalling her every moment with Damien—the heaven of his voice, his touch, the wonder of his nearness, the healing power of his warm mouth on hers. There had been such emotion in their sharing, their kiss, the promise of worlds to explore between them.

She was falling in love with this tormented, passionate man.

Damien and Sarah grew closer with each passing day. It was as if on that first night when they had truly shared, both had opened a floodgate, and now their feelings poured forth. Each night they sat together on the window seat, holding hands and sharing amid Vincy's moonlight-washed paintings, even as Olympia's haunting music drifted up from downstairs.

Damien talked endlessly of Vincy, and Sarah talked of Brian. Damien told her of his and Vincy's grand tour of Europe back when they had both come of age and of how they'd gone to Natchez to race horses. She told him of Brian's brilliance on the violin and his concert debut. She chose her every word quite carefully to disguise the fact that she had come from another century. When Damien asked gently, "And Brian died in the war?", she replied simply, "Yes," knowing that to each of them, there was only one war.

They talked about the good times. They skirted the pain of their loss. In the sharing alone, there was healing. In the sharing alone, there was a deep and abiding love building between them. Indeed, as the days passed, they touched and kissed with increasing frequency, their physical intimacy mirroring the emotional and spiritual bond deepening between them.

Even though Damien held back discussing Vincy's death and that of his wife, Lucy, Sarah became acquainted with him in other ways. She came to understand his values and philosophy. She discovered that Damien's thinking was surprisingly modern and practical, identical to her own in so many ways. She learned that he had never believed in slavery, that he had been seriously considering freeing the slaves at Belle Fontaine when war had broken out. She learned that he had fought in the war due to loyalty to the South, not due to loyalty to the institution of slavery. She learned that he believed in God, but that he had felt alienated from formal religion ever since he'd lost his brother. She learned that he, too, felt displaced and cut off in the age in which he lived.

She learned that in every way, Damien was her soul mate.

Both Olympia and Baptista seemed to take note of the budding friendship between Sarah and Damien. While Sarah had never questioned Damien concerning Baptista, to her relief she had not again seen the black woman slipping into his bedroom at night. And Baptista's attitude toward Sarah certainly hinted that perhaps she was no longer Damien's mistress; she often treated Sarah with scarcely veiled antagonism.

Olympia's disapproval was expressed in more subtle ways. One crisp autumn morning as she and Sarah shared tea in the courtyard out back, she remarked with a frown, "I've noticed that you and my nephew have become friends."

"Have you?" Sarah replied cautiously.

"Well, a time or two, I've heard you talking as I've passed the salon at night."

Sarah took a long sip of her tea. "We've Vincy's work to discuss. In doing repairs such as these, I find it helpful to understand the artist."

Olympia set down her teacup. "Ah, yes, you've said as much before. Why is it, then, that I feel that what you and Damien are building goes beyond that?"

Sarah stared Olympia straight in the eye. "Damien and I are becoming friends, Miss Fontaine. Don't you think your nephew needs someone with whom he can share his thoughts and feelings?"

Olympia frowned. "I'm not so sure. Damien did want to have Vincy's paintings repaired, but sometimes I wonder if having the work done, and bringing you here, hasn't opened a Pandora's box."

Sarah felt her spine stiffening. "What do you mean?"

Olympia's chin came up slightly, and she cast Sarah a cool glance. "Sometimes the pain of the past is best left buried."

Sarah was quiet, frowning, for a long moment. "Miss Fontaine, at risk of contradicting you, isn't it the pain of the past that has made Damien a recluse in the first place?"

Olympia leaned forward intently, her hazel eyes gleaming as she spoke in a low, intense tone. "Ah, but how can you know that bringing all that suffering to the surface will really improve Damien's lot? On the contrary, it might be enough to drive him quite mad."

Sarah was silent, disturbed by Olympia's arguments. Would Damien's sharing with her ultimately drive him deeper into himself?

She didn't know. But she did find herself wondering if Olympia Fontaine truly wanted her nephew to get better.

That night, Damien asked, "Will you go with me to Vincy's grave, Sarah?"

They were sitting at their window seat, holding hands. Damien's question caught Sarah off guard, and she glanced at him quickly, curiously. Noting the intent expression in his dark eyes as he waited for her reply, Sarah realized that she'd just made a breakthrough with him.

Over the past few days, Damien had shared his relationship with Vincy, but he'd invariably stayed on the light side, telling her of the good times he and Vincy had shared. Was he now ready to make that ultimate leap of faith and tell her of the dark side as well, sharing his pain and grief with her?

"I'm honored that you would ask," she said at last.

He glanced off toward the window, a faraway look in his eyes. "I go there often to place flowers. He's buried in a bower north of here, not far from the river. It's a lovely place with many trees." Hoarsely, he finished, "Lucy is buried there, too—as well as my son."

"Oh, Damien!" Sarah cried, tears springing to her eyes as she viewed his anguish. So Damien's wife and stillborn son were also buried with Vincy.

And now, at last, he was beginning to share all of his feelings and torment with her. Yet could she really risk going with him to the graves? Would she be safe outside the walls of the house? She just didn't know. Her fear of the outside world remained real and strong, as was her premonition that if she told Damien the truth about where she had come from, she might break the spell and be propelled back to a world where she had always felt she didn't quite belong.

Damien stroked her cheek with his fingertips. "Well, Sarah? Will you go with me?"

There was such need in his touch, his words. She stared at him through sudden, stinging tears. She couldn't deny him; his asking her had cost him too much, she knew. But she needed some time to figure out the mystery of the invisible barrier threatening her. Even now, she could feel its ominous energy just beyond them near the glass. Damien had never felt it, she knew, or he would have mentioned it. He was safe, yet she still feared she wasn't.

"Can we go in a day or two?" she cautiously replied. Watching a cloud cross his eyes, she squeezed his hand and added in a rush, "I do so want to go with you, but right now, I'm finishing up Vincy's street scene of the Vieux Carre. The colors have been quite challenging, and I can't risk losing any of the light until the repairs are completed."

Damien smiled, seeming totally satisfied by her explanation as he glanced off at the painting, which sat near them on an easel. "Ah, yes, you are doing such a fine job of restoring Vincy's street scene. We mustn't chance breaking your concentration until the work is done. But you'll go with me then?"

"Oh, yes, Damien, yes!"

Damien drew her close and kissed her then. Over the past days, the character of his kisses had changed. His advances were becoming more passionate, more demanding. Even now, he held her close as his lips moved with hot mastery over her own, and his tongue took full, intimate possession of her mouth. Sarah moaned and hugged him tightly, feeling totally enraptured. Tremors of excitement raced down her body, bombarding her womanly core until she ached with desire. Her heart beat at a giddy pace as she pressed herself into him, kissing him back with a need that matched his own. Never before had a man excited her as Damien did! He'd awakened in her a deep yearning that she'd previously thought herself incapable of. Now, she longed to draw as close to him physically as they'd been drawn spiritually.

After a moment, they both pulled back to catch their breath, and Damien smiled down at her. "I like your hair down," he whispered, plucking the pins from her coiffure. As her thick blond hair tumbled about her shoulders, he ran his fingers through the silken tresses and whispered, "My beautiful Sarah."

"Oh, Damien," she whispered back, shuddering

129

with her desire for him, as well as her fear of the future, of losing him. "Kiss me until I can't breathe."

He kissed her, then, with such power and passion, that when they at last reluctantly parted, her lips were sweetly bruised.

The next morning, Sarah paced the salon like a caged animal. Since the morning was chilly, she wore a long woolen frock and a light shawl. The heels of her high-topped shoes clicked on the polished floorboards as she moved to and fro.

Last night, Damien had asked her to go with him to see Vincy's grave. He had transcended his own pain and reached out to her. And she had lied to him out of fear, telling him she must first finish Vincy's painting.

How could she deny him now? He had become her soul mate. She knew she would have to find some way to leave the house and go with him to the graves. Maybe then he could begin to share his pain with her about Vincy and Lucy. And maybe then he would come to love her as deeply as she loved him.

Yet Sarah still felt so fearful of the world beyond the front windows of the house. She still felt she would not be safe outside, and she only half-understood her own anxieties. She knew she could never even begin to explain her fears to Damien. She couldn't do so without telling him where she had come from, and if she did, surely he would think her mad. She was still very much afraid that if she told Damien the truth, she would break the spell, and that prospect frightened her as much as did the thought of leaving the safety of the house.

She knew she could no longer run from her fear, not without hurting Damien. She would have to see what the strange, invisible border truly meant. She would have to go out the front door of the house. And she would have to face this alone—without Damien. She could not risk doing him harm.

Sarah took a quiet moment to fortify herself, then she left the salon and went slowly down the stairs. The downstairs hallway was swept with sunshine, patchwork patterns of light dancing on the Persian runner. No one was around, she noted with relief.

Slowly, Sarah approached the front door. She felt the eerie vibrations encroaching, but she pressed on.

Opening the door, she could feel the energy bombarding her, as if she were caught in the crush of an invisible crowd. The electricity was beating her back, warning her, but she had to forge on for Damien's sake. "Give me strength," she murmured, a quiet, plaintive prayer.

Sarah stepped forward forcefully through the portal. She reeled, as if suddenly, rudely shaken. Caught fully in the grip of the barrier, she began to spin, the energy bombarding her with such vigor that she could barely stand on her feet. Colors spun by her, and the whole universe seemed to crack open beneath her feet. She thought she heard a voice crying out, and she couldn't even tell if it was her own.

The next thing Sarah knew, she was clinging to a slender column. The barrier was gone now, but she was dizzy, blinking to clear her vision.

The first thing she saw was that the column was weathered and gray.

"Oh, my God!" she gasped, whirling, horrified, to stare at the gray, abandoned house, the house she had left ten days ago. "It can't be. It just can't be!"

Sarah dashed madly back into the house. It was

barren, scarred; all the furnishings, all the people, gone. "No!" she cried desperately, rushing from room to room. "No! Oh, Damien, please, no!"

Endlessly, she raced through the rooms, calling Damien's name brokenly, looking for any vestige, any clue of the life she had known mere seconds before. There were none—save for the old-fashioned dress she still wore.

Ten minutes later, Sarah sat on the front gallery of the abandoned house, tears streaming down her cheeks as she stared ahead at the forest where the fallow field should have been.

"Oh, Damien," she sobbed, beating her fists on the gray planks of the porch. "What happened? Where are you? I don't understand anything. But I'm sorry—so sorry!"

She was back in the twentieth century. Damien—and everything that mattered to her—was gone.

Chapter Nine

Despondently, Sarah walked back toward Miss Erica's house. She stayed close to the trees, hoping no one would spot her in her old-fashioned clothing.

She wondered what on earth had happened to her. One minute, she'd been living in the year 1871, and the next, she'd been propelled back to the present. It was almost as if her experience in the past had never occurred—but then, how else could she account for the nineteenth-century clothing she still wore? How else could she explain the fact that her mouth still held the taste of the rice fritters she'd eaten for breakfast?

Sarah let herself into the house with the keys she'd left under the mat ten days ago. When she walked into the den, she could hear the vacuum cleaner running toward the front of the house. Ebbie was here, she realized. So was her painting of the house and Damien. It still sat on its easel where she'd left it.

Glancing at the painting wistfully, Sarah ducked into her bedroom. Casper was perched on the bed waiting for her, and he sprang up at once and meowed, as if to scold her for being gone so long.

Sarah petted the cat gently. "Hello, boy. I wish I could say I'm happy to be here, but I am happy to see you again." As he purred in response and arched his back against her hand, she added, "We'll get reacquainted later, but for now, I must change, before someone spots me and carts me off to an asylum."

Sarah stripped off the old-fashioned dress, her undergarments and shoes, and hid everything at the back of the bedroom closet. Donning a bra and panties, she let down her hair and brushed it out, then dressed in gray wool slacks, a maroon sweater and loafers. She realized she had no idea what day it was here in the present, or what kind of reception awaited her. She may as well find out.

Sarah walked out into the living room. Ebbie was in the dining area running the vacuum, her stooped back to Sarah. "Ebbie?" she called.

The little woman dropped the vacuum attachment and whirled, her eyes huge, her hand flying to her heart. "Miss Sarah!"

"Good morning, Ebbie," Sarah said awkwardly. "I didn't mean to startle you. Could you turn off the vacuum for a minute, please?"

With a trembling hand, Ebbie reached down and switched off the Electrolux. She still looked stunned as she stared at Sarah. "Miss Sarah, we don't know where you be. You gone ten days, child."

"Oh, I'm sorry," Sarah murmured. So the time

she had spent in the past had passed concurrently in the present. Somehow, this fact seemed to lend even more legitimacy to her experience. "I didn't mean to make you worry," she added stiffly. "I should have let you know of my plans." As if she had known herself, she thought.

"We don't know where you be, child," Ebbie repeated. "We thought you was drowned in the river or lost in the swamp. Maudie, she go for the sheriff this morning."

Oh, Lord, Sarah thought, this was getting serious.

Before Sarah could even absorb all this, the doorbell rang. "I'll get it," she told Ebbie. Nervously, she went to the door, frowning as she glanced through the peephole. Maudie Wilson stood on the stoop with a pot-bellied man wearing a khaki uniform and a silver star on his chest. Bracing herself with a deep breath, Sarah swung open the door. "Good morning," she said to her guests.

"Why, forevermore, child!" Maudie Wilson gasped. "Where on earth have you been?"

Sarah stiffened her spine at Maudie's imperious tone. "Won't you two come in?" she asked.

Sarah showed the two into the living room, and Maudie introduced Sarah to Sheriff Claude Thibideaux. Ebbie, who had been watching the exchange from the dining area, grabbed the vacuum cleaner and retreated into the kitchen.

After Sarah and her guests were seated, the sheriff leaned toward her with his hat in his hands. "We don't mean to intrude, little lady, but Maudie here has been mighty worried. Seems you disappeared for ten days."

"Yes," Sarah replied calmly. "I was just telling Ebbie that I didn't mean to cause any worry, and I do apologize to all of you."

"So what happened to you, Miss Jennings?" the sheriff asked with a frown.

Catching Maudie's disapproving countenance through the corner of her eye, Sarah gathered her fortitude. During the intervening moments, she'd managed to think up an excuse for her disappearance. She braved a smile at the sheriff. "Really, the explanation is quite simple. You see, an old college friend of mine lives in New Orleans. On the spur of the moment, Brenda invited me down to stay with her, and I accepted."

"Your car was still here," Maudie pointed out.

Sarah's chin came up slightly as she turned to Maudie. "My friend came out and got me."

"You didn't take your purse. It's still on the table in the entryway," Maudie added triumphantly.

Sarah shrugged with a bravado she hardly felt. "I took a different purse."

Maudie was opening her mouth to protest, when Sheriff Thibideaux cleared his throat. "Well, I guess that solves the mystery," he said with a relieved smile. He stood and clapped on his hat. "I'm right glad you're okay, little lady, but next time you up and decide to go off with your girl friend, you might tell someone hereabouts what you're aimin' to do." He drew himself up stiffly. "I'm not sure just how you was reared up back in Atlanta, but folks tend to look out for each other here in Meridian."

"I understand, Sheriff," Sarah replied. "And again, I apologize for my thoughtlessness. Next time I decide to leave, I promise I'll inform Ebbie of my plans."

Sarah saw the sheriff out, then turned back to face a very suspicious-looking Maudie Wilson. The older woman stood with arms akimbo as she stared at Sarah through narrowed eyes. Again, Sarah was struck by how much Maudie resembled Olympia Fontaine. "Is there something else?" she asked.

Maudie's scowl deepened. "Well, I must say that I never would have expected you to be this inconsiderate, Miss Jennings, disappearing as you did, without leaving any word of your whereabouts. Why, not even Mr. Baldwin knew."

"Oh, no! Don't tell me you told Mr. Baldwin about this, too!"

"Why, of course."

Sarah struggled to hold onto her patience. She realized that her conduct must have seemed remiss to those she'd left behind, but she had already apologized several times, and Maudie's overbearing attitude and nosiness were beginning to rankle. "You needn't have assumed that I met with some dire calamity just because I left for a few days," she informed the other woman coolly. "I am a free agent, Miss Wilson, and quite capable of taking care of myself."

"Well, I never!" Maudie said huffily. "Obviously, my concern is misplaced. I'll see you tomorrow then, when I come to do the books."

Watching Maudie square her shoulders and leave, Sarah sighed. She did feel badly about the way she had treated everyone, but Maudie had an uncanny ability to rub her the wrong way.

Sarah went to the bedroom and phoned Mr. Baldwin, letting him know she was fine. Afterward, she began to feel as if she were suffocating in the house. She knew she had to leave and go find a quiet place to think, a place to analyze everything that had happened to her. Grabbing her purse from the entryway table, she went to the kitchen and told Ebbie, "I'm going for a drive. And don't worry—I *will* be back for lunch."

"Yes'um," Ebbie mumbled from the sink.

Sarah left the house through the front door and walked around to the carport. She backed out her Mustang and put down the top. Then she drove out to River Road and followed the contour of the river northward toward the old house. The day was crisp and bracing, the breeze tugging at Sarah's hair, the trees on River Road ablaze with autumn colors. But the glory of nature was largely lost on her at the moment.

Soon, she spotted the old place just off the roadway. She parked her car beneath some trees and walked to the abandoned house. She sat down on a tree stump out in the yard and stared at the gray mansion longingly. What had happened to her during the past ten days? Had she lost her mind? Had she had another breakdown? Had she gone so deeply into meditation that she had hallucinated the entire experience in the house?

If so, how could she explain the ten days that had passed? And again, how could she account for the old-fashioned clothing she had worn back to the present?

Sarah shook her head. No. What had happened to her couldn't have been a dream or an hallucination; her experience had simply been too real. Damien was too real, and her feelings for him were too real. Bizarre though it might be, the only explanation that made sense to her was that she had gone back in time—and had fallen in love with a man who lived in another century.

But *how* had she gone back in time in the first place, and how had she made her way back to the present? She thought over the mystery and decided her meditation had somehow taken her back in time. As to how she had returned to the present, she knew it must have something to do with the subtle vibrations she had felt near the front walls of the house. She had been safe as long as she stayed within the confines of the house, or even out back in the courtyard, where the walls of the house extended. But when she'd come out the front door for the first time this morning, she'd found herself instantly propelled back to the present.

That was it, then. A window in time existed just beyond the front door of the house.

Sarah climbed the steps of the old mansion and stood for a moment at the front portal. She examined the old archway carefully, passing her hand to and fro through the doorway. Nothing happened. If the portal truly was a door in time, then there was no sign of it here in the present. That meant that the mystical passageway that had brought her back to the present existed only in the past. It all made sense in an uncanny way.

Sarah went back down the steps and sat down on the stump. She propped her chin in her hands, her expression deeply troubled. Could she make her way back to the past again? Even if she could, she would probably be safe only within the confines of the house itself. If she left the house again, she'd likely be propelled back to the present once more. So, in essence, even if she could make her way back to the past, she would be trapped in the house.

And yet Damien was there, and they needed each other so desperately. How could loving him ever be a trap? She wondered if he had already noted her departure back in the past. Did he already miss her as much as she missed him?

Or was life still even going on in that fantastical

world she had left? Had Damien's world existed only because she had been there? Oh, it was enough to boggle the mind.

But again, Sarah's instincts told her that life was still going on in that past world and that Damien must surely feel baffled and hurt by her abrupt departure. If only he could know how unwilling she had been to return here, and how she ached to be back with him.

Sarah realized that she would have to try her meditation again, that she would have to try to get back to Damien. But even as she yearned to try right this minute, she knew she would have to wait until at least late tomorrow. Maudie Wilson would be at Miss Erica's house all day tomorrow, working on the accounts, and Sarah couldn't risk disappearing again while that woman was around. She would also have to make adequate preparation before she attempted to leave; if she simply disappeared once more, the authorities might well contact her parents this time.

The thought of her parents brought up the whole Pandora's box of her future. If she could make her way back, would she stay with Damien forever this time? Could she even pull it off, considering the tenuous hold she had on that past world? Oh, it was all too much to consider at the moment. She couldn't settle the entire issue of her future right this minute. For now, all she knew was that somehow she must return to Damien.

"Oh, Damien," she whispered, staring at the house. "Be patient, my love. Somehow I'll find my way back to you."

The wind swirled then, almost as if in answer to her words. A dreamy light drifted over the house, and suddenly Sarah recalled Damien's asking her to go with him to Vincy's grave. She couldn't make that journey with him in the past, but couldn't she try in the present?

Yet where *were* the graves? Sarah concentrated fiercely. Damien had said the graves of Vincy, as well as those of Damien's wife and child, were in a bower north of the house. Would they still be there? Wouldn't the headstones have crumbled away by now? The graves might even be gone entirely, replaced by a field or building. But she could at least try.

Sarah walked beyond the house, heading north through the forest. Since she'd never come this way before, she used the river as her touchstone; as long as she could see the distant glow of it through the trees, she knew she would be safe.

A dappled light guided her path, and a crisp, woodsy breeze swirled around her, caressing her skin. Instinct seemed to guide her on toward a towering grove of sycamore trees. They were glittering in the breeze beyond her, their leaves the fiery red of autumn.

When Sarah reached the stand of trees, she stepped through a curtain of greenery, then gasped. At the center of the cool, shadowy grotto stood three ancient graves. Sarah would have expected the headstones to be covered with vines and the area surrounding them to be heavily entangled. Instead, the small enclosure was remarkably clean and clear with the headstones unobstructed, the ground looking as if it had been recently swept. There were even flowers, dead and dry, sitting in old soda bottles by each marker.

Who tended these graves?

In an attitude of reverence, Sarah knelt, studying the markers closely. The stones were heavily eroded

141

and covered with lichen, but a few letters were still visible. On the first marker, she was able to make out the name, "Lucy." That would be Lucy Fontaine, Damien's wife, she thought excitedly.

Staring at the headstone, Sarah felt filled with both joy and sadness. Sadness for the young woman who had died so long ago, while her husband was off fighting a brutal, destructive war. Joy at this proof that Damien Fontaine had truly existed, that she had surely spent the past ten days in his world. How else could she have known about the brother, wife and son Damien had buried here?

Sarah eagerly studied the other two graves. The first, with its smaller marker, was obviously the grave of Damien's stillborn son. Her heart twisted with sadness for the precious small life that had been lost. Sarah carefully brushed away the lichen with a leaf, but, to her frustration, she could not make out any letters or numbers on the stone; the limestone was simply too heavily eroded.

With a sigh, Sarah turned to the last stone. She caught a sharp breath as she read the faded name, "Vincy," and the year "1863."

"Oh, Vincy," Sarah whispered, tears stinging her eyes. She felt as if she'd just been reunited with her dearest, oldest friend. She touched the stone with a trembling hand. "Vincy, I feel I know you already, through Damien. I know your beautiful art. And now here you are, your brilliance lost to the world forever."

Not lost.

Where the words came from, Sarah was not sure. But even as she heard the haunting message, the breeze shifted again, rustling the trees and blowing a cool, wet leaf across her face. Sarah stood and looked up through the dense arc of branches, glorying in the hazy light that drifted down upon her.

"It's not so bad here, Vincy," she whispered poignantly. "Damien chose the spot well. It's really very peaceful, a rather nice place to spend eternity."

Not lost. Again the words echoed through her mind. It was a moment of affirmation and profound insight for Sarah. A moment that told her that Vincy's brilliance would not be lost to the world, that what she and Damien shared would not be lost. Somehow, she must find her way back to him—to repair Vincy's paintings, to repair her and Damien's souls.

Tears streamed down her cheeks as she thought of the special relationship Damien and Vincy had shared. No wonder Damien had wanted to bring her here. Just standing by the graves, she felt a deeper bond with Damien and Vincy; she felt she understood both brothers so much better.

"I just wanted you to know that I came, Damien," Sarah whispered to the wind. "I just wanted you to know that I came."

Chapter Ten

"Sarah! Sarah, where are you?"

In another century, Damien Fontaine stood by the same graves in the same grotto of trees, trees that were little more than saplings now.

He'd been searching for Sarah everywhere, ever since the moment when he'd gone into the salon looking for her and had found her missing. He'd searched the house, the grounds, but there'd been no trace of her anywhere at Belle Fontaine. It was as if she'd vanished into thin air.

And unfortunately, his aunt had not been at home this morning, having gone to see a friend, Mary Broussard. Damien had questioned Ben, the stable-boy, as to whether Sarah might have gone with Olympia, but Ben had sworn that Olympia had left alone in the buggy. Damien had prayed the boy was mistaken, that Sarah had simply gone calling with his aunt.

He'd come to Vincy's grave in desperation, remembering that he'd mentioned the grave to Sarah. He'd hoped desperately that she might have come here on a whim; yet again, she was nowhere in sight.

Why was it then that he almost could feel her presence here, especially when the wind shifted? He felt closer to her here, somehow.

Oh, God, surely he had not lost her, after knowing her for such a short time!

Damien thought over the past week and a half. His life had radically changed ever since Sarah Jennings had come here. From the instant he'd laid eyes on her, he'd sensed in her a gentle, kindred spirit. His evenings spent talking with her had been heaven. He'd at last seen a brief glimmer of light in the walls of darkness, grief and despair that had imprisoned him for so long. Sarah understood him, just as she understood Vincy and Vincy's paintings. For the first time in eight agonizing years, Damien had been able to share with another human being his torment over his brother. Sarah empathized totally, for she, too, had lost a brother. Just yesterday, he'd mused that in time he might be able to reveal to her all the dark demons of his past—his constant guilt over Lucy as well as Vincy. In time, he might be able to share the memoirs with her. In time, they might be able to seek true happiness together.

Yet how could they, if Sarah were indeed gone?

Even as his mind asked the tormenting question, the wind ceased its haunting music, and Damien no longer sensed Sarah's presence. He crossed himself and uttered a supplication to the Holy Virgin for the souls of Vincy, Lucy and his son. Then he left the grove of trees and strode to his horse. He mounted the black stallion and rode hard for Belle Fontaine.

In front of the house, he left his horse with Ben,

then hurried up the steps. Inside, he burst into the parlor, where he found his aunt knitting by the window. "Aunt Olympia, have you seen Sarah this morning?"

Olympia frowned and set down her knitting. "Actually, I haven't. I stopped by her room early this morning—you see, I was going to invite her to come calling with me—but I couldn't find her there or in the salon. Quite odd, don't you think?"

Damien raked a hand through his hair. "Yes. I can't find Sarah, either. Did she say anything to you about having plans?"

"No, not at all."

"Damn. She could have gone for a walk and gotten lost. There are some real quagmires in the swamps hereabouts."

"I suppose that's true." Olympia bit her lip. "Only . . ."

"Yes?" Damien asked, stepping forward, his features creased with tension.

Olympia slanted a sympathetic glance at him. "Well, nephew, I hate to say this, but I wouldn't be that surprised if Miss Jennings simply left. She had some—well—peculiarities."

He scowled fiercely. "What do you mean?"

"Like the clothing she wore when she first arrived here. It was quite bizarre."

Damien shrugged. "We're doubtless not that familiar with fashions in Atlanta or New Orleans these days."

Olympia harrumphed. "No offense, nephew, but this attire was—well, quite strange and bordering on indecent."

Damien had been listening with a preoccupied frown. "You'll have to excuse me, Aunt Olympia. I must continue searching for Sarah."

Leaving the parlor, Damien hurried up the stairs. What had his aunt meant by saying that the clothing Sarah had worn when she arrived here had been bizarre?

In the upstairs hallway, he headed first for the salon, praying that Sarah had somehow miraculously returned, unnoticed by either him or his aunt.

Yet the salon remained empty, Vincy's painting of the New Orleans street scene sitting on its easel, just where Sarah had left it last night. The repairs were still half-finished. "Oh, Sarah, how could you do this?" he asked in sorrow. "Leaving without even finishing your work on Vincy's paintings?"

Damien knew how much these repairs had meant to Sarah, which made her disappearance even more frightening and difficult to figure out.

With a heavy heart, Damien left the salon and crossed over to Sarah's bedroom. As he feared, a knock on her door brought no response.

Damien slipped inside the room. The bed was made, and there was no sign of Sarah. He searched the dressing table and the armoire, looking for some sign, some hint of what her thoughts were or where she might be. But there was nothing, beyond the subtle, sweet essence of her that still lingered in the room.

Then he spotted the cedar chest beneath the window. He hurried over and threw back the lid. He sighed as he stared at Lucy's old dresses, dresses Sarah had worn over the past week and a half. He felt a stab of guilt that the garments brought to mind no lingering feeling toward Lucy, but only his love and anguish for Sarah.

Damien pulled the dresses out of the chest and tossed them on the bed. At the bottom of the chest, he found the odd garments his aunt had spoken of.

First, he pulled out a blue and gold calico dress. It was quite strange-looking, with its straight lines and no fullness in the skirt. Turning it over, he found the back was held together with quite an odd device, like a miniature pulley sliding on metal teeth. He pulled the device up and down; it was like a magical seam that miraculously opened and shut.

Setting the dress aside, he pulled out the other items. There was a peculiar set of drawers, fashioned of some silky pale blue fabric, lace trimmed and very brief. He stared at a label that read, "Vanity Fair." There was an even odder device, some sort of skimpy corset, fashioned mostly of beige-colored lace, that had cups which obviously restrained the breasts. Across the back of it was a springy, rough fabric and metal teeth to hold the device together.

There was also a long, straight-lined petticoat and the strangest pair of shoes Damien had ever seen. They reminded him of the sandals he'd seen on men's feet in Biblical paintings. Yet the shoes were far too small for a man to wear. Nevertheless, it seemed incomprehensible to him that Sarah might have worn these shoes or any of the other unconventional items.

Damien was starting to replace the items in the chest when the light glinted off another item. He leaned over and picked up the queerest device he'd ever seen. It was like a miniature pocket watch, yet it had no cover and was mounted on a leather band. Damien stared at the face of the small clock; it read "Timex."

The object seemed from another world, and all at once, a chill gripped him as he remembered a night long ago, a night that he and Vincy had spent talking with a riverboat pilot on the Mississippi. The man had suggested fantastical possibilities. Could it be . . .?

"Oh, Sarah," he cried. "Where did these things come from? And where did you come from?"

Back in the present, it was midafternoon and Sarah was back at Miss Erica's house. She sat in the den, staring dismally at a television documentary on tensions in the Middle East and Africa. The footage was violent and grim, depicting recent wars and uprisings. Sarah watched with a sense of sadness and unreality. She could cope here in the twentieth century, just as Dr. Hogan had often so often told her, but, more and more, she felt she belonged in another time.

"Oh, Damien," she whispered, "how I hunger to be back with you."

Sarah flipped off the TV and went out to the kitchen, where she found Ebbie gathering her purse and coat. "Ebbie, I just wanted to let you know that I may be going off again," Sarah said awkwardly. "I'm planning to return to New Orleans and stay with my friend for a few more weeks. I anticipate doing quite a lot of painting while I'm there. I may leave tomorrow or perhaps a few days later—as soon as I can make the arrangements—so don't be surprised if you don't see me for a while."

If Ebbie was perturbed by Sarah's announcement, she did not show it. "Yes'um," was all she said.

"My car will remain here," Sarah added casually. "You see, my friend will be coming out to get me again."

"Yes'um," Ebbie repeated.

After the little woman left, Sarah breathed a sigh

of relief. Her explanation to Ebbie should suffice when she disappeared again—and she fully intended to disappear again.

Sarah shook her head in wonder at her own thoughts. Only two weeks ago, she would have considered to be totally bizarre what she now accepted as normal—that she had traveled back in time, that she now hungered to live the rest of her life in another century with the man she loved.

The thought of returning to the past brought to mind her family, and Sarah felt a stab of guilt. She certainly needed to call her folks. They might try to contact her after she went back again, and she needed to make provision so that they wouldn't worry.

Yet wouldn't they worry when she disappeared from their world entirely?

The question brought a lump to her throat. Sarah loved her family, of course, yet she had to acknowledge that she hadn't really felt that close to her folks ever since she'd left for college. In a sense, both she and Brian had been mavericks in the family—Sarah with her passion for art, Brian with his passion for music. Neither had shown any interest in the family shipping business. Certainly, her parents had taken the death of Brian very hard, but now they seemed to be pinning all of their hopes on young Teddy.

It would be difficult, of course, never to see her parents or Teddy again, and she hated the thought of causing her loved ones any pain. But she had no doubt that her family would survive, even prevail, without her. Ultimately, Sarah knew that no one in this world or any other meant as much to her as did Damien Fontaine.

Feeling the strength of this new resolve, Sarah sat down on the couch in the den and dialed her parent's number in Atlanta. Seconds later, she heard her mom's voice over the fuzziness of the connection. "Hello."

"Hi, Mom. It's Sarah."

"Sarah! I'm so glad to hear from you. Teddy gave me your message and I tried calling you the other night, but there was no answer."

"I've been in and out a lot."

"How are you doing, darling?"

"Much better," Sarah answered truthfully. "And how are you and Dad and Teddy?"

"We're all fine. Teddy is back at boarding school, and Richard and I are getting ready to go off to our house in Myrtle Beach for a few weeks. Richard has invited a few of our best customers to come out and golf with him, sort of a working vacation."

"I'm sure you both need it, Mom."

"How are things progressing there?"

"Oh, Cousin Erica's lawyer is getting the estate settled, and I'm really enjoying staying in her house."

There was a tense pause, then Margaret Jennings asked, "Sarah, you aren't planning to stay there indefinitely, are you?"

Sarah bit her lip, feeling very torn. "I do like it here, Mom. And I've been able to paint again."

"Have you? That's wonderful." After another pause, Sarah's mother added, "What about Bill?"

Sarah's hand tightened on the receiver. "Mom, as I explained to you before I left, it's over between the two of us."

"Sarah, don't you think you're being a bit hasty? Bill called the other day, and he's still hoping that you'll be able to come home in time for all of us to go to the Picasso opening in New York."

Sarah sighed. How could she tell her mother that

the thought of seeing Pablo Picasso's contemporary sculpture left her cold? How could she tell her mother that she'd discovered a new artist of unbelievable depth and brilliance and turbulent emotion, an artist who had lived in another century?

How could she tell her mother where she'd been the past ten days? Or what she'd done? She couldn't, of course. If she did, her mother would assume she'd lost her mind. So, instead, she said, "Mom, I just don't think I can make it back for the opening. You know how it is—one doesn't disturb the juices when they're flowing. As for Bill, please, just don't hold out hope for us."

"But why, Sarah?"

Sarah hesitated. Could she tell her mother that she refused to marry a man who had had himself sterilized without even consulting her? No, she decided, she couldn't. It was too much of a violation of Bill's privacy. "Mom, what can I say?" Sarah asked. "I love Bill in my way, but there's just no passion there between us."

"Oh, Sarah," her mother scolded, "you're such an incurable romantic. Passion, my foot. A truly solid marriage is founded in values much more lasting, like friendship and honesty and trust."

I agree, Sarah thought to herself, but Bill lost my friendship when he withheld the truth from me and violated my trust. To her mother, she said, "Mom, I can't force my own feelings into some convenient mold."

She heard her mother sigh. "All right, dear. We won't argue about it right now. Just come home as soon as possible, won't you?"

Sarah felt a new twinge of guilt. "Actually, it may be some time before I return. For one thing, I've renewed my acquaintance with an old friend in New Orleans."

"Oh? Who might that be?"

"Brenda Birmingham, my old roommate at Sarah Lawrence."

"Oh, yes, I remember Brenda. Isn't she the one you once brought home for Thanksgiving?"

"Yes."

"How is she doing?"

"Just fine. I stayed with Brenda and her family on my way down here. And I wanted to let you know that I intend to spend more time with her in New Orleans."

"But why, dear? I know you're fond of her, but—"

"Mom, New Orleans is really a horn of plenty for an artist. There's the levee, the market, the French Quarter, plus Brenda lives right in the heart of the Garden District."

"Well, I suppose all of this is true."

"Anyway, if you should call here and get no answer, don't worry."

"Could you give me Brenda's number in New Orleans, then?"

"Well, I . . ." Sarah's voice trailed off, then she blurted, "I have it, but I can't put my hands on it right now." Hating herself for telling the lie, but knowing it was necessary, she added, "Tell you what. I'll drop you a card soon with Brenda's address and phone number. Okay?"

"Okay, dear. Take care, will you?"

Sarah said good-bye to her mother, praying that her parents wouldn't become unduly worried if they couldn't get in touch with her in coming weeks. She had traveled fairly frequently when she had lived in

Atlanta, and she was sure her mother would assume she'd simply forgotten to send the card with Brenda's phone number and address. Such absent-mindedness was all-too-common for her. Her mother would be annoyed, but not alarmed.

Sarah started to set the phone back on the end table, then stopped herself. She decided that she had better call Dr. Hogan, too. She had no intention of discussing her experience with him, since she was sure he would never believe her—indeed, he'd probably decide she'd had a relapse—but she did need to check in.

Sarah called Hogan's office in Atlanta and was relieved when his secretary told her that he had already left for the day. She asked the secretary to give him a message—that she was doing fine, and that she was planning to go off to New Orleans for a few weeks.

Hanging up the phone, Sarah breathed a sigh of relief. Her various alibis were falling into place. Now, the problem was finding her way back to Damien.

As sunset approached, Sarah found herself drawn back to the old house. She drove her Mustang to her parking spot off River Road, then headed off through the trees, taking along a flashlight.

She paused before the mansion, feeling mesmerized, as always. The house appeared awesome and majestic in the fading light. Ghostly sprays of light drifted down through the tree limbs and Spanish moss, creating a patchwork effect on the roof. In the distance, an owl hooted from his perch high in a tree.

Sarah went to stand on the ancient porch. She watched the sun set and watched the stars appear. A cool wind whipped about her, rattling the old shutters and raising gooseflesh on her skin. The evening was growing quite chilly, but she didn't mind. She somehow felt closer to Damien here, even though he was actually a world away.

Should she try to make her way back to him now? She shook her head sadly. She'd never before tried meditating in the house at night, and she seriously doubted she'd be able to relax in the darkness, with all the creepy sounds of night surrounding her.

No, she'd best wait. Tomorrow she would return here and try to go back in time again.

Sarah stared at Venus, glittering brightly in the sky above her. She thought of John Keats's words, "Bright star, would I were stedfast as thou art."

"Oh, Damien," she breathed, as the night throbbed around her. "Where are you?"

Almost a hundred years away, Damien Fontaine stood on the same gallery, looking out at the same star and remembering the same poet's words: "Bright star, would I were stedfast as thou art."

His voice rose in anguish to the cold night sky. "Oh, Sarah, where are you? My love, where are you?"

Chapter Eleven

The next morning, Sarah awoke vowing that she would make it back into the past today. If meditation had gotten her there before, she would try meditation again until she made her way back to Damien. She decided she would dress in her old-fashioned garb, so that if she did make it back, she wouldn't astonish Damien and his aunt with her twentieth-century clothing.

But Sarah knew that she couldn't leave the house in the odd garments, not with both Ebbie and Maudie working there today. Giving the women the day off probably would only make Maudie suspicious and confuse and offend Ebbie, she decided. Ebbie in particular clung tenaciously to her routine.

Thus Sarah spent her day pacing, trying to paint or read. At four o'clock, after both women had left, she breathed a deep sigh of relief. Dressing in her old-fashioned clothing, she scribbled Ebbie a note:

"Have gone back to New Orleans to stay with my friend. Please call Mr. Baldwin if you need anything." She prayed that when Ebbie found the note tomorrow she'd be well back into the past.

Sarah left Miss Erica's house, placing her keys under the back mat. She walked to the old place, staying close to the trees so as not to attract attention. Casper followed her for a time, then he disappeared into a field.

Sarah was just leaving the swamp when she spotted the old, white-haired woman again in a stand of trees beyond her. Sarah called out and waved, but as always, the woman in black disappeared without responding in any way. Sarah had long since begun to call the old woman "the ghost." Sometimes she wondered if she existed at all.

Sarah climbed the steps to the old house and settled herself inside the parlor. She chanted her mantra and tried to get into meditation, but she was simply too tense and couldn't. An hour later, she was pounding her fists on the floor in supreme frustration. No matter how hard she tried, she couldn't relax.

Perhaps she wanted it all too badly. "Oh, Damien, if only you could know how I ache to be with you," she whispered through tears.

Finally, Sarah gave up for the day and went home. She took the note she had left for Ebbie, folded it and placed it in the pocket of her dress. Each day, she would leave the note out while she went back to the house to meditate. She wouldn't give up until she made her way back to Damien.

The next two days brought no change in the pattern. Each day after Ebbie left, Sarah dressed in the old gown, went back to the house and tried to get into her meditation. Each time, she was too tense to get in. She went home angry and frustrated. She was beginning to doubt her own sense of reality and fear she had dreamed her entire experience in the past.

Sarah used her spare time to start going through and packing up Miss Erica's things, and the simple physical activity did help take the edge off her tension. She decided to split much of Miss Erica's clothing between Ebbie and Reuben Voisin's wife, and she was grateful that Maudie Wilson wasn't around to voice her disapproval. Ebbie seemed genuinely pleased with the three boxes of clothing and costume jewelry that Sarah insisted she take, and the maid then helped Sarah carry the two remaining boxes out to Reuben Voisin's wife, Laticia. Laticia and her children were equally thrilled with the clothing, yard goods and linens Sarah brought them.

On Friday evening, Sarah went through Miss Erica's desk, sorting through her various papers and journals in the hope that she might discover more information about the old house. She didn't make any real breakthroughs concerning the old place, but she did learn plenty about Erica Davis. Indeed, Miss Erica had kept journals and old letters dating back to the turn of the century.

Sarah read through one sheaf of old letters and discovered them to be love letters written by Miss Erica's fiancé, Lesley Wharton, who had been sent to Europe with the Army during the first World War. The tone of the letters was deeply romantic, filled with the angst of lovers separated for the first time. Why hadn't the two married? Sarah wondered. Noting that the letters abruptly ended in the summer of 1918, she feared she knew the reason.

She found the answers she sought in Miss Erica's journals. The entries from 1916 and 1917 spoke of Erica's love for Lesley. One entry read: "After Lesley and I marry, we're going to go live in the old place. Mama and Papa said we could have it as a wedding present. Lesley will finish his education, then he'll start his law practice here in Meridian. Oh, everything shall be perfect!"

Sarah smiled at this glowing evidence of a young woman's optimism and romanticism. But that rosy outlook changed as the United States was swept up in the first World War. An entry from January of 1918 read: "Lesley has been drafted into the A.E.F. I'm so frightened!" Then came the entry Sarah had feared, from July of 1918: "Lesley's parents came out from New Orleans to tell us he was killed at Chateau-Thierry. I can't believe it! My life is over. I shall never love again."

Reading the entry, Sarah blinked at a tear; she realized that with that one fell stroke, Erica's youthful idealism had been shattered, just as hers had been when she lost Brian.

Later entries revealed why Miss Erica had never lived in the old steamboat gothic house. An entry from August of 1919 read: "I went to the old house today, and I thought I saw Lesley. I shan't go there ever again. It's too painful. I must go on and find strength in my faith. There's nothing else left for me."

Sarah reread the entry, and a chill swept her as she paused once more on the words, "I thought I saw Lesley . . ." So Miss Erica had thought she saw the ghost of her fiancé at the old house. She had stayed away to avoid the pain and had found sustenance in her faith.

Had Miss Erica really seen Lesley at the old place?

Or had the ghost been Damien? She might never know.

Sarah packed Miss Erica's papers and mementos in a box, wondering what she would do with them. Perhaps she could give the collection to the local library or historical society. She decided that, if she were still here next week, she would begin making some inquiries locally to see who might be interested in the papers. And she would also need to see if she could find records on the Fontaine family, since her search through Erica Davis's papers had spurred more questions than it had answered.

Sarah, help me! Please, help me!

The next morning, Sarah awakened in a cold sweat, her heart hammering furiously. She sat bolt upright in bed, gasping for breath, rocking back and forth to steady herself.

She glanced wildly at her surroundings, the sunswept bedroom and Casper, who sat at the foot of her bed with his ears perked, eyes wide with alarm.

"Oh, God," she gasped after a moment, burying her face in her hands and sobbing. The nightmare of Brian had come again—the terrifying episode where she heard him screaming for help and was powerless to go to him. She knew the dream had no logic, yet its impact was devastating, nevertheless.

Sarah hadn't experienced the dream the entire time she had been back in the past. Obviously, she was safe from the nightmare in the past—but not here in the present. Being with Damien truly held some mystical, healing quality. She had to find her way back to him.

Sarah climbed out of bed and hurried to the bathroom. Since it was Saturday, neither Ebbie nor

Maudie would be here, so she was free to go to the house right away.

Sarah had a quick breakfast of cereal and toast, dressed in her old-fashioned garb and left for the house in the coolness of morning. This time, for the first time since she'd been back, Casper followed her all the way to the house. He even climbed up the steps with her, and, inside the old parlor, he curled up in her lap. The cat had acted rather distant toward her since her return, and his presence now soothed her. Obviously, she had at last been forgiven for leaving.

And with the cat there snuggled close to her, something magical happened. Sarah was able, at last, to relax. She stroked Casper and mouthed her mantra, giving herself over to the restful, deep darkness and the fanciful images.

Gradually, thought faded. But two thoughts remained for a time.

Morning. She had gone back before in the morning. Perhaps morning was the key.

And *Casper.* The cat had been there with her when she'd gone back in time before.

Morning was the key. Casper was her guide.

Then peace washed away all reason, and Sarah gave herself over to the images. The piano played, beckoning her to another age.

Sarah blinked, shaking her head as she stared at the room around her. The music—Olympia's piano music—had stopped, and the first thing she noticed was that she was back in Damien Fontaine's nineteenth-century parlor. Everything was just the same as she had left it—the book on the coffee table, even the old clock ticking away on the mantle.

Sarah knew an instant of joy so blinding, it

161

actually hurt. Then she noticed that Casper was still with her, curled up in her lap. The cat stared up at her with his beautiful gold eyes; he did not seem the least bit astonished that the room had just changed so radically.

"Well, I'll be damned," Sarah murmured, stroking the cat with trembling fingers. "You came all the way back with me, didn't you, boy?"

Sarah had no sooner said the words, then she heard a swish of skirts and a sharp gasp. She looked up to see Olympia Fontaine's plump form standing over her; the spinster was staring down at Sarah in consternation.

"Why, Miss Jennings," she cried, "whatever are you doing down there on the floor? Where have you been? And what manner of animal life is that in your lap?"

Sarah fought to gather her wits. She was just coming out of deep meditation and was unprepared to handle intense interrogation. She struggled to her feet, with Casper still in her arms. "I'm sorry, Miss Fontaine," she said awkwardly. "I didn't mean to startle you."

" 'Startle' is a rather mild word under the circumstances," Olympia replied archly, her face screwed up with displeasure. "Where on earth have you been these past three days, child? Don't you know that Damien has been beside himself trying to find you?"

The mention of Damien made Sarah's heart well with joy. She hungered to see him, but knew she had Olympia's indignation to deal with first. "I'm sorry," she repeated. Quickly, she fabricated an explanation. "You see, a friend of mine was suddenly taken ill in New Orleans and sent her manservant here to fetch me. It was barely dawn when we left, and I didn't want to disturb you or Damien."

"So you simply left—with no note, no explanation whatever?" Olympia cut in irately. "Where are your manners, child?"

"Again, I apologize, Miss Fontaine," Sarah said. "I promise it won't happen again."

Olympia harrumphed, then glanced at Casper. "And where did that animal come from?"

"Oh, this is my friend's cat, Casper," Sarah hastily explained, wondering at the ease with which she had learned to spin lies. "I'm caring for him until my friend is better. That is, if you have no objection?"

Olympia's stern countenance softened just slightly. "Well, I suppose he can help rid the stable of some of its vermin."

"Oh, no," Sarah said quickly, horrified at the thought of Casper's going out the front door. Casper was a creature of the twentieth century, just as she was, and if he did leave the house, he'd probably be propelled back to the present, just as she had been. And she knew now that Casper was her guide, and that fact made her cling to the cat, as well. "He's quite used to staying inside, so if you don't mind, I'd prefer that he be confined to the house and garden."

Olympia studied the cat with a frown. "Well, he is quite a striking thing, with that flat face and those large golden eyes. I swear, I've never seen anything quite like him."

"He's a Persian," Sarah put in, coughing nervously. "Well, then, I am back, so I suppose I should get upstairs to the salon and continue with my duties."

"Not so quickly, Miss Jennings," Olympia put in coldly, her eyes narrowing. "You'll have to speak with Damien first, of course. As I already told you, you caused my nephew great distress with your disappearance."

Sarah felt keenly dismayed by the thought that she had made Damien worry. "Oh, of course I'll speak with him, then. But isn't this the time of day he writes? Do you truly want me to disturb him?"

Olympia drew herself up huffily. "Yes, I definitely think you should clear your presence here with my nephew. Following your irresponsible behavior, I'm not at all sure he'll want you to continue with your duties."

Olympia's words were filled with rebuke, and Sarah's spirits sank. With an effort, she bucked up her courage. "I'll speak with Damien at once, then, Miss Fontaine."

Slanting Sarah a last, disapproving glance, Olympia turned and left the room. A moment later, Sarah heard her resume her piano playing in the dining room.

Sighing, Sarah left the parlor with Casper in her arms. She was dying to see Damien, but still quite concerned that her actions may have caused him confusion and fear.

Then, out in the hallway, something strange happened. Casper bolted out of her arms and streaked into the dining room.

"Casper, no!" Sarah cried in a hoarse whisper. She followed the cat, appalled at the thought that he might disturb Olympia at the piano.

At the archway to the dining room, Sarah paused in her tracks as she viewed a wondrous sight. Casper hopped up into Olympia's lap as she played, and, after a moment of startled hesitation, Olympia petted the cat then placed her hands back on the ivories. Casper curled up contentedly as the spinster continued playing with an expression of pleasure on her face.

Sarah was amazed. So Casper loved music. She recalled poignantly how the cat had in some mystical way reminded her of Brian. This thought gave her new resolve and courage.

Sarah turned and started back down the hallway for Damien's study. She took a deep breath, then rapped on his door.

A deep voice called out irritably, "Come in."

Sarah entered the small office and closed the door, leaning against it for support. Damien sat at his desk, his back to her as he wrote. The sight of him was heaven to Sarah; her heart pounded with joy, and her eyes filled with bittersweet tears.

"Damien," she whispered.

At once he was on his feet, his eyes incredulous. "Sarah!"

In two strides, he was across the room, and she was caught roughly in his arms. His kiss was bruising, his mouth passionately taking hers, his tongue thrusting deeply into her mouth. All his need and frustration and frantic fear were poured into his kiss and crushing embrace. Sarah clung to him, reeling with joy to be back in his arms again, drowning in the heat of his lips, awash in his scent. Back home, she thought achingly.

"My God, Sarah," he said, drawing back to hold her by the shoulders. "Where have you been? I'm been searching for you everywhere—distraught and terrified that you might have come to harm."

"I-I'm sorry," she said lamely. "A friend took ill suddenly, and I was called away to New Orleans."

At once she felt him stiffening. Then he pulled

away, staring at her with eyes filled with angry reproach. "So you just left without a word and let me think the worst? Let me fear I might never see you again? How could you, Sarah? I thought we meant much more to each other than that."

Sarah felt wounded by his just fury. "I'm sorry," she repeated, gesturing helplessly. "You're right. I should have left word. I made a mistake, Damien. But I'm here now, and I give you my word that I won't give you such a scare again."

"Oh, you give me your word, do you?" he asked bitterly.

Sarah swallowed hard as she stared up at him. All at once, he seemed like a remote stranger standing across from her, his face a stony mask, his dark eyes gleaming with suspicion. Why was he so angry at her?

Marshaling her courage, she stepped forward and touched his arm, her eyes shining with love and regret. "Yes, Damien, I give my word. I know I acted thoughtlessly, and, again, I do apologize. But can't you just forgive and forget, and we'll go on from here? I missed you so."

Yet he turned away, his rigid back to her. "There's more to it than simply forgiving and forgetting. There's a matter of trust, a trust I gave you as I've given no woman before, a trust you violated with your departure."

Sarah bit her lip. How could she get through to him, make him understand without giving away too much? He had been hurt so much in the past. She knew it had been a supreme leap of faith for him to trust her at all, and now she had shattered their fragile rapport with her own unwitting departure. "Just give me another chance," was all she could manage to say. "Things will be the same again, I promise. You'll see."

Yet Damien shook his head as he turned to her. "Things won't be the same again." He gripped her arms, and his eyes gleamed with an intense light. "Because you lied to me, didn't you? All this nonsense about a friend taking ill. It was all a sham, wasn't it? Tell me, where did you really go? And who were you with?"

Staring up into his angry eyes, Sarah felt electrified by his incisive questions. Oh, God, how much did he know? How much had he guessed? Should she risk all and tell him the truth? Or was it too late? Had she already destroyed herself in his eyes?

She was on the verge of spilling everything out, when some instinct warned her not to tell Damien where she had really come from. Don't break the spell, the voice warned. You may lose him forever.

But I've already lost him, she thought dismally.

"Well?" Damien prodded, shaking her slightly.

She stared up at him with tears in her eyes. "You don't understand," was all she could say.

But he only laughed cynically. "How little did it mean?" he whispered fiercely. "All the things we shared—how little, Sarah?"

She wanted to answer, "It meant everything," but she couldn't. Her emotions felt too exposed, too raw. Instead, she hung her head and whispered, "Do you want me to continue repairing the paintings?"

"Yes," he replied tersely.

For a moment, they stared at each other, a sea of anguish stretching between him. Then Damien turned his back on her, and, with a low cry, she fled the room.

Outside, Sarah leaned against the door for support, tears streaming down her face. She was back, but nothing was the same. She had violated Damien's trust with her departure, and now he might never again look at her as his friend, his soul mate.

She could understand his hurt and bewilderment, but she was stunned by the depth of his anger and his sense of betrayal. Why had he dismissed her story? Why had he accused of her lying? Again, she wondered how much he knew. She could ask him outright, but instinct still warned against it. For if she broke the spell, if she lost him for good, she would surely die.

He needed her. She knew this. She needed him just as much. Somehow, she would find a way to win his love and rebuild his trust.

After Sarah left, Damien found himself unable to write. Sarah had come back, and instead of rejoicing, he had treated her quite badly. Yet he had felt frightened and hurt by her disappearance, and her lame explanation just now had angered him because it had afforded him no real answers. After all they had shared, he just couldn't take her lying to him this way—and he knew damn well she was lying. Even if he had never found the strange items upstairs, he still would have guessed of her subterfuge; her eyes and tone of voice gave her away. Where had she really gone? Would she leave again? And why hadn't she told him the truth?

A sharp rap at his door interrupted his troubled thoughts. He called out, "Come in," hoping that Sarah had come back. Yet when he turned, it was to watch in disappointment as his aunt swept into the room. "Yes, Aunt Olympia?"

"Good morning, Damien. I was wondering if I might have a word with you."

"Of course." Damien crossed over to his desk, indicating a chair on the nearby wall for Olympia. Once both were seated, he asked, "What's on your mind, Aunt?"

"It's Miss Jennings."

"Yes?"

Olympia shifted in her chair. "Well, don't you think her behavior has been irresponsible, to say the least?"

Damien scowled. "In what way?"

"Why, the girl disappeared for over three days, leaving no word as to her whereabouts. I find it quite reprehensible that she would just walk out on her duties that way."

Damien's scowl deepened. While he still felt hurt and confused by Sarah's actions, he refused to let his aunt cast aspersions on the woman he had come to love. Stiffly, he replied, "Sarah was no doubt distraught, with her friend taking ill suddenly. I'm sure she meant to leave word, but perhaps in the panic of the moment—"

"Are you telling me you actually believe that arre story about her going off to New Orleans to with a sick friend?"

"Do you have any reason to believe she would lie?"

Olympia hesitated, biting her lip.

"Well?"

In a rustle of her taffeta skirts, Olympia got up and walked over to the window. With her back to Damien, she admitted, "Nephew, after Miss Jennings first came here, I made inquiries."

"What do you mean?" Damien asked tensely.

169

Olympia turned with a sigh. "As I've told you before, the clothing Miss Jennings wore when she first arrived here was—well, eccentric, to say the least. I've had my doubts about the girl from the start, so I recently wrote to Mr. Rillieux in New Orleans, asking him about her."

"And?"

"Two days ago he wrote back saying that he's never heard of Sarah Jennings."

"What?" Damien shot to his feet.

Olympia stepped forward, her eyes gleaming with triumph. "Mr. Rillieux did commission an artist to come out here, but the hapless young man came down with a bilious fever and died over a month ago. Mr. Rillieux wrote that he has been trying to find us a replacement ever since, but that he's had no luck."

"I see," Damien murmured, thrusting his fingers through his hair.

Crisply, Olympia continued. "Now that you're aware of Miss Jennings's subterfuge, you'll dismiss her, of course?"

"No," Damien said coldly, "that's out of the question."

"But the girl is an imposter," Olympia cried out indignantly.

"She's an eminently qualified artist."

"That may be, but it still doesn't change the fact that she came here under false pretenses."

Damien shrugged with a bravado he hardly felt. "Perhaps Sarah knew the young man who died or heard of the assignment from a friend. Perhaps she simply decided to take advantage of it."

"Then that would make her an opportunist, at the very least." Olympia drew herself up with dignity. "I

170

think you should discharge Miss Jennings at once and find another artist to complete the restoration of Vincy's paintings."

Damien's jaw clenched in fury. "Aunt, have you taken leave of your senses? Do you realize that Sarah has been able to emulate Vincy's style with virtual perfection? Do you realize that our chances of finding another artist with her particular gift are practically nonexistent?"

Olympia stepped forward, placing her hand on Damien's sleeve. She spoke with quiet urgency, her pain and worry reflected in her hazel eyes. "Damien, I've noticed that you spend much time with her. I know her kind; you can't trust her. Perhaps she will complete her work here—perhaps not. But at any rate, she'll soon be gone, and I just can't bear to see you hurt again."

Damien pulled away and walked over to the window, his broad back to Olympia. "Whether or not Miss Jennings leaves after she completes her task is up to her, don't you think? As for myself, I'm not a child any more, Aunt Olympia. I've long since become capable of handling my own affairs—and my own tragedies."

"Damien . . ."

He turned to her, raising an eyebrow. "Was there anything else, Aunt?"

She sighed in defeat. "No, Damien."

After his aunt left, Damien stood at the window for a long time, a troubled frown creasing his brow. So, just as he had suspected, Mr. Rillieux had never sent Sarah out from New Orleans. In that, she had lied to him, too. Who was she really, then? And why had she come here?

More importantly, would she indeed leave again

after the paintings were repaired—or even before —as his aunt had argued she would? For despite all his feelings of betrayal and hurt, Damien knew now that Sarah was the true ray of hope shining at the end of the tunnel of blackness where he dwelled. Now that he had her back, he couldn't bear the thought of losing her again.

Chapter Twelve

No one seemed to want her back.

All day, Sarah felt an alien in the world to which she had returned. Olympia continued to act coolly toward her, while Damien shut her out completely. Even Baptista's attitude seemed hostile. When Sarah passed her in the hallway, the negress merely muttered, "So you back," staring at Sarah with dark, accusing eyes.

The rejection by one and all devastated Sarah. She spent the day working in the salon repairing one of Vincy's paintings and trying not to think of how isolated and hurt she felt. She and Damien had shared so much, and now that fragile bond had been broken. How could she get across to him that it wasn't her fault, that she hadn't meant to leave him, when she didn't even feel safe telling him where she'd come from?

In her despair, she even considered going back to the present and remaining there, yet she knew she must finish her work on Vincy's paintings first. By then, she would surely know whether or not Damien would forgive her. If he wouldn't, she may as well leave. What kind of existence was this anyway, when she couldn't share Damien's world with him outside the walls of the house itself?

Yet even as Sarah asked herself this central, troubling question, she realized that she would go to any length and make any sacrifice to stay here—if only Damien would forgive her.

She didn't see him all day; he remained sequestered behind the study doors, writing. Both luncheon and dinner were quiet, strained meals Sarah passed with Olympia in the dining room. Even Casper had deserted her; he seemed to have adopted Olympia, and vice versa.

That evening after dinner, Sarah went to her room, feeling disconsolate. Then a knock at her door brought new hope. "Yes?" she called out, praying that it would be Damien asking her to join him in the salon.

Yet her spirits sagged as Baptista stepped into the room. "I come to turn down the bed, mam'zelle," the negress said sullenly.

"Go right ahead," Sarah replied, sitting down at the dressing table. She might as well take down her hair and get ready for bed, she thought.

But even as she reached for the first pin, she heard Baptista gasp behind her. Sarah turned to watch the negress stare at the bed in horror, her eyes enormous as she hastily crossed herself.

Sarah rose. "Baptista, what is it?"

But Baptista merely backed away, pointing a

shaking finger at the bed. Sarah walked forward, frowning, and spotted an odd, small red flannel bag on the white sheet. "What on earth . . . ?" she muttered, reaching for it.

"No, mistress, don't touch it!" Baptista cried.

Sarah pivoted with her hand still poised. "But what is it?"

Baptista swallowed convulsively. "It the *gris-gris*."

"*Gris-gris*?" Sarah repeated.

"Voodoo," Baptista added meaningfully. "It evil."

"Oh, is that all," Sarah said, waving her off. "Don't tell me you hold with such nonsense." She picked up the small bag. "Here, will you throw it away?"

But Baptista was backing away, shaking her head violently. With eyes dilated with terror, she whirled and fled the room.

Sarah sighed, staring at the strange little bag tied with a piece of braid. She lifted it and took a whiff, then sneezed. It smelled vile and peppery. She decided she had no desire to view the contents of the little bag.

She wondered who had placed the *gris-gris* on her bed. She knew that the practice of voodoo had its roots in African tribal religion, yet she found it impossible to believe that one of the maids, Hattie or Jane, had placed the odious object on her bed.

That left Baptista, who was most likely the culprit, she decided. Sarah knew the negress felt jealous of her and Damien's relationship. After all, since she and Damien had become friends, she'd seen no real evidence that he had continued his liaison with the black woman. Baptista had no doubt resented Sarah's reappearance here and had

175

probably planted the voodoo charm to scare her away. If this were so, she'd also done a consummate acting job just now in order to put the finishing touch on her little con job.

Well, it wasn't going to work. Sarah didn't hold with voodoo, and the first thing she intended to do was to get rid of this foul-smelling charm.

With the token still in hand, Sarah went downstairs and approached the backdoor. She found Casper perched near the door, a splash of cottony whiteness amid a pool of rosy, fading light. Spotting Sarah, he meowed at her plaintively.

"Need to go outside, boy?" While Sarah had already decided that the cat should be safe in the courtyard, she nevertheless hesitated a moment at the thought of actually letting him out.

Then the cat meowed piteously, and Sarah knew she had no choice. She opened the door, and the cat streaked out. She breathed a sigh of relief when he didn't disintegrate into thin air.

Sarah went to stand on the back veranda, watching Casper slip into some bushes. She took careful aim and tossed the *gris-gris* over the courtyard wall. So much for voodoo, she thought.

The wind whipped up then, cool and scented with autumn, and the fading sun bathed the lush courtyard with a golden glow. A nightbird began to call. It was so odd, Sarah mused, that she was safe here, within the courtyard walls, but that she couldn't go out the front door without returning to the present.

Soon, Casper rejoined her. He followed Sarah back up to her room, then curled up at the foot of her bed and began licking his paws and washing his face. Sarah smiled at this evidence that the cat hadn't completely deserted her in favor of Olympia.

"What do you make of all this, boy?" she asked,

scratching his ears. But Casper merely closed his eyes and purred.

Sarah went to bed soon afterward. Her sleep was turbulent, haunted. A low, almost indistinguishable voice kept repeating, *Go away, you don't belong here.*

In the middle of the night, she awakened, shaking and sweating in the coolness. The wind was howling outside, Casper was gone, and she was alone—more alone than she'd ever been in her life.

Go away, you don't belong here.

Still, the message haunted her dreams.

The next morning, Sarah joined Olympia for tea out in the courtyard. The morning was briskly sunny, almost wintry; both women wore wool frocks and knitted shawls. Olympia's attitude was aloof, if courteous, as she served Sarah tea and rice cakes.

While Sarah suspected that Olympia still resented her presence here, she was also growing desperate for someone to confide in regarding Damien's withdrawal and rejection. And who would better understand him than his aunt?

Setting down her tea, Sarah ventured, "Miss Fontaine, I'm worried about Damien. Ever since I came back, he's remained sequestered in his study."

"You might remember your own behavior," Olympia admonished.

Sarah repressed an urge to grit her teeth. "I do apologize again. However, my concern now is for your nephew."

Olympia sighed and stirred her tea. "Damien is like that, I'm afraid. Ever since the war ended, he's been consumed with the idea of writing Vincy's memoirs. Days and sometimes weeks go by with him barely leaving the study."

Sarah frowned. "I just wish there was some way to ease his torment, to bring him out of himself more."

"There isn't," Olympia said bluntly. "Damien has the life he has chosen."

"Are you so sure it's the life he wants?" Sarah countered. "You know, I've lost a brother, too—Damien and I have discussed it—and I just can't believe that he would choose to enmesh himself in the pain for the rest of his life. Surely he must want to find a way out of it. Lord knows how I've tried to find answers myself."

Sarah paused then, realizing she had revealed to Olympia so much more than she had intended, perhaps through her own frustration at being cut off from Damien. Now, Olympia was staring back at her with a mixture of suspicion and displeasure. After a moment, the spinster leaned forward and said earnestly, "My dear, I have noticed that you and Damien have spent much time together. I suppose that is only natural, since you do need to understand Vincy's nature in order to repair his paintings with the proper amount of sensitivity. But I also suspect that you may have misinterpreted my nephew's kindnesses, that you may have become attracted to him."

Sarah's chin came up. "I won't deny it."

Olympia clucked to herself as she leaned back in her chair. "Oh, my dear, I do fear you have set yourself up for a terrible fall. You must understand something about Damien."

"Yes?" Sarah stiffened in her chair, listening with every fiber of her being.

"Damien will never love again," Olympia said feelingly. "Any capacity for loving was destroyed in him during the war. Thus, for your own sake, I hope you'll plan to conclude your work here as quickly as possible and return to New Orleans."

Sarah was devastated by these words, which seemed to confirm all her worst fears. "Thank you for the advice," she said stiffly. "Now, if you'll excuse me . . ."

Sarah fled for the safety of the house.

That evening after Sarah completed her work, she returned to her room to find a black candle burning on her dressing table. The wax had been shaped in the image of a woman—obviously, a symbol of herself. Beneath the burning image were written the words, "Go away," in a reddish brown powder.

Sarah gasped at the sight. Cursing under her breath, she brushed a few flecks of the powder onto her fingertips and smelled it. She frowned, at once recognizing the mixture as ocher, an oxide of iron and earth which was used as a pigment. Indeed, there was a small jar of ocher with Vincy's paintings supplies in the salon.

Sarah blew out the candle, wondering who was trying to terrorize her with these voodoo tokens. She picked up the candle and moved to the open window. Standing at a safe distance, she tossed the odious object out through the parted lace curtains.

Afterward, Sarah paced the room wearing a troubled frown. Obviously, there was a malevolent presence here in the house, someone who didn't want her here. This was rather daunting to her, since the house represented her only safety. Who was now threatening that safety?

While Baptista had seemed the obvious choice before, Sarah now realized that someone else might have left the voodoo tokens in her room to throw suspicion on Baptista. Could the culprit be Olympia? Or Damien himself? That possibility was so devastating to Sarah that she dismissed it at once. While Damien might be angry at her, she could never imagine him resorting to anything this insidious and cruel.

At bedtime, Sarah still had no answers. Again, that night, she felt restless and had difficulty sleeping. Again, she heard the low, ominous voice saying, *Go away, you don't belong here.*

Finally, she got up, donned her wrapper and went into the salon. She shivered in the coolness, staring at the window seat where she and Damien had shared so many beautiful hours. Her heart twisted with painful longing. "Oh, Damien," she whispered, "what happened? Why won't you speak to me? Why do you keep shutting me out?"

The wind whistled against the windowpane, a low, mournful sound as Sarah blinked at tears. Then she heard a voice ask, "Are you thinking of going back again?"

Sarah whirled to find herself facing Damien. He stood across from her, all in black, staring at her with his beautiful, haunted eyes. Her heart sang with joy that he had come to her. "Damien, have you forgiven me at last?"

She seemed to fly across the room into his arms. She kissed him feverishly, trembling as he clutched her close. Excitement raced along her nerve endings as he groaned and kissed her back with a vehemence to match her own.

When the kiss ended, she rested her cheek against his shirt front, inhaling his scent and listening to the comforting sound of his heartbeat. Being in his arms again was ecstasy. "Damien, I've missed you so," she said brokenly. "Please don't hold yourself away from me again."

He drew back and brushed a tear from her cheek with his thumb. "Are you thinking of going back again?" he repeated anxiously.

Sarah blinked at him. In her joy at seeing him, she hadn't really heard his question the first time. "You knew," she whispered as realization dawned. "You knew I came here from another time!"

He nodded soberly. "I suspected there was something ephemeral about your presence here."

"But how?"

"After you left, I questioned Aunt Olympia. She mentioned your odd dress when you first arrived here. I went to your room and found the clothes you wore that day." He shook his head in wonderment. "Your clothing and that strange pocket watch of yours—they're not from this time, Sarah, are they?"

"No, they're not."

"Are they from the future, then?"

She shook her head in amazement. "Yes. I can't believe you truly knew this."

"Actually, I had doubts, at first. I puzzled endlessly over your abrupt disappearance and the bizarre items you'd left behind. Incredible as it all seemed, the only explanation that made sense was that you had come here from another century, and that when you left, you went back to your own world."

Sarah continued to feel astounded by his words. "You believe in time travel, then?"

He sighed. "Vincy and I used to discuss such possibilities."

"You did?"

"Yes." A slight, ironic smile pulled at his mouth. "You see, I haven't always been a recluse here at Belle Fontaine. At one time, Vincy and I traveled the continent on powerful trains and crossed the ocean on sleek new steamers. We saw the fantastic modern

181

factories in the east and in England." A wistful quality entered his voice. "And there was a night long ago, before the war, that Vincy and I spent talking with a young riverboat pilot on the Mississippi. The man had a master intellect and keen wit. He spoke of the great strides mankind has made and the possibility that one day man might overcome space and time itself."

A chill swept Sarah at his words. "What was this man's name?"

Damien shrugged. "Sam—Samuel something."

"You met Mark Twain?" she cried.

He frowned. "You're referring to Twain, the writer? Funny, I've seen a book or two of his in recent years, but I've never connected him with the man Vincy and I met."

Sarah was shaking her head. "This is amazing. You're amazing! Then you knew I had gone back in time."

"Suffice it to say, I knew you hadn't merely slipped off to New Orleans to sit with a sick friend."

"So that's why you were so angry when I returned here."

A cloud crossed his eyes. "Yes. I knew you had lied to me."

"But you don't understand," Sarah said, gesturing in entreaty. "I didn't want to lie—truly, I didn't—but I was so afraid that if I told you the truth you would think me mad. Afraid I'd break the spell and be propelled back to the present, that I'd lose you forever."

He drew her close again. His breath was hot against her cheek as he ran a hand through her hair. "You're not going to lose me, Sarah, and I don't think you're mad. Not everything makes sense to me as yet, but I fully believe now that you did come here from the future. I also feel that there must be a reason you came here—and a reason you returned a second time. I'm not going to let you slip away again. I need you too much."

"Oh, Damien, I need you, too."

He took her face in his hands. "Forgive me my anger, darling. I know I behaved callously, shutting myself off from you, but you must know that it's not easy for me to trust—"

"I know," Sarah cut in, staring up at him with eyes filled with love and tears. "I know because I feel your hurt, your need. I realize now that your anguish is what drew me across time to you. There's so much we can share, so many ways we can help each other."

"I know that, too. Oh, my love."

Damien kissed her, a long, passionate kiss filled with emotion and need. Sarah pressed herself into him eagerly and kissed him back, drawing love and joy and sustenance from his wonderful embrace.

Afterward, Sarah felt as if a deep, aching wound had been healed inside her. She drew a breathless sigh. "You can't know how happy I am to have you back. I thought you were lost to me forever. Your aunt said—"

He drew back and frowned. "What did Aunt Olympia say?"

"She said that any capacity for loving was lost in you during the war."

He expelled a heavy breath and released her, walking off toward the window. He stood with his back to her, a dark, imposing figure awash in moonlight. "Ah, sometimes I think my aunt is right. There's something broken inside me, and I'm not sure it can ever be fixed." He turned to her with a sad smile, the chiseled planes of his face outlined in silvery relief. "I'm not sure how much I can offer you, Sarah—another reason I've stayed away."

"Oh, no!" she cried. "Please don't doubt yourself. For there's no doubt in my mind that you can give me everything I could ever possibly want. I know we can find great peace and healing and love together. There's just . . ." She paused, feeling a shiver of fear wash over her. "So much we must overcome."

He nodded. "I know, my beautiful, brave Sarah. You have borne too much on your own shoulders for far too long." He stretched out his hand to her. "Come sit with me at the window, love."

"Oh, yes!" Eagerly, she came to his side and took his hand. At the window seat, he kissed her tenderly, while in the heavens above, their bright star beamed down on their blissful reunion, on two souls that had been wrenched apart and were now one again.

Damien stroked Sarah's moon-washed hair and whispered, "Tell me all, darling. Tell me how you got here, and how you went back again."

Sarah bit her lip, recalling her recurring premonition that she shouldn't tell Damien the truth, that she shouldn't risk breaking the spell. She glanced at him in uncertainty. "Damien, I'm afraid."

He squeezed her hand. "You're safe here with me."

She drew a shaky breath. "If you're sure."

"I am." Damien smiled at her. "Tell me of your world, my love."

Chapter Thirteen

"I don't know where to begin," Sarah said.

"Just start at the beginning," Damien urged. "Tell me where you came from, how you got here."

Sarah collected her thoughts. "I came from Atlanta, Georgia. From the year 1967."

"My God!" Damien gasped.

"Do you believe me?"

"Yes, I do," he said. "I knew you had come from the future, but, Good Lord, that's almost a hundred years away."

"I know."

"Please continue, love."

She shook her head. "There's so much—it boggles the mind."

"Then tell me only what's necessary to explain your presence here. We can go into greater detail later."

She nodded and smiled at him. "The world I

came from is vastly different from your own. There have been enormous strides in technology, science, medicine, you name it. And there have been more wars—many wars."

"Ah," Damien murmured. "Then perhaps your time is not that different from my own, after all, is it?"

She nodded. "Perhaps not. Anyway, as to how and why I came here, one of these wars caused a major change in my life. My younger brother was drafted by the Army. He was sent overseas and was killed."

Damien's eyes gleamed with intense empathy as he squeezed her hand. "My darling, I'm so sorry. This is the brother you spoke of?"

"Yes. Brian. He was only eighteen years old." She drew a painful, shuddering breath. "Soon after I learned of his death, I—fell apart. I had a nervous breakdown."

"Nervous breakdown?" Damien repeated.

"A mental collapse."

"I see."

"Then a gifted doctor treated me and gradually brought me back to reality. But I had earned my living as an artist, and when Brian died, it seemed like everything creative in me died, as well."

"I understand," Damien murmured sympathetically.

"My doctor suggested transcendental meditation as a way to break through my artistic block and also to heal my pain. So I took instruction, if reluctantly." She paused. "It was about this same time that I learned that I had inherited an estate in Louisiana from a distant relative."

Damien laughed in disbelief. "You inherited this land, this house?"

She nodded. "You see, eventually, this house and

the land became the property of a cousin of mine, Erica Davis."

"This is all fantastic," Damien put in, shaking his head.

"I know."

"So you inherited the house—then what?"

"Well, I came here to Louisiana to see to Cousin Erica's estate."

"Did you live here, in this house?"

"No. I would have loved to, of course, but I'm afraid your house is vastly different in the year 1967. The house is abandoned. My cousin left me a new, modern house in which to live. When I came here, I settled into this newer house. Soon, I discovered your house—the old place—here by the river. The house was old and gray, but structurally sound. Rumor held that the house was haunted."

"Indeed?" Damien smiled.

"Yes. At any rate, I soon came to believe the rumors. I became fascinated by the old place and started coming here to meditate. I sensed that the house held the answers I was seeking, answers to my pain."

"How amazing."

"I know. And as I began to meditate here, I began to see images from another age. I began to see you, Damien."

His eyes glittered with excitement. "Did you?"

"Yes. Many times I saw you. I began to realize that the ghosts did exist, but I was never afraid, only eager to come back here again and again."

"Were you?" His fingertips caressed her cheek, and he smiled tenderly.

"Oh, yes, Damien. So eager. And I began to paint again, to paint like one possessed, with more clarity and energy than I had ever possessed before. I

187

painted the house, and yet when I finished, your face was superimposed on the canvas."

"My God!" he gasped.

Sarah continued speaking with intense emotion. "It was you I saw, Damien. You haunted me in the sweetest possible way. When I came here, I saw you, always dressed in black. I called you my dark cavalier. And sometimes you spoke to me— comforting words like, 'Don't ask why.' Sometimes, I heard music—Olympia's piano music. Usually 'Beautiful Dreamer.' Sometimes, I heard Brian's violin, as well. And one day I awoke here in another century."

"That's truly astonishing. But how . . .? Do you suppose your transcendental meditation brought you back here?"

"I suppose it must have, but I also feel you drew me here."

"Ah, perhaps I did. I've been searching for something, too, but I didn't quite know what it was until you came here, Sarah. At any rate, it must have been a shock for you to awaken here."

She laughed dryly. "Indeed, it was. In fact, I was sitting in the parlor, just gaining my bearings, when Olympia walked into the room. She said something like, 'Are you the artist we sent for from New Orleans?'"

"How fascinating," Damien murmured. "You know, we did send for an artist to repair Vincy's paintings."

"But none ever came."

"You came," Damien said tenderly.

"That's just my point."

He nodded. "Actually, we found out later on that the artist we had sent for took ill with a bilious fever and died. You see, Aunt Olympia checked into the matter."

Sarah uttered a cry of dismay. "How terrible that the artist died." She bit her lip. "Then if your aunt found out that I was never actually sent here, she must be very suspicious of me."

He sighed. "Don't worry about that now, darling. Just continue with your story. How did you feel when you first realized you had arrived in another century?"

"Well, I was stunned, to say the very least. At the same time, I was fascinated—by you, by everything. So I did my best to adapt myself to my life here."

"I must say that you made a remarkable transition under the circumstances. But then you went back to your world again. Why? Didn't you want to stay here with me?"

She squeezed his hand and spoke vehemently. "Oh, I did, Damien. The world I left—I never felt I truly belonged there. I felt somehow displaced. During the past year, the only real peace I've known was during my ten days here with you. And you must understand that I didn't leave you willingly."

"Then why?"

She sighed. "The door in time."

He scowled. "Door in time?"

She stared warily at the window. "There's something out there—some sort of ominous, mystical border. I feel it when I venture too close to the front windows of the house. You see, I'm safe within the confines of the house or even out back in the courtyard, surrounded by the high brick walls. But if I leave the front door of the house, as I did that day last week . . ." Her voice trailed off and she shuddered.

"What happened?"

"Let me backtrack a minute. Do you remember when you asked me to go with you to Vincy's grave?"

"Yes."

"I felt that was such a breakthrough for us, and I so wanted to go with you. But I was fearful of the strange, electric border I felt each time I approached the front of the house. I felt so torn. I wanted to accompany you, but I couldn't subject you to possible injury from the invisible boundary. So I decided I first had to test the area out myself, alone."

"And you did?"

She nodded.

"What happened?"

She shook her head in wonderment. "I walked out the front door, found myself spinning around, and the next thing I knew, I was back in the present."

"My God, that's incredible!"

"It truly happened, Damien. And it was every bit as amazing to me as I'm sure it is to you."

"Then you risked all that for me, for us?" he asked poignantly. "Even sensing the danger?"

"Yes."

"Sarah, you could have been hurt."

"I wasn't—although losing you hurt in a way I cannot even begin to describe. You must understand that I never would have risked testing out the border, except that I yearned to see Vincy's grave. I wanted to go there with you. And as things turned out, I did find his grave—but back in the twentieth century."

Damien smiled in amazement. "You know, I went

there, too. I sensed your presence, but I couldn't find you."

"And I sensed you, too, but couldn't find you, either. It was exquisite frustration, like reaching for a brass ring that forever eluded me. I sensed you again when I looked at the sky that night from the porch of the house. I gazed at a bright star—"

"And I gazed at the very same star, that very night," he cut in passionately. "I cried out for you, Sarah."

"And I cried out for you."

The emotion of the moment became too much, and Damien pulled Sarah close, kissing her hungrily. Sarah reeled with pleasure, opening her mouth to him eagerly and tangling her fingertips in the thick silk of his hair. She loved him so. God, how she loved him so.

"Darling, I've missed you so much," he whispered after a moment, pressing his lips against her temple.

"I've missed you, too."

He drew back to stare at her intently. "And again I must ask your forgiveness, for my anger when you first came back. I just didn't understand."

"It's all right, Damien. There's nothing to forgive."

"How did you get back to me?"

She sighed. "I tried meditating again. For three days. But at first I was just too tense and couldn't get in. Finally, I was able to get in deep enough. Casper was my guide this time."

"Casper?"

"The cat I brought with me."

"Ah, yes. Aunt Olympia has pretty much adopted him."

"I'm not sure just what his role was, but when he was with me, I was able to make it back to you."

"I'm so grateful, my love. You're here with me now, and all is well."

Sarah frowned. "But all is not well, Damien. What about the window in time? I can't exist here with you beyond the doors of this house. I'm terrified that if I walk out the front door, I'll return to the year 1967 and I'll never find you again."

"Then don't walk out the front door, darling," Damien whispered intensely. "The house is enough for us, is it not?"

Sarah thought that over a moment. "I don't know," she answered truthfully.

"Enough talk, now," Damien said, kissing her hair. "You're exhausted and confused. We'll talk again when you're ready." A husky note entered his voice as he added, "For now, it's time to welcome you back properly."

"Oh, Damien."

Damien pulled Sarah into his lap and kissed her passionately. She moaned in ecstasy, curling her arms about his neck and kissing him back. She felt no shame sitting in his intimate embrace wearing only her nightclothes. There was only the unearthly rapture of being cocooned by his strength, sheltered by his warmth, awash in his scent. The bold thrust of his tongue in her mouth aroused her exquisitely, and when his rough fingertips caressed her taut nipples through the cloth of her gown, hot flames of excitement and fierce need streaked down her body, settling in her aching center. When those same bold hands kneaded her breasts, claiming mastery, she was sure she could endure no more. After a moment, she wrenched her mouth free from his just to breathe.

Damien caught a ragged breath and pressed his mouth against the throbbing pulse on her throat, searing her anew with his heat. Sarah broke out in shivers, and he whispered a soothing endearment as his hot mouth captured hers once more.

He held her there and kissed her until she was mindless. Never had she felt so cherished, so needed, so welcomed.

Afterward, he cradled her close on the window seat. Together, they gazed out at their bright star.

Later, when Sarah went to her room, she seemed to be walking on air. She and Damien were together again—truly together. Their relationship was stronger, deeper, more passionate than ever before.

Yet when she flipped back the covers on her bed, she found another ugly red *gris-gris* awaiting her on the sheet. Cursing under her breath, she picked up the odious object and tossed it out the window. She considered going to Damien to tell him of the threat, then decided she had already worried him enough over the past few days. Besides, while someone was obviously trying to frighten her, surely the devices themselves were harmless enough. Sarah refused to believe that the little red bags and black candles actually had the power to bring disaster hurtling down upon her.

Nevertheless, her sleep was troubled, and she again heard the low, ominous voice, saying, *Get out—you don't belong here*, all through the night.

Chapter Fourteen

The next morning another strange event occurred. Sarah came downstairs to find Casper at the front door, meowing to be let out.

"No, boy," she said, frightened at the prospect of the cat's leaving the safety of the house. "You'll have to go out back."

She picked the cat up, but he let out a protesting wail, clawing to get down again. Growing exasperated, Sarah scolded, "No, Casper, you can't—"

"Is there some problem?" a feminine voice inquired.

Sarah turned to find herself facing a frowning Olympia. "Casper wants to go out the front door," she explained. "I don't mind his going out back to the courtyard, but I'm afraid that if he goes out the front, he may—get lost."

"Nonsense," Olympia said stoutly. "That animal is quite clever and not about to get lost. And it's high time he started ridding the stables of some of their mice."

Before Sarah could even protest, Olympia had stepped forward and taken the cat from her arms. The spinster then walked briskly to the front door and flung it open.

"No!" Sarah cried.

Too late. Olympia had already set the cat down. Casper bolted out the front door, went down the steps and into the yard.

He didn't disappear.

Sarah was flabbergasted, her mouth falling open.

Olympia, meanwhile, took it all in stride. Shutting the door, she turned calmly to the wide-eyed Sarah. "If you're so worried about the cat, would you care to go after him?" she asked imperiously.

Sarah could only shake her head in mute horror.

Later that morning, Damien sat at his desk as Baptista poured him a cup of hot tea.

"Will there be anything else, m'sieur?" the negro woman asked.

Damien set down his pen and glanced up at her, feeling a stab of compassion as he noted the thinly veiled hurt in her chocolate brown eyes. "No, thank you, Baptista. You're most kind."

Nodding, Baptista set down the teapot and took her leave. Damien sighed as he heard the door click shut. For years, Baptista had been his mistress, the only comfort he had known during hellishly lonely, tortured nights. Yet ever since Sarah had arrived here, he'd declined what the negress had so generously offered before. Even during the long, tormenting days of Sarah's absence, he'd been not the least bit tempted to take his ease with Baptista. He knew she didn't understand, and he was certain she resented Sarah. But out of fierce loyalty to him, she would never voice a complaint.

He turned his thoughts to Sarah, his beloved soul mate. He'd been so frightened and frustrated when she'd disappeared, and angered when she'd returned. For he'd known by then that she was lying to him, unwilling to share with him the truth regarding the world from whence she'd come.

Yet soon his anger had faded in the force of new fears of losing her again. Thus, last night, he had gone to her, and he was so glad now that he'd set aside his own anger and wounded pride. Sarah had told him the truth about her world and the strange forces that had brought her here. Now he understood everything. Poor Sarah, caught here on the precipice of time. Afraid that if she even spoke to him of her mystical hold on this century, that fragile link might be broken. It all seemed almost beyond comprehension, yet he knew in his heart that she had spoken the truth. And it was truly frightful to think that one day time might take her from him again. Was she even capable of becoming a permanent part of his world?

He loved her so much now that the idea of losing her was terrifying. He wanted to know more about her world, to learn everything about her. He didn't care if they never left this house again. Since she'd come, he'd noted a wondrous change in himself. He'd felt alive for the first time in many, many years. In time, he might even show her Vincy's memoirs.

Vincy. That was where the rub came in. He stood and walked over to the window. Clasping his hands behind his back, he inhaled the aroma of late-blooming honeysuckle and watched patterns of light dance about in the verdant courtyard. It was a lovely, crisp fall day. Ah, Vincy, he thought, if only you could be here to share this beautiful day. It should have been me, my brother. It should have been me that hellishly hot day at Gettysburg eight years ago.

He knew that if he gave himself over entirely to his love for Sarah, sooner or later that love would chase away his guilt and grief over Vincy. He couldn't love Sarah and still live with his demons; there was no room in his heart for both.

Was he ready to let the past go?

For now, he knew no answer to the puzzle, but he knew he would love Sarah, taking all that time would offer them. As far as the future was concerned, perhaps they could seek answers together.

Chapter Fifteen

All day long, Sarah wondered about the amazing event she had witnessed that morning—Casper leaving the house and yet remaining in the nineteenth century. What mystical power did the cat hold over time and space? If he could remain in this century outside the house, if he could defy the invisible barrier with a flip of his snowy tail, why couldn't she?

After the cat left the house, Sarah had ventured toward the front door. She had felt the eerie vibrations, strong as ever. Why was the forbidding boundary there for her and not for the cat?

Then she thought over the mystery from another angle. Perhaps Casper possessed no special powers at all. As an animal, he simply accepted things at face value. Perhaps he saw no distinction between past and present. Perhaps he simply was; he simply believed.

And perhaps her own belief was not strong enough to hold her here. Yet how could she increase her faith? How could she remain fully integrated in the past and not just nebulously cling to the house?

It was an enigma. Yet even this mystery could not dampen her joy that she and Damien were truly together again, that they were soul mates once more.

Perhaps together, they might yet find answers.

That night after dinner, Sarah went to the salon. The half-dozen paintings she had already completed were displayed toward the center of the room, where they sat proudly on their easels, now perfect in every detail, shimmering in pools of moonlight. Sarah was about a quarter of the way through the restorations, and she found this fact strangely threatening.

The manner in which she had signed her repairs reflected her anxieties in a subtle, if humorous, way. She walked around the easels to study each canvas from behind. On the back of each painting, she had inscribed her bold signature and had entered the date the restoration had been completed; then, as a final, whimsical touch, she had added an hourglass beneath her signature on each panel. On the first completed painting, she had drawn the hourglass with the top full of sand; yet with each subsequent painting, a few more of the precious grains had filtered away.

To Sarah, the hourglass seemed symbolic of her tenuous existence here. She knew that her work on Vincy's paintings was somehow inexorably linked to her fragile hold on the house. When her work was completed, would her grasp on the past weaken, just as the sands of the hourglass would eventually all trickle away?

It was a disturbing thought. But Sarah banished it, thinking instead of Damien. She knew he would join her shortly for their nightly rendezvous.

Indeed, at that very moment, she heard his voice at the portal behind her. "Good evening, Sarah."

She turned with a smile, stepping forward through the easels. Damien looked so handsome standing beyond her, his eyes gleaming with vibrant happiness at the sight of her. "Good evening, Damien."

He strode to her side and took her hand, glancing with approval at the finished paintings. "Every time I look at your work, it's truly uncanny, Sarah. It's as if Vincy has just set down his paintbrush."

Her heart welled with joy at his ardent praise. "I know of no higher compliment that could be paid me."

He smiled. "Come, now, darling. Sit with me by the window. Tell me more of your world."

They settled themselves on their window seat and held hands, their silhouettes outlined in the silvery light of their bright star. Sarah spoke for hours, telling Damien everything she could of the 96 years separating their worlds. He listened in fascination, occasionally making a comment or asking a question.

She began with the Industrial Revolution, then told him of the invention of the telephone, of electricity, the automobile and the airplane. She spoke of the great strides in medicine, in inoculation, childbirth and surgery, and of how researchers were even now finding ways to combat cancers. She told him of the two great wars. When she described the invention of the atom bomb, he was appalled. "Do you mean to tell me that man has created a weapon so powerful that it is capable of destroying his very way of life forever?" he asked incredulously. Sarah could only nod sadly.

She continued, moving on to the Korean war. As she told of how man had begun to overcome space and was even now planning a journey to the moon, Damien was fascinated.

When she got to the Vietnam conflict, her talk turned more personal. "It's a war our country never should have gotten involved in," she related bitterly. "It has caused great unrest and anti-war demonstrations in our country, especially in this last year. And it took away my beloved brother."

Damien squeezed her hand. "Tell me more about Brian."

Sarah smiled poignantly. "Brian was such a free spirit. He was blond and blue-eyed, like me, and he had this fabulous gift for the violin. He made his debut with the Atlanta Symphony Orchestra at the age of sixteen. He was wonderfully talented, and yet so cavalier."

"In what way?"

"When the Vietnam conflict started really heating up a few years back, young men were drafted to fight there. Brian had a full scholarship to the Juilliard School of Music in New York City. If only he had gone off to college as he was supposed to, he could have been exempted from the draft, but he was such a died-in-the-wool romantic. He thumbed his nose at the scholarship and went off to Europe bicycling with some friends. When he returned home, the draft notice awaited him. He was inducted into the Army, sent to Vietnam, and three months later he was killed there."

"Oh, Sarah, I'm so sorry. And that's when you had your breakdown?"

"Yes."

Damien shook his head grimly. He stood and walked off toward the center of the room. "Our worlds are not that different then, are they, Sarah?" he asked ironically. "Ah, what a combative people we are! I suppose there will always be wars to destroy the best of our humanity—our violinists, our artists, our dreamers."

She nodded soberly. "But, Damien, since I know what the future will hold, I also know that from now on you'll be living in a long period of relative peace—easily forty years. It could be a good time for you, a time to rebuild."

He turned to her, gesturing resignedly. "I'm not sure that what I've lost—what the South has lost—can ever be recaptured. For me, everything seemed to go with Vincy's passing."

"I understand that." Sarah's eyes beseeched his. "But perhaps something new and different can come in its place. It could be a time for us, Damien."

At her words, his expression at once softened, and he returned to her side, squeezing her hand. His words were tender but laced with an underlying fatalism. "What we have is here and now, Sarah. This is our time. I'm not sure we dare hope for anything beyond that."

"But—"

"And besides, darling, you can't go beyond this house. We must live within your limitations here."

Sarah sighed. "I've been meaning to tell you something about that. This morning, your aunt let

Casper out the front door. Yet he remained here in the past."

Damien looked perplexed. "Is that significant?"

"Well, yes, I think it is. Don't you understand? The cat is also from the future, but he's somehow found a way to remain here in the past, even outside the house. There must be an answer there for me, and I'm hoping we can find it together."

Damien stroked her cheek with his fingertips. "Perhaps we can, love, but if we never have more than we have at this moment, it is enough for me." As she glanced away guiltily, he added, "I only wish it were enough for you."

They fell into an unhappy silence. Sarah wished she could tell Damien that staying here in the house with him forever would be enough, but she wasn't sure it ever could be. And she was disturbed that he showed no interest in rebuilding his own world and going forward. She realized that she was asking him to do more than he was capable of right now; she was asking him to transcend the walls of his own grief and embrace a new and different world. He simply wasn't ready yet. This she understood, for sometimes she didn't know if she could ever completely let go of her own grief.

After a moment, he asked, "And what are the values and philosophy of the age in which you live? How do twentieth-century people think?"

Sarah gathered her thoughts. "We're still a God-fearing people, but I'd have to say that morality is much looser in the age in which I live. You see, Damien, you're living in the middle of what will later become known as the Victorian Age. But standards changed greatly with the advent of the Gay Nineties, the Roaring Twenties, the two great wars. In the 1960's, I'd have to say there's more hustle and bustle and technology, more self-absorption, and much less courtesy and soul-searching and caring for one's fellow man. There are forces for change, of course, and many cries of 'Down with the Establishment.' But I'm not really sure any of the rebels have come up with a better plan. There are others, like the Hippies, who have tried to escape entirely, establishing their own communes." She smiled at him lamely. "It's not an age I think you would particularly like."

"I presume not."

"Of course, not all changes have been negative. Much of the technology has benefited mankind through modern conveniences. In my age, we possess the ability to wipe out most hunger and communicable disease. And there have been enormous strides made in areas such as Civil Rights and women's rights. For instance, women in the United States were given the right to vote around 1920."

"I find that an admirable decision."

"Do you?" Sarah asked with a laugh. Damien was constantly amazing her with his modern thinking.

"I do. And what of relationships between men and women in your society?"

"Well, there's a little more equality between the sexes now. Women are starting to come into their own in the workplace. And we have made some progress toward abolishing the double standard."

"Double standard?"

Sarah laughed. "You should know all about the double standard. It comes straight from your age."

Yet he scowled. "Does it? Pray, explain."

"The double standard is the traditional fallacy in a man's thinking—that it's all right for him to sew his wild oats prior to marriage, but that his bride should come a virgin to the marriage bed."

Now Damien chuckled, too. "Ah, yes, I know exactly what you mean. And is this double standard still a part of the thinking of the twentieth-century man?"

"Pretty much," Sarah conceded, "but things are changing. For instance, if a woman makes love with a man she really cares for, she's no longer automatically labeled a trollop."

"And she shouldn't be."

"Really?" Sarah asked with a disbelieving laugh.

He drew himself up and spoke forthrightly. "I think that if a man expects purity from his bride, then she has every right to expect the same from him."

Sarah could only shake her head. "Damien, you amaze me. You know, if you lived in my century, you'd be called a free thinker."

He smiled. "Would I? I suppose I've never had too much patience with the artificial constraints of the society in which I live."

She nodded bitterly. "But my society definitely has it's problems, as well. I've never felt quite comfortable in the twentieth century. It's always been as if I belonged somewhere else."

He stared deeply into her eyes. "We're both displaced souls, aren't we, Sarah?"

"We have each other," she whispered back.

"Yes," he murmured, leaning over to kiss her. "We've found our place in time together. And that is everything, my love."

The next night, as they sat on their window seat, their talk became more personal. "Sarah, I want to know more about you," Damien said. "Tell me about your life before—your upbringing, and how you became such a wonderful artist."

"Well, what I told you previously was pretty much true," Sarah admitted. "I do come from Atlanta, Georgia, where I was born into a prominent family in Ansley Park. My forebears date to the time when Atlanta was still called Marthasville, so my parents are definitely part of the city's Old Guard. My family accumulated its wealth from the railroads, and even now we own a highly successful shipping business."

"Are you close to your family?" Damien asked.

Sarah was quiet for a long moment. "Are you trying to ask if I would leave them?"

He nodded, gazing at her in uncertainty. "I suppose I am."

Sarah sighed as she mulled over the question. Then she looked him in the eye. "It would be difficult. My parents have already lost a son. But, yes, I would leave them to seek my own destiny. I love my family, but they pretty much have their own lives, and I have mine."

He squeezed her hand, looking greatly reassured by her words. "I'm glad. Now, tell me more about your art."

She laughed. "My mother used to say I was born with a paintbrush in my hand. By the time I was in my mid-teens, my work was placing in the local shows. I had my first private show at eighteen; then I shocked the socks off my parents by going off to Sarah Lawrence to study art."

"Sarah Lawrence?"

"It's a very liberal women's college in New York State. Anyway, I got my degree and came back, devoting myself full-time to my painting. I became a member of the Atlanta Art Association and a part-time teacher at the Art School. Soon, my work was hanging in galleries all over town, and I began to get commissions from banks, department stores, doctors, lawyers, that sort of thing. I became a commercial success, which is something rare in the world of art."

"I'm not at all surprised, not with your gift." He paused. "And what of your personal life, Sarah? Was there someone special for you back in your world?"

She sighed. "Yes, there was a man. Bill Bartley. He's a lawyer in Atlanta. We were friends all our lives, and a few years back, we became engaged."

She felt Damien's hand tensing over hers. "Are you still planning to marry this man?"

Sarah shook her head. "No. He betrayed my trust."

Damien scowled. "With another woman?"

"No. He had himself sterilized without discussing it with me."

"He did what?" Damien looked incredulous.

"He had a surgical procedure done that's called a vasectomy. It renders a man sterile, unable to beget children."

Damien was still staring at her in amazement. "But why would any man willingly have this done to himself, destroying his very manhood, robbing himself of any potential heirs?"

Sarah spoke slowly and carefully. "You must understand that I come from a nuclear age. There's always the threat of the bomb hanging over our heads, and we're living in the midst of what's known as the Cold War, a time of great international tensions. Bill's argument regarding the sterilization was, why bring children into a world that may blow apart tomorrow? At least that's what he said. And unfortunately he didn't inform me of his decision until after the fact."

"You seem to doubt the explanation he gave," Damien remarked.

She sighed. "Oh, I believe he convinced himself that he had the vasectomy done for the noblest of reasons, but I always wondered if Bill simply wasn't too selfish to become a good father."

"So you called off the engagement after he did this thing?"

"Oh, yes."

"I'm glad."

"I felt so betrayed when he did it," she confided in a small voice.

Damien drew her close, pressing his lips against her hair. "I'm sure you did, poor darling."

"After Brian died, even after I recovered from my breakdown, I just felt so dead inside. I desperately needed to reaffirm life." She looked up into his eyes, her own brimming with tears. "I wanted a baby," she finished breathlessly.

"Oh, Sarah." His eyes lit with exultation. "I do understand."

"Do you?"

"Yes." He kissed her tenderly, making her senses swirl with excitement. Afterward, he looked down into her eyes and whispered, "I love you, Sarah. And I'll give you a baby."

It was an electrifying moment for both. Sarah gazed up at her beloved, her heart pounding with such joy that she could barely hear him. He was willing to give her a baby? He was offering to take their two souls, which had merged so beautifully and perfectly, and create a third soul together?

Then reality intervened. "Do you understand what you're offering?"

He smiled. "I do. Perfectly."

"But I fear you don't understand," she cried in torment. "Damien, I'm a soul in transit. I don't know where I belong."

Damien clutched her close. "You belong with me, darling. We've shared more intimately than two human beings ever could."

"I realize that."

His arms trembled about her. "Then tonight, let's make our union complete. Let's chase away the shadows of the night together. Let's create a new life out of all this death and hurt and betrayal."

"Are you sure?" she asked with anguish and love.

"Do you love me, Sarah?" he asked.

"Oh, yes! I do love you so."

"Then take my hand."

She slipped her trembling fingers into his.

Chapter Sixteen

Silver washed over Damien's room. He led Sarah in and closed the door behind them. She thrust herself eagerly into his arms, clinging to him. Her heart was pounding so hard, she could barely catch her breath. She would be his tonight, she thought achingly. His, at last. Perhaps tomorrow, time would rip them apart again, but time was their friend tonight. They had this wondrous night and their love to sustain them.

She had never been in Damien's room before, but she hardly noticed the furnishings as they crossed over to his bed. He cast off his coat, then they fell across the soft mattress together. Quicksilver light played across the counterpane, bathing their bodies with a mystical beauty.

Damien propped himself next to her, resting his weight on his elbow as he gazed down at her with eyes filled with love. "Oh, Sarah," he whispered, "I've yearned for this moment ever since I first laid eyes on you."

"Me, too."

As he unbuttoned a tiny pearl button at the throat of her gown, she knew a moment's unease. "I must tell you—"

"What, my love?" He leaned over and nuzzled her neck with his burning lips.

She shivered in delight, but forced herself to continue. "I—I'm not a virgin."

He drew back and stared down at her. His gaze seemed glazed, a mirror of the moonlight, and she couldn't really read his feelings.

She cleared her throat and continued awkwardly, "As I explained before, things are somewhat different in my time. My fiancé and I—it wasn't that often, but—"

Damien pressed his fingers to her lips. "Shhhh. It's all right, Sarah. You don't have to explain. It doesn't matter."

"Are you sure?"

He nodded. "Let's make tonight a beginning. What happened before—for either of us—is meaningless."

"Oh, Damien!" She threw her arms about his neck, her eyes filling with tears of joy. In a small, choked voice, she added, "He never made me feel what you do. No man has ever excited me so."

He drew back, caressing her cheek with his fingertips. "Then tonight will be a first for you, won't it, love?"

"Yes!"

Damien leaned over and kissed her then, thrusting his tongue deeply into her mouth. Sarah moaned inarticulately and kissed him back. Heat was swimming in her veins, desire and love swelling in her heart and soul.

Damien made love to her with a slow and thorough expertise that made her feel she had never been loved before. With infinite care, he removed the pins from her hair, kissing the heavy silken tresses and inhaling their sweet fragrance. He drew his tongue over the lobe of her ear, down her neck, over her cheek and chin. Sarah broke out in gooseflesh and tossed her head, unable to bear the sweet torture. Damien smiled and gripped her chin, his tongue repeating the provocative sexual dance, this time between her lips. Hot and tantalizing, his tongue flicked across her trembling mouth, finally darting inward to taste the sweetness within. With a moan, Sarah raked a hand through his hair and brought his mouth crushing down on hers. In the core of her, her need for him twisted with painful intensity; never before had she known such a hot, wild yearning.

After a moment, he pulled his lips from hers and stared down into her eyes. "Wouldn't it be wonderful if we could make a child tonight, a child born of our love. Do you want my child?"

"Oh, yes. So much!"

"A child could be a link between our worlds."

"I pray that it's true. Oh, love me. Please love me now."

He smiled at her eagerness, but still took his time as he unbuttoned the tiny buttons traveling down her bodice. Only then did he slip his fingers inside her frock, moving aside her chemise and caressing her breast. Sarah writhed and gasped, her nipple tautening to painful arousal beneath his titillating touch. "Damien, I need you so badly, it hurts."

At her words, he slid a hand up inside her dress, traveling upward until he found the very, throbbing spot. His fingers pressed boldly against her through the handkerchief linen. "Where does it hurt, love? Here?"

She nodded convulsively.

He leaned over and kissed the pulsing spot through the gauzy linen of her pantalets. Sarah caught an achingly sharp breath, tangling her hands in his hair as his lips moved to her stomach. But then he pulled down her skirts again, frustrating her exquisitely as his mouth moved to capture her lips once more. His breath was sweet and hot on her face, his eyes blazing with desire above her. "Let's wait until neither of us can stand it, until we're both dying of want. Let's savor every second."

"I can't stand it now." Indeed, his words alone made her weak with desire, made the ache inside her turn to a burning need. She kissed him with desperate desire, pulling at the buttons on his shirt. She thrust her fingertips inside, feeling the warm heat of his chest, the rough hair. How she hungered to feel that roughness next to her tender breasts!

He pulled back then, staring at her quizzically, and it occurred to her that perhaps he was not used to a woman behaving so wantonly. "Don't you want me to touch you, Damien?" she asked breathlessly.

"Ah, yes, I do want you to, love." He grinned, then admitted, "I guess it just takes a little getting used to."

Sarah snuggled closer and pressed her lips against his bare male nipple, teasing the areole with her tongue. She delighted to his agonized moan, to the way he suddenly trembled, the way he thrust his hands into her hair. "Then tonight can be a first for you, too, darling?" she whispered.

"Ah, yes," he said hoarsely. "Tonight can be a first for us both."

A moment later, he was pressing her back into the pillows, as if he couldn't endure any more. He undressed her, his hands trembling and his breathing rough; yet still he maintained his control, removing each garment slowly, kissing every inch of her satiny flesh that his lips revealed. When she was naked to the waist, he caught her hands above her head and stared down at her, watching the rise and fall of her lovely breasts, devouring her with his eyes and listening to her rapid breathing. His dark eyes were deeply dilated now, blazing with hunger. "I could take you now," he whispered, thrusting against her through the layers of their clothing. "Just like this."

"Please," she whispered back.

But he only continued slowly torturing her, undressing her. He made love to her breasts with his mouth, teasing each tight nipple gently with his teeth. Sarah feared she was losing her mind. When at last she lay naked beneath him, when his fingertips touched the downy curls beneath her legs, she could take no more. "Damien, please, love me," she whispered, tears springing to her eyes. "Heal this hurt inside me. I'll die if you don't."

That reached him. He threw off his shirt and covered her body with his. She cried out in ecstasy as his rough chest abraded her bare breasts. "Don't cry, love," he whispered, kissing away her tears. "I'm here. I just wanted you to need me as badly as I need you."

"Oh, I do," Sarah cried. "Take me now."

His muscled thighs drew hers apart, and she felt his hand briefly between them. Then he was hers. He penetrated with absolute confidence and mastery, probing deep, stretching her tender flesh to an unbearable tautness. Sarah gasped, arching her back at the hot, swollen magnitude of him. Throbbing and vibrant, he filled her with intense, indescribable pleasure.

Above her, Damien could feel her trembling, could feel her tight flesh struggling to receive him. "There, love. You're so sweet, so small. Am I hurting you?"

"Just a little—it's been a while," she managed. Feeling him tense, she dug her fingers into his buttocks, beseeching, "Please, I want you to. Don't hold back."

"Oh, Sarah." He slipped his hands beneath her and thrust powerfully, devouring her with all the love and need in his body. She pressed her aching lips on his to keep from crying out at the unbearable rapture. He possessed her insatiably, and she met each stroke fully, melting, softening to his heat.

Soon Sarah was on fire, her skin hot, her instincts taking over. She moved against Damien with a primitive abandon that broke his control as well. He moaned like a man in pain and spiraled into her, deeper and deeper.

Just when she thought she could endure no more, Damien lifted her high and held her fast against his final, convulsive thrusts. That's when Sarah knew complete ecstasy for the first time in her life. Her entire world shredded apart with a beautiful searing cataclysm and then became whole again in the aftermath. She heard Damien's groan as he reached the pinnacle right after her. Then he collapsed against her and they lay together, mouth to mouth, their breaths, their bodies, as one.

* * *

"I should go," she said later.

"No," he replied simply, lacing his fingers through hers.

"But if I'm here with you in the morning—"

"I'll marry you, Sarah," he said simply.

She sat up and stared at him. Damien looked magnificent lying beside her, his dark eyes reflecting the moonlight, his perfect male body outlined in silvery relief. Her heart twisted at the impossibility of their situation. "Damien, no. What we just shared was so beautiful, but we mustn't hope for anything that permanent yet. As I've told you before, I don't know if I'll ever be able to exist here beyond the house."

"And I've told you that the house is enough." He stared at her searchingly. "Think of how we gave ourselves to each other so completely. How can you say that what we have is not enough?"

She gestured miserably. "I'm not saying that, it's just . . ."

Sarah wished she could go on, yet fear held her back. What they had was enough for her; she realized that now. She loved Damien so much that she would be content to spend eternity in this house with him. But how could what they had ever be enough for him? Surely at some point, he would want to become reintegrated into his world, and she could never join him there. It wouldn't be fair to hold him back when the time came. And what if there were a child? What they had would never be enough for a child.

Finally, she thought of the dark presence that didn't seem to want her here—the voodoo charms in her room, the ominous voice whispering, *Go away*. She hadn't told Damien of the presence as yet;

she was almost afraid to voice her fears, for that would give them power, legitimacy.

Noting her troubled expression, Damien lifted her hand to his mouth and kissed each lovely, tapered finger. "Don't fret about it now, my love. We have the rest of the night to chase away."

"Oh, Damien, I love you so."

"I love you, too."

Sarah leaned over to kiss him, her hair falling in a silken swath across his face. This time she made love to him, worshiping his beautiful body with her lips. She kissed his handsome square jaw then drew her lips down his throat. She licked his skin, glorying to the slightly salty taste of him, flicking her tongue over his chest, his nipples. But when she drew her lips even lower, he groaned and pulled her astride him. With their eyes locked, he pleasured her with his bold fingers. He stroked her deeply even as he moved upright, pulling her into his lap and catching her tender, aching nipple gently between his teeth. When she whimpered in ecstasy, he growled contentedly, drawing her breast deeper into his mouth.

Sarah was floating in a liquid pool of rapture, being sucked into a hot vortex of unbearable sweetness. "Damien, let me—"

But he wouldn't. Even as she reached for him, he plunged into her again, filling her aching, sensitized flesh once more. She dug her hands into his shoulders and clung to him; he hooked his arms about her waist and possessed her more deeply still. Sarah tossed back her head and joined in the rhythm, riding him, clenching about his wonderful hard heat.

"Oh, Damien!" she cried. "Devour me until nothing else exists."

"Nothing but this," he whispered back convulsively.

Together they chased away all the shadows of the night, their only reality this aching oneness, this need to know each other deeper, to penetrate their very souls until those souls fused and pleasure obliterated all pain.

Chapter Seventeen

The following night, Damien asked Sarah to dance. He brought her a wreath of flowers from Olympia's garden—sweet gardenias and lily of the valley—and pinned the garland in her hair. Then he swept her about the moonlit salon, as Olympia's haunting music drifted up from downstairs, tonight the sweet, sad strains of a Chopin waltz.

They held each other close as they whirled among the half-finished paintings. Sarah could not remember a moment when she had felt happier. She was in Damien's arms, he was smiling down at her, and her heart was filled with love.

Petals fell at their feet as they glided about, and Sarah laughed giddily. "What is it?" Damien asked with a smile.

"Back in the time I came from, I was sometimes called a Flower Child," she explained.

He grinned. "Ah, the name suits you."

"I certainly feel like a Flower Child tonight," she confided. "Even this dress . . ." She glanced down at the brown calico dress she wore, another of Lucy's. "You see, old-fashioned clothing had become popular in the world from which I came."

"Like the dress you wore the day you first arrived here?"

"Yes."

Damien was quiet for a moment, his expression abstracted. "Do you miss your own time, Sarah?"

Sarah pressed her face against his chest, inhaling the exciting scent of him and listening to the comforting cadence of his heart. "No, not really. Not now that I have you."

He pressed his lips against her brow. "Do you like this century more than the one from which you came?"

She smiled. "Yes, I do. And I think that you should give this world—your world—another chance. If only I could . . ."

"I know," he whispered tenderly, clutching her closer as the song reached its crescendo.

Later, Damien swept Sarah up into his arms and carried her off to his room, where he made love to her, wildly and recklessly. It amazed Sarah that this man, usually so consumed with his own torment, became someone else in her arms—masterful, passionate, totally confident. Damien's lovemaking showed her a side of him that she had assumed was long dead. When they were together this way, he seemed a man reborn, a man who took joy in living and in loving her.

Afterward, they rested on his bed and drank wine, the covers drawn up to hold the chill of night at bay. Sarah realized that Olympia's distant music had stopped. "Do you think your aunt suspects anything?" she asked him.

Damien shrugged. "She may. But I'm not the least bit ashamed of what we have. Are you?"

"No, of course not." She bit her lip. "I'd just prefer that we not cause Olympia any distress."

"You're ever thoughtful, darling." He kissed her quickly and possessively. "At any rate, I still intend to marry you."

Sarah sighed deeply, setting down her goblet and nestling herself closer to his warmth. "I don't even know if I'll be allowed to stay here with you."

They fell into an unhappy silence, listening to the cold wind rattling the windowpane. After a moment, Damien leaned over and picked up the brown calico dress Sarah had tossed in a heap on the floor moments earlier. Folding the garment carefully, he laid it across the footboard, then turned to her with a smile. "I'd like you to make a new wardrobe. I'm sure my aunt will help you. It's a shame that you must wear Lucy's old clothes. They're drab and ill-fitting."

Sarah stiffened. "And perhaps a painful reminder to you of your loss?" When he didn't reply, she continued, "You never speak to me of her. Of Vincy, yes—but never of Lucy."

He nodded with painful resignation. "Our time together was so brief. Lucy was only seventeen when we married; she was little more than a child. Sometimes I can hardly even remember what she looked like. I feel badly at those times."

"But you shouldn't feel guilty. It was so long ago. I think that sometimes forgetting is a merciful opiate our mind grants us. Lord knows, how I've hungered to forget at times."

He clutched her hand tightly in his. "I know, love."

Feeling the tension in his grip, Sarah forged on. "But there's much you can't forget, isn't there, Damien?"

"Ah, love, you know me so well," he said ironically.

"You've never spoken to me of how Vincy or Lucy died," she added quietly.

At once, his hand left hers. She watched the chiseled lines of his face tighten. "And I never shall."

Sarah's eyes beseeched his. "Damien, do you remember last night when you said that if we could have a child he or she could be a link between our worlds?"

"Indeed, I do."

She continued with growing passion. "Well, maybe our sharing is the true link. And maybe we're meant to share even more." Before he could comment, she added, "I want to read Vincy's memoirs."

He turned to stare at her, his expression both pained and incredulous. "Do you realize what you're asking?"

"I'm asking to understand you completely," she said, her eyes reflecting her own torn feelings. "And I'm asking for help. I can't completely let go of Brian. You can't completely let go of Vincy. There must be an answer there, or else why were we drawn together in the first place? Perhaps if we shared all—"

Damien pressed his fingers to her mouth. "Not yet, Sarah. You're asking too much."

"But our sharing could be the key."

"Our love is the key, Sarah," he said, leaning over to kiss her.

Damien made passionate love to her again. Soon, Sarah was lost in the sweetness, the heat of desire. Ah, yes, she thought, their love was the key. But that love was still captive, still earthbound. They were two wounded souls clinging together. Only with the truth could they soar and know healing and wholeness once more.

By the time a week passed, Sarah was feeling stir crazy. She spent her days repairing the paintings, her nights with Damien. Being with him was paradise, yet part of Sarah bristled against her continuing confinement in the house, and her mind remained troubled. From time to time, she still found voodoo charms in her room, and she still heard the ominous voice urging her to leave.

Sarah continued to feel frightened of the world outside the windows of the house, the world of Damien's century that was forbidden to her. In a way, she felt that she and Damien had both become prisoners of the house. The house seemed symbolic of the shared grief neither of them could quite let go of. She loved him with all her heart now, yet as a human being, a vibrant, healthy young woman, Sarah couldn't help but feel trapped.

While Damien still spent much of his time sequestered in his study, writing Vincy's memoirs, in other ways Sarah sensed that he could be on the brink of a dramatic change. He laughed regularly now; the old Damien had rarely even smiled. He brought her flowers and sweet wines nightly; they danced in the salon; they talked for hours on end and made beautiful, joyous love together.

And there were other subtle changes. One morning as Sarah paced the salon, she heard hoofbeats. Approaching the window, she saw Damien below, standing next to his horse before the fallow field. He was looking out at the barrenness, the snarl of weeds and vines, as if he were making some grand plan. Was he thinking of turning Belle Fontaine into a working plantation again? she wondered. She watched him carefully as he remounted his horse and rode toward the house. The stableboy met him in the yard, taking his horse, and as Damien climbed the steps to the house, she noted a thoughtful smile on his lips, a ruddy glow about his complexion.

Two days later, another startling event occurred. Sarah was taking an afternoon break, sharing tea in the parlor with Olympia, when Damien burst in with a bolt of exquisite white eyelet in his arms. His hair was wind-ruffled, his eyes gleaming, and he smelled of crisp autumn foliage.

"Sarah, you must make yourself a dress out of this," he began excitedly. "I had some business in town and saw this in the window of the dry goods store." He summarily dumped the bolt into Sarah's lap, then grinned at his aunt. "Don't you think the eyelet is perfect for Sarah, Aunt Olympia?"

"It's quite fine, nephew," Olympia commented stiffly.

Damien now pulled several yards of rolled-up, blue satin ribbon from the pocket of his frock coat. He grinned at Sarah as he handed her the roll. "I thought pale blue for trim. Do you agree?"

"Oh, yes," she said, touched by his thoughtfulness. "It's lovely."

"Sarah, you should see the fall foliage over River Road," he went on with growing animation. "It's so glorious, with the trees changing colors. I must take you—"

Abruptly, Damien stopped talking, and the two of

them exchanged an anguished look. "Yes, Damien," Sarah said bravely, fighting the sting of tears. "We must go there sometime."

He backed away then, looking much sobered, and suddenly the atmosphere between them was unbearably awkward. Damien drew out his pocket watch, then forced a smile as he glanced from Sarah to his aunt. "Well, then, ladies. I must get back to my study. There are still a few good hours of daylight left, and I'm behind on my writing schedule. So if you'll excuse me?"

Damien took his leave, and Sarah stared at the fabric and ribbon in her lap. The ribbon gleamed in the light as her fingers trembled and shifted. A tear slid down her cheek and splashed onto her hand. Never before had she seen the reality of her and Damien's situation with such clarity. While he might not acknowledge it as yet, she knew now that Damien was taking those first small steps toward recovery, toward embracing the future, his future. Damien was ready to start healing; he was ready to start repairing the jagged pieces of his soul, just as she was repairing Vincy's paintings. These thoughts filled her with both joy and pain. Joy for the resurrection of his spirit. Pain, that when his wholeness came, it would inevitably, one day, take him away from her.

For it was her love that bound him to the house, to the past.

Would their love never know freedom?

Olympia's voice interrupted Sarah's musings. "Well, that's quite a handsome gift my nephew brought you," she said. She rose and walked to Sarah's side in a swish of her heavy woolen skirts. She reached out and fingered the eyelet. "But white—an odd choice of color, don't you think?"

Sarah stared up at Olympia, and the two women exchanged a meaningful look. Sarah was well-aware of the thinly veiled hostility that flickered in Olympia's hazel eyes.

Neither needed to say the obvious—that the white eyelet was just what a bride would wear.

Another week passed, and Sarah discovered that her menstrual period was late. While she realized it was too soon to really know anything, the possibility that she might be pregnant filled her with a myriad of emotions—joy, hope, affirmation, as well as fear, confusion and despair. There was the wonder of knowing that perhaps even now Damien's seed grew inside her; yet there was also the wrenching angst of knowing that she and Damien might never find true happiness together, as long as her existence here was limited to the house. And what if the child shared its mother's limitations?

While Sarah realized it was too soon to speak to Damien with any certainty regarding her possible pregnancy, that night in bed she broached the subject in general terms. They had been lying together for a long time, sipping wine, when she asked, "Damien, what if we did have a child? What if the child should be like me—not firmly grounded in this century? What if at some point the door in time took us both away from you?"

Damien caught her close and spoke in a trembling, vehement voice. "I won't ever let that happen, love."

"But what if it does happen, anyway? What if this mystical force turns out to be stronger than both of us?" As he started to protest, she added, "Please, Damien, I must know. I can't bear the thought of you suffering additional regret or loss."

He caressed her cheek and stared down at her with eyes brimming with love. "Sarah, I told you I'd give you a child. If I tried to take it back, it wouldn't be a gift, would it?"

"Oh, Damien." She clung to him, and he stroked her hair.

Damien pressed his lips against her cheek and whispered, "No matter what happens, I'll never regret what we've had. I want you always to remember that."

"I will."

"And do not fear, my love. I know we'll be together always—you, me, and our child."

Damien kissed her, and Sarah wished she could share his confidence. She loved him with sweet desperation that night. For though it was breaking her heart, she knew now that she must seek answers —answers that did not exist here in this house or in this century.

Answers that quite possibly did exist back in the twentieth century.

Chapter Eighteen

The next day Sarah was restless again, trying her best to avoid the devastating conclusions she had reached last night. She knew it was time for her to go back to the present again. She must try to find out more information about Damien—and about herself. Did records exist regarding the Fontaine family? Could she discover whether or not she had truly lived—and died—here in the past with Damien? She needed these answers, especially now that it was possible that she was carrying Damien's child.

Sarah worked hard that day completing repairs on one of Vincy's paintings, a vivid portrait of a carriage clopping down River Road beneath a mantle of fiery autumn colors. She remembered yesterday, when Damien had told her how he yearned to take her to glimpse firsthand the autumn majesty which was even now emblazoning the countryside. Oh, she must find a way to share Damien's world with him!

By the time Sarah had completed her repairs, it was late afternoon. She studied her work critically and found she was pleased. As she cleaned her brushes, she glanced about the salon. She'd fully repaired seven paintings now, but there were still a good 17 left needing attention. Some of the most badly damaged works she hadn't gotten to as yet. Studying them now gave her confidence that she wouldn't become trapped in the present, that she would find her way back here to complete her work, her mission—and most importantly of all to love Damien.

Should she tell him she was going? She shook her head. If she did, he would no doubt try to convince her to stay here, and it was hard enough to get up her courage as it was.

Thus she went to her room, sat down and wrote him a letter:

My dearest Damien,

My darling, I must go back again. There are answers that I simply can't find here. Please tell your aunt that I've gone to visit my friend in New Orleans again.

If I've angered you with my departure, I pray for your forgiveness. I will be back, my love. Never doubt it!

Yours forever,

Sarah

Sarah blew on the finished letter, folded it and placed it in an envelope. Where could she put the letter so that Damien and no one else would find it?

Under his pillow seemed the logical choice. Leaving her room, Sarah headed down the hallway. Yet she paused before his door as she heard him inside humming, "Beautiful Dreamer." She smiled through her tears as she imagined him inside standing near his armoire, dressing for dinner. Could she leave him this way, causing him untold anguish?

Sarah hurried away from his door before she could lose her nerve. She went downstairs and was relieved to note that the central hallway was deserted. She went quickly to Damien's office, opened the door and swept inside. Quietly closing the door, she tiptoed over to his desk, upon which sat a neat stack of manuscript pages. She studied the manuscript with intense longing. Damien's memoirs of Vincy were sacrosanct, she knew; no one in this house would ever dare read them.

Sarah quickly lifted the top manuscript page and hid her letter underneath. As she set down the page, she couldn't resist reading the entry from March, 1861, written in Damien's beautiful, bold script:

Vincy, Lucy, Aunt Olympia and I spent another week in New Orleans—a last celebration before my brother and I must do our duty fighting for states rights. We heard Adelina Patti sing in *Dinorah* at the French Opera house. There's much posturing here against the Yankees—military parades and rousing speeches.

My child-bride issues daily supplication
that she may conceive before Vincy and I are
called off to fight. She dreams of an heir—I
fear, in the event that I should not return to
her.

Vincy is eager to return to Belle Fontaine
and continue with his duties as captain of our
regiment. He has every female in the parish
busy sewing uniforms.

Ah, my brother, have you no idea what war
truly means?

Finishing the entry, Sarah wiped a tear. She set
the page down, feeling like an eavesdropper. Yet
reading the page only underscored her determination to return to the present. Until she found the
answers she so desperately needed, both she and
Damien would be trapped here, trapped in their
grief.

Sarah left the office and shut the door. Taking a
deep breath, she walked steadily toward the front
door of the house. Shadows shifted on the floor and
an eerie wind rattled the door, as if to dare her to
proceed.

Yet she went on, although by now her heart was
pounding so furiously, she feared it would burst.

Sarah opened the door and stepped forward. The
mystical barrier slammed her in powerful, violent
waves. Just as she began to whirl, she heard
Damien's anguished voice behind her, screaming,
"Sarah, no! Don't go!"

She tried to turn to him, tried to reach for him,
but it was too late. She was sucked into the twisting
vortex of time again, carried away.

Seconds later, she found herself back in the

twentieth century, clinging to a weathered post, utterly bereft.

Back in the present, in the chill of late afternoon, Sarah crossed through the woods and returned to Miss Erica's house. She took the key from beneath the mat and let herself in the backdoor. Inside, she called out, "Anyone home?" and breathed a sigh of relief when no one answered. A scattering of lights had been left on, and the house appeared clean and normal. Her painting of the old house and Damien still sat on its easel in the den. She stared at it sadly.

Sarah went to the bedroom, stripped and hid her old clothing, then dressed in green and gold plaid slacks, a yellow ribbed turtleneck sweater and brown loafers. She had brushed out her hair and was thinking of going to the den and starting a fire, when she heard the doorbell ring.

Sarah cursed under her breath. Who could be calling? She prayed it wasn't nosy Maudie Wilson trying to stir up trouble again. Surely after she had left Ebbie the note, no one had panicked at her departure this time.

Hurrying to the foyer, Sarah gazed through the peephole. She was stunned to spot a familiar, brown-haired man out on the stoop. What on earth was her ex-fiancé, Bill Bartley, doing here? He looked impatient as he frowned at his watch. He wore a sports shirt, dark slacks and a navy poplin jacket.

She swung open the door. "Bill! What on earth—"

"Sarah!" he exclaimed, staring at her incredulously. "Thank God! I didn't know what had happened to you, where you might be—"

"What are you doing here?" she cut in with amazement.

"Isn't it obvious?" he replied. "I came to see you."

She sighed. "Come in."

Sarah showed Bill into the living room. They stood for a moment in awkward silence, staring at each other like strangers.

"Can I get you something to drink?" Sarah asked at last.

"A Scotch and water would be nice," he replied stiffly.

"I'm afraid there's no bar in the house," she said, "but I think I have a bottle of wine in the refrigerator."

"Fine."

Sarah went out to the kitchen, took the bottle from the refrigerator and poured two glasses of white wine. When she returned to the living room, she found Bill seated in one of the Chippendale wing chairs. Watching him start to rise, she said quickly, "No, please don't get up," and handed him his drink. She sat down in the matching chair across from him, and for a moment they sipped their wine in strained silence.

Then Bill set down his drink and leaned forward. "All right, Sarah. Would you tell me where you've been?"

Feeling uncomfortable, Sarah stared at his thin, handsome face. "Didn't the maid explain things to you? Ebbie was aware that I'd gone off to New Orleans to stay with a friend."

He emitted a tired sigh. "Yes, your maid told me as much. But you didn't leave any address or number where you could be reached. And the maid expected you to be gone for only a few days, not for over two weeks."

"Is that how long you've been here?"

"Actually, I've been here just over a week. When I arrived in town, you'd already been gone about eight days, and your maid was expecting you back at any time."

Sarah sighed. No wonder Bill was so impatient now, if he'd waited around for her all this time, expecting her to appear at any moment. "Bill, I'm sorry, but if you wanted to see me, you should have phoned first."

"I did. Your mother gave me your number here several weeks ago. I tried calling you before I left Atlanta, but there was no answer. I tried calling your folks, too, but there was no answer there, either. So I just decided to come on."

"My parents went off to their house in Myrtle Beach for a few weeks," Sarah explained. "I'm sure they shut down the Atlanta house, as they normally do when they go on vacation, so there would have been no one around to answer your call."

Bill shook his head. "No wonder I couldn't find out where you'd gone."

Sarah set down her wine and leaned forward. "Why did you come to see me?"

He drew himself up in his chair and spoke defensively. "I wanted to check up on you. After your breakdown, and what happened between us in Atlanta, I was very concerned about you. Then, when I arrived here, and found you'd disappeared . . . Well, you must admit that your behavior seems odd, and I feared—"

"I didn't disappear," Sarah cut in with strained patience. "Nor did I flip out, as you seem so subtley to be hinting. I went to New Orleans to stay with

Brenda Birmingham, my old roommate from college. And furthermore, I don't even know why I'm explaining all of this to you. You have no right to interfere in my life—not any more."

Sarah regretted her words as soon as she saw an expression of hurt cross Bill's eyes. She watched him distractedly rake a hand through his hair. They'd been such good friends once, and even though he had hurt her by having the vasectomy done without discussing it with her, she realized that she had hurt him, too, by calling off the engagement. Now, she found she disliked the idea of causing him additional pain. She had to admit to herself that he'd gone to a lot of trouble and had come a long way to check up on her, and she felt sure that his concern for her was genuine.

But how could she ever make him understand that there was no room for him in her life anymore, that it was over, that she had found her life and love in another century?

She couldn't, not without confirming what he already so obviously suspected—that she had gone over the edge again. And while her life during the past few weeks seemed bizarre even to herself, never in her life had she so strongly believed in her own sanity.

"Look, Sarah," he said, "I didn't come here to fight with you. As a matter of fact, I'm starving, and I was wondering if there's some place around here where we can have dinner."

Sarah smiled and nodded. Given the tensions between them, she actually welcomed the thought of finishing their discussion in a more neutral setting. "Where have you been having your meals?"

"Well, there's only one small hotel in town. I've been staying there and eating at the café on the square. The food's okay, if rather monotonous."

Sarah nodded. "There's a small restaurant on the outskirts of town run by a Cajun and his wife. I think you might find the food there more interesting. Just let me get my jacket."

Sarah grabbed her purse and a plaid jacket, then left the house with Bill. As they approached a shiny blue Buick Riviera in the yard, she asked, "New car?"

"No. I flew in to New Orleans and rented a car there."

Bill drove them out onto River Road in the gilded light. The evening was crisp, and Sarah rolled her window down. Above them, the trees wore the bright scarlet and russet and gold colors of autumn, and the crisp scent of the foliage, mingled with the earthier smell of the river, was a marvelous opiate for her senses. The smoky light drifting down through the trees was exquisitely beautiful as well, and she realized how much she had missed the out-of-doors recently.

If only she could be seeing this brilliant autumn parade in another century, sitting next to Damien in his carriage as they laughed and clipped along, perhaps on their way to a *soirée* at a neighboring plantation. Later on, they might drive their baby to the parish church to be christened. These images filled Sarah's heart with intense longing.

Bill turned the car off River Road onto the cutoff that led to town. They passed the familiar cottage of Madame Tu on the outskirts of Meridian. Sarah spotted the negro woman out in her yard; she wore a flowered dress and a floppy hat and was industriously weeding her marigolds. Madame Tu turned at the sound of the approaching car and Sarah waved to her, but the black woman merely stared back.

Soon, they arrived at Gerard's Restaurant and were shown to a cozy window booth. Sarah ordered a bowl of gumbo, while Bill had a big plate of jambalaya. At first, their talk was general. Bill told Sarah about some new corporate clients he had landed.

As he finished his account, Sarah asked, "Didn't it cause you problems to leave the firm for this long?"

He shrugged as he buttered his cornbread. "I had several weeks of vacation coming to me."

And you've wasted them all on me, she thought.

Bill in turn asked Sarah about her life here. She told him all about the vast holdings she had inherited and how the estate was moving through probate.

As they finished their entrees, Bill set down his fork and stared at her, tension obvious in his expression. "Are you planning to stay here permanently, Sarah?"

"Yes," she answered without hesitation.

He whistled. "Have you told your parents about this?"

"Not exactly—not yet. But their lives are pretty full, and they have Teddy, thank God. I have to find my own way."

"And you've found it here?"

"Yes."

Bill sighed as he pushed his plate away. "I've always admired your independence, Sarah, but to cut yourself off from all you hold near and dear—"

Sarah almost said, I've found all I hold near and dear in an ancient house, in a time and place you could never understand. But instead, she said, "I've been able to paint again."

At that, he smiled. "Have you?"

She nodded. "There's something very healing

about being here. Life seems simpler somehow."

He shot her an admonishing glance. "I just hope you're not trying to avoid reality again."

At one time, Sarah would have bitterly resented Bill's remark. He had always put her down, had never taken her seriously. But tonight, she found herself tempted instead to laugh at his criticism. Bill had no comprehension of what her reality actually was now or of how beautiful it was to her.

Quietly, she asked, "Are you going to tell me why you've come here?"

"Isn't it obvious?" He stared at her earnestly. "Sarah, I've missed you terribly. I want you back."

Sarah glanced off at a potted plant in a corner, feeling quite ill-at-ease. "I thought it was that."

He reached across the table and took her hand, forcing her to meet his eye. "There's no reason for you to continue staying in this hick town. Just think—we could fly back to Atlanta tomorrow. We could get married, then settle the legal technicalities here later on. And if we leave right away, we could still see the Picasso exhibit in New York City. I know how much you've looked forward to it."

Now Bill had gone too far. Sarah's jaw tightened with resentment as she yanked her fingers from his. "Wrong, Bill. I haven't looked forward to the Picasso exhibit at all. You're the one who insisted we attend. But this is just another example of your not hearing anything I say—including my often repeated statement that you and I are no longer engaged."

At her words, Bill paled. But even as he recovered his composure and attempted a reply, the proprietor's wife stopped by. The friendly little woman poured them more chicoried coffee and questioned them at length about the food in her half-English, half-French. After they assured the woman numerous times that everything was delectable, she swept off, beaming, to repeat her queries at the next table.

Bill nodded to Sarah exasperatedly. "Look, why don't you come with me to my hotel room where we can have some privacy? We need to do a lot more talking."

But she shook her head adamantly. "I want to talk here."

He sighed. "All right." In a low, anguished voice, he asked, "Why won't you give us another chance?"

Feeling a stab of guilt at his question, she stared at him sadly. "Things would never work between us. We're just too different."

"In what ways?"

Sarah stifled an impatient sigh. "I'm a Flower Child, you're a dyed-in-the-wool conservative. You're on the fast track to success at the law firm, and I want a simpler existence. We don't agree about anything, Bill—not about race, politics or children."

"I know you're still angry at me about the vasectomy," he put in patiently, "but you really do need me, Sarah. I've been so concerned about you, concerned that you might have another relapse."

Now Sarah gritted her teeth as Bill's manipulative words made her feelings of regret surge into anger. "I need you, do I? So you think I'm going to come running back to you because I fear another nervous breakdown? You know you're very clever, trying to prey upon my anxieties this way."

"Sarah—"

"Tell me, Bill, did you have a vasectomy because you were afraid our children might end up crazy—like me?"

With a stunned gasp, Bill fell back against the

banquette, even as a twangy Cajun melody spewed forth from the Wurlitzer jukebox. They stared at each other for a charged moment. Then, in a cutting undertone, Bill demanded, "That's it, isn't it? This is all about the vasectomy I had."

Her eyes flashed with anger. "Well, it seems to me that you gave up any claim to me when you made a major decision about our future without even consulting me."

He clenched a fist on the tabletop. "Sarah, you know how strongly I felt about our not having children."

At his words, Sarah illogically smiled, feeling a surge of pride and joy at the thought that, even now, she might be carrying Damien's child, the child she had wanted for so long. To Bill, she said tersely, "Then go find a woman who feels the way you do."

Bill shook his head incredulously. "I can't believe you'd break up with me only because of the children issue."

She leaned toward him and spoke intensely. "It's not just our views on children. We're just not well-suited in so many ways. We were friends growing up, and we should have kept it that way as adults. We never should have given in to the pressures from our families to marry or tried to take our relationship further."

"You're talking about sex now?" he asked in a tense whisper, a muscle twitching in his jaw.

"Sex—and much more. The spark just isn't there, at least not for me. And I never could have been the kind of wife you needed, Bill—someone whose life revolves around you."

Suddenly, he emitted a short, bitter laugh and stared at her as if seeing her for the first time. "You've found someone else, haven't you?"

240

Sarah knew she couldn't deny it; indeed, her sudden, hot blush gave her away. But she raised her chin proudly and stared him in the eye. "Actually, I have."

He snapped his fingers. "So that's why you stayed away so long in New Orleans."

Let him think it, Sarah decided. Still meeting his gaze, she said, "Yes."

Bill shook his head. "You know, you're changed, Sarah. You're stronger now."

"And you don't like me that way, do you, Bill?"

He glanced away guiltily. Both of them knew that her question required no answer.

Later, they were quiet as he drove her home. On the porch, she didn't ask him in; she knew he didn't expect her to now. Studying the taut lines of his face and the disappointment in his eyes, Sarah felt a twinge of sadness for what they'd once shared. Still, it seemed incredible to her now that she had ever been involved with him; he was so totally different from the man she truly loved.

At last, she took his hand and said earnestly, "Bill, it was good of you to come here, but go home now, please. Tell my parents I'm fine. Tell them I'm happy here. And go find yourself someone else. I'm sure she'll be a very lucky woman."

Bill nodded and kissed her cheek quickly. "Take care of yourself, Sarah," he said gruffly. "I hope you're very happy with him."

She stood on the porch and watched him stride away. She didn't draw a comfortable breath until his taillights faded into the obscurity of night.

Chapter Nineteen

The next morning dawned cold, rainy and gray. Sarah awakened to her nightmare of Brian. She bolted upright in bed, gasping for breath as thunder boomed out and rain pelted the roof. She hugged her pillow and sat there for a long moment, rocking and crying. Never had she so ached for Damien's comfort and love.

When at last the harrowing images receded, she recalled that this last time when she had gone back in time she had again been safe from the nightmare. Obviously, there was no protection from the demons of her grief here in the present. True, the past held its own terrors, as evidenced by the voodoo presence she had felt in the house this last time. Yet neither the *gris-gris* nor the ominous voice held the power to lacerate her heart as did her nightmare of Brian. The answers she needed might be here in the present, but she was convinced now that true healing and love lay with Damien in the past. And now that it was possible that she was carrying his child, she longed to move away from the grief and despair she'd known for so long and move toward love, affirmation and life itself.

As Sarah was donning her robe, Bill Bartley phoned to say good-bye. They shared a brief, awkward conversation, and then it was over. Bill was off for Atlanta, and Sarah knew he wouldn't contact her again. She set down the receiver with a feeling of relief.

Yet Bill's visit had driven home to her the fact that if she did want to live permanently in the past she couldn't just turn her back on the present. She would need to make some provision for her estate. And what about her family? How could she ever explain to her parents the drastic turn her life had taken since she had come to Louisiana? How could she make them understand that, while she loved them, she'd discovered that her life, her future, lay in another century? If she told them the truth, they'd surely think she'd had another nervous breakdown.

Nevertheless, before she could resolve her future, she had to seek the answers she needed about the past. Were their records in the parish of her and Damien marrying? Of their deaths? The very possibilities made her shiver.

Sarah ate the breakfast Ebbie prepared for her out in the kitchen. Afterward, she dressed in gray wool slacks and a sweater, clipping her hair back in a ponytail. Donning her raincoat and grabbing her umbrella, she left the house and drove toward town, deciding that she would first visit the parish courthouse.

The courthouse was a colonial brick building on

the center of the square. It was still pouring when Sarah parked her car. She hurried for the imposing edifice as icy rivulets slashed against her back and pelted her umbrella.

Inside the building, Sarah closed her umbrella and shivered as she glanced about to gain her bearings. The interior was dark, cold and smelled of a mixture of rain and must. A young black janitor was sweeping the corridor.

"Excuse me," Sarah said. "I'm looking for the office that keeps the parish records."

"Third door on the right, miss," he told her, pointing down the hallway.

"Thanks."

Sarah proceeded to a door whose mottled glass panel read "Parish Clerk." Inside the office, behind a counter, a silver-haired, plump little woman sat making entries in a large record book. She glanced up as Sarah entered. "Good morning, miss. May I help you?"

Sarah smiled. "Good morning. I'm Sarah Jennings. I inherited the Davis plantation outside town."

The little woman closed her book, stood and walked over to the counter. "Why, of course," she said, extending her hand with a smile. "You'd be Erica's cousin, then. I'm Miss Faith Hamilton, the parish clerk."

Sarah shook the woman's hand and smiled back. "Pleased to meet you. Did you know my cousin?"

"Indeed, I did. Erica and I belonged to the same church." Studying Sarah quizzically, she added, "You know, once, when I was at Erica's house for tea, she showed me a lovely painting of yours. It was your painting, wasn't it?"

Sarah brightened at the compliment. "Yes, it was. I'm surprised you remember."

"Oh, honey, that painting was a marvel. Erica was so proud that you'd given it to her." The woman clucked to herself. "Such a shame about her passing, but then, she did have a good, long life."

"Yes, she did."

"Well, how can I help you, dear?"

Sarah bit her lip. "Actually, I've come here because I'm trying to gather some history on the estate I inherited. I'm particularly interested in the Fontaine family, who once lived in the old plantation house north of Miss Erica's place."

The little woman frowned at that, laying a finger alongside her cheek. "You're talking about the haunted house?"

Sarah laughed. "I suppose I am."

"And you say some people named Fontaine once lived there?" she continued skeptically.

"Yes."

Miss Hamilton shook her head. "If I may ask, how did you come up with that name, Miss Jennings? I've lived here in Meridian for forty years now, and I've been keeping the parish records for almost thirty. And I've never heard of any Fontaines hereabouts."

Sarah thought quickly, manufacturing an explanation. "I believe some of the papers and deeds pertaining to the estate mention the Fontaine family as the original owners of the plantation. Mr. Baldwin, who is handling my cousin's estate, has shown me these documents."

"Ah, yes." Faith Hamilton seemed to take Sarah's explanation entirely in stride.

In a rush, Sarah continued, "Anyway, the information I am seeking would date from the mid-nineteenth century through the early part of this century. I'm interested in records of births, deaths, marriages—anything having to do with the Fontaines."

Miss Hamilton's expression sagged. "Oh, dear! If those are the years you are researching, I'm afraid you're out of luck."

Sarah was quite taken aback. "I beg your pardon?"

"You see, the old parish courthouse burned to the ground in 1910. This one was built a year later. And I'm afraid all the records prior to 1910 were lost."

"Oh, no!" Sarah cried.

"Of course, you can go up to Baton Rouge and see what the state has on file," Miss Hamilton continued, "but I'm sure it won't be much, not if you're looking for information from the last century. Why, around these parts, a number of births, deaths and marriages are still recorded only in family Bibles."

"I see." Sarah frowned a moment, then snapped her fingers. "Would the churches here in town have records?"

"I'm sure they do, although I can't vouch for how extensive or accurate their records might be. You could try the local history room at the parish library. And there used to be a Historical Society here."

"Used to be?"

"Actually, the Historical Society was the brainchild of Celeste Boudreau. During her lifetime, Celeste amassed quite a collection on local history. But when Celeste died five years ago, the society pretty much fizzled out. Her daughter moved off to New Orleans, and I believe Ann donated Celeste's papers to a museum there."

"Do you know the name of the museum?" Sarah asked.

Miss Hamilton shook her head sadly. "Afraid not, dear."

"Do you know how I can get in touch with this Ann Boudreau?"

"No. But I can surely ask around. There are several women living here who were in Celeste's Bible study group, and I'm sure one of them will have Ann's address in New Orleans. Tell you what— I'll see what I can find out, and why don't you drop back by in another week or so?"

Sarah smiled. "I will. Thanks for your help, Miss Hamilton."

The little woman waved her off. "Oh, it's my pleasure, dear. Actually, it's quite a thrill to find someone interested in local history. Not many folks around these parts are, you know."

The two women said their good-byes, and Sarah left. Her spirits sank as she walked down the darkened hallway toward the door. Finding information on Damien and his family was going to be a lot more difficult than she had originally anticipated, especcially with the parish records she needed having been reduced to ashes so many years ago.

As she arrived at the exit, the young janitor came forward to open the door for her. Sarah braved a smile at him.

"Did you find what you wanted, miss?" he asked.

Sarah shook her head, a little startled by his question. "I'm afraid not. The records I need burned long ago."

She started out the door, but the man called after her, "Oh, miss?"

She turned. "Yes?"

247

Shyly, he said, "If you troubled, go see Madame Tu."

Sarah's lips twisted in a mixture of curiosity and amusement. "Madame Tu?"

"Madame Tuchet."

"Oh, yes," Sarah said with a laugh. "Madame Tuchet, Reader and Adviser. I've seen her sign on the outskirts of town."

"She help my wife," the man added awkwardly, shifting from foot to foot.

"Did she, now? Well, thanks for the suggestion," Sarah said politely.

Opening her umbrella, Sarah swept out the door. Rain was still falling as she proceeded carefully down the brick steps. She shook her head at the janitor's odd suggestion. He had seemed sincere enough. He'd said Madame Tuchet had helped his wife.

Or maybe he was on Madame's payroll, she mused cynically. Perhaps he collected a finder's fee for each pigeon he sent her way. The very thought of going to see a reader and adviser made Sarah roll her eyes as she conjured an image of a turbaned con-woman dripping with gold jewelry, looking into a crystal ball, reading tea leaves and palms. Sarah had never held with such nonsense.

But then, how could she explain what had happened to her? On second thought, she decided to file the suggestion at the back of her mind.

Sarah's next stop was the local Catholic church, St. Jerome's. She had recalled that, while she was in the past, Olympia had several times left to attend mass at a nearby Catholic Church. She had also seen a crucifix or two, as well as some rosary beads, in the house. Although she knew that Damien, like herself, had become disenchanted with formal religion, she prayed that the church might have the family records she sought.

Again, she was disappointed. The priest she spoke with was young and eager to be of help, but he assured Sarah that the church had little, if any, records dating back to the period she was researching. He confirmed that Saint Jerome's had been the only Catholic church in the parish during the nineteenth century, but explained that record-keeping had often been haphazard at best and that many records had been lost during the two moves the church had made before settling in its present edifice. The priest did promise to search through the church archives for any possible clues he might glean, but like Miss Hamilton, he urged Sarah to look elsewhere, particularly at the parish library.

Thus, Sarah's last stop was the old red brick library building off the square. Inside, Sarah introduced herself to a pleasant young assistant librarian, Frances Gatlin. Miss Gatlin brightened visibly when Sarah mentioned that she was thinking of donating some of Erica Davis's papers to the library. Then Sarah explained that she was doing research on the Fontaine family, who were the original owners of the Davis plantation.

Like Miss Hamilton, Frances Gatlin was thrilled to find someone interested in area history. She led Sarah into the library's small, musty local history room. Sarah glanced about at the dusty, cluttered room, at shelves of ancient-looking books, at tables cluttered with various yellowed documents, at walls dotted with pictures and shadow boxes containing everything from old dueling pistols to lace tatting, hair pictures and even a collection of square nails.

"I'm afraid we don't have any organized records of births, deaths or marriages in the region,"

Frances explained. "But we do have much nine-teenth-century material dealing with the parish—old family Bibles and photographs, diaries, journals and letters, that sort of thing." Throwing Sarah an encouraging smile, she added, "And of course we'd be delighted to add Miss Davis's papers to our collection."

"I'll be sure to bring them in soon," Sarah replied, smiling back. She glanced again at the daunting sea of clutter. "Do you have any index to your holdings?"

France bit her lip. "Yes, but I'm afraid it's not very comprehensive." She went to one of the tables, picked up an oblong wooden file box and handed it to Sarah. "We're perpetually short-handed here, as well as low on funds. Suffice it to say, our local history collection is rather informal. When some-one donates an item, we basically shove it away in here and fill out a card when we have the time." She glanced about, then shrugged apologetically. "Well, please make yourself at home, Miss Jennings."

"Thanks."

Watching the librarian leave, Sarah sighed. She took off her raincoat and rolled up her sleeves, then sat down at one of the tables and began flipping through the file box. First, she tried to find a listing under "Fontaine." No luck. Then she began reading through the index cards one by one, looking for clues. Soon, she gave up this time-consuming task as pointless as well. She decided she may as well dive into the contents of the room itself.

Over the next few hours, Sarah perused old maps, deeds, letters and early editions of the town newspa-per. When this search proved fruitless, she turned to the metal shelves housing the books. She glanced through the old diaries, journals and family Bibles, but could find nothing written by or about the Fontaine family.

So consumed was Sarah with her task that she worked on through the lunch hour. Toward midafternoon, the rain at last stopped, and the sun belatedly appeared through the high, grimy windows of the small room. Late afternoon found Sarah sitting on the floor in the corner in a dusty beam of light. Her clothing was soiled, her hands filthy, and a dark smudge marred the loveliness of her face. In her lap were the last of the books she was laboriously sifting through.

"Miss Jennings?" a voice called out.

"Yes?" Sarah glanced up to see Frances Gatlin standing in the doorway.

"Please don't get up," Frances said as Sarah started to rise. "I just wanted to let you know that we close in twenty minutes."

Sarah's spirits sank. "Thanks."

After Frances left, Sarah glanced ruefully at the remaining two volumes in her lap. One was labeled, "Diary of Media Grant," the other, "The History of the Ladies Beneficent Society of St. Christopher Parish."

Sarah tiredly flipped through the volumes. Her eyes were beginning to hurt, she had been sneezing constantly due to the dust in the room, and she was developing a splitting headache. To top it all off, neither of the volumes in her lap looked promising.

So much for the records in St. Christopher Parish, she thought dismally. Unless the parish clerk or the Catholic priest turned up something in coming weeks, she would have to look elsewhere for the information she so desperately needed.

Sarah was on her knees reshelving the last two volumes, when she caught a glimpse of another dusty, thin volume, wedged between the back of the shelf and the wall. Was the book worth reaching for?

Sarah hesitated a moment, then reached through the bookcase, stretching to grasp the slim black book. At last her fingers clutched a frayed edge, and she pulled the book out. She dusted it off, and then her heart leaped into her throat as she read the narrow printing on the spine.

VINCY, it read. *By Damien Fontaine.*

An incoherent cry split the silence of the library, a cry of raw ecstasy. Sarah felt as if she had just been handed the keys to her future on a silver platter. She held in her hands both the proof that Damien was real and the means by which she could at last understand the man she loved.

Clutching the precious volume to her heart, Sarah rocked and cried.

Chapter Twenty

"Miss, is something wrong?"

Sarah glanced up at Frances Gatlin, who stood at the portal to the small room. Frances's expression was twisted in a mixture of concern and alarm as she studied Sarah kneeling near the bookcase and clutching the slim black book, her face smudged and tear-streaked.

"No, nothing's wrong," Sarah responded hastily, wiping her tears and struggling to her feet. "I didn't mean to cry out that way. It's just that I've found what I'm looking for."

"Oh. Well, good, then." Awkwardly, Frances glanced at her watch. "You're welcome to come back tomorrow and spend as much time as you like here."

"Tomorrow? Oh, no!" Sarah cried. The idea of parting with the precious volume she'd just found filled her with panic, and she clutched Vincy's memoirs even tighter. "Please, may I take the book home—just for the night? It took me all day to find it, and I haven't even had a chance to open it as yet."

The librarian's expression was sympathetic, but she shook her head. "I'm sorry, Miss Jennings, but library policy forbids checking out any materials from our local history collection. However, I suppose we could ask Mrs. Hodges."

"Please, we must," Sarah cut in feelingly. "If you'll just let me take the book home, I promise I'll have it back by the time you open tomorrow. And I'll leave any deposit you may require. How does a hundred dollars sound?"

Frances was biting her lip when an older woman stepped up to join her. "Frances Jean, what is the problem here?" she asked as she adjusted her reading glasses. "We must get this library closed."

Frances glanced lamely at Sarah, then back at the older woman. "Mrs. Hodges, this lady would like to take a book from the local history room home for the night. I explained our policy to her, but—"

"Please, you must let me take the book home," Sarah repeated plaintively, moving closer to the two women.

As the older librarian turned to frown at Sarah, Frances explained, "Mrs. Hodges, this is Sarah Jennings, who has inherited the Davis plantation outside town. In fact, Miss Jennings is thinking of donating Miss Erica's papers to our collection."

"Oh, is she?" Now the older woman's frown was replaced by a quizzical smile.

"Yes, I'm definitely planning to donate my cousin's papers," Sarah put in, pressing her advantage. She gestured at the cluttered room. "And I'd also like to make a suitable donation so that you may hire someone to complete the cataloging of your local history collection. You see, Miss Gatlin explained to me that you're short-handed, and I'm sure that this is the least my cousin would want me to do."

"Well, if that's the case . . ." Now the older librarian looked as if she were definitely wavering.

"As for this book," Sarah continued, holding up the volume, "I explained to Miss Gatlin that I'd be happy to leave a substantial deposit. I promise I'll bring the book back first thing in the morning—along with my cousin's papers, of course."

Mrs. Hodges glanced at Frances, then stepped closer to Sarah. "Let me see what you have there, Miss Jennings."

Reluctantly, Sarah handed Mrs. Hodges the book. "It's called *Vincy* by Damien Fontaine."

Mrs. Hodges scowled as she opened the volume. "It appears to be some sort of journal. To tell you the truth, I can't recall ever seeing this book here before."

"It was wedged between the bookshelf and the wall," Sarah explained.

"May I ask why you're so interested in it?"

"Certainly. You see, the Fontaine family originally owned my cousin's plantation, so of course I'm most eager to read the journal. It's really the first concrete information I've been able to find on the history of the plantation."

With a shrug, the librarian handed the book back to Sarah. She nodded to Frances. "Well, I think we can manage to part with this book for the night, don't you, Frances? I feel confident Miss Jennings won't abscond with it." She glanced back at Sarah.

"Tell you what, Miss Jennings—if you'll come with me to the circulation desk, we'll make the arrangements."

Sarah beamed with gratitude. "Thanks, Mrs. Hodges."

Ten minutes later, after filling out a card and leaving a check for the deposit, Sarah left the library with the precious volume wedged under one arm. The weather was clear and cool as she walked to her car. She drove out of town quickly, glancing frequently at the book on the seat next to her, as if she were afraid it might disappear.

As Sarah veered out onto River Road, she almost collided with a pickup truck. The overall-clad driver honked and waved a fist at her, and Sarah called out an apology. Following the frightening incident, she pulled her car off the road beneath a tree. She realized that she was trembling all over and that she felt dizzy, half-sick. She took several deep breaths, resting her forehead against the steering wheel. Then she remembered that she hadn't eaten since breakfast. She scolded herself silently. If she were indeed pregnant, then she must take better care of herself than this. And she'd never get to read the precious memoirs if she got herself killed on her way back to Miss Erica's house.

Sarah drove the rest of the way carefully, albeit her fingers trembling on the steering wheel. She walked into the house to the tantalizing aroma of hot chicken. Bless Ebbie's heart, she thought. Going straight to the kitchen, she set the memoirs down on the counter, then grabbed a pot holder and opened the oven, pulling out the foil-wrapped plate Ebbie had left her—a fried chicken breast, mashed potatoes with gravy, green beans from the garden and one of Ebbie's wonderful homemade yeast rolls.

Grabbing a glass of milk, Sarah sat down at the kitchen table and ate her hearty supper. She felt much better afterward. She tidied up the kitchen, then took the memoirs into the den. Putting the book down on the coffee table, she started a fire, then settled herself on the couch with her prize. As the cedar logs snapped and blazed in the grate, filling the room with a spicy scent and comforting warmth, Sarah opened the precious volume.

The first page was blank, and Sarah turned it carefully, since the paper was old, yellowed and quite fragile. The next page contained only the title and author: "VINCY, by Damien Fontaine."

"Oh, Damien," Sarah whispered as she stared, captivated, at the old-fashioned lettering. "How I wish you could be with me at this moment. For I'm holding in my hands the very proof that you did exist—and that what we have is real."

On the next page, Sarah found the publisher and date of publication: "Henry Clark, New Orleans, 1876."

With a deepening sense of awe, Sarah turned to the next page, which turned out to be an introduction written by the publisher himself:

Dear Reader:

It is with great pride that I publish this volume. By expanding his own diary entries covering a period of over twelve years, the author has produced a faithful and moving portrait of a time now lost to us all. With unerring accuracy, Mr. Damien Fontaine has recreated life on a Louisiana sugarcane plantation prior to the War Between the States; and with this same incisive honesty, the author has written a poignant account of how the war destroyed that way of life forever.

On a deeper level, this book is the story of a love between two brothers, a deep, abiding love that this same, cruel war ripped asunder. Do not expect to read this account, dear reader, and not be moved. I vow to you that no heart embarking on this journey will remain untouched, that no spirit traversing these pages will leave without forever bearing their imprint.

It is most fitting, then, that the author should name this volume in simple, humble tribute: VINCY.

Finishing the introduction, Sarah shivered. Beneath it was printed, "J. Henry Clark, New Orleans, December, 1876."

Sarah quickly turned the page. On the next page was a single quotation from the Bible: "Greater love hath no man than this, that a man lay down his life for his brother."

"Oh, Damien," Sarah whispered. Already, she was beginning to understand.

Sarah quickly flipped to the next page and began reading the journal. The first hundred or so pages were filled with life and vitality, a compelling portrait of life on a Louisiana sugarcane plantation in the mid-nineteenth century. Together, Damien and Vincy attended balls and barbecues, spending countless afternoons on fragrant verandas wooing fair belles. Sarah laughed over one entry, dated December of 1859:

Vincy and I went visiting for over a fortnight. So long was our disappearance that Aunt

Olympia sent Old Jacob to fetch us. We attended the harvest ball at La Branche Plantation, imbibing great quantities of rum punch. It was quite a memorable night. Vincy and I acted as seconds for an impromptu duel held between the son of the house, Edward La Branche, and his erstwhile friend, Charles Reynaud. It seems young La Branche considered his fiancée insulted when Charles had the temerity to spill punch on darling Fifi. La Branche promptly challenged Reynaud to a duel and dragged Vincy and myself along. Luckily, given the intoxicated state of the principals, both men missed their aim and afterward promptly declared the matter settled. They then departed back to the house, laughing and clapping one another across the shoulders.

Vincy and I drank and danced into the wee hours, and when the La Branche daughters begged prettily that we must take them to see the sunrise over the Mississippi, Vincy and I promptly indulged the twins. Luckily, I had the foresight to drag along one of the serving girls as duenna. Sitting in our barouche at the edge of the levee, we laughed and shared a bottle of champagne as the sun rose. Ah, 'twas a glorious sight!

Unfortunately, upon returning to the big house, we were met by the twins's irate papa, who assured us that they were irrevocably compromised and demanded that we make honest women out of his daughters. Vincy quickly defused the situation by declaring our eternal devotion to the twins and promising that we would wed them posthaste. The twins

259

were horrified, of course. Young Bettina had
hysterics, crying buckets that she and her
sister Regina, only sixteen, were being con-
signed to the terrible fate of becoming wives of
wicked old men in their twenties such as
ourselves. When the serving girl confirmed
that nothing untoward had happened, Papa at
last relented. But he banned Vincy and me
from his estate for at least the next fortnight.

If only M'sieur La Branche had known how
eager we were, at that point, to depart!

Finishing the entry, Sarah again laughed. No
wonder Damien mourned the loss of this way of life;
it seemed he had lived a nearly idyllic existence, that
he and Vincy had found their own Utopia at Belle
Fontaine.

Sarah read of Damien and Vincy's travels to the
east and England. As the entries moved into the
1860's, they grew more sober. One, dated in June of
1860, read simply: "I am to marry Lucy St. Pierre,
as was arranged between our families at her birth.
The bride will become seventeen shortly." An entry
from later that summer read: "The entire South has
become consumed with secession fever. If Lincoln
is elected, war is certain to follow. May God preserve us all."

A longer entry from early 1861 read:

Louisiana has seceded. Vincy and I will, of
course, answer the call. I'm deeply troubled
about the pending outbreak of war against our
brothers in the North. Vincy, on the other
hand, is rallying to the call, determined to
defeat the "Yankee cravens" and preserve our
way of life.

My dear brother, I fear our way of life is already doomed.

Aunt Olympia says the wedding must be effected before Lent. My child-bride is willing.

An entry from early February read:

Today I married Lucy St. Pierre. Vincy stood up for me. I'm off with my bride to New Orleans for a proper honeymoon. In the interim, Vincy will continue organizing a regiment from our parish. While he drills the troops daily along River Road, I'll be providing for our progeny.

Sarah paused, confused by an undercurrent of cynicism that she detected in Damien's writings about his wife. Had he resented the arranged marriage? What had his true feelings been about Lucy? It was hard to tell from his cryptic comments here. Yet she could already sense Damien's pain, his foreseeing the disaster war would bring while Vincy continued to live his dreams of glory.

Moving on, she found an entry that read: "Vincy and Aunt Olympia joined Lucy and me in New Orleans for Fat Tuesday. Mardi Gras this year has become a celebration of secession. Can no one foresee the catastrophe coming?"

Then, to Sarah's wonderment, she again found the entry from March, 1861, that she had discovered on Damien's desk in the past only two days ago. A chill streaked down her spine as she reread it:

Vincy, Lucy, Aunt Olympia and I spent another week in New Orleans, a last celebration before my brother and I must do our duty fighting for states' rights. We heard Adelina Patti sing in *Dinorah* at the French Opera House. There's much posturing here against the Yankees—military parades and rousing speeches.

My child-bride issues daily supplication that she may conceive before Vincy and I are called off to fight. She dreams of an heir—I fear, in the event that I should not return to her.

Vincy is eager to return to Belle Fontaine and continue with his duties as captain of our regiment. He has every female in the parish busy sewing uniforms.

Ah, my brother, have you no idea what war truly means?

This was followed by a terse entry from April, 1861, that read: "We learned today that the Confederates opened their guns on Fort Sumter. The war has begun."

There were more entries dealing with the training of the regiment and how they awaited instructions from the Confederate command. Then, an entry from August read simply: "My wife is pregnant, and Vincy and I are off to fight with our regiment."

Sarah read accounts of early skirmishes Damien and Vincy encountered during the war. Only in the late spring of 1862 did the magnitude and reality of the conflict begin to sink in:

Vincy and I are home, fresh from the horror of Shiloh. We arrived in New Orleans on the train bearing the Confederate dead from the battle. Our mission was no happier than that of the hapless train.

My wife and son are dead. We secured

special leave to come home and bury them at Belle Fontaine. Louis, my dear son, was stillborn, and Lucy succumbed to childbed fever three days later. Aunt Olympia is taking the deaths very hard. Vincy spends much time on the veranda, gazing out at the barren cane fields.

Soon after we arrived home, New Orleans fell to Farragut. Belle Fontaine is at risk, but Aunt Olympia refuses to evacuate. I haven't the heart to argue with her. Vincy and I are back off to fight this senseless, interminable war.

The entries that followed were sketchy, briefly describing other battles and telling of the deprivations the Southern soldiers had to endure—the lack of medical supplies, food and clothing, the dysentery and epidemics, the long winter marches in rain and mud.

An entry from May of 1863 provided a gleam of hope: "Today we defeated Hooker at Chancellorsville. Perhaps the Cause is not lost, after all."

For a time after that, the entries grew more detailed. Vincy and Damien were with Lee's army, part of his invasion of the north. The entries described the large army's march through the Blue Ridge Mountains toward Pennsylvania. Damien was a Colonel now, Vincy a Major; as such, they were included in the strategy sessions for their corps and had even met with Robert E. Lee himself on a few occasions. Damien spoke of his admiration of Lee: "I see a sadness in his eyes. I know that he, like me, abhors this war. But, like me, his loyalty is with the South."

As Sarah followed the account of the Confederate

Army's march on into Pennsylvania, she felt herself
tensing. She knew the tragedy of Gettysburg was
soon to come.

At last she came to the entry, dated July 2:

We are now at Gettysburg, Pennsylvania,
involved in the greatest battle of the war, three
mighty divisions deployed against the Federals. Today, we routed the Yanks at the Peach
Orchard and Devil's Den. Vincy is jubilant,
sure that total victory is imminent, but I do not
share his confidence. Meade's army is very
strong, and the Federals continue to hold onto
Cemetery Ridge and Little Round Top. I fear
that this conquest, if it comes, will be hard-
fought.

Sarah sighed as she read the chillingly prophetic
words. The remainder of the entry mirrored
Damien's pain and personal anguish, his sense of
impending doom:

Oh, Vincy, what brought us to this juncture?
We have lost so much, my brother. Will the end
of this war see us safely home or forever torn
asunder? You still dream of victory; I dream
only of peace.

Then came the tragic, anguished entry Sarah had
been waiting for, dated July 3, 1863:

The light has gone out of my life. Vincent
Paul Fontaine was killed today in the charge
on Cemetery Ridge. He died a hero among
many heroes.

When Major General Pickett asked for additional volunteers for the hapless charge, Vincy was the first to spring up with the rebel yell and volunteer our regiment. I begged him not to go on what I was certain was a suicide mission, but he only laughed and told me the war had made an old woman out of me. Ah, how I saw the old Vincy in that moment, his eyes alive with laughter and courage, his heart filled with visions of glory. It was almost as if you knew, my brother, almost as if you greeted the dark messenger with an ardent embrace. Within seconds, I, too, had caught the fever and sprung up, yelling the battle cry.

Casualties were heavy, the fighting soon hand-to-hand. Oh, my brother, why did you step in front of me, catching the lance that was aimed for my heart? I dispatched your assassin to hell, but for you, it was too late. Beneath a mighty tree in the shadow of the ridge, you died in my arms. Oh, my brother, your spirit was so invincible. You thought that the war could never truly touch you, but it caught up with you today.

I asked you, "Why?" And you told me in a death rattle. "Do not mourn me," you said. "If one of us had to go, I wanted it to be me. Now I can be with Lucy." And then you died.

You loved her, Vincy. What a fool I was never to see it. You never told me. Looking back, I can see it all now—the shy, anguished glances the two of you exchanged, the brave smiles when all of us were together. She loved you, too—surely she did.

You shared everything with me, Vincy. Why did you never tell me this?

I never loved her. It is my greatest shame. I

would have given her to you, so eagerly. Oh, Vincy, my brother, where are you now?

There, Sarah stopped reading, overcome by tears. At last she was beginning to understand Damien's private torment. To have his brother lay down his life for him. To find out at the moment of his brother's death that Vincy and his wife had been in love, that they'd forsaken that love so as not to hurt him.

"Oh, Damien," Sarah whispered, "my poor darling." Never had she loved him as much as she did at this moment.

At last, she was able to go on to the final entry, dated July 5, 1863:

Today I asked for special leave to take Vincy's body home. My request was denied. Afterward, I simply stole a wagon and left with my brother's body. My plan is to follow the retreating troops back into Virginia. Traveling will be perilous until we're out of the North. Surely somewhere south of here, I'll find a railroad not yet destroyed by the Federals to bear us back to New Orleans.

I am not a deserter. I will return and see this tragic war through to its ignoble conclusion. But first, I will return home and bury my brother next to the woman he loved.

Sarah finished the entry, her heart aching for Damien. But one central truth shone through the pages of the journal, a truth she was sure Damien could not see, a truth she knew she must go back and reveal to him.

Vincy did not want Damien to spend the rest of

his life as a recluse, mourning his brother's passing. Vincy had died in Damien's place not to make him a prisoner, but to set him free. And somehow, she'd been sent back in time to accomplish what Vincy's death had not.

The journal ended soon thereafter, but on the final page, Sarah found a postscript:

> Several years have passed since I completed these memoirs of my beloved brother Vincy, and it is with joy that I greet their publication by Mr. Henry Clark of New Orleans.
>
> And it is with joy and exultation that I finally lay you, my beloved brother, to rest. May you know peace, dear Vincy, the peace I have at last come to know in my own life.
>
> For I have found her now and she has taken away all my pain.
>
> Damien Fontaine
>
> Belle Fontaine Plantation
> St. Christopher Parish
> October, 1876

With tears streaming down her face, Sarah reread the final line: "For I have found her now and she has taken away all my pain."

Sarah closed the volume and clutched it to her heart. For the first time since this spiritual journey began, she knew a moment of sublime joy and peace.

Chapter Twenty-One

The next morning, Sarah awakened nauseated. For a wrenching moment, she feared she was going to vomit. She remained on the bed, her head between her knees, and after a dizzying interlude, the spasm passed.

Leaning back against the headboard and drawing a deep breath, she smiled. Her period was quite late now, and she had an increasingly strong feeling that she was indeed pregnant. She realized that it was time to go see a doctor to have her intuition confirmed.

The likelihood that she was pregnant filled Sarah with deepening wonder and excitement. After reading the memoirs, she knew for certain that Damien Fontaine had existed. And if she was, indeed, carrying his child, then this would prove conclusively that her encounter with him in the past had really happened.

In her heart, she had never doubted it.

Sarah glanced at the nightstand where she had laid the precious memoirs. She had reread the volume in bed last night, drinking in every word, staying up until the wee hours. When she had again come to the words, "I have found her now and she has taken away all my pain," she had wept once more in exultation. How she yearned to go back to Damien to tell him of all she had discovered!

But first, she must find out for certain whether or not they'd be having a child together. What doctor should she see? She frowned. Maudie Wilson had mentioned a Dr. Nugent in town who had recently delivered one of her grandchildren, yet the idea of seeing a local doctor made Sarah uneasy. She didn't want to risk stirring up any gossip. No, she decided, it would be far better to try to find a doctor in New Orleans, a doctor with whom she could pass as married.

Sarah picked up the phone and dialed the number of her friend, Brenda Birmingham. Sarah hadn't spoken with Brenda since she had stayed with the Birminghams on her way out from Georgia.

Brenda seemed delighted to hear from Sarah again, although she sounded harried and Sarah could hear the loud, raucous sounds of small children in the background. "I'm so glad you called, Sarah," she said. "Excuse the noise, but I'm trying to get this brood fed. Anyway, Charles and I have been wondering how you're faring up there in Meridian."

"Oh, I'm doing fine," Sarah said. She bit her lip. "But I was wondering—do you have a gynecologist you see there?"

Brenda laughed. "Try obstetrician. Dr. Ferguson delivered all three of these monsters."

Sarah chuckled, recalling the exuberance of Brenda's young children. "Do you like him?"

"Why, of course I like him. Do you think I'd let a doctor deliver three children for me if he wasn't a real doll?" Brenda paused, then asked tensely, "What's up, Sarah?"

Sarah sighed. She decided her best course was to be as honest as possible. "Brenda, I've met a man here, and—well, to tell you the truth, I think I may be pregnant."

She heard Brenda whistle. "This guy you met— would he be willing to marry you?"

"Yes, of course," Sarah hastily assured. "As a matter of fact, we're deeply in love, and I'm sure he'll be thrilled if I am pregnant. The only thing is, I need to see a doctor as quickly as possible. Today would be ideal. You, see, my friend and I are planning to go off for a while."

"How romantic," Brenda interjected. "I can't tell you how much Charles and I long to get away from the brood for a while. Tell you what—why don't I call Dr. Ferguson's office now and see if they can fit you in? Frankly, we've spent a fortune there in the last few years, and the doc definitely owes me a favor or two at this point."

"Oh, Brenda, would you?"

"Of course. Only, what do you want me to tell him about your—er—situation?"

Sarah bit her lip. "Why don't you tell him I'm already married, and that I'm leaving on a vacation with my husband tomorrow?"

"Sure, if that's what you want, Sarah. But if you think Dr. Ferguson would be the type to pass judgment, you're wrong. He's very forward in his thinking."

"I'm sure he is. But still, I'd prefer that he think

I'm married. Just tell his office that I'm Mrs. Jennings, okay?"

"Fine, Sarah. Look, why don't you just sit tight, and as soon as I get these hellions fed, I'll call Dr. Ferguson and get right back to you. What's your number there?"

Sarah gave Brenda the number, thanked her, and the two women hung up.

By the time Sarah had finished breakfast, the phone rang. "They want you to come in at one-thirty," Brenda told her. "Actually, Dr. Ferguson is pretty well booked up for today, but when I told him you're about to leave town, he promised to fit you in."

Sarah heaved a sigh of relief. "Brenda, I can't thank you enough."

"What are friends for? Look, Sarah, if you can get to town by noon, why don't we meet for lunch? The maid is coming in an hour, and she can watch the pack for me. We could have a great visit, and you can tell me all about this new man in your life. I could even show you where Dr. Ferguson's office is on my way home."

"Sounds wonderful, Brenda. Where do you want me to meet you?"

The two women arranged to meet at Antoine's at noon.

After breakfast, Sarah dressed in a gray sweater, a navy wool skirt and boots. With Ebbie's help, she packed Erica Davis's papers and journals in a box; then she left the house. On her way through Meridian, she stopped at the library to drop off Vincy's memoirs and Erica's papers. She also wrote the library a generous check to help pay for the organization of the local history room.

Sarah hated to part with the precious memoirs and had to restrain herself from grabbing them back from Frances Gatlin. But she promised herself that one day soon she would get to read the original version—back in the past, with her beloved Damien.

Sarah enjoyed the drive to New Orleans in the cool autumn weather. Just inside the city limits, she stopped at a five-and-dime and bought herself a cheap gold wedding band. She dropped the ring in her purse for use later on when she went to the doctor's office. Then she drove into the French Quarter and parked her car on Toulouse Street not far from Antoine's. She smiled as she approached the famous old restaurant, with its historical façade and iron lace balconies. On the corner, three negro street musicians were entertaining the tourists with banjos and tambourine. The air was laced with the tantalizing aroma of Creole cuisine, mingled with the crisp saltiness of the air.

Sarah was looking askance at the long line in front of the restaurant when Brenda rushed up to greet her, grabbing her arm and taking her straight to the front door, amid the scathing looks and mumbled criticisms of the waiting tourists. After Brenda knocked, a smiling maitre d' admitted them, greeting Mrs. Birmingham by name and promptly escorting them to a beautifully set corner table.

Sarah greatly enjoyed chatting with her old friend as the two women sipped white wine and perused the menu. Brenda was a lively, pretty woman in her late twenties. She had a cute, petite figure, a heart-shaped face and red curly hair. When Sarah had stayed with Brenda when she first arrived in Louisiana from Georgia, she had met Brenda's husband, a naturalized Englishman named Charles Birmingham. Sarah remembered thinking what a fine couple they made, Brenda's vivaciousness complementing Charles's quiet reserve. Charles was quite wealthy, his English family being the owners of the Birmingham Hotel chain that was so prominent in Europe. Already, he had established five branches of the hotel here in the United States.

The two women were served a fabulous lunch— Oysters Rockefeller, trout *amandine* and crusty French bread. Soon, Brenda broached the subject of the new man in Sarah's life. Choosing every word with great care, Sarah explained that she had met Damien in Meridian. She then described him in as general terms as possible, telling her friend that he was a writer and a very sensitive, intelligent man. When Brenda asked where they were planning to go tomorrow, Sarah was noncommittal, telling Brenda that they were planning simply to get in the car and travel east to watch the trees change color.

"Oh, how romantic," Brenda cried, stirring her *café au lait.* "I wish Charles and I could do something like that."

"Hah!" Sarah put in. "You get to go to England every summer to visit your husband's family."

"Sure. The kids and I get to stay in the country with Charles's mum, bored silly, while he and his father travel all over the continent seeing to the family hotel business."

Sarah laughed. "As the children get older, I'm sure the situation will improve for you." Saying the words, she thought of her own unborn child, the one she prayed was growing inside her.

Brenda seemed to pick up on Sarah's thoughts. Reaching across the table to touch her hand, she asked, "Sarah, how do you feel about the possibility of being pregnant?"

273

"Wonderful," Sarah replied honestly, her eyes gleaming with joy.

Brenda smiled. "I'm so glad. And this Damien—you're sure he'll want to marry you?"

Sarah nodded. "Positive."

"You know I'd love to meet him," Brenda went on. "Is there any chance the two of you could have dinner with us tonight?"

Sarah felt a prickle of unease at the back of her neck. With an effort, she forced a thin smile. "Thanks, Brenda, but I'm afraid that's impossible. You see, Damien and I will both be busy tonight—you know, getting ready for our trip and all."

Brenda winked at Sarah. "And I suppose you'll want some time alone with him to share the happy news?"

Sarah smiled with relieved pleasure. "Yes, of course."

"Oh, I'm so thrilled for you," Brenda continued gaily. Then, guiltily, she added, "And I hope I haven't given you the wrong impression about children. I know I complain a lot about my brood, but I can't tell you how much they've enriched our lives. Charles and I remark on it all the time."

"I can't wait to experience it all firsthand," Sarah replied feelingly.

"And don't worry about this afternoon," Brenda went on. "I promise you, Dr. Ferguson is a real gent."

After the meal, Brenda insisted that Sarah should follow her to the doctor's office. "Really, it's on my way home," she said. "And if you like, I'll be delighted to stay with you at the office and hold your hand."

"Don't be ridiculous," Sarah said with a laugh. "You've done plenty for me already. Just showing me the way to the office will be quite enough."

As the two women left the restaurant, Sarah promised to let Brenda know the results of her doctor's visit. She then thanked her friend for everything, and the two women parted company to go to their cars.

Sarah followed Brenda's Mercedes out of the Vieux Carre toward the west part of town. The doctor's office turned out to be in a converted Victorian mansion on the edge of the Garden District. Brenda slowed down and pointed as they passed the elegant old house; Sarah waved her friend on, then parked her car. Taking the wedding band from her purse, she slipped it on, then left her car and went inside.

Sarah had a lovely time fantasizing about her future child as she sat in the beautifully furnished waiting room with other, obviously pregnant women. She picked up the latest issue of a magazine for expectant parents and read with interest an article on fetal growth and development.

When the nurse finally called her name, Sarah found Dr. Ferguson to be every bit as nice as Brenda had promised. He was middle-aged and soft-spoken, with a very reassuring smile. His examination was thorough but gentle, and after Sarah dressed, he spoke with her in his office.

"Is your husband here?" was his first question.

Sarah felt a tiny frisson of discomfort, but her smile did not waver. "No. I'm afraid he couldn't make it this afternoon."

"Too bad. I like to speak with both husband and wife at this juncture, whenever possible." Abruptly, he broke into a grin. "Well, young lady, you should have some good new for your husband tonight. I'm almost certain you're pregnant."

Sarah's face lit with joy. Then she asked, *"Almost* certain?"

He flashed her a kindly smile. "All the physical signs are certainly there, but we'll be one hundred percent sure when the result of your pregnancy test comes back tomorrow. In the meantime, I don't see why you can't go ahead and tell your husband. Given the absence of your period and the changes I observed during your examination, I don't think there's much doubt."

Sarah was beaming. "Yes, I'll tell my husband at once."

"Now, what exactly was the date of your last period?"

Sarah told the doctor that her last period was on September 24th, and he figured her due date to be July 1st of '68. "I'll want to see you again in a month from now," he said, scribbling on a prescription pad. "In the meantime, here is the name of some vitamins I want you to start taking, assuming that the result of the test is positive. And we'll need to make an appointment with the lab for some routine blood work."

"Thanks," Sarah cut in, taking the slip of paper he extended, "but actually, I can't make any more appointments right now. You see, my husband and I are planning to move, so I won't be continuing to see you. For now, I just wanted to find out for certain whether I'm pregnant."

He looked taken aback for a moment, then smiled. "Oh, I see. In that case, it might be best if you have the rest of your tests with your new doctor. Why don't you send me his name, and I'll forward your records?"

"Of course."

Dr. Ferguson promised he'd call Sarah in the

morning with the results of her pregnancy test, and the two said good-bye. After paying the bill, Sarah left the office and headed out of the city, feeling elated. She stopped at a drugstore on the edge of town, picking up the vitamins Dr. Ferguson had prescribed. Then she continued on toward Meridian, thinking of the precious baby growing inside her. "Oh, Damien," she whispered, "it really did happen. We really did meet and love and create a new life together. Oh, my darling, I can't wait to get back to you and tell you the wonderful news."

Then Sarah sobered as she remembered the ominous presence she had sensed in the house—the voodoo tokens, the frightening voice telling her to leave.

If she did return to the past and Damien, would her precious child be safe there?

Chapter Twenty-Two

It was late afternoon by the time Sarah drove back through Meridian. She couldn't wait to get home and make her plans to go back in time again.

But as she drove past the outskirts of town toward River Road, something made her pull her car off the road in front of Madame Tu's Victorian cottage. She glanced at the lovely frame house in the gilded light of dusk. The white paint looked fresh, and the shutters were a cheery yellow. A railed gallery spanned the front; there were rockers sitting on the porch, as if in welcome, and flowering baskets spilled their lush fragrance from the eaves. The tall front windows were draped with lacy white Cape Cods; on the center of each windowsill, a yellow candle glowed.

Staring at the house, Sarah remembered the young negro man at the courthouse yesterday, and how he'd urged her to go see Madame Tu. She was doubtless a fool, she thought, but she found that something was compelling her toward the cottage. And she had long since stopped questioning forces she couldn't see or understand.

Sarah turned off the engine and got out, approaching the house. She didn't even know if the mysterious Madame Tu was at home, but her knock was promptly answered by the tall, heavyset negro woman. Today Madame wore a maize-colored shirt-waist dress and metal-rimmed glasses. A broad smile crinkled her face as she spotted Sarah on her porch.

"Hello, honey. I been expectin' you," she said.

"Have you?" Sarah asked, taken aback. Madame Tu spoke in a rather nasal, sing-songy *patois* similar to some of the Cajuns Sarah had heard in town. "I'm Sarah Jennings."

"Yes, I know," Madame Tu replied. "Come on in, honey."

Entering the cottage, Sarah was entranced. The parlor and dining room were filled with beautiful Victorian furniture in the style of Duncan Phyfe. Thick pastel carpets dotted with dusky pink roses covered the polished wooden floors. The interior of the house was dark, but candles gleamed everywhere amid the shining mahogany, and a musky sweetness like incense filled the air.

Madame Tu led Sarah straight into the dining room, where she showed her guest to a chair. "I get tea," she said.

Seated at the carved mahogany table, Sarah inhaled the comforting smells of hot scented wax and furniture oil. She glanced about at the handsome sideboard and corner cabinets, studying Madame's lovely hand-painted dishes. Near the archway, on a small, carved table was laid an large, opened Bible;

above it was a portrait of Jesus.

There was something so homey and comforting about this cottage, Sarah mused. A feeling of serenity washed over her.

Within minutes, Madame returned with a tray bearing a china teapot and two cups. To Sarah's surprise, the negro woman didn't attempt to read the tea leaves or whip out a crystal ball. Handing Sarah her tea, she simply asked, "What troubling you, honey?"

Sarah took a sip of the strong, hot brew. She stared at Madame's face and saw wisdom and experience reflected in her weathered features and dark, soulful eyes. "First, would you mind explaining to me how you knew who I am and that I was coming to see you?"

Madame shrugged. "Everybody here know who you is."

"But did the janitor at the courthouse tell you I was coming?

Madame shook her head. "No one tell me. I see the signs in the moon and the stars."

Sarah hesitated a moment. The woman's last words sounded bizarre, albeit her mannerisms and voice came across as lucid enough. "I see," she murmured frowningly, although she didn't understand at all.

Madame reached out and briefly touched the cheap gold ring that was still on Sarah's finger. "You married, honey?"

"No," Sarah answered awkwardly, quickly pulling her hand away and placing it in her lap.

"You expecting a child?" Madame asked.

The breath left Sarah's body in a sudden whoosh at the woman's uncanny insight. "Yes. How did you—"

"You go to the haunted house, up by the river, *n'est-ce pas?*" Madame went on with a slight, knowing smile. "You go there many times, no?"

"How can you know these things?" Sarah asked incredulously.

"Madame know," she replied. "Madame know you deeply troubled. You tell Madame everyt'ing. Okay?"

Staring into Madame's intelligent, chocolate-brown eyes, Sarah wasn't sure just why she trusted this woman, but she did. Of course, some people might dismiss Madame's insights as shrewd guesses, yet somehow Sarah knew that Madame's perceptions went far beyond that. She realized that she'd found a kindred spirit.

Sarah took a deep breath and spilled out everything to Madame Tu—how Brian had died; how she had inherited Erica Davis's estate; how she had come to Louisiana; how she had gone back in time and had fallen in love with a man who lived in the year 1871. Madame listened without batting an eyelash as Sarah told of how she'd walked out the front door of the house and had ended up back in the present, of how she'd gone back to the past a second time, and of how she'd just learned that she carried the child of a man who lived in another century. She also spoke of the dark presence that didn't want her to stay in the past. She told of the black candles and the voodoo tokens she'd found in her room and of the ominous voice she'd heard urging her to leave.

"I want to go back in time again," Sarah finished, "but I just don't know if I—or my child—will be safe there." Eyeing Madame guardedly, she added, "Do you believe me?"

"I do," Madame answered without hesitation.

"But why?"

Madame shrugged. "I understand these t'ings of the spirit."

"Do you have any idea who might want to do me harm?"

Madame frowned thoughtfully as she sipped her tea. "It not your man—that I know. Who else with you in that house?"

Sarah told Madame about everyone else she'd known at Belle Fontaine—Olympia, Baptista and the town girls, Hattie and Jane. She explained why she felt both Olympia and Baptista had cause to feel jealous of her.

"It Baptista," Madame said when Sarah had finished.

Sarah's fingers clutched the tabletop. "Are you sure? Are you certain she's the one who's been trying to scare me away?"

Madame nodded. "She the one. You try to steal her man, so now she try to voodoo you, no?"

Sarah frowned. "Well, I suppose that makes sense. But are you certain it couldn't be Damien's aunt?"

Madame Tu shook her head. "It a black person. The voodoo and the white person—dey not mix." Madame inclined her head slightly. "You going back there again, honey?"

Sarah nodded. "Yes. I want to be with Damien. I want to share the child with him." She leaned forward and spoke intently. "But aside from the danger I told you about, there's another major stumbling block. Even if I can manage to go back in the past again, I'm sure that as soon as I leave the house, I'll return to the present once more."

Madame nodded matter-of-factly. "You not grounded."

Sarah snapped her fingers, her eyes glowing with realization. "Yes, that's it exactly. I'm not grounded, and my only safety in the past is within the walls of the house. But unfortunately, whatever it is that wants to hurt me is also right there in the house with me."

Madame's brow was now deeply puckered. "When you going back again, child?"

"As soon as possible."

"Then you wait here."

As Sarah watched in puzzlement, Madame left again. A moment later, she returned with a small wooden chest. She opened it and pulled out two small red flannel bags tied with black cord. A pungent odor assaulted Sarah's senses, and she instinctively recoiled.

"Those are *gris-gris*, aren't they?" she asked Madame suspiciously, staring wide-eyed at the frightful objects.

"How you know about the *gris-gris?*" Madame asked.

"Baptista told me what they're called when we found the first token in my room."

Madame nodded smugly, wagging her index finger at Sarah. "She the one, I tell you." She extended the bags toward Sarah. "Now you take dese, child."

Sarah was horrified, waving Madame off. "But aren't those used to put curses on people?"

"Not dese," Madame said. Even as Sarah tried to protest again, she took the girl's hand and pressed two of the red bags and a small bundle of feathers into her palm. "Dese good *gris-gris*. You take dese. You put them in your room in that house. They keep the voodoo away."

Sarah was still frowning as she stared down at the objects. "You mean they combat the bad *gris-gris?*"

"Oui. You take these with you, child, when you go back into the past again. They protect you and the child."

At last Sarah nodded, setting the tokens down next to her car keys. Then she cast the negro woman an anguished look. "Madame, how can I manage to stay back in the past this time?"

Madame sat down. "You in love with that man, child?"

Sarah nodded vehemently. "Oh, yes."

Madame shook her head. "Then you got to believe."

Sarah considered this a moment. "When I went back last time, I took my cat with me. He's still back there in the past, but he can come and go from the house without returning to the present."

"The animal believe," Madame said simply. "That the nature of the cat."

"But how can I make my own belief stronger?"

Madame shook her head sadly. "That you got to find for yourself, child."

Sarah thanked Madame and talked her into accepting a ten dollar bill for her time and advice. She left the cottage with the good tokens in her purse and decided she would take the charms back with her into the past, along with the bottle of vitamins. The charms surely couldn't hurt, she rationalized. And if the person tormenting her in the past saw them in her room, he might even be warned off and cease his insidious attempts to frighten her.

She didn't know why, but after talking with Madame Tu, Sarah felt strangely at peace.

The next morning, bright and early, the phone rang. After Sarah picked it up and mouthed a sleepy hello, Dr. Ferguson's cheerful voice boomed forth on the other end.

At once Sarah became completely alert. "So what's the verdict?" she asked, knowing full-well from his tone of voice that the news would be good.

"Congratulations, Mrs. Jennings," he said brightly. "It's official now. You're definitely pregnant."

Sarah whooped for joy, then thanked the doctor for calling. "Don't forget to send me your new address," he added, "so I can forward your records."

Sarah was tempted to reply, Send my records to Belle Fontaine Plantation, care of the year 1871.

Sarah made preparation to leave again. After calling Brenda to tell her the good news, she wrote a note for Ebbie, telling the maid that she was leaving on an extended trip and might not return for several months. She then phoned Jefferson Baldwin and told him much the same story. He informed her that the will still hadn't gotten through probate and added that they could settle everything when she returned.

Finally, Sarah sat down and wrote her parents, telling them not to worry if they didn't hear from her for some time, since she was going with Brenda Birmingham and her family to Europe for the winter. Sarah hated telling the lie, but she knew that at this point telling her parents the truth would serve only to frighten them, causing them untold anguish and grief.

Chapter Twenty-Three

She was back.

This time, Sarah's return to the past came much more readily. Sitting in the abandoned house in her old-fashioned dress, with the vitamins and Madame Tu's good *gris-gris* stuffed in her pockets, she was able to get into meditation quite easily. As she chanted her mantra and drifted away from all earthly care, her last conscious thought was of how Madame Tu had told her simply to "believe." She realized that every day now, her critical belief was growing stronger.

Moments later, she awakened back in the past in Damien's nineteenth-century parlor. She looked around at the familiar furnishings and drapes, watching the fire snap in the grate and inhaling its homey cedar scent. A wondrous smile lit her face that she'd truly made it back again.

And this time, to her relief, she was greeted not by

Olympia but by Casper. The cat bounded into the room, meowed at her then jumped into her lap. Sarah laughed in joy, petting him. Casper purred and stared up at her with his magnificent golden eyes. "So, did you miss me, boy?" she asked. "I thought you had permanently adopted Olympia and forgotten all about me."

At her words, the cat purred all the more and rubbed his face against her hand. "What's your secret, Casper? Why is it you can come and go in the past, but I can't?"

Casper's inscrutable eyes offered no answer.

Hearing a noise coming from the dining room, Sarah decided she'd best get out of the parlor quickly, before Olympia or Baptista discovered her here. Putting Casper down, she stood, smoothed down her heavy skirts and inched toward the archway. She could see Olympia arranging flowers at the dining room table; her back was to Sarah. Sarah tiptoed out into the hallway, then made a dash for the stairs.

Upstairs in her room, she hid the *gris-gris* and her bottle of vitamins at the back of a dresser drawer. She adjusted her coiffure, then decided it was time to go find Damien.

She went downstairs and rapped on his office door. A second later, his preoccupied voice called out, "Come in." Sarah's heart welled with joyous anticipation.

She slipped inside the office, closing the door behind her. Damien was at his desk, writing away. Even though he sat with his back to her, the very sight of him thrilled her senses. His dark wavy hair caught the bright light of the sun, and his shoulders were beautifully broad and straight, the muscles rippling as he worked.

287

"Damien?" she whispered.

Hearing her voice, Damien lurched to his feet and whirled to face her. His handsome features twisted in a mixture of surprise and anger. "Sarah! Thank God you're back! I've nearly lost my mind worrying about you."

In two strides, he was across the room, hauling her into his arms. His kiss was passionate, filled with pent-up emotion. Sarah kissed him back with equal fervor, glorying in the feel of his strong arms about her and the taste of his warm lips on hers, after their seemingly endless separation.

"Oh, Damien!" she cried, kissing his chin, his neck, and inhaling his exciting scent. "I'm so glad to be back."

He drew back, clutching her shoulders with trembling fingers. "Sarah, where have you been? My God, when I saw you disappear—"

"You saw me?"

"Yes. You walked out the front door—and then you were gone." He shook his head wonderingly. "It was incredible, the way you simply vanished. It was just as you said it would be."

"Did you doubt it?"

He clutched her close, pressing his lips to her temple. "I prayed it wouldn't be true, love," he said in a choked voice.

"I know." She drew a deep, shuddering breath. "I thought I heard you calling me—I mean, when I left."

Damien pulled back and regarded her sternly. "You still haven't answered my question. Where have you been?"

"Didn't you find my note?"

"Yes. But your letter didn't really tell me much, and you've been gone so very long."

"I know," she said, flashing him a quick, apologetic smile. "But I felt I had to return to the present. I had to find answers—answers that just don't exist here."

"So you just left? Sarah, you didn't even discuss it with me."

"I knew what you would say if I did," she confessed in a small voice, lowering her eyes.

Damien glowered at her for a long moment, then sighed, drawing her into his arms again, tucking her head beneath his chin and pressing his lips against her fragrant hair. "Ah, what the hell. I love you so much, I can't stay angry at you. I'm just so damned relieved that you're back. Now you must promise me that you'll never leave again."

She pulled away and bit her lip. "I'll try not to leave again, Damien. But don't you even want to know what I found out back in the present?"

At last, he smiled, brushing a strand of golden hair from her brow. "What did you find out, darling?"

Knowing that he had forgiven her, she found her revelations pouring forth in a rush. "I found your memoirs of Vincy. They were published by a New Orleans publisher. At the end, you said, 'I have found her now and she has taken away all my pain.'"

"My God," he gasped, his features incredulous.

Then Sarah threw her arms around his neck and finished triumphantly, "Oh, Damien, I love you—and we're going to have a baby!"

Now a look of stark joy flashed into Damien's eyes. He held Sarah at arm's length and looked her over as if she were a fragile china doll. "A child? Are you sure, Sarah?"

She nodded ecstatically. "In my century, we have what's known as a pregnancy test. There's no doubt,

Damien. Our child will be born next summer."

"Oh, darling. A child. Just think—an affirmation of our love—of life itself."

"I know. It's proof that what we have really does exist."

"Did you ever doubt it?" he asked.

"Not in my heart," she whispered back.

For a moment they clung together, kissing hungrily, sharing their bliss. Then Damien whispered tenderly, "We'll have to marry now, you know."

She glanced at him uncertainly. "Are you sure that's what you want? As far as I know, I still can't exist here beyond the house—"

He pressed his fingers to her mouth. "You know that never mattered to me, Sarah. What we have is enough."

At his loving words, Sarah's eyes stung with sudden tears. For in reality, they both had to know that what they had could never be enough, especially not now that there was a child to consider. Yet as always, Damien was being so sweet; he seemed willing to make any sacrifice to keep them together.

Damien drew back and stared down into her eyes, his own eyes gleaming with intense emotion. "Sarah, will you marry me?"

Sarah smiled, then a frown drifted in as other practical considerations flitted to mind. "What about your aunt and Baptista? How did they react to my departure? And how do you think your aunt will feel about our marrying?"

Damien sighed. "As you suggested in your note, I simply told my aunt and Baptista that your friend in New Orleans needed you again. As for how Aunt Olympia will feel about our marriage, I'm really not sure, but it is not her place to protest."

"But, don't you think we should—"

Her words were cut short as Damien clutched her close and pressed his lips against her temple. "Just think, we could marry out back in the garden. Didn't you say you're safe there?"

"Yes, but—"

"Say you'll marry me, Sarah. Say it, please."

Sarah found she could no longer resist him. "Oh, yes, Damien," she cried, clinging to him. "Yes!"

But inwardly, she remained troubled.

"Isn't it wonderful that Sarah has returned, Aunt Olympia?"

It was several hours later, and Damien, Sarah and Olympia were gathered in the dining room for the noon meal. In the background, Baptista was quietly making her rounds, serving them a main course of crawfish *étouffée*, with stewed lima beans and "dirty" rice on the side. As the maid moved about in her dark dress and white apron, she cast occasional, resentful glances toward Sarah.

Observing the negress, Sarah sighed. Her reception by Olympia had been no friendlier, and she inwardly winced as she anticipated the spinster's response to Damien's question. However, Olympia merely shot Sarah a cool glance as she replied to Damien in a wooden tone, "Indeed."

Damien took a sip of his white wine and announced evenly, "Aunt, Sarah and I are planning to wed."

At Damien's abrupt announcement, Sarah's hand flew to her mouth, while Olympia's teacup clattered into its saucer. Baptista, meanwhile, dumped her serving tray onto the table, shot Sarah a searing look and left the room.

Sarah felt as if the floor had just been pulled from beneath her. She took a ragged breath to steady herself and dared to glance at Olympia, who appeared flabbergasted.

"Damien, surely you jest," Olympia said at last.

A dangerous glint flickered across Damien's dark eyes. "Why would I jest, Aunt?"

"Well . . ." Obviously flustered, she sputtered, "You hardly know this young woman."

Damien addressed his aunt in a cold, firm voice. "Sarah and I have had ample opportunity to become acquainted over the past few weeks, and we're both of an age to know our minds on the subject. Indeed, the wedding will be performed just as soon as I can make the arrangements."

"I see." Recovering some of her composure, Olympia flashed a brittle smile first at Damien, then at Sarah. "Well, congratulations to you both, then."

As Sarah and Damien muttered "Thank you," in unison, Olympia added to Damien, "I presume you'll be speaking with Father André?"

"Nay," he replied. "Sarah and I shall not be marrying in the Church."

Olympia's eyes grew enormous as she automatically crossed herself. "Not marrying in the Church! But, Damien, we're Catholic! How can you even think—"

"Sarah is not Catholic, Aunt," Damien cut in evenly. "And, as you're aware, I've felt alienated from the Church for some time now." He paused to smile at Sarah. "Sarah and I prefer to have a small service in the courtyard. The wedding will be performed just as soon as I can find a parson who's willing to come out and marry us."

"Well, I never!" Olympia gasped.

Sarah winced inwardly at Olympia's indignant response. She couldn't really blame Damien's aunt for being outraged that he would thumb his nose at his religious upbringing this way. And since Olympia obviously disapproved of Damien's choosing her as his bride, his refusal to have a Catholic wedding only added more tension to an already charged situation.

"Miss Fontaine," she said tactfully, "I would be delighted to marry Damien again in the Catholic Church—later on. But for now, we really don't want to wait."

"I hope you both realize that you'll be living in sin until you're wed by a priest," Olympia put in heatedly.

At once Damien shot to his feet, his eyes gleaming with anger. His hands gripped the tabletop; his knuckles were white, and his voice, when he spoke, brooked no challenge. "Aunt, that is quite enough. I love Sarah and she is to become my wife—in the eyes of the law as well as in the eyes of God. If you have any objections, then perhaps I should arrange for accommodations for you elsewhere, where my presence and my bride's won't be such a trial for you."

"Damien!" Sarah cried, appalled that he would threaten his aunt this way.

Yet Damien merely shot Sarah a quelling glance, then turned back to his aunt, who was now trembling in mortification. "Well, Aunt? I vow to you that I'll see you never lack for anything, but I'll not have you sit in my house and talk ill of my future bride. So the choice is yours—either give us your blessing, or I'll be forced to arrange for your lodging elsewhere."

For a long moment, Olympia struggled visibly. Finally, in a low, choked voice, she said, "You have my blessing, Damien."

Then, without glancing at either of them, Olympia tossed down her napkin, lurched to her feet and fled the room.

The instant Olympia was out of earshot, Sarah flashed Damien a beseeching look. "Damien, don't you think you were being a bit harsh with your aunt?"

He shook his head adamantly as he walked over to her side. "No, Sarah. She must accept our marriage."

"I know. But you did tell her so abruptly, and she seems very upset about everything."

"I realize that, but there's really no time to break the news to her gently. Besides, Aunt Olympia has been far too protective of me for too long."

"You wouldn't honestly cast her out?" Sarah asked worriedly.

He sighed, reaching down to cup her chin with his hand. "I will if she refuses to accept you as my wife." Watching her features blanch, he leaned over and kissed her quickly and possessively. "Don't worry, Sarah. I'd buy Aunt Olympia a house in town and establish a generous account in her name. She has friends in Meridian, and I'm sure she would be just fine."

"But, still, to cast out your own aunt—"

"Hopefully, it will never come to that," Damien said. He forced a smile. "Anyway, when she finds out about the child, she'll be so delighted that she'll forget all about her doubts."

"Well, let's not tell her about the child right away," Sarah put in ruefully. "I think we've provided the poor woman with enough shocks for one day."

"Indeed," he concurred with a laugh. "Well, my pet, I'm off to town to arrange for a marriage license and find us a parson. While I'm gone, why not start working on your wedding gown? The white eyelet I bought you would suit nicely, don't you think?" Winking at her, he added, "Do hasten, love, since I promise you, I'll be giving you little time to do the sewing."

"All right then, Damien," Sarah replied with a smile.

He kissed her again, and then he was gone. A moment later, Baptista came into the room with a tray and began sullenly gathering up the dishes. Feeling the force of the negro woman's antagonism, Sarah decided it would be best to leave. But as she headed for the archway, she was shocked to watch Olympia walk in briskly, carrying a sewing basket.

"Well, Sarah," she said with crisp self-possession, "since Damien wants to wed you so quickly, don't you think we'd best start on your gown? I've a pattern or two here that might suffice—that is, if you'd like to fetch down the fabric Damien bought you recently?"

"Of course. How kind of you," Sarah said with a smile.

Olympia didn't return Sarah's smile. But she was polite, even helpful, as the two women spent their afternoon cutting out the simple, straight-lined gown, basting the seams and fitting the frock to Sarah.

At dinner, Damien announced to Sarah and his aunt, "I've arranged for the license, and I've found a minister to marry us two days hence—a Reverend Turner of the Cumberland Presbyterian Church. He recently arrived here from Tennessee, and he's establishing a circuit in the area."

The announcement was received with a smile by Sarah, a stoic nod from Olympia. "Well then, Sarah," Olympia said, "we will have to hurry with our sewing now, won't we?"

Sarah smiled at Olympia, but inwardly she wished she could do something to diminish the strong tension in the room.

That evening, Damien and Sarah met in the salon. He lit a fire in the grate to ward off the chill in the room. From the distant downstairs, they could hear Olympia's haunting piano music, tonight Foster's "Come Where My Love Lies Dreaming."

With only the moonlight and the flicker of the fire to guide them, they danced among Vincy's paintings. It was their own private celebration of their reunion and their coming child. Damien's gaze was filled with a riveting intensity as he led Sarah about; she curled her arms about his neck and stared up at him with adoring eyes.

"I can't believe we're actually going to have a child," he said joyously.

"We are," she replied ecstatically. "Do you want a boy or a girl?"

"I don't care," he said. A shadow crossed his eyes as he added, "As long as the child is healthy."

Sarah hugged Damien close, tears stinging her eyes as she thought of the tiny son he had buried so many years ago. "I'm sure our child will be fine," she said, her voice rapt with hope.

"I do hope so, darling." He grinned down at her.

"Actually, I think a girl might be nice. A girl who looks like you."

"Or a boy who looks like you," she added.

Later, they ended up on their window seat in each other's arms, kissing hungrily. "Damien, I missed you so much," she said breathlessly. "Take me to your bed, please, darling."

He drew back and stared down at her searchingly. "Let's wait till our wedding night, dearest. Let's hold out until neither of us can stand it."

"But I can't stand it now."

"Good," he whispered tenderly, the flames of the fire dancing in his dark eyes. "Then I'll not have to worry about you leaving me before the wedding can be performed."

Feeling a stab of guilt, Sarah hugged him quickly and tightly. "Damien, I'm not going to leave you."

He drew back, taking her face in his hands. "Not ever?" he asked poignantly.

She sensed the tension behind his words. "I can't promise I won't ever go, because there are still too many things I don't understand. But I can promise you this—I'll not go away again without discussing it with you first."

He stroked her soft cheek and sighed. "Then I suppose I must settle for what you're willing to give," he said resignedly.

Sarah snuggled close to him, wishing she could reassure him more.

After a moment, Damien whispered, "Tell me more of your time away from me, my love."

She drew back and stared up into his eyes. "What do you want to know?"

"Everything."

She paused to gather her thoughts. With a sheepish frown, she began, "Well, when I first got back, Bill Bartley was there, waiting for me."

Damien's expression grew thunderous. "Bill Bartley? You mean your former fiancé? How dare he—"

She touched his arm. "Damien, it was all right. You see, I broke up with Bill rather abruptly back in Georgia, and I know he came to see me out of genuine concern."

"And that was all?" He laughed cynically. "Forgive me, Sarah, but I find that rather hard to believe."

"All right, it wasn't all," she admitted. "Actually, Bill came to see me because he wanted me back." Watching Damien's eyes glitter dangerously, she held up a hand and continued quickly, "But in a way I'm really glad he came, because I was able to convince him—for once and for all—that it's really over between us."

"Truly?" Damien still appeared skeptical.

"Yes, truly."

"Did the cad try to force himself on you?" Damien asked darkly.

Sarah laughed. "No, Damien. You know, in some ways you really are a man of your century." As he continued to glower at her, she added, "Don't worry, Bill didn't try anything. He's not the type who would."

Damien nodded in satisfaction. "Good. Just so he understands that he's no part of your life any more."

"He does."

They drifted into a comfortable silence, holding each other close, awash in the light of their star. Then, to Sarah's confusion, Damien got up and walked off toward the paintings, his hands clenched behind him. He paused for a long moment before

Vincy's self-portrait, staring at it intently.

"Tell more of your time away from me," he said at last, his words muffled and tense.

Sarah sensed he was avoiding the real issue troubling him. "What exactly is it you want me to tell you?"

He turned to her, his jaw tight. In a hoarse voice, he said, "This morning, you mentioned that you found my memoirs of Vincy."

She nodded. "Yes, I did find a copy of the memoirs at the parish library in Meridian."

He strode forward. "They were published?" he asked tersely.

"Yes—five years from now."

He shook his head. "I find that incredible."

"But it's true. Don't you believe me?"

He moved closer, the moonlight wafting over his tall, striking figure and illuminating the intense gleam in his eyes. "Did you read the memoirs, Sarah?"

She nodded.

He turned his back on her. "Then you know everything now?"

Sarah got up and walked to his side, placing her hand on his rigid shoulder. "I think I understand you now." Feeling his muscles tighten even more, she continued, "Damien, before we marry, don't you think we should discuss—well, things?"

He turned to her, his eyes gleaming with turbulent emotion. "You're talking about Vincy and Lucy."

"Yes."

"That's impossible," he said gruffly.

"But don't you understand that eventually the whole world will know about . . . ?" Watching him wince, she bit her lip and decided to try a new tack.

"Tell me of how you've written the memoirs."

He lifted an eyebrow. "I beg your pardon?"

"The memoirs are in diary form, are they not? I found that aspect so interesting as I read them. There was such a sense of immediacy about them. Did you keep a diary for the entire period you wrote about?"

He hesitated a moment, then nodded. "For years, I kept a journal—albeit, a rather sketchy one. Actually, my work since the war has largely been expanding and polishing the entries I made previously. I've been able to supply a great deal of detail, since I do remember everything so clearly." He drew a hand through his hair and finished hoarsely, "But there are some parts that I just can't face completing."

She watched his shoulders sag, and her heart ached for him then. She realized that Damien's grief was ever-present, always ready to spill back to the surface, even in his fleeting moments of joy. Yet only sharing could exorcise his demons, she knew. And if he couldn't even write about his own, deepest anguish, however would he be able to share his feelings with her?

Quietly, she asked, "The parts you can't finish— you're talking about the entries regarding Lucy and the part where Vincy died?"

He stared at her, his gaze filled with despair. He started to speak, but no words came forth.

Sarah quickly took his hand, squeezing it reassuringly. "I'm not saying these things to cause you pain. I'm saying these things because I realized something when I went back. Vincy and Lucy never intended for you to suffer this way."

He gripped her fiercely by the shoulders. "How can you know what they wanted?"

"I just know—I mean, after reading—"

Something seemed to break in him then, as he cut in passionately, "Do you realize that I never loved her?"

"Her? You mean Lucy?"

"Yes!"

"Damien, that wasn't your fault."

Yet he seemed not to hear her as he went on in an agonized voice, "Do you realize that Vincy loved her, and she loved him, and I never even realized . . ."

His voice broke then, and his hands fell to his sides. Sarah threw her arms around him, holding his body close. Yet, once more, he was rigid in her embrace. She could literally feel him withdrawing from her, could sense him internalizing his pain.

"Damien, no, don't blame yourself this way," she pleaded. "It's the last thing that either of them would have wanted for you. Why, in the memoirs you said in your own words that you found a woman who took away all your pain." She drew back and looked up at him beseechingly. "Please, let that woman be me. You must learn to talk about your grief. You must learn to let Vincy go."

"I can't, Sarah," he replied in a choked voice, breaking away from her. "Oh, God, it should have been me that day so long ago."

Then he was gone, leaving Sarah bereft among the cold shadows.

Sarah had a hard time getting to sleep that night. The wind was howling outside her window, and she hungered for Damien's warmth. She didn't know if their discussion of the memoirs had helped him or had made things much worse. In a way, he'd come out of himself more tonight than he ever had before, but afterward he'd only retreated further into his own grief and despair.

Would her love ever bring him true healing?

When at last Sarah drifted into a restless sleep, she heard the prophetic words again, for the first time in many weeks: *Elissa . . . The three gifts . . . The answer is Elissa. . . .*

Damien, too, had trouble sleeping that night. Part of him hungered to go to Sarah, to take her in his arms and make love to her, especially after their wrenching scene in the salon. Yet he knew he was too locked up in his own grief tonight to offer her much comfort. Besides, as he had already told her, he wanted to wait, to make their wedding night very special.

Thank God he had her back! His days apart from her had been hell, and he had been so very relieved and happy when she had at last returned. And now they were to have a child together. It was a miracle, indeed.

Yet, even though Sarah's return had thrilled him, the discoveries she had made back in the twentieth century had opened an old wound. To think that she had actually found Vincy's memoirs and had even read them! It all seemed to defy comprehension. To think that one day, the entire world might read of his private despair and shame, of aspects of his life that he had long held sacred.

He thought of the words Sarah had quoted to him, the words he himself had presumably written: "I have found her now and she has taken away all my pain." Would he, indeed, write those words one day? Would he at last know true freedom from the agonizing guilt he had carried for so long? Would Sarah be the one to help him let go of his pain, of the past? Was he capable of doing so? Did he even want to?

Ah, his feelings were in turmoil. Yet through it all, one truth loomed foremost. He wanted nothing more than to love Sarah and their coming child.

Perhaps the rest of the answers would come in time.

Chapter Twenty-Four

The next day, Sarah saw little of Damien. Since the minister was coming the following afternoon to perform the wedding, Sarah and Olympia worked all day and well into the evening finishing Sarah's gown. Most of the work was done in Olympia's small sewing room adjoining her bedroom. Sarah found Olympia's Elias Howe sewing machine crude compared with the machines she was used to in the twentieth century, but at least the device speeded up what would have been an interminable task of sewing her dress by hand.

While Olympia tried her best to act cool and reserved around Sarah, she was not totally immune to the excitement of the coming wedding. Sarah noted an occasional, grudging smile pulling at Olympia's tight mouth as the two women worked with the lovely fabric and trim. Nor could Olympia totally resist the sense of camaraderie building between her and Sarah as they worked so closely together. Sarah commiserated with Olympia when the spinster pricked the same finger twice while putting in button holes, and they both laughed when Sarah put in a seam backwards.

It was almost midnight by the time the two women finished. When the last stitch was put in the hem and Sarah donned the gown for a final fitting, Olympia stood back and studied the young woman critically. The gown was quite simple, in the fashionable Empire style; it had a modest, high neck and long sleeves with lacy cuffs. Tiny seed pearls added an elegant touch to the neck and cuffs. A wide blue ribbon was tied beneath the bodice; from there the full skirt fell to the floor in graceful folds.

"Ah, Sarah, you do make a beautiful bride," Olympia said.

Sarah beamed back at Olympia, recognizing the words as a small breakthrough. "Thank you. And I just want you to know that I understand your concerns about Damien."

Abruptly, a mask closed over Olympia's features. "Do you?"

"Yes, I do. And I want you to know that I'll do everything in my power to make your nephew happy."

Olympia turned away and began gathering up scraps on the sewing table. "I'm sure you will," she muttered.

Just then, Baptista swept into the tiny room; she carried a tray with a steaming teapot and two cups. Not even glancing at Sarah, she said to Olympia, "Madame, I thought you might like some tea before retiring."

Olympia turned to Baptista, smiling. "Indeed, yes. Just set the tray on the sewing table, if you will."

As the negress set the tray down, Olympia added, "Doesn't Sarah look lovely?"

Baptista turned to stare at Sarah with scarcely veiled hostility. "*Oui*, madame," she said stiffly, turning and leaving the room.

Once Baptista was out of earshot, Sarah sighed. "What is her problem?" she asked Olympia. "She looks at me as if she wishes I would drop dead."

"Oh, I would not take Baptista's sulkiness too seriously, my dear," Olympia responded smoothly. "Like me, she's fiercely protective of Damien."

And she used to be his mistress, didn't she? Sarah was tempted to ask. But she didn't, of course, not wanting to risk letting anything threaten the tenuous rapport she'd managed to reestablish with Olympia.

"Tea, my dear?" Olympia asked.

Sarah forced a smile. "Of course. But I think I'll change out of my dress first. I don't want to risk soiling it before tomorrow."

Later, Sarah wandered into the salon. To her surprise, she found Damien there waiting for her, seated at their window seat.

Sarah hurried over to join him. Their eyes locked, her gaze filled with love and uncertainty, his filled with tenderness and anguish. She leaned over to kiss him, and he groaned and pulled her down into his lap, taking her lips ravenously, plunging his tongue deeply into her mouth. Sarah whimpered and kissed him back, thrilled by the potency of his need. It was as if the distance between them last night had miraculously evaporated.

At last Sarah pulled away to catch her breath, staring up at him in delight. His eyes were so dark and sexy, smoldering with intensity, and she adored him for waiting for her, for wanting her so much. "I'm surprised you're still up this late," she murmured. "Have you been waiting long?"

He smiled. "I'll wait forever for a good-night kiss from you, my lady. Tell me, is the wedding gown ready?"

She nodded. "Everything is in readiness for tomorrow. And I think your aunt is warming up a bit." I just wish I could say the same for Baptista, she added to herself ruefully.

"Good," Damien said, his eyes gleaming with pleasure. "I knew Aunt Olympia would come around."

Sarah bit her lip, then said, "Damien, about last night—what we discussed. I hope I didn't—"

"Shhh," he cut in soothingly. "I'm the one who must apologize for my abruptness with you. Don't give it another thought, darling."

"But when will we talk? I mean, *really* talk."

His hand clutched hers, and he spoke earnestly. "Sarah, I have to be ready. What happened to you back in the present, when you found and read the memoirs—it was just too soon for me. Please, don't try to force things that aren't meant to be as yet."

She sighed. "All right then, Damien."

Abruptly, he smiled, as if quite relieved to have put the matter aside. "Now, kiss me again, you captivating creature."

Damien hooked his arm around her neck and captured her lips hungrily, his kiss a promise of the passion to come between them. Arousal consumed Sarah with hot, hurtful intensity. As Damien flicked his fingertips tormentingly over her painfully tautened nipples, she said breathlessly, "Damien, are you sure we can't—"

"Can't what, darling?"

"Oh, you know quite well what I mean. You're driving me insane!"

"Good," he said with a wicked grin. He nuzzled her neck, sending delicious chills down her spine. "Tomorrow, my love. Tomorrow."

Much later, in the middle of the night, Sarah jerked awake to a noise, sensing a presence in her bedroom. A shadow flickered at the window, and to her horror, she spotted the sinister outline of a woman stretched over the bed.

The woman's hand held an object shaped like a dagger!

Stifling a scream, Sarah cowered beneath the covers, wondering desperately what she would do. Her first thought was that she mustn't let this intruder bring harm to her unborn child. Yet she could hardly even hear her own thoughts over the fierce, terrorized pumping of her heart.

"Get out," the phantom now hissed in a low, chilling voice Sarah could not recognize. "You don't belong here! Go back where you belong!"

The words turned Sarah's blood to ice. She watched, paralyzed, as the intruder edged even closer, her dagger poised to strike.

At last Sarah reacted. She began to scream as if the house were on fire.

In an instant, her attacker fled, a white shadow streaking through the opened doorway, but Sarah continued to scream. Then another shadowy shape leapt into the room, lunging for her.

Sarah struggled briefly with her attacker. Then she heard Damien's hoarse, alarmed voice. "Sarah, don't fight me! It's me—Damien."

"Oh, Damien!" she cried, clinging to him and sobbing her relief. "Someone was trying to k-kill me! She c-came into my room with a knife and she was going to s-stab me!"

An instant later, a wavering light spilled over them, and a shocked voice murmured, "Nephew, what in God's name is going on here?"

The two jumped, turning to stare at Olympia, who stood at the portal in her robe and nightcap, a lantern in hand. She was staring, appalled, at the sight on the bed—Damien and Sarah embracing, wearing only their nightclothes.

Damien did not budge from Sarah's side. Stroking her trembling back, he informed Olympia calmly, "Aunt, someone tried to hurt Sarah."

Olympia's brows rose in shock, and she took a step into the room, glancing from Damien to Sarah. "Indeed?"

"Did you hear or see anything, Aunt?" Damien continued.

Olympia shook her head. "I was sound asleep across the hallway until a moment ago, when I heard Sarah screaming. I lit the lantern and came at once to investigate."

Damien nodded, then turned back to Sarah. "Can you identify the person who tried to hurt you?"

She shook her head convulsively. "I only know that—it was a woman and she had a dagger."

"How awful!" Olympia gasped.

Damien was silent for a moment, then he asked his aunt meaningfully, "Where's Baptista?"

"I assume she's asleep out back in the kitchen, as usual," Olympia replied.

Another tense silence descended, then a second lantern-toting figure appeared at the portal. Sarah recognized Baptista, who also wore her nightclothes. The negress was surveying the scene with expressionless brown eyes.

Baptista addressed Damien. "M'sieur Fontaine, is everything all right?"

"Someone tried to frighten Miss Sarah," he replied in a voice of controlled fury.

Baptista glanced at Sarah. "I hear her scream, so I come."

Damien stood. "You heard Miss Jennings scream all the way out back in the kitchen?" he asked suspiciously.

Baptista's dark features betrayed no hint of emotion. "*Oui*, m'sieur."

Damien stepped forward aggressively, glowering at the negress. "Baptista, are you the one who crept into Miss Jennings' room just now and tried to frighten her with a knife?"

Now Baptista's eyes flashed with fear, and she shook her head violently. "No, m'sieur."

As Damien continued to scowl fiercely at the negress, Olympia moved toward Sarah. "My dear, are you certain someone was actually in your room?" she asked in a kindly tone. "I mean, perhaps with all the excitement over the wedding tomorrow—"

"Are you implying that Sarah imagined the encounter, Aunt?" Damien demanded, turning furiously to her.

"Not at all, nephew," Olympia assured. "I just know how easy it is to become fooled in the darkness. I recollect it has happened to me more than once. I've awakened during the night, frightened and certain there was an intruder in my room. Then I would discover that it was only a curtain moving in the breeze or a bird flying across the window—"

"That was not the case here," Sarah cut in vehemently. "I've had similar experiences myself, of course. But tonight, there was definitely a real person in my room with a real dagger."

A charged silence fell in the wake of Sarah's words. Then Olympia asked soberly, "Sarah, do you really believe that someone in this house would want to do you harm?"

"I'm not sure," Sarah answered honestly, her chin coming up.

"Well, it's obvious that we won't be solving this mystery tonight," Damien put in distractedly, running a hand through his hair. "Aunt Olympia and Baptista, why don't you go on back to bed. It'll be light in a few hours, and in the meantime—" his gaze rested meaningfully on Baptista "—I'll be outside in the hallway every minute, guarding Sarah's room with my pistol."

Baptista received Damien's words in stoic silence, while Olympia gasped sharply. "Why, Damien, don't you think you're overracting here?"

"Not at all, Aunt," he replied evenly. "I intend to see to it that nothing happens to my bride."

Shaking her head and muttering under her breath, Olympia left the room. Baptista blinked at them sullenly, then followed suit.

As soon as the two women were out of earshot, Damien hurried back to the bed, taking Sarah in his arms. "Poor darling," he murmured tenderly, stroking her hair and kissing her temple.

"I was so frightened, Damien," she said clinging to his strength and inhaling his soothing scent. "What if whoever it was—had hurt our child?"

"Oh, Sarah." Damien groaned and drew her closer, kissing her cheek, the corner of her mouth. "Darling, I'll never let anyone hurt you or our child."

311

She pulled away and frowned. "Who do you think it was?"

He released her, stood and began to pace, his expression grim. "I fear it was Baptista," he said at last.

"Was she your mistress?" Sarah asked quietly.

He turned to her with an anguished nod. "But only before you came." Returning to her side, he took her hand and continued earnestly, "Please don't hate me for it, Sarah. I suppose I took what comfort I could where I could find it."

Sarah squeezed his hand and gazed up at him with love. "I would never hate you for it."

He gathered her close, kissing her forehead. "After you came here, Baptista came to me and offered herself that night. But I sent her away, and I haven't been with her since. You see, from the moment I first laid eyes on you, Sarah, I knew you were someone very special. And from that very moment, my dearest dream was that we would find what we now have."

She hugged him fiercely. "So you think Baptista did what she did tonight out of jealousy?"

"It's quite possible," he acknowledged.

"There's more," she added quietly.

"What?" he asked tensely. "Tell me."

Sarah told Damien of the ominous voice she had heard several times before and of the voodoo charms she had found in her room. He listened, his expression one of alarm and deep concern. "Sarah, why didn't you tell me of these things before?" he demanded. "To think that you were in grave danger all this time!"

"But I didn't believe I was truly in danger, Damien," she explained. "I dismissed the voodoo tokens as insidious mischief, and as for the voice, I wasn't completely sure whether I heard it or whether it was part of a nightmare. You see, ever since I lost Brian, I've had troubled dreams. Anyway, while I was back in the present this last time, I met a woman who knows of these things—Madame Tu. She convinced me that whoever was tormenting me with the voodoo charms had a much more harmful motive in mind."

"Indeed!" Damien exclaimed. He got to his feet and began to pace again. "That does it," he said with a furious gesture. "Baptista goes, first thing in the morning."

Sarah sighed. "But what if she isn't the culprit?"

He blinked at her incredulously. "Who else could it be?"

She bit her lip. "There's your aunt," she said in a small voice.

"Surely you jest," he said with a short, dismissive laugh. "Whyever would Aunt Olympia torment you with voodoo tokens? It makes no sense."

Sarah sighed. "I suppose you have a point there. And Madame Tu pretty much said the same thing. Still, I hate the thought of you casting Baptista out without any real proof that she's the one who has been trying to terrorize me."

"Sarah, she tried to kill you tonight."

"*If* it was her," Sarah put in. She frowned thoughtfully for a long moment. "And now that I think about it, I really feel that whoever came to my room tonight did so mainly to frighten me. The person made a lot of noise. She wanted me to awaken and hear her voice and see the knife. If she had intended to kill me, it seems that she could have done so quite easily while I slept."

"Oh, Sarah!" With tears in his eyes, Damien rushed forward to embrace Sarah again, clutching her tightly to his heart. "The very thought of you being harmed sears my soul. Are you sure you don't want me to send Baptista away?"

"Why don't you talk with her for now, warn her," Sarah suggested. "After all, we'll be married tomorrow, and I think I'll feel safe after that."

"Indeed," Damien said. "I'll be watching your door until morning, and then I'll be off to town to find a locksmith to put a stout lock on my bedroom door. You needn't worry about our being interrupted on our wedding night, my love."

Sarah snuggled closer to him, but inwardly she remained troubled. Was she being a bit too liberal and twentieth-century in her thinking, giving Baptista the benefit of the doubt until she was proven guilty? Still, she hated the thought of casting the woman out when she might indeed be innocent. Besides, on every night hereafter, she would have Damien by her side to protect her.

The thought lifted her spirits and made her heart fill with love, keeping her demons at bay for the moment.

Later, Damien sat on a chair outside Sarah's door, his pistol in his lap. He was deeply concerned for Sarah's safety now, and there was no doubt in his mind that Baptista was the one who had terrified her earlier. As he had already confessed to Sarah, he and Baptista had shared a relationship once, and in a way he owed Baptista much. Yet the woman had no cause to try to harm Sarah. After all, he was the one who had broken things off; Sarah was in no way responsible.

He planned to interrogate Baptista first thing in the morning, and if he received any confirmation of his suspicions, she would be cast out, his promise to Sarah notwithstanding.

For he would take no chances with the lives of the woman and unborn child he loved.

Chapter Twenty-Five

Early the next afternoon, Damien was frowning as he stood in his room getting dressed for the wedding. He'd been on edge ever since the horrible moment last night when he'd heard Sarah screaming out for help down the hallway from him.

The rest of the night had passed without further incident, yet Damien remained troubled, very concerned for Sarah's safety. First thing this morning, he'd gone out to the kitchen and had confronted Baptista. His purpose had been to make her confess to terrifying Sarah, but, to his chagrin, he'd gotten nowhere with her. Baptista had sworn repeatedly that she'd done nothing to harm Sarah. She'd also begged Damien not to cast her out, evidently guessing what was in his mind. Despite himself, Damien had been moved when she had said, "Please, Master Damien, I got nowhere to go."

Damien had felt very torn then, especially considering his past relationship with the negress. In a kinder voice, he'd said, "Baptista, it is not my intention to be cruel, but it's over between the two of us. You're aware that I never made any promises to you. I love Sarah, and she's going to be my wife now. There's nothing you can do to stop it."

"I know that, Master Damien," Baptista had said. "Just don't cast me out."

Damien had at last given in. "Very well, Baptista, you may stay for now. But I swear, if Miss Sarah should ever again be caused the slightest distress—"

"Ain't nothin' more going to happen to Miss Sarah."

Damien had stepped forward aggressively at that. "Then you're admitting that you—"

"Nossir. I ain't admittin' nothin', but ain't nothin' goin' to happen to Miss Sarah. I give my word, Master Damien."

Perplexed by Baptista's cryptic reply, Damien had nevertheless stood by his pledge to let her stay. "Just remember that your future here will depend on that promise," he'd warned her.

Recalling his admonition, Damien wondered if he'd been too lenient, if he should have, indeed, thrown her out. He sighed. Such action doubtless would have upset Sarah and cast a blight over their wedding day. He preferred to hope that he'd managed to put the fear of God into Baptista. Beyond that, he'd keep a watchful eye on her; if there were any hint that she was making further attempts to frighten Sarah, then he'd evict her without a flicker of remorse.

After speaking with Baptista, Damien had gone off to town. He'd bought Sarah a wedding ring and had brought back with him a craftsman to install a strong bolt on his bedroom door. Even now, he glanced with approval at the door, where the new brass bolt gleamed, ready to keep at bay all intruders. He and his beloved Sarah would be safe tonight.

Just to think that in a short hour she would be his! When Sarah had been gone this last time, Damien had feared she was lost to him forever. Now she was back, ready to marry him. Now they were going to have a child together. His dearest desire was that she never walk out the front door of the house again.

He sighed. He knew that Sarah was not satisfied to stay here in the house with him. The house—and the love they shared—were not enough for her, even though they were enough for him. Of course, he understood her longing to become fully integrated into his world. There was the child to consider, as well. Perhaps they could solve the mystery of the window in time.

Until then, nothing mattered more than to keep her here with him, to love her and keep her and their child safe from all harm.

Sarah and Damien were married at two o'clock in the courtyard behind the house. Nature herself seemed all decked out for the celebration. The air was thick with the perfume of late-blooming jasmine and honeysuckle. Olympia's flowers—marigolds, petunias, and pansies—fanned out in lush rows flanking the bride and groom, who stood before the black-robed minister. Their altar was the gleaming fountain, its cascades of sparkling water adding a special brilliance and sweet music to the scene.

Sarah looked radiant in her lovely white gown and a simple veil of lace. She wore her hair down, with fragrant blossoms of baby's breath interlaced through her golden tresses. Damien had never looked more handsome; he wore a formal suit of black velvet, a ruffled linen shirt and lace jabot. The day was sunny and cool, the bright light casting jet highlights in his thick, wavy hair and illuminating the pride and happiness shining in his brown eyes.

In the background on wicker chairs sat Olympia and the minister's wife. The women looked as festive as fall flowers themselves, Olympia in a frock of mauve silk with matching hat, and Mrs. Turner in a full-skirted dress of pale blue organza.

Sarah was in heaven as she repeated her vows. She held Damien's hand and stared at him with eyes brimming with love as she whispered, "To have and to hold, from this day forward . . . till death do us part." Somehow, she vowed, she and Damien would find a way to be together for the rest of their lives—and then some. She vowed that neither time nor death would rip them asunder.

Damien's thoughts were identical as he repeated his own vows in his deep, confident voice. He marveled at how beautiful his bride was, how lucky he was that she was his. He and Sarah exchanged a joyous smile as he slipped the gold band on her finger. Soon it was over and they were officially man and wife; Damien drew back Sarah's veil and kissed her tenderly. "I love you, Mrs. Fontaine," he whispered, staring down into her eyes with tears in his own.

"I love you, too, Mr. Fontaine," she whispered back, hugging him joyously.

Then they pulled apart like two shy adolescents. The minister pumped Damien's hand and grinned, while his wife rushed forward to congratulate them.

After the necessary papers were signed and witnessed, Olympia served everyone cake and punch in the dining room. To Sarah's pleasure, the atmosphere was quite gay, mainly thanks to Reverend and Mrs. Turner. The Reverend was a robust, jovial man who at once led a toast to the newlyweds. His wife, an effusive little woman, kept remarking on what a perfect couple Damien and Sarah made and urging them to attend her husband's church. Sarah caught Olympia's forbearing expression as Mrs. Turner described the various churches on her husband's circuit. Sarah knew that Olympia remained scandalized that she and Damien had not married in the Catholic Church, but at least Damien's aunt was being outwardly supportive and had made no further comments about Sarah and Damien "living in sin."

Baptista was in evidence now, too, bringing in trays of refreshments and clearing away dirty dishes. As usual, her presence was innocuous, her expression inscrutable; she never even looked at Damien or Sarah.

Once the Turners had departed, Damien poured another round of punch for his bride, Olympia and himself. Holding up his cup, he said, "Another toast—to my beautiful bride."

Sarah smiled, although inwardly she felt uneasy, knowing that Damien was testing his aunt. But Olympia was wise enough to follow suit; she, too, smiled and said with forced cheerfulness, "To Sarah," dutifully clinking her cup against the others.

"Well, Damien," Olympia said afterward, "are you going to take Sarah on a wedding trip? Perhaps to New Orleans?"

Sarah shot Damien a troubled glance. But he

merely smiled at his aunt and said smoothly, "Sarah and I prefer to stay here for the time being. After all, what more secluded spot could a bride and groom ask for?"

At Damien's forthright reply, Olympia blushed. Muttering, "Indeed," she nervously raised her napkin to her lips.

"Actually, Miss Fontaine, I've only recently been to New Orleans," Sarah put in tactfully. "If you want to know the truth, I'm rather weary of traveling at the moment."

At her words, Damien threw back his head and laughed. Olympia looked confused, but Sarah and Damien exchanged a special, tender smile at the secret only the two of them shared.

That night, Sarah and Damien sipped champagne in his bed. Beyond them, a fire snapped in the grate, bathing the room with a cozy warmth. Sarah wore a white handkerchief linen gown; her golden hair flowed freely to her shoulders. Damien wore his silk brocade dressing gown. Sarah feasted her eyes on the beautifully sculpted planes of his face, the muscular lines of his body. How lucky she was that he was hers!

"Just think, darling," he whispered, kissing her hair. "By next July, we'll be holding our beloved child in our arms."

Sarah nodded, but inwardly she was stabbed by a needle of anxiety. At last, she dared to voice her most gnawing fear. "Damien, what will we do if the child is like me, not firmly grounded in this century?"

He frowned, his arm tightening about her waist. "Darling, you should not trouble yourself with such matters."

321

"But I must," Sarah said. "I'm not even completely sure I belong here."

He laughed shortly. "You're not sure? How could you marry me today if you're not sure?"

Sarah sighed. "I love you, Damien, and perhaps I'm selfish to cling to whatever time we can have here together."

He nuzzled her neck with his masterful lips, and she shivered in delight. "You're not the least bit selfish, darling."

Nevertheless, she pulled back and stared at him soberly. "I am realistic enough to know that, for our child's sake, what we have here in this house will never be enough."

"How can you say that?" Before she could say more, he took the champagne glass from her hand and placed it, with his, on the nightstand. "Darling, enough fretting," he continued, drawing her close. "Let's not let our troubles spoil our wedding night. Besides, hasn't there been a purpose to everything that has happened to us?"

"That's true," Sarah conceded.

"I'm not an overly religious man," he continued with a rueful smile, "much to my aunt's chagrin, but I do believe that whatever god brought us to each other will find a way to keep us together."

Her heart welled with joy and renewed hope. "Oh, Damien, I do hope you're right."

"We must have faith, my darling."

"Yes," she concurred, her eyes lighting with realization. "You know, faith was what we both lacked when we first met. We'd both lost all joy, all interest in living. And now, we're starting to get it all back—faith, hope—"

"And love," he added hoarsely, kissing her.

Sarah moaned in ecstasy as Damien pressed her

beneath him on the sheet. She clung to him eagerly, rejoicing in the joy of their wedding night. His lips were hot and sweet on hers; his tongue, swirling deeply in her mouth, tasted headily of champagne. They kissed each other hungrily, insatiably, until their lips were bruised and trembling.

Damien drew back and flung off his dressing gown, and she feasted her eyes on his magnificent nakedness, outlined by the flickering fire. Copper highlights danced in his hair, and love gleamed in his beautiful, mesmerizing dark eyes. His manhood stood beautifully erect, straining to bring them both pleasure. She loved him so much in that moment. And she knew that no matter what happened to them in the future, she would bear his image in her heart forever.

Swimming in happiness, Sarah ran her hands over the rough texture of his chest, the hard muscles of his back and thighs. When she pressed her mouth against his nipple, he moaned, his trembling fingers reaching for the tie on her gown. He drew the delicate garment off her slowly, caressing her silky flesh. Soon, they were both naked against the cozy quilts, secure in the warmth of their love.

Damien feasted his eyes on Sarah—on her lovely oval face and bright blue eyes, the sleek column of her throat, the shapely curves of her breasts, the downy triangle that led to her innermost delights, and her long, shapely legs. "My God, you're so incredibly lovely," he whispered, his heart swelling at the corresponding joy that flashed in her eyes.

Damien kissed Sarah all over, starting at her hair and lingering at her mouth. His warm lips moved slowly, tormentingly, down her throat, drawing gooseflesh in their wake. Her breathing quickened as he fastened his mouth on her tender nipple. His hands kneaded the firm globes, and he glanced up at her wonderingly. "Your breasts are so much fuller now, darling."

She nodded. "It's a change that comes with pregnancy. My nipples are much more sensitive, too."

She felt him stiffening at her words, and his fingers ceased their seductive rhythm. "Does it hurt when I touch you there?"

She shook her head. "No, Damien. In fact, in a way, it's better. I feel you that much more."

"Oh, darling." He made love to her breasts gently, running his tongue over each aching nipple, at once delighting and frustrating her exquisitely. She thrust her fingers into his hair and pulled his mouth tightly to her breast. "Damien, please," she whimpered. "I want to feel you, *really* feel you."

Her words brought a feral groan rising in his throat. He drew hard on her nipple, sucking the tip of her breast deeply into his mouth. Sarah tossed her head and bucked with such violent pleasure that Damien clamped an arm across her hip to hold her still. He nibbled delicately at the underside of her breast with his teeth, sending hot needles of arousal shooting through her body.

Rapturous moments later, his mouth moved to her stomach. His lips searched the smooth contours for any sign of thickening. He found none as yet, but he nestled his cheek against her, whispering, "Little life. Precious little life." Sarah felt so deeply touched that tears welled in her eyes.

Then he parted her thighs and kissed her there, and Sarah went wild with sensation, bucking and catching her breath in sharp, desperate gasps.

"It's all right, darling," Damien said, holding her

thighs apart. "Just relax and let me show you pleasure."

He did. She drew her hands wildly through his hair as he prepared her—teasing, then withdrawing, igniting the flames then banking them, wanting her to know that ultimate pleasure only with him inside her. She tossed her head and begged him to quench her burning need.

Just when she could bear no more, he drew upward, fastening his mouth on hers and thrusting into her. Sarah cried out in reckless joy, arching violently into his thrusts, trembling, clinging to him as he pressed deeper, stretching and probing to know her fully.

"Take me, Damien," she whispered breathlessly. "Oh, please take me."

He groaned and claimed her lips fiercely as their loins mated and melded. Their movements were fearless and uninhibited, two souls reaching out to become one, becoming galvanized in a shattering moment of passion, a blinding flash of light. When the paroxysm came, their eyes locked and they both cried out their love.

Afterward, Damien collapsed on her, kissing her tenderly. "Oh, Sarah. Never, never leave me."

"Never, my darling," she whispered back, tears spilling onto her cheeks.

Chapter Twenty-Six

On a warm morning in late May, 1872, Sarah Fontaine stood in the upstairs salon, putting the finishing touches on the last of Vincy Fontaine's paintings. The landscape of a summer sky at midnight, with its bright stars beaming down on a dark forestline, now gleamed back at her with its finishing coat of varnish.

Rubbing her aching lower back, Sarah glanced about the room at Vincy's other paintings, all now beautifully restored. Seeing the shining proof of her accomplishments filled her with great pride.

She went to the work table to clean her brushes, her movements awkward due to her advanced pregnancy. Her child was due in just over a month now. Damien grew more excited each day, as did she.

Sarah smiled. The months since they had been married had been wonderful in so many ways.

Damien was not just her life mate but her soul mate as well. Together they had shared so much; they had found great healing in each other.

But Sarah remained deeply troubled about the window in time which prevented her from sharing Damien's world with him completely. The barrier seemed even more ominous and threatening now that her work here was finished. After all, she'd been brought here for a purpose, to repair Vincy Fontaine's brilliant paintings. Now that her goal had been accomplished, would her tenuous hold on the nineteenth century weaken even more? The thought was truly frightful.

Her anxieties had been increased by the fact that Casper had disappeared from the house a few months ago. Sarah had questioned Olympia and the servants at length, yet no one had seen a trace of the animal since early spring. Sarah didn't know if the cat had run off, if he had taken ill and had gone off to die, or if he had simply walked out the front door one day and had disappeared back into the present. Sarah strongly suspected the latter, which hardly increased her confidence about being able to stay here permanently.

Through cleaning her brushes, Sarah walked over to the window. Damn! Why was it she could see the outside world from here, yet she remained captive behind some invisible curtain, unable to experience its wonders firsthand?

Sarah hadn't left the house in almost seven months now. Only Damien's love had kept her here, sustaining her, behind these walls. Still, there were days when she paced like a caged animal, growing desperate to figure out the time barrier's secret. Damien would often find her thus and would comfort her, saying endlessly, "Sarah, what we have is enough. The house is enough. You must calm down now and think of our child."

Sarah never had the heart to tell him that the house had become her prison. Somehow, she still sensed that her being trapped in the house was linked to her grief over Brian's death and Damien's grief over Vincy. If they could both transcend their grief, could they also overcome the door in time itself? Endlessly, she puzzled over this.

She knew she was becoming ready to give up her grief over Brian. The first anniversary of his death had passed recently, and she had honored this occasion in the past as she would have in the present. While the day had brought sadness, on another level it had seemed to mark a beginning in her life.

Sarah sensed, too, that Damien was almost ready to give up his grief over Vincy. He'd told her recently that Vincy's memoirs were almost finished. "But not quite," he'd said. While he hadn't admitted it in so many words, Sarah suspected that he still couldn't force himself to finish his account of how Vincy had died or really address his guilt over the love Vincy and Lucy had shared.

However, in other ways, Damien showed signs of being ready to become reintegrated into his world. Often now, as she glanced out the upstairs window, she would again see him sitting on his horse at the edge of the fallow field, as if he were planning new seasons, new plantings. He'd mentioned once that he might use part of the money his father had left him in the English bank to do some refurbishing of the plantation. But when Sarah had encouraged him to do just that, his expression had grown guarded, and he'd abruptly dropped the subject. She knew he'd been thinking only of her, aware of her limitations here and afraid to cause her anguish.

Nevertheless, Sarah did everything she could to encourage Damien to embrace his world again. He did go to town a little more often now, though he was careful never to be gone long or to cause her the slightest worry. Once, as they'd been talking and laughing gaily over a newspaper account of Mardi Gras in New Orleans, he'd said in a rush, "Oh, Sarah, I must take you to New Orleans some time." Then, seeming to realize his *faux pas*, he'd hugged her and said passionately, "Sarah, I'm sorry. It doesn't matter."

But Sarah knew it *did* matter. It mattered to them both. Sometimes, when Damien didn't know she was looking, she could see the stark fear in his eyes—and that same fear gnawed at her—that one day the door in time might separate them forever. Also, there was the child to consider. Keeping the child trapped here in the house was, of course, out of the question. But what if he, or she, was like Sarah, not really grounded in this century?

And there was the even greater question of their destinies—hers and the child's. What if she or the child—or both of them—were actually meant to live their lives back in the twentieth century and not here? And an equally tormenting question often loomed in her mind. In staying here, was she holding Damien back, ensuring that he would never completely let go of his grief? Was she interfering with *his* destiny?

Sarah knew that over the past months, she'd been living in a dream world, postponing the inevitable. Sooner or later, she must confront the reality of her tenuous existence here. She must seek answers again. She must find her rightful place in time and her baby's rightful place in time.

Sarah was grateful that over the last seven months there had been no further attempts to terrorize her. Ever since the day she'd married Damien, she had not heard the ominous voice during the night, nor had she found any more of the frightening *gris-gris* in her room. As Damien had predicted, his aunt had come around and seemed to accept their marriage. Olympia had seemed pleased when, a couple of months after Sarah and Damien had wed, they'd told her about their coming child. She had even knitted an afghan for the baby and had taught Sarah how to knit booties and sweaters.

Yet while Olympia's attitude had softened, Baptista had remained aloof and inscrutable. On several occasions while Sarah had been in the salon, in the parlor or hallway, she'd been startled to find Baptista standing behind her. Indeed, the servant had developed an annoying habit of creeping up behind Sarah at the oddest moments; several times, she had rebuked Baptista because of this. Baptista's behavior was not overt enough for Sarah to go to Damien, but she was beginning to suspect that he'd been right, that Baptista was the one who'd been tormenting her before. Certainly, the frightening incidents had ceased ever since the morning when Damien had warned Baptista off.

Hearing the sound of horse's hooves, Sarah moved over to the window. Looking down, she smiled as she watched Damien ride up on his black stallion. He looked quite dashing in his chocolate brown frock coat, buff-colored trousers and brown planter's style hat. She was pleased that he was now dressing more fashionably and wearing colors other than the perpetual black he'd worn for so long to mourn Vincy. This, to Sarah, was another sign that he was ready to end his seclusion here.

He dismounted his horse, and as the stableboy rushed up to take the animal away, Damien untied a burlap sack that was hanging from the saddle horn. Looking up, he spotted Sarah. He removed his hat and bowed to her gallantly. "Good afternoon, my lady," he called up with a grin. "Now don't move. I'll be right up."

As if I could go anywhere, Sarah thought to herself ironically.

Moments later, Damien burst into the salon. His hair was ruffled, his features flushed from the ride, his dark eyes gleaming. Never had he looked more handsome to her. He hurried to Sarah's side and set the burlap sack down on the windowsill. "Ah, darling, you look radiant, as always," he said with a grin, hugging her gently as he swooped down for a kiss.

Sarah smiled as she kissed Damien back and inhaled his scent, a comforting mixture of sweat, leather, tobacco, and a trace of spring foliage. "Damien, I'm so glad you're back."

He drew back and placed a loving hand on her belly. "How's our little marvel doing today?"

The baby kicked against its father's hand, almost as if he or she had heard the question. They both laughed, and Sarah replied ruefully, "Active."

Damien's eyes gleamed with joyous anticipation. "Ah, it won't be long now, will it, love?"

"No, it won't be long," Sarah replied, biting her lip. When the baby came, would she have any real answers? Afraid to think of these uncertainties, she asked, "What did you do in town?"

He grinned, then picked up the burlap sack. "I

almost forgot, darling. These are for you—or rather, for our child." Upending the sack, he dumped the contents out on the window seat.

"Oh, Damien," Sarah cried. Sitting down, she sifted through the tall stack of handmade baby clothes—lovely handkerchief linen gowns edged in lace, crocheted booties, knitted blankets and shirts in lovely pastel colors. Her eyes gleamed as she stared up at him. "These are divine."

"I've had a black woman in town working on the layette for months now," he announced proudly.

She laughed, shaking her head. "Between these and all the things your aunt and I have knitted, we'll have the best-dressed baby in the parish."

He caressed her cheek with his fingertips and smiled down into her glowing eyes. "Only the finest for our child, darling."

Sarah stood and hugged him. "Damien, you're wonderful."

He hugged her back, then said more soberly, "Sarah, there's something I've been meaning to talk to you about."

"Oh?"

He drew back slightly, brushing a wisp of hair from her eyes. "Lately when I've been in town, I've noticed quite a lot of blacks—and even whites—needing work. You see, toward the end of the war, a number of our slaves here merely walked off the plantation. I understand that some of them traveled north to seek their fortunes there. Now, a number of our former slaves have returned to Meridian, and many of them are badly in need of work. I've been approached a number of times, and I was thinking—"

"Yes?"

He hesitated a moment. "I was thinking of hiring

on a crew soon and starting up a crop of cane next spring."

"Oh, yes, Damien, I think you should," Sarah concurred at once. "It's not right that your land should lie fallow. Belle Fontaine was once a working plantation, and it should be again."

Damien braved a smile, but she didn't miss the shadow of anxiety crossing his eyes. "Sarah, you must understand that if we start planting again, I'll have to be away from you more. I'll need to supervise the work crew personally for a time, leastwise until I can find a reliable foreman and hire an overseer. And there will be needed trips to New Orleans to see my factor." Quickly, he added, "Of course, if you should feel the least bit threatened by this—"

She pressed her fingers to his lips. "Damien, the last thing I want to do is to keep you from fulfilling your own destiny. You're meant to become reintegrated into your world." She frowned, then continued with determination, "And somehow, I—and our child—must find a way to join you."

Damien clutched Sarah close, a frown drifting in about his eyes. "Darling, please, you're not thinking about leaving the house again, are you?"

She sighed. "No, not at the moment."

His arms tightened about her. "The house is enough for us."

She gazed up at him, shaking her head sadly. "But it isn't enough. Not for you or our child. Your future plans and dreams more than demonstrate that. You deserve a woman who can share all of it with you and be a proper mother for your child."

"Sarah, don't say that," he cried, gesturing his frustration. "You'll be a wonderful mother. And how can you think that any other woman would ever do for me? Look, if my talk of refurbishing the plantation is bringing on these doubts, then that's the end of it."

"No," Sarah said fervently. "I really want you to get the plantation running again. I just wish I could be out there in your world with you, by your side more."

"Oh, Sarah, don't you know that already you share everything with me, my dearest heart?"

He kissed her tenderly, but afterward she was still frowning. Noting her troubled expression, he rubbed her back and said, "You look tired, darling. You've been standing too long again, haven't you?"

She shook her head. "I'm all right, really." Then she gestured about the room, her eyes gleaming with pride. "Look, I just finished repairing the last of Vincy's paintings."

He glanced about the room, a wistful quality in his eyes as he studied the refurbished paintings. "Indeed, you have, darling. I can't begin to tell you what a magnificent job you've done." He walked over to study the landscape Sarah had just completed, drawing back to scrutinize it from various angles. He shook his head wonderingly. "If only Vincy could be here to see this day," he said tightly.

"I know. I would have loved to have known him," Sarah whispered.

"You do know him, Sarah," Damien whispered back. "Indeed, you do."

They shared a look of poignant understanding. Then Damien walked around behind the painting and studied Sarah's signature on the back of the canvas. "I like the way you've signed each painting and entered the date of restoration," he remarked. Then he frowned quizzically. "However, why is it you persist in signing your name 'Jennings?'"

Sarah laughed as she took a step forward. "Strictly for the sake of consistency, darling. You see, I fully expect these paintings to end up in a museum one day. I thought it would be less confusing to future generations if I use the name 'Jennings' on all of them to identify me as the sole restorer."

He nodded, then said firmly, "Just so you understand that in all other matters you're Sarah Fontaine."

She looked at him with eyes brimming with love. "I'm Sarah Fontaine in every way that matters."

He grinned back at her, seeming satisfied. Glancing downward, he added, "The hourglass beneath your signature is another interesting touch. However, I've noticed that each hourglass is somewhat different. Take this one, for instance. Most of the sand seems to be on the bottom."

Sarah laughed dryly. "You're very observant." She walked over to join him at the back of the painting. "You see, when I signed the back of the first painting, I sketched in an hourglass beneath my name. I did it—" she shrugged, then said "—I don't know, sort of on a whim. Anyway, the top of the hourglass was almost full when I first sketched it in, but on each successive painting I completed, I sketched in the hourglass with a few more of the sands having trickled away. It's something I did by instinct, I guess." She stared at the painting and drew a heavy breath. "Now, almost all the sands are gone."

Damien sighed fiercely and wrapped an arm about her shoulders. "Then we'll just have to invert the hourglass and start all over, won't we, darling?"

She looked up at him bravely. "I hope we'll be able to."

They exchanged a long, emotional look. Then

Damien forced a smile and clapped his hands together. "Well, this calls for a celebration, don't you think?"

"A celebration?"

"Yes, of your completing the repairs. I think we should host a *fête*—after your confinement, of course. We could invite some of our neighbors from the parish. The reception could be held in honor of your restoration of Vincy's paintings and, of course, to celebrate the arrival of our child."

Sarah smiled at him, despite the sudden sting of tears. Damien was so ready to embrace his world again, to cut his ties with the past, with his grief. Now, not only was he thinking of starting up the plantation again, he was making plans to begin socializing with the parish once more. And while he might not acknowledge it consciously, every step he took in the healing process took him further away from her and made it more critical that she find a way to share his entire world with him.

For it was unthinkable that he not become whole again, that he remain a prisoner of his grief, a prisoner with her in this house.

Still, he was contemplating a big, drastic step, and Sarah's protective instincts rose up. "Damien, are you sure you're ready for something like this?"

"What do you mean?"

She glanced about the room. "Would you be willing to share Vincy's paintings with others—with strangers?"

Damien followed Sarah's gaze about the room, his features gripped in a struggle. Then he turned to her and nodded. "Yes, I think I am ready to share Vincy's paintings with others. I'm just so damned proud of your accomplishments, Sarah."

"Oh, Damien." She hurried forward to embrace

him, her heart bursting with joy that she had pleased him so. Resting her cheek against his chest, she listened to the soothing thud of his heart. "If that's the case, then I think a reception would be lovely."

Damien kissed the top of her head. "If you can't venture out in the world, my love, I'll bring the world here to you."

She drew back and stared up into his eyes. "I love you so."

"No more than I love you."

They shared a sweet, ardent kiss. Afterward, Sarah pulled back slightly. "What about Vincy's memoirs? Wouldn't it be wonderful if they could be finished before the reception, as well?"

At once, she felt him stiffen, then he shook his head grimly. "I haven't finished the memoirs as yet, nor am I ready to share anything that intimate with the world."

"But you don't understand. In time, you *will* share the memoirs with the world. In time, you'll share everything about Vincy."

Damien took her hand, squeezing it. "For now, we must be content with what we have, Sarah."

Sarah didn't press the point, yet she remained uneasy. Their love, the house, their grief—all seemed impossibly locked up together. And in a way, they were both afraid to let go completely of any of it, even their deepest, darkest pain.

That night at dinner, Damien said to Olympia, "Aunt, Sarah and I are thinking of hosting a *fête*. After her confinement, of course."

"Why, how nice," Olympia murmured with a slight smile.

"I've finished repairing Vincy's paintings," Sarah

explained. "Damien would like to show them off to the parish."

"And the occasion will honor the arrival of our child, as well," Damien added.

"I think we should have some sort of reception," Olympia agreed. "Once Sarah's up to it, of course. It's high time we brought some gaiety back into our lives here at Belle Fontaine." She nodded to Sarah. "How nice that you've finished your work before your confinement, dear. Now you can devote all your energies to the child."

"Yes, that is nice," Sarah said. She and Damien exchanged a smile.

Then Sarah's smile faded as she watched Baptista walk into the room and sullenly begin gathering up their soup bowls.

Chapter Twenty-Seven

The next day, while Damien was out riding through the fields, Sarah was knitting in the parlor when Olympia walked in. "Sarah, I would like to have a word with you," she said.

Sarah laid down the baby blanket she'd been knitting and glanced up at Olympia. She noted that the spinster looked unusually tense today. Her plump features were clenched, and her hazel eyes were gleaming strangely. "Of course. Please sit down and we'll have a chat."

"Thanks, but this won't take long," Olympia said enigmatically.

"Oh?" Growing confused, Sarah asked, "Is something wrong?"

"Yes," Olympia said, stepping closer. "Something is most definitely wrong."

Watching beads of perspiration break out on

Olympia's upper lip, Sarah leaned forward in her seat. "What, then? Is it Damien, or—"

"It's you." Saying the words, Olympia abruptly drew a small pistol from the pocket of her gown.

"My God!" Sarah gasped.

With a trembling hand, Olympia pointed the pistol toward Sarah. "I think you should leave."

"You—what?" Sarah stammered. She stared helplessly at the deadly barrel of the gun, feeling terrified for the safety of her unborn child. Her hands moved protectively to her belly, and her eyes beseeched Olympia. "Please, you must put that gun down before you hurt someone."

Yet Olympia was shaking her head adamantly, her eyes glowing with a fanatical light. "No. Not until you leave."

At last realization dawned on Sarah. She blinked at Olympia, aghast. "You're the one—the one who's been tormenting me?"

"Yes." Olympia smiled maliciously. "I bought the voodoo tokens from a conjure woman and placed them in your room."

"And yours was the voice I heard?"

"Yes."

"But why?" Sarah cried.

Olympia stepped closer, her hand on the pistol trembling all the more as she said hoarsely, "Because I'll not allow you to destroy Damien."

"Destroy Damien?" Sarah repeated, utterly perplexed. "Whyever would I do that?"

Olympia snorted a contemptuous laugh. "Because I know you don't belong here." Watching Sarah go pale, she continued, "Oh, I was suspicious of you from the start, after you arrived here last fall wearing those odd clothes. Then a week or so later, I saw you walk out the front door and disappear."

"You saw me?" Sarah repeated, her heart thudding.

"Yes. I don't know where you're from, Sarah, or where you're bound, but I do know one thing—one day you'll leave this house and disappear forever."

Sarah cut in plaintively, "No, I wouldn't."

Olympia waved the gun wildly. "You will! And I won't allow you to do that to Damien. He almost died when he lost Vincy, and now I won't stand idly by and watch his life be shattered again."

"No, I would never do that," Sarah repeated, growing desperate in her attempts to get through to the woman. "And don't you understand that if I leave now, Damien will be destroyed anyway? He'll lose me and his child."

A muscle jumped in Olympia's fleshy cheek as she continued in a trembling voice, "He should have lost you both long ago as far as I'm concerned. You've finished your work on Vincy's paintings, so now we have no further need of you. I want you out of here before the child is born, so Damien won't become attached to it. Now get out!"

"Please," Sarah begged. "You're making a terrible mistake. Don't do this."

"Leave!" Olympia hissed, gesturing with her gun.

Suddenly, the entire picture became clear to Sarah. "You don't want Damien to get better, do you?" she accused. "You want him tied to this house—and to you."

"I said, get out!"

Olympia's face was livid now, and she looked close to the breaking point. Her hand was trembling so badly on the pistol that Sarah was terrified that she might accidentally discharge it. She realized that it was futile trying to argue with this hysterical, surely demented woman, and that she had no choice at the moment but to follow her orders.

Sarah got up and walked toward the archway, surprised that her trembling limbs even supported her. Her heart was pounding, tears filling her eyes as she thought of the possibility of never seeing Damien again. And her child—her poor, unborn child—thrust back in time again, possibly never seeing its father.

She reached the hallway and hesitated, staring terrified at the front door.

"Go on!" Olympia hissed from behind her.

Swallowing hard, Sarah inched toward the door. Olympia followed at a safe distance.

Then, even as Sarah was reaching for the doorknob, even as she was struggling frantically to think of a final plea to Olympia, she heard the sound of a scuffle behind her. She whirled to see Olympia and Baptista struggling over the gun.

Sarah watched in horror as the two women flailed wildly at each other, both wearing grim, determined expressions. Olympia put up a valiant fight, but the younger woman was much stronger than she. Within a few seconds, Baptista had wrenched the pistol away from Olympia. Olympia shrank back, her eyes those of a hunted animal as she glanced wildly from Baptista to Sarah. Then, uttering an anguished cry, she ran toward the stairs.

There was a moment of charged silence. Sarah stood with her hand over her heart, struggling to catch her breath; Baptista stood watching her warily.

Then Baptista set the pistol down on the hall table and came forward, placing her hand on Sarah's arm. "You all right, Miss Sarah?"

She nodded convulsively. "Thank you, Baptista. I owe you my life—and that of my child's."

For the first time since she'd been here, Sarah saw Baptista smile. "You sure you not hurt?" the negress repeated.

Before Sarah could answer, Damien burst in the front door, looking exuberant from his ride. "Good morning, dar—"

Then he paused in mid-sentence, noting Sarah's pale expression. He strode quickly to her side and wrapped an arm protectively about her waist. His gaze flicked accusingly to Baptista. "What's going on here?"

Sarah glanced at Baptista, then turned sadly to him. "Damien, I'm afraid it's about your aunt."

"My aunt?" Damien lifted an eyebrow in perplexity. Then he spotted the pistol on the hall table, and all color drained from his face. Releasing Sarah, he walked over and picked up the gun. "What in God's name is *this* doing here?"

Sarah and Baptista exchanged helpless glances, then Sarah repeated, "Damien, your aunt . . ." Her voice trailed off, and she bit her lip.

Damien's brow was furrowed in a deep frown. "Let's go into the parlor," he said grimly.

Damien took Sarah's arm and led her toward the archway. As Baptista started to slip away, he turned to her and said firmly, "You, too, Baptista."

The three seated themselves in the parlor, Damien and Sarah on the settee and Baptista across from them on a side chair.

Damien laid the gun down at his side and turned to Sarah sternly. "All right, my dear, now tell me everything."

Miserably, Sarah said, "Damien, a moment ago, your aunt confronted me in here with a pistol—"

"My God!" he cried.

"And I'm afraid she demanded that I leave."

343

"She *what?*" he asked, his expression stunned.

"She told me I must leave. She claimed I was ruining your life." Sarah drew a ragged breath, then continued, "Anyway, your aunt was forcing me toward the front door, when Baptista intervened and wrestled the gun away from her."

They both glanced at Baptista, who nodded soberly to confirm Sarah's story. Then Damien squeezed Sarah's hand and said, "Oh, my poor darling. Are you sure you're all right?"

"Yes, Damien, I'm fine."

In a lower voice, he asked, "My aunt—knew about you, then?"

She nodded. She knew there was no need to mention the ominous barrier directly; they were both well-aware of the potentially disastrous implications of Olympia's actions a few moments ago.

Damien sighed fiercely, drawing a hand distractedly through his hair. "My God, I should have known it was Aunt Olympia tormenting you all along. To think that you could have been hurt or—"

"Damien, I'm fine—thanks to Baptista," Sarah said. She flashed the negress a grateful smile.

Damien turned to the black woman. "Baptista, we both owe you a debt of great gratitude, and I owe you a sincere apology, as well."

At Damien's words of praise, Baptista modestly lowered her eyes. "Thank you, sir."

Damien frowned quizzically at Baptista. "Then you must have known for some time that Sarah was in danger from my aunt?"

"Yessir." Baptista's gaze shifted to Sarah. "When Master Damien accused me of tryin' to hurt you, I swore it was lies. And I swore to myself that I was going to find out who done you bad."

"Then that's why you've been watching over me all these months," Sarah put in.

"Yes, madame." Baptista's chin came up slightly as she turned back to Damien. "And I gone to the conjure woman and foun' out that Miss Olympia, she the one that bought the *gris-gris*."

"Good Lord!" Damien said. "Baptista, why didn't you tell me?" Then, watching the black woman's eyes flash first with resentment, then with fear, he held up a hand and added, "No, please, you don't have to answer that. After all, I accused you of being the culprit, didn't I?"

Baptista nodded.

Sarah smiled at Baptista. "How can I ever thank you?"

For once, Baptista looked Sarah squarely in the eye. "Miss Sarah, I ain't goin' to lie to you. I ain't happy you took Master Damien away from me, but he be happy wi'd you. And I ain't never gonna let no one hurt Master Damien's child."

"Baptista, we owe you so much," Sarah said, her eyes gleaming with gratitude. "And we're both so sorry for misjudging you."

"Amen," Damien added.

Abruptly, there was a sound at the portal. All three turned to see Olympia standing at the archway, her face puffy, her cheeks streaked with tears. Her voice was filled with piteous pleading as she extended her arms toward Damien and said, "Nephew, please forgive me. I only wanted what was best for you."

Yet Damien was unmoved. He got to his feet, his expression immutable. "Aunt, I believe it's a bit late to ask for forgiveness." He leaned over to pick up the pistol from the settee, holding it barrel-down.

345

"You just endangered the lives of my wife and child, a matter most grave."

Olympia came forward, her expression beseeching. "Damien, the gun was not loaded. I thought Sarah was bad for you, and I only wanted to scare her away. It was never my intention to hurt her."

At his aunt's words, Damien checked the cylinder of the gun. "You've spoken the truth on that score. The gun is not loaded," he conceded, setting the pistol down on the coffee table. "Nevertheless, that fact does not diminish one iota the despicable nature of the act you just committed." Damien's voice was like ice. "Pack your trunks, Aunt. I'll see that you're found suitable quarters in town."

"Damien!" Sarah cried, tugging at his sleeve. Now, even she felt sorry for his aunt, and her expression begged him to relent.

Yet Damien's countenance did not waver at all as he turned to Sarah. "No, my dear," he told her quietly. "I'll take no chances with the lives of you and our unborn child."

Sarah could only sigh and nod in unhappy agreement, as Olympia uttered a cry of dismay and fled the room.

After Olympia left, Baptista said tactfully, "I go get tea, Master Damien."

"Thanks, Baptista."

Once they were alone, Damien sat down next to Sarah and hugged her. "Darling, are you quite certain you're unharmed?"

"Yes."

"You know, last fall when I confronted Baptista, accusing her of trying to frighten you, she denied everything so vehemently that I feared she might not be the one. But I just couldn't force myself to believe it was Aunt Olympia."

"I know, Damien. It's hard for me to comprehend, too, but she did believe she had your best interests at heart."

"Perhaps so." His jaw tightened, and his eyes gleamed implacably. "Still, I can't allow her to stay here any longer. The potential threat is simply too great."

Sarah sighed, recognizing once more that he was right. After a moment, she said quietly, "She knew about me, Damien."

He nodded. "Yes, I surmised as much from our conversation before. But how did she know?"

"She saw me walk out the front door and disappear that first time."

He shook his head. "My God. That makes what she did today all the more contemptible." Before Sarah could comment, he went on, "Do you think Baptista knows?"

Sarah shrugged. "I'm not sure. She may." She sighed heavily. "Oh, Damien, it breaks my heart that your aunt must leave, although I understand what you're saying about the safety of our child. Still, I feel like I'm ruining your life."

He drew her close and spoke hoarsely. "Nonsense, darling. Don't you know by now that far from ruining my life you've been my sole salvation?"

Sarah hugged Damien back, but her heart was heavy, laden with the unhappy choices and heartbreaking decisions she knew she could no longer postpone.

That night, Damien found Sarah sitting on the window seat in the salon. His heart was full of love at the sight of her. She was perched in a beam of moonlight, her long blond hair gleaming silverwhite, her features softly beautiful, her belly large

347

and ripe. Her expression was wistful as she stared out at their bright star. She looked like an ethereal vision to him tonight, like a misty dream that might soon vanish. A poignant sadness filled his heart as he wondered if his love was strong enough to hold her here.

He came to sit beside her and took her hand. "Darling, are you all right?" he asked, stroking her cheek gently.

She turned to smile at him. "I'm fine. But after you forced me to nap most of the afternoon, well, I guess I'm feeling restless tonight."

They fell into silence. They both knew the main reason Damien had insisted that Sarah stay in her room was so that she wouldn't be present when he evicted Olympia from the house. Even now, the eerie quiet of the house—the absence of Olympia's beautiful piano music drifting up from downstairs —seemed to scream out at them both.

"Did you get your aunt settled in Meridian?" Sarah asked at last.

He nodded. "She'll be staying with her friend Mary Broussard until I can buy her a house. I've already got my eye on a vacant cottage." Watching Sarah frown, he added, "Darling, I swear I'll see to it that she never lacks for anything."

"Except her nephew's company."

"I'll go visit her regularly." His features tightened. "But she'll never set foot in this house again."

"Which means she'll never get to see the baby."

"What does she care about the baby?" he asked with cutting bitterness. "She was going to cast you both from the house."

Sarah wiped at a tear, shaking her head. "It was me, Damien—not the baby—that she wanted to be rid of."

"Hell," he said grimly, "if it'll make you happy, I'll take the child to see her."

"But we don't know about the baby," Sarah cried with sudden frustration. "We don't even know if he or she will be safe outside the house." Miserably, she finished, "We don't know anything."

"Oh, Sarah." Damien pulled her into his arms and stroked her back, but she remained stiff in his embrace.

After a moment, she pulled back and said with quiet resignation, "I've got to go back again, Damien."

"Sarah, no!" he cried, his eyes wild with fear.

"Damien, I must." She turned toward the window, her eyes mirroring a world of anguish as she continued sadly. "You see, I'm not like our star, Damien. I'm not steadfast."

He took her face gently in his hands, turning her to him. "But you are, Sarah," he said passionately. "You're the greatest—the only reality in my life."

She could only shake her head. "I must find out where I truly belong and where our child belongs."

He looked crestfallen. "Are you considering this because of what happened today with my aunt?"

"It proved to me once more how tenuous my existence is here."

He gestured beseechingly. "But, darling, when you went back the last time, didn't you find my very own words? Didn't I say, 'I have found her now and she has taken away all my pain?'"

She nodded, then said in a choked voice, "But how can I know that I'm the one you spoke of?"

He pulled her into his arms. "My God, Sarah, how can you ever doubt that?"

She clung to him, tears streaming down her cheeks. Her heart was breaking at the thought of leaving him again, but she realized now that she had no choice. "Damien, I must return to the future one more time and try again to find records, anything that will prove conclusively that the child and I do belong here."

"Sarah, no—"

But she pushed him away and continued vehemently, "Listen to me, Damien. It's the child. Don't you see that it all revolves around the child now? We have no right to impose a destiny on this precious life we have created together. I must find out where our baby is truly meant to live."

He stared at her in anguish for a long moment, then sighed. "If you must do this thing, then let me come with you."

She shook her head resignedly. "Damien, you would not belong in my world any more than I feel I do. You must stay here and finish Vincy's memoirs."

He stared at her through her tears. "Sarah, I beg you, don't do this thing."

She grasped his hands. "Darling, think. When the baby comes, it won't be enough, not if we're all still trapped here. I don't know just what the answer is, but I think it has something to do with the grief that drew us together in the first place."

"The grief?" he repeated confusedly.

She nodded. "I think our being prisoners here has to do with our grief. I think we must let it go entirely in order to be free. I know that knowing you has helped me deal with my feelings over Brian. And you must let go of Vincy, too."

As he turned away in sudden despair, she squeezed his hands and continued, "Vincy didn't mean for you to spend the rest of your life mourning him. That's why it's so crucial that you complete the memoirs while I'm gone. And Damien, you must tell everything this time—including how he died."

At last his haunted eyes met hers. "Everything?" he repeated brokenly.

She nodded. "You've got to let him go, Damien, and you've got to do it alone. I'm not even sure you can do it with me here."

"How can you say that?"

"It's the only way."

At last, he nodded. "But what about the baby? You're due so soon now and going back to the present might harm you both."

"I don't think so. The time barrier has never hurt me before, but I'll be careful. And I promise you, I'll be back before our child is born—with answers."

"Oh, Sarah." Damien's arms trembled as he embraced her. "Godspeed, my love. Come back soon."

That night, they held each other close, both fearing that this could be their last time together.

The next morning, Sarah awakened before Damien. She kissed his lips tenderly. He shifted in his sleep, smiling, and her eyes stung at the unbearable sadness of leaving him. She glanced at him longingly as she dressed, saying a silent prayer that soon they would all be reunited—the two of them and their precious child. The thought that this good-bye might be forever was too tormenting to be borne.

Once she was ready, she stared at him again for a last, long moment, until his image blurred in the mist of her tears. Then she went down the stairs, opened the front door and slipped out of his life once more.

Chapter Twenty-Eight

Moments later, Sarah was walking through the forest toward Miss Erica's house. The morning was mild, and the twentieth century looked much the same as she had left it. Fall had passed, of course, and after it, winter. A new year had arrived, and now spring's glory had ripened into the heady verdancy of early summer. Taking deep breaths of the dew-scented air, Sarah realized that, as much as it had saddened her to leave Damien once more, she had keenly missed the out-of-doors. In a way, she felt like a flower denied the nourishing light of the sun for too long.

As she crossed a footbridge, she spotted the familiar, white-haired woman walking near the swamp. As always, Sarah called out to her and waved; as always, the woman merely slipped away without acknowledging her. Sarah shook her head wonderingly. The old woman seemed almost like a talisman, marking her comings and goings.

Soon, Sarah arrived at Miss Erica's house and found the key just where she'd left it, under the mat. She let herself in the backdoor, breathing a sigh of relief when she noted that Ebbie hadn't arrived yet. The house appeared normal, the rooms quiet and orderly. She walked around, hunting for Casper and calling his name. Since the animal had disappeared from the past several months ago, she had hoped he had returned here. The cat was nowhere in sight, and there were no feeding dishes set out in the kitchen.

Sighing, Sarah went into the bedroom. She stripped off her nineteenth-century clothing and hid it, then hunted around for something to wear. Given her advanced pregnancy, she found that none of her old clothing fit her. At last she was able to squeeze her swollen form into an old sweatshirt and a pair of loosely fitting sailor slacks with a cord-tied waist. Glancing at her pear-shaped reflection in the mirror, she wondered what the people here in Meridian would think when they learned of her pregnancy. She sighed. Doubtless, she'd soon become the subject of gossip. There was no real cure for that, since there was no way she could tell anyone here what had really happened to her. At any rate, she had too much on her mind right now to worry unduly about what the local citizens might think.

Sarah was in the kitchen making coffee when Ebbie walked in. The maid stopped in her tracks at the sight of Sarah, gasping and jerking a gnarled hand to her heart. "Miss Sarah!"

"Hello, Ebbie," Sarah replied, turning to her with an apologetic smile. "I didn't mean to startle you. Did you find the note I wrote you before I left this last time?"

Ebbie nodded. "But you gone a long time, Miss Sarah." Ebbie's eyes widened as they fixed on Sarah's enlarged middle.

Sarah forced a smile and stepped forward. "Well, as I said in my note, I did go off on a very long trip with some friends. And, as things turned out, I—er —met a man and—"

Sarah was debating whether or not she should tell Ebbie that she was married now, when the phone rang.

"That your mama," Ebbie informed Sarah. "She call every day now. She worried about you."

"Oh, dear," Sarah muttered.

Ebbie turned and picked up the receiver, answering, "Davis residence," out of longstanding habit. She listened a moment, then nodded vigorously. "Yes, ma'am, Miz Jennings. She back. Your Sarah here now." Scowling fiercely, she extended the receiver to Sarah.

Sarah swallowed hard as she stepped forward and took the phone. Watching Ebbie tactfully retreat into the den, she said tremulously, "Mom?"

"Sarah!" Her mother's voice sounded nearly frantic. "Thank God you're back! We've been about to send out the National Guard. Where on earth have you been, child?"

"Mom, didn't you receive my letter saying I was going to Europe with Brenda Birmingham and her family for the winter?"

"Yes, we did receive that letter, but it's been almost seven months now without so much as a postcard from you."

"Mom, I'm sorry. Look, I'm fine. It's just that I was having such a good time that I forgot to write."

She heard her mother sigh fiercely. "You and

Brian. Such free spirits. Neither one of you could ever be bothered with such trivia as writing letters."

A painful silence fell in the wake of Margaret Jennings' words. At last, Sarah said, "Mom, again I apologize."

"Very well, dear. It's spilt milk at this point, I guess." There was another pause, then Margaret abruptly asked, "Sarah, can you come home?"

Sarah frowned, taken aback. "Is something wrong—with you or Dad or Teddy?"

"No, we're all fine. It's just that we've missed you so, honey. And next week—well, as you know, it's Brian's birthday."

Sarah sighed heavily, her heart twisting with sadness. "Oh, Mom, I'm so sorry."

In a low voice, her mother continued, "I can't believe he was killed just weeks before his nineteenth birthday. He would have been twenty next week, if only . . . Anyway, your father is taking it hard, Sarah, much harder than I thought he would. We're having a small memorial service, and it would mean a lot to all of us if you could attend."

Sarah struggled a moment, feeling saddened and quite torn by her mother's request. She knew that her time back here in the present would necessarily be quite limited and that there were so many things she needed to do—records to trace, decisions to make.

Yet Sarah also realized that she needed to see her family. Indeed, her mother's call had brought this reality crashing in on her. She had truly neglected her folks and Teddy, and this might be her last chance to say good-bye to them—and to make her peace with Brian.

She knew now that these were things she must do.

"Okay, Mom, I'll try my best to come," she said. Thinking of her pregnancy and the shock it would surely pose to her parents, she added, "Only, there might be—well, a complication."

"What do you mean, Sarah? You're not ill or—"

"No, I'm not ill. It's just that—" She took a deep breath, then said in a low voice, "I met a man while I was in Europe. In fact, I'm married now."

"You're married!" her mother gasped. "To—to some European? And you didn't even let us know?"

"I'm sorry, Mom. It all happened so fast."

"So it appears! And just where is this new husband, Sarah? Will he be coming home with you?"

Sarah bit her lip. "No, he can't make it this time. Anyway, I'll tell you all about Damien when I get there."

"Damien?"

"That's my husband's name." She cleared her throat awkwardly. "And I'm afraid you're going to be in for an even greater shock."

"Yes?" Sarah could hear her mother's voice rising.

"My husband and I—we're expecting a child soon."

"Good Lord, Sarah!"

Trying to sound calm, Sarah continued, "So I'll need to check with a doctor before I fly home. But I do want to make the memorial service if I can—and see all of you, of course."

There was a moment of stunned silence on the other end.

"Mom, are you okay?"

"Yes. Just flabbergasted, dear."

Sarah had to laugh. "Look, Mom, I promise that I'll explain everything when I get home. And I'll call you and let you know when my flight will get in."

"Okay, Sarah. Take care, dear."

"I will, Mom. Thanks."

After Sarah got off the phone, she sat down in the den with a cup of coffee, wondering what she should do first. The very thought of all she needed to accomplish during the coming weeks was exhausting. All her instincts told her that if she was to live with Damien permanently in the past, she would need to return to him before their child was born.

Yet her instincts also urged her to go home to Atlanta—and to search for records here to find proof that she and the child *had* remained in the past with Damien. She also needed to contact Mr. Baldwin about settling the final details of her cousin's estate. Indeed, she felt pulled in a hundred directions at once, and unfortunately, now that she was in her ninth month of pregnancy, even the most routine activities soon exhausted her. She would need to pace herself quite carefully if she were to accomplish all her goals during the coming weeks.

First things first, then. The memorial service was four days away, which didn't give her much time. She would need to have a checkup before she went home. Sarah hadn't seen a doctor since Dr. Ferguson had confirmed her pregnancy in New Orleans last fall. She was concerned for the welfare of her child, and she also needed to check with a physician before she considered flying this late in her pregnancy. Driving to Atlanta was, of course, out of the question, given her general lassitude these days and the shortness of time.

Thus, Sarah first picked up the phone and called Dr. Ferguson's office in New Orleans. She explained that she would be in town briefly during the next two days and that she would like to have a checkup before she flew on to Atlanta. Sarah was relieved when the nurse said they could fit her in for an early morning appointment two days later.

Next, Sarah made a reservation to fly home three days from now, then she called her friend Brenda Birmingham in New Orleans. Brenda was delighted to hear from Sarah again. Sarah explained that she and Damien were married now and that she had come back to Meridian to settle some details of the Davis estate. Then Sarah asked, "How would you like to have a houseguest for a couple of nights?"

"Oh, Sarah, you know I'd love to have you anytime. Can Damien come with you?"

"I'm afraid not this time. As a matter of fact, Damien is—well, he's away on business at the moment. I'll be joining him in a few days. But first, I've made an appointment with your doctor for another checkup, and there's some business I need to take care of in New Orleans, as well."

"Come right on, then, Sarah. I can't wait to catch up on everything with you."

Sarah thanked Brenda and told her friend to expect her by noon the following day. As she set down the receiver, she felt her baby kick against the constriction of her sweatshirt, and she smiled. She definitely needed to buy some maternity outfits to wear here in the present. There was no way she could spend the next week or so in slacks and a sweatshirt.

Sarah decided she would go to town and buy some clothing; while she was there, she could also go see the parish clerk to see if Faith Hamilton had found any leads regarding the local historical society papers that had been donated to a museum in New Orleans. And she needed to stop in at Mr.

Baldwin's office, as well, to let him know she had returned.

At a clothing store in Meridian, Sarah selected several maternity outfits—two street dresses, a pair of slacks and a blouse, and a sedate navy-blue coat-dress to wear at Brian's memorial service in Atlanta. The saleslady was very helpful, cutting the tags on one of the casual dresses when Sarah announced that she wanted to wear it out of the store.

Her next stop was the parish courthouse. The parish clerk, Faith Hamilton, remembered Sarah at once. Thankfully, the polite little woman made no comment regarding Sarah's pregnancy.

"I'm sorry to be so late getting back to you on my inquiry," Sarah told Miss Hamilton. "But have you been able to find out the name of the New Orleans museum which received Celeste Boudreau's historical papers?"

"Yes," Miss Hamilton replied. "As a matter of fact, I spoke with Ann Boudreau soon after you came by the courthouse last fall. She said she donated all of her mother's papers and artifacts to the—oh, what was that name?" The little woman snapped her fingers, then finished with a triumphant smile, "The Miro Collection in New Orleans. That's what it was."

Sarah frowned. "The Miro Collection? I've never heard of it."

"I believe Ann said the collection is housed in a mansion in the Garden District. The house is owned by one of the local historical societies, I understand. Evidently, they give tours, and there's also a museum on the ground floor. At any rate, I'm sure you can look the museum up in the New Orleans telephone directory."

"Thanks, Miss Hamilton," Sarah said eagerly. "I can't tell you how much you've helped me."

After Sarah left the courthouse, she decided to walk on over to Jefferson Baldwin's office and let him know she was back in town. She'd spoken with him briefly last fall, telling him she was leaving town on an extended journey. He'd told her then that they could settle the final details of Cousin Erica's estate when she returned.

The thought of seeing the lawyer also brought to mind the whole question of her future. Perhaps she should have a will drawn up. Whether or not she would be able to live her future with Damien, all her instincts told her she needed to settle her affairs in the present. That way, if she should disappear from the present entirely—as she fervently hoped she would one day—her estate here would be in order.

Yes, Sarah decided, she would definitely ask Mr. Baldwin about drawing up a will. As the baby once again kicked, she had to chuckle. Wouldn't Mr. Baldwin be in for a shock when he saw her and learned that she was now married and eight months pregnant?

Then Sarah frowned. Should she actually tell Mr. Baldwin that she was married now? Was her marriage to Damien even legally binding here in the present? That particular question was mind-boggling.

Yet the more Sarah thought about it, the more distressed she became by the potential legal ramifications if she told the lawyer that she was now married. Her knowledge of Louisiana law was quite limited, but she was aware that this was a community property state. If, as a married woman, she were to have a will drawn up, she might be legally required to make some provision for her husband. Worse yet, what if she were required to provide proof of her marriage or her new name? What if she should even need Damien's signature on some of the documents pertaining to the will or to settling Erica's estate? There was certainly no way she could tell Mr. Baldwin that she was married to a man who lived in another century. And it was even conceivable that her will might be invalidated later, if she used a name that wasn't legally hers here in the present.

Sarah shuddered at the possibilities. Telling Mr. Baldwin that she had a husband would definitely be a complicating factor, and right now she couldn't afford any complications. Her time here was simply too limited.

No, she decided, despite her obvious pregnancy it would be far better to pretend with Mr. Baldwin that she was still single. As far as the laws here were concerned, she probably *was* still single. And so far, she hadn't actually told anyone here in Meridian that she was married.

Her decision made, Sarah slipped her wedding ring off her finger and into her pocket just before she swept through the door to Jefferson Baldwin's office. Mr. Baldwin's middle-aged secretary greeted Sarah with a wide-eyed stare followed by a nervous laugh.

"Well, hello, Miss Jennings. How was your trip?" the woman asked, after she recovered. "I mean, Mr. Baldwin told me you were going to be gone for some time."

"My trip was wonderful," Sarah replied. Glancing

toward the door to the inner office, she added, "Is he in? I was hoping I might slip in for a moment and let him know I'm back in town."

The secretary bit her lip. "Oh, dear. I'm afraid Mr. Baldwin's tied up with a client, but if you'd like to wait—"

"Yes, I believe I will," Sarah said.

Sarah sat down on the vinyl couch and used her waiting time to sift through a stack of news magazines on the coffee table. She caught up on world events over the past seven months. She felt deeply saddened by news of the assassination of Dr. Martin Luther King, the Pueblo incident, and the Tet offensive in South Vietnam. At least peace talks were at last starting in Paris—a small ray of hope.

Sarah was still deeply immersed in her reading, when the secretary at last piped up, "You can go in now, Miss Jennings."

Sarah thanked the woman, got up and walked toward the inner office. Even as she was reaching for the doorknob, Jefferson Baldwin emerged to greet her. He wore his familiar seersucker suit and looked as if he hadn't aged a day since she'd left.

"Why, hello, Miss Jennings," he began with a grin. Then, spotting her advanced pregnancy, he colored and added in a low, awkward voice, "That is, if it *is* still Miss Jennings?"

Sarah's chin came up. "It is."

Jefferson Baldwin recovered his composure in remarkable time. "Well, please come in, my dear."

Once they were both seated in the inner office, Mr. Baldwin said, "This is a most pleasant surprise. How was your trip?"

"Excellent, thank you."

"I'm pleased to hear it, and of course it's good to

have you back. So what can I do for you, dear?"

She leaned forward in her chair. "I came to check on my cousin's estate. The last time I spoke with you, the will still hadn't gotten through probate."

He nodded. "Actually, the will passed probate months ago. Just a matter of getting the final papers ready for your signature."

"Good. Can we set up a date, then? Actually, I'm about to leave for Atlanta, but I should be back in a little over a week."

"Well, we could set up an appointment for, say, ten days from now."

"That would be great."

An awkward silence stretched between them, then Baldwin smiled kindly and said, "Sarah, is there some other way I can help you?" His color deepened as he added, "I mean, my dear, I can't help but have noticed that your—er—situation has changed since you were last here."

Sarah couldn't resist a chuckle. "You're right, Mr. Baldwin. I'm expecting a child now. And I would like to discuss with you having a will drawn up."

"Oh?" He scowled, drumming his fingertips on the tabletop. "I don't mean to pry, but does this mean that you're planning to raise your child alone? I mean—" he paused to cough nervously "—what of the baby's father?"

Sarah spoke stiffly. "There's a possibility that we'll marry." Watching Baldwin's frown deepen, she added with determination, "But in any event, I won't be giving up my child."

"I see." He cleared his throat. "Then this man is willing to marry you?"

"Yes. But we've made no definite plans."

Again, Baldwin's fingertips rapped his desktop,

and he looked deeply immersed in thought. "Perhaps—that is, if you are considering a fairly imminent marriage—you might hold off on the drawing up of your will until afterward. You see, your legal status will change then, and you'll almost certainly have to amend and reexecute your will."

"I want to proceed with the will now, thank you," Sarah said smoothly, feeling relieved that she had decided not to tell Baldwin of her marriage to Damien in the past. "I can always consult with another attorney later on—when my status changes."

"As you wish, then," Baldwin said. He picked up his pen and a legal pad and flipped to a blank page. "Basically, what kind of terms do you have in mind for this will?"

Sarah bit her lip. "That's something I haven't completely thought through as yet. I came by today mainly to let you know I'm in town. As for the specifics I want included in my will—can I call you in a few days?"

"Certainly. In fact, if you can get back to me fairly soon, we might be able to execute the will the same day we settle Erica's estate."

"Yes, I would like that. I'll be sure to call you soon, then."

Sarah and Mr. Baldwin shook hands and said their good-byes. Moments later, as Sarah drove out of town, she passed the local Catholic Church and remembered asking the priest to search for records on the Fontaine family. She stopped in a St. Jerome's, but the young father informed her with regret that he'd been unable to find anything. Sarah thanked him and left.

By the time Sarah arrived home, she felt exhausted. Obviously, she'd be able to find no further records on her or Damien here in Meridian. Her only hope now was that the answers she needed could be found in New Orleans.

Chapter Twenty-Nine

The next morning, Sarah packed for her trip home to Atlanta, then she drove on to New Orleans to stay with Brenda. Her friend was delighted to see her and exclaimed over Sarah's advanced pregnancy. Brenda wanted to know all about Damien and what he and Sarah had been doing over the past months. Sarah answered Brenda's incessant questions in as vague terms as possible, saying that she and Damien had been traveling for some time, and that even now he was waiting for her in Atlanta. Sarah hated lying, but she was much more afraid of the consequences should she tell her friend the truth.

After lunch, Sarah was at last able to break away gracefully, telling Brenda that she must run some errands about town. She left Brenda's home and drove to the Miro Collection, which the telephone directory had said was on nearby Carandolet Street.

A Tryst in Time

The old Greek Revival mansion was filled with wonderful period furnishings; however, Sarah hardly gave the fabulous rooms more than a passing glance as she headed through the hallway for the museum collection, which a sign had informed her was housed at the back of the first floor.

Sarah entered a large, well-organized room filled with bookshelves, glass display cases and shadow boxes on the walls. She explained to the guide in charge of the room that she had come from Meridian and that she wanted to see any historical papers that had been donated to the museum by Ann Boudreau.

The middle-aged woman knew exactly what Sarah was referring to. She showed her to a table, then graciously brought her a cup of tea. Moments later, the guide began depositing large stacks of aged documents and dog-eared volumes in front of Sarah.

Sarah sifted through the records. They were a hodgepodge—everything from old diaries and journals to letters, marriage certificates, newspaper clippings and family Bibles.

She worked all afternoon, occasionally getting up to walk around the room and relieve some of the pressure on her aching back. As the hours trickled by, she found references to some familiar names in Meridian, but disappointingly nothing on the Fontaine family.

Sarah had just finished with one huge stack and was starting on another when the woman in charge of the room said apologetically, "I'm sorry, ma'am, but we have to close now."

Sarah thanked her and said she'd be back the following day.

* * *

The next morning, Sarah had her appointment with Dr. Ferguson. He examined her, confirming that she was in excellent health and that the baby seemed to be thriving; Sarah was thrilled when he let her listen to her child's heartbeat. He told her to expect her child in about four weeks.

When Sarah asked Dr. Ferguson about flying home to Atlanta the next day, he expressed some initial misgivings. But when she explained about the memorial service, he agreed that she needed to go, cautioning her to get plenty of rest and not to overtax herself.

Immediately after her appointment, Sarah went back to the museum on Carandolet. She worked well into the afternoon, stopping for a brief lunch. As the hours passed, she again discovered nothing helpful in the records. Indeed, she was about to despair of finding anything on Damien and his family when she opened an ancient black book and found it to be Olympia Fontaine's Bible.

Sarah stared at the aged book in awe. Attached to the first page was a yellowed note written by Celeste Boudreau. The note explained that the Bible had been found 30 years ago; it was discovered in the attic of an old cottage being torn down in Meridian. With amazement, Sarah realized that the Bible must have been found in the very house Damien had bought for his aunt.

Eagerly, she began turning the pages. She found the Family Record and went down the listings of births, deaths and marriages. There were listings pertaining to Damien's parents and Olympia and entries of the births of Damien and Vincy. Damien's marriage to Lucy was also entered, as was her death and that of their stillborn son. Vincy's death was listed, too.

But there, to Sarah's frustration, all information on Damien ended. There was no record of his death, of his marriage to her, or of their child. The last listing was of Olympia Fontaine's death on September 16, 1886. The death was entered in a different handwriting, perhaps that of a priest or friend, Sarah mused.

Sarah closed the Bible with a sigh. Why hadn't Olympia recorded her marriage to Damien or the birth of their child? The lack of these listings did not bode well for her future with Damien.

Had Olympia left her and the child out of the listings because they never again returned to the past? Or was her bitterness and resentment toward Sarah so deep that spite had motivated the deliberate omissions?

She might never know.

The next day, Sarah flew home to Atlanta where her parents met her at the airport. As she stepped into the terminal, she spotted them waving at her—a tall man in an impeccable suit and a slender woman in a tailored linen dress. Sarah smiled and waved back, hurrying toward them. Her folks also rushed forward, only to pause awkwardly before her, studying their pregnant daughter in her maternity dress. Then the uncomfortable moment ended as Margaret Jennings forced a smile and hugged Sarah warmly. "Oh, darling, it's so good to have you back."

"It's good to be home, Mom," Sarah replied.

Her father stepped forward and embraced his daughter briefly, kissing her forehead. "Welcome home, Sarah. How was the flight?"

"Just fine, Dad."

Richard Jennings clapped his hands together and

said with forced cheerfulness, "Well, then, guess we'd better get your luggage. Right, honey?"

As the three of them walked off to the baggage area, Sarah studied her folks more closely. Richard and Margaret Jennings were much alike, a tall, sophisticated middle-aged couple who had aged markedly in the last year. Sarah noted that her mother's beautifully coifed hair was now more silver than blond, and her father's hair was practically snow-white. Both her parents looked as if they'd lost ten pounds since she'd last seen them, and the lines on their faces had deepened conspicuously. The change in her folks—the aura of frailty and aging about them—filled Sarah's heart with sadness.

The car ride back to Ansley Park was also awkward, filled with strained conversation. When Margaret Jennings asked Sarah about Damien, she told her parents a story she had concocted on the airplane—that she had met and married him while she was in Europe with Brenda, that she had returned here to the States to settle her affairs, and that even now Damien was waiting for her in France. When her father asked gruffly what her husband did, she told him that Damien owned an estate in the South of France. Her parents accepted her story outwardly, but from the meaningful glances they exchanged, Sarah knew that they remained deeply shocked, even suspicious, regarding her sudden marriage and advanced pregnancy.

Sarah couldn't blame them for being stunned and surely disappointed at her behavior. She marveled at the web of deceit she had spun about herself in order to cover up what had truly happened to her over the past nine months, but telling her friends or family the truth seemed out of the question at this point. She was sure that no one would believe her, and she couldn't risk having anyone take steps that might prevent her from returning to Damien.

When they pulled up to her parents' palatial colonial mansion, Sarah's 11-year-old brother Teddy burst out the front door even as she was getting out of the car. "Sis, you're back!" he called out exuberantly, sprinting down the walk toward her.

Watching her brother approach, Sarah was stunned to see how much Teddy had changed in the last nine months. He seemed half a foot taller, and his voice had also deepened. His more adult clothing—tailored slacks and long-sleeved shirt—added another layer of maturity to his visage. While Sarah was delighted to see her brother, her heart twisted with sadness at the thought of all she had missed in his life—and all that she might again miss in the future.

Teddy hugged her warmly. "Sarah, I'm so glad to see you."

"Hi, Ted, I'm glad to see you, too," she returned brightly, ruffling his blond hair. She drew back and added, "Let me take a better look at you. Good grief, you're as tall as I am now. I can't believe how much you've grown in the last year."

"So have you," Teddy quipped back with a charming flash of dimples.

Sarah had to chuckle at her brother's forthright remark, yet her parents only looked on in grim silence. Oh, dear, she thought, it was obviously going to be a long, awkward visit.

Inside the house, Sarah shared tea with her parents and Teddy who was full of questions about Sarah's life in Louisiana and especially about her expected baby. Sarah answered his queries as calmly and honestly as possible, but she once again felt the strain as her parents sipped their tea in sober silence. As soon as she could slip away gracefully, she excused herself and went upstairs to take a nap. To her surprise, she slept around the clock, not stirring until the maid brought in her coffee the following morning. She got up and dressed for Brian's memorial service.

Rain was pouring down as Sarah and her family left for the downtown church. The service, attended by about 50 relatives and family friends, was brief and uplifting. Sarah watched her mother dab at tears as the minister spoke of resurrection and life everlasting; her father's expression was stony. Only Teddy turned to smile at Sarah and bravely squeezed her hand. He reminded her poignantly of Brian in that moment, and Sarah's eyes misted with tears. She felt oddly at peace.

By the time they left the church, the rain had stopped and the sun had broken through the clouds. Sarah saw this as a good portent. Glistening droplets gleamed on the crepe myrtles and peach trees as they drove back to Ansley Park to receive their friends.

At her parents' home, Sarah's mother greeted her guests with typical poise as the servants circulated with trays of food. Sarah spoke briefly with some colleagues from the Art Association and with a couple of old girlfriends with whom she'd made her debut. Yet she noted that her father stood apart from the others, his expression grim.

Sarah went over and hugged her dad. "I think the memorial service was great," she told him with a brave smile.

Richard Jennings shrugged. "It was your mother's idea."

"It was a very good idea." Biting her lip, Sarah

added, "You know, Dad, we're meant to let him go."

Her father frowned. "I beg your pardon?"

"Brian—we have to let him go," Sarah said feelingly. "I think that was really what the service was all about, and I know Brian would have wanted it that way."

Richard Jennings sighed and stared at his feet. Suddenly, he looked very old and tired to Sarah, and her heart filled with tenderness toward him. "It's not easy for a man to lose a son, Sarah."

"I know, Dad." Sarah nodded toward the couch, where Teddy sat with an elderly friend of the family's. "But you have Teddy. He needs you. Look to him now."

Unexpectedly, Richard Jennings looked up and stared at Teddy for a long, poignant moment. Then he turned to smile at his daughter. "I'm glad you came. And glad you're doing so well. Now, when are we going to get to meet this husband of yours?"

"In time, Dad," Sarah hedged. "But just remember that I'm happy. I really am."

He nodded. "I can tell. You're truly aglow."

Later, after the guests had left, Sarah's mother took her aside in the dining room. As Margaret Jennings dabbed at a stain on the linen tablecloth with a napkin dipped in club soda, she asked, "Sarah, you're not thinking of flying back to Europe now, are you?"

Sarah bit her lip. "Actually, Mom, I'm flying back to Louisiana in a couple more days. I still have business to settle there regarding Cousin Erica's estate. After the baby is born and I'm fully recovered, the two of us will fly on to France to join Damien."

Margaret Jennings appeared aghast, her mouth dropping open as she tossed down her napkin. "You mean your husband won't be there when your baby is born?"

Sarah replied stiffly, "Mom, I'm afraid it's just impossible for Damien to get away right now."

Margaret drew herself up stiffly. "Then I must come with you to Louisiana, dear. You'll need help."

Sarah shook her head adamantly. "I have all the help I need there in Meridian. Besides, Dad really needs you right now."

Sarah's mother frowned suspiciously. "Sarah, does this husband of yours even exist? If you're in trouble, dear, please know that you don't have to invent a husband in order to spare our feelings."

Though Sarah felt herself flushing, she continued to face her mother bravely. "Mom, I'm not lying. Damien does exist. I didn't invent him. The fact that he can't be with me right now is not his fault. And furthermore, my husband can't wait until I and our child can return to him."

"Very well, then," her mother said resignedly.

Yet Margaret Jennings appeared highly skeptical and worried.

As the day had passed, Sarah had felt increasingly compelled to go see Brian's grave, which she hadn't visited in over nine months. It was as if she needed to hold her own private memorial service, to say her own benediction.

Thus, late that afternoon, Sarah borrowed her dad's car and drove toward Westview Cemetery, where Brian was buried. She stopped en route and bought a bouquet of yellow roses. Moments later, she stood holding the flowers on the shady, rain-washed knoll where her brother rested. The site was warm and quiet, bees buzzing about in the thick, nectar-scented air. Standing there so close to her brother, Sarah was filled with a sense of peace so profound that tears again filled her eyes.

"Happy birthday, Brian," she said at last. "I think you're the real reason I came home. You know, I've learned a lot during the past year. I've learned what grief means, and I've learned what love means—and I've learned about letting go. That's why I'm here today. But you always knew that, didn't you? You always wanted that for me."

Sarah paused, choking out a laugh that was half a sob. "You know, Mom always called the two of us free spirits, but you're the one who was always truly free. You understood so many things I never did. I've been a prisoner ever since you died, Brian. I've been dead inside. But I know about freedom now. I know how it feels to be truly alive. You see, Damien brought me all the things you always wanted me to have. You'd like him, Brian. I only wish you could have known him. He's like you in a lot of ways—so sensitive, intuitive and wise. We're going to have a child together now, and my dearest hope is that I may find him again and spend the rest of my life with him."

Sarah stared at Brian's headstone until the marble blurred with her tears. She could feel the pieces of her heart becoming whole in that moment. "I'm free now, Brian," she said at last. "Damien's love has set me free."

Sarah laid down the flowers and let Brian go.

In another cemetery, almost a hundred years away, Damien Fontaine stood holding a bouquet of flowers before Vincy's grave.

"Vincy, I've come to tell you that the memoirs are finished now," he said in an emotional voice. "I did what Sarah asked me. I told it all, including how you died. I think that something was healed inside me in that moment, just as Sarah always knew it would be."

Damien smiled. "Sarah has finished repairing your paintings now, Vincy. You should see them; you should see how they shine. They're whole again, just as I have become whole since she came into my life."

Damien paused, then went on in a choked voice, "Sarah's gone now, seeking answers she feels she must find before our child is born. But my most fervent hope is that she'll come back to me—and soon.

"I've come to thank you, Vincy, to thank you for the gift of my life, a life I hope I may now share with Sarah. You'd like her, if only you could have known her. But I know now that you're at peace, that you're with the woman you truly loved. I'm sorry I never recognized what you and Lucy shared, but I can't feel guilty about it anymore, Vincy. Sarah's love has filled my heart and left room for nothing else. And I realize now that she was right. You and Lucy never would have wanted me to suffer this way. It's time to let you rest—both of you—here in this lovely, serene place. May the two of you find in eternity what you could never have on this earth. And, if God wills, may I find my beloved Sarah again and hold her and our child close to my heart forever."

Damien laid down the flowers and let Vincy go.

Chapter Thirty

The next three days passed quickly for Sarah in Atlanta. She spent time visiting with her parents and Teddy and dropped in on some old friends. She also called Dr. Hogan and spoke with him briefly, letting him know that she was doing fine. She glossed over the subject of her marriage to Damien and their expected child, making her life now sound very settled and upbeat.

On the day after Brian's memorial service, Sarah sat down in her bedroom with pad and pencil and attempted to jot down a list of the basic terms she wanted included in her will. She knew she needed to call Jefferson Baldwin right away, if he was going to have the will prepared in time for their appointment next week.

For several days now, Sarah had been debating about what she should do with her property in Louisiana. Since her parents were quite wealthy, leaving her estate to them would be little more than an encumbrance.

One of her major concerns was the old house and what might happen to it in the future, if she should indeed spend the rest of her life with Damien. She hated the thought of its possibly being torn down, but knew that restoring it would be logistically difficult and perhaps prohibitively expensive. She toyed with the idea of donating the house to the state as a historic site. Yet she knew that setting up that type of endowment would be quite complicated, and she simply had no time to arrange for any sort of elaborate trusteeship. She finally came to the unhappy conclusion that, if she were to return to Damien, she had to let go of all her affairs in the present.

With this goal in mind, Sarah roughed out a list of basic terms. She then picked up the phone and called Jefferson Baldwin in Louisiana. When his secretary learned that Sarah was calling long distance, she put the call right through to Baldwin.

"Why, hello, Sarah," Baldwin began. "My secretary tells me you're in Atlanta?"

"Yes, that's right," Sarah replied. "Look, Mr. Baldwin, I've been doing a lot of thinking about Cousin Erica's estate and the terms I'd like included in my will. I'd really like to discuss it all with you now, if that's okay."

"Sure," he replied. "Just let me grab my pad and pencil here . . . Okay, Sarah. Shoot."

"Basically, Mr. Baldwin, after my child is born, I'm planning to do some extensive traveling in Europe. It's possible that I may never return to Louisiana. For this reason, I'd like for you to arrange to sell most of the property I've inherited."

"I see. You say you want to sell most of your property?"

"Yes, with the exception of the acres Reuben Voisin is farming. I'd like that parcel of land and the cottage given to him and his family outright."

"I'm sure that can be arranged."

"Good. And after the rest of the land is sold, I'd like five percent of the proceeds given to Ebbie."

There was a brief pause on Baldwin's end. "You realize, of course, that Erica already set up a generous annuity for Ebbie?"

"Yes, I know that, but I still want Ebbie to be given an additional five percent of the proceeds."

"Very well, then. So you basically want everything liquidated?"

"That's right."

"You're talking about generating a substantial amount of cash, Sarah."

"I'm aware of that. Which brings me to my will. Once everything is sold, I'd like the proceeds placed in trust. I'd like my will to provide that half of my estate will go to my child or children, and the other half will go to the Juilliard School of Music in New York City."

"Juilliard?" Baldwin repeated confusedly.

"Yes, Juilliard. You see, I had a brother who was destined to become a world-class violinist. He would have gone to Juilliard, except that he got drafted by the Army and was killed in Vietnam."

"Sarah, I'm so sorry," Baldwin said sincerely. "And I'm sure that sort of bequest will present no problem."

"Good." Sarah took a deep breath, then forged on. "I'd also like my will to provide that if I should die or be declared legally dead, and no child or children of mine are found within a five-year period, then the entire estate will revert to Juilliard."

She heard Baldwin whistle. "My, you've really given this a lot of thought, haven't you?"

"Yes, I have."

"Clients usually don't come to me with such complicated bequests in mind. Tell me, are you expecting to die or be declared legally dead any time soon?"

"No, of course not," she answered smoothly. "However, my child and I will be traveling in some rather obscure locales in Europe, and I think it best to provide for any contingency."

"Well, I guess you know what's best, then."

"Can these particular terms be included?"

"I see no real legal stumbling blocks."

"And how soon can everything be ready?"

"Well, drafting the will itself shouldn't take too much time. However, as for selling all your land, and setting up the trust—"

"I'll want you to handle everything, of course," Sarah put in hastily. "As I told you, I'm not going to be returning to Louisiana for long."

"Then I'll need a power of attorney."

"Just prepare any documents you'll need, and I'll sign them. Look, Mr. Baldwin, do you think you can have everything ready for my signature when we settle Cousin Erica's estate next week?"

He whistled again. "That's kind of pushing things a bit."

Sarah's hand clenched on the phone. "Please, it's very important to me. Like I said, my time here is quite limited."

"Very well, then. I'll try my best to have all the documents ready to be executed then."

Sarah thanked Baldwin and gave him her number

in Atlanta, in case he had any questions in the next day or so. She breathed a sigh of relief as she hung up the phone.

Sarah's final two days at home were marred by the news of Robert Kennedy's assassination in Los Angeles. The country reeled in shock, and Sarah felt more displaced than ever, here in the twentieth century. More than ever, she felt she belonged in a simpler, earlier time with Damien.

Nevertheless, her parting with her family at the airport was a tearful one, especially as she hugged her parents and her little brother good-bye for the last time. "Take good care of Mom and Dad," she whispered in Teddy's ear, clutching him tightly.

"I will, Sarah," he promised with a smile.

Then she was off for the boarding ramp, waving to her family bravely, knowing in her heart that she would never see any of them again. Before she exited the terminal, she turned to catch one last glimpse of them. They all stood near a window in a broad beam of sunlight—a tall, slender couple with their son. Her father had one arm around Teddy's shoulders, the other around his wife's waist. All of them were smiling at her, and Sarah smiled back through tears. She realized that her visit home had somehow drawn her family closer, and this insight gave her a small measure of peace.

Still, once the plane took off, she wondered how she could convey to her parents and Teddy a final good-bye, assuming she could stay permanently in the past with Damien. She knew her mother was already suspicious about her alleged husband in Europe. She would have to offer them some sort of explanation before she disappeared from their world entirely. What should she do? Write them a letter and tell them the truth? They would never believe her, and they might worry even more afterward.

Sarah sighed. She could only hope she would find more information in New Orleans. If she found the answers she needed regarding the past, that same knowledge might help her resolve the present, as well.

Back in New Orleans, Sarah returned to Brenda Birmingham's house. She spent a day recuperating from her trip and visiting with her friend. Then she set out on another search for records.

The next few days brought Sarah no definitive answers. She went to other museums in New Orleans and to the Public Library. In all her investigations, she found only one glimmer of hope. In some old records of the Daughters of the Confederacy, she found a listing of prominent families who had contributed to the building of a war memorial in Jefferson City. One listing read: "$1,000 was contributed in the name of Mr. and Mrs. Damien Fontaine of St. Christopher Parish, on December 6, 1885."

At first Sarah was jubilant, sure she had discovered absolute proof that she had remained in the past with Damien. Then doubts began to seep in. The phrase "in the name of" troubled her. If she had disappeared before 1885, Damien might still have contributed the money in both their names, or he might have gotten tired of waiting for her. He might have later had their marriage annulled and married someone else. It was even possible that a third party had contributed the money in the name of Damien and his wife.

Nevertheless, Sarah drove to the monument itself

in Jefferson City on the off chance that some of the names of the contributors might be inscribed on the monument. She was, of course, out of luck; the monument bore only an inscription to the glorious Confederate dead and the date the Daughters of the Confederacy had erected it.

At one of the last museums Sarah went to, the curator suggested that Sarah go up to Baton Rouge to contact state agencies or write to the National Archives in Washington, D.C. But Sarah had no time for another long trip, nor could she wait for answers to arrive by mail.

Indeed, she was running out of time. She knew in her soul that if she was going back to Damien, she had to go soon.

Sarah finally made her breakthrough early the following week. She was touring a charming old museum on Royal Street when she walked into a large back room and spotted half a dozen of Vincy Fontaine's paintings hanging on the walls.

Sarah stopped dead in her tracks and gaped at the hauntingly familiar paintings. The eeriest feeling crept over her. It was as if she had gone home again, home into the past. Indeed, most of her favorites were among the paintings on the walls, including Vincy's self-portrait and his painting of the house. All six looked as vivid and beautifully restored as they had the day Sarah completed her repairs.

As she continued to stare, mesmerized, at the works of art, an elderly docent sprang up from her desk and rushed to her side. Touching Sarah's arm, she asked, "Ma'am, are you all right? You turned so pale, all of a sudden."

Sarah turned to the kindly woman and braved a smile. "I'm fine. It's just that I was rather shocked to see these paintings. They're by Vincy Fontaine, aren't they?"

The woman laughed in pleasant surprise. "Why, yes, they are. Perfect examples of expressionism, don't you think? May I ask how you're so familiar with Mr. Fontaine's work?"

Sarah quickly improvised an explanation. "I'm on the board of the High Museum of Art in Atlanta, and I believe I've seen some of Mr. Fontaine's work in a catalog there."

The woman frowned, laying a finger alongside her jaw. "Now that is odd. Mr. Fontaine was a very talented, but quite obscure, artist. I wasn't even aware that any others of his paintings were in circulation, Mrs.—er, what did you say your name was?"

Sarah smiled. "I didn't. I'm . . ." About to say, "Sarah Fontaine," she stopped herself in time, realizing that this woman might find it odd that she had the same last name as Vincy. "I'm Sarah Jennings," she finished instead.

"Sarah Jennings!" the woman gasped.

Sarah frowned in perplexity. "Yes, that's right."

The woman shook her head in amazement. "Why, what a coincidence! Sarah Jennings is the name of the artist who restored these paintings back in the 1870's."

Sarah felt all color draining from her face. "How do you know this?"

"Well, the restorer signed and dated the backs of all the paintings," the woman explained. "She also sketched in an hourglass on each one—a rather whimsical touch, don't you think?"

Sarah's heart seemed to climb into her mouth. "May I see the backs of the paintings?"

The woman frowned. "Well, we'd have to take

them down off the walls, and our policy does forbid—"

Sarah gripped the woman's sleeve and spoke intently. "Please. It's such a remarkable coincidence, don't you think? I really would love to see the restorer's signature. And, like I said, I'm on the board of the High Museum of Art, so I'm quite accustomed to handling old works of art."

The woman sighed. "Well, I suppose there's no harm in your seeing the backs of the canvases. It *is* a fun coincidence about the names, isn't it? I'll just call in our custodian, then . . ."

During the next few minutes, Sarah was able to examine the backs of all six paintings. All bore her bold, unique signature, the date of the restoration, and the hourglass. Sarah was filled with a growing excitement as she studied each panel. Examining the last of the six, she asked the docent, "How long have these paintings been here?"

The woman frowned a moment. "Since 1920."

"Since 1920!" Sarah gasped. "Tell me, do you have any proof of the date the paintings were acquired? Are they logged in somewhere? And do you know from whom they were acquired?"

"Well, we could examine the records, I suppose."

The woman brought out several old log books, and she and Sarah perused them until they found the listings for Vincy's paintings. Sarah stared at the faded handwriting in wonder. She learned that the six paintings had been donated to the museum in September of 1920. The artist's name was entered, as well as her name as restorer, but unfortunately there was no other helpful information. All six paintings had been an anonymous gift.

After scrutinizing the listings for a long moment, Sarah asked the docent, "If I send some people here to see you, would you show them the backs of the paintings and this log book?"

The woman frowned. "Well, I'm not sure. This is a rather peculiar request."

Sarah offered the woman her most engaging smile. "I know it must seem a strange request to you, but a friend of mine—and my family—would truly be fascinated by the coincidence of the names. You see, I'm an artist myself."

The little woman brightened. "Oh, are you?"

"Yes. Which makes the entire coincidence so much more interesting, don't you think?"

"Why, of course."

"And therefore, I'd really appreciate it if you would show my family and friend these items."

"Well, I suppose it couldn't do any harm."

"Great. Whom should I tell them to ask for?"

"I'm Mrs. Ida Lee Carpenter."

"And are you here every day, Mrs. Carpenter?"

The little woman drew herself up proudly. "Yes. Haven't missed a day for almost forty years now."

Sarah shook Mrs. Carpenter's hand. "Thanks. I can't tell you how much you've helped me."

Driving back toward Brenda's house, Sarah felt elated. She now had positive proof to offer her parents and Brenda that she *had* lived in the past with Damien. Now, she needed to arrange for them to find this proof—after she went back again. She mulled over the problem for a moment, then nodded as realization dawned. She would write them letters to be opened and read later. That was the perfect solution.

But as she pulled into Brenda's driveway, her spirits sagged again. Sure, she could now prove that she had lived for a time in the past, but she still had no actual proof that she and her baby belonged there.

Inside Brenda's house, the maid informed Sarah that Mrs. Birmingham was out, that she had gone to drop the children off at Vacation Bible School for the afternoon. Sarah thanked the maid and went upstairs. Actually, she was grateful for the moments alone, for she knew she had much to do.

In the guest room, Sarah at once pulled out writing paper and a pen and got to work. She began with the letter for her parents and Teddy. Her opening sentence read:

"By the time you read this, I will be living in the year 1872 with the man I love."

Sarah reread the first sentence and whistled. Would her parents ever believe her bizarre story? She wasn't sure, yet all her instincts urged her to tell them the truth this time—to put an end to the web of deceit she had spun about herself—before she left them forever. Surely she owed her parents and Brenda that much.

Thus Sarah bucked up her courage and continued writing. She told her parents about her experience with time travel, how she had gone back to live in the past with Damien and had fallen in love with him. She told them that she planned to live the rest of her life with him. She left out the problem of being trapped in the house. She told them about her will and why she had decided to have it drawn up in her maiden name.

Then Sarah wrote,

"I know you will find all of this hard, if not impossible, to believe, but I do have proof to

*offer you that I have actually lived in the past.
You see, while I was in the past, I repaired
some paintings done by Damien's brother. On
the back of each painting, I signed my name
and entered the date of restoration. Anyway,
several of these paintings are now housed in
the Vieux Carre Museum on Royal Street in
New Orleans. The paintings have been there
since 1920. If you'll go to the museum and ask
for Ida Lee Carpenter, she'll show you the
backs of the paintings with my signature. And
she'll also show you the log book with the date
the paintings were acquired and my name
entered as restorer. These items I offer you as
positive proof that I have actually lived in the
past with Damien Fontaine."*

Sarah ended with,

*"Please, Mom and Dad, don't worry about
me. Just love each other and Teddy. Be happy.
Please know that I love you and miss you, but
I realize now that my destiny is not to be
found in this century. My true happiness can
be found only in the past with the man I love."*

As Sarah finished the letter, she prayed that the
words she had just written would later prove true.
She sealed and stamped the letter, then wrote a
similar one for Brenda. Afterward, she took both
letters downstairs and went hunting for Brenda.

Sarah found her friend drinking tea in the large,
sunny living room. As soon as Sarah stepped into
the room, Brenda sprang up from the couch, looking quite anxious. "Sarah, please come in. We need

to talk. I've been quite worried about you—all these mysterious comings and goings—"

Sarah held up a hand. "Really, Brenda, I'm fine. I know I haven't been much of a houseguest, but, as I explained before, I had some business to settle here. And now—well, I have a rather big favor to ask of you."

"Oh? Sit down, then. We'll have tea and talk."

Sarah sat down and took the cup of warm tea Brenda handed her. She started to speak, then hesitated, setting down her cup and staring at the precious letters tightly clutched in her other hand.

"Do you want to tell me what this is all about?" Brenda prodded. "Does it have anything to do with those letters you seem to be holding onto for dear life?"

Sarah glanced up at Brenda, smiling sheepishly. "You know me so well. Actually, I have here one letter for you and one letter for my parents."

Brenda paled visibly. "My, how dramatic you are."

Sarah laughed ruefully. "Wait till you hear the rest."

"Yes?"

Sarah took a deep breath, then met Brenda's troubled gaze. "Brenda, I want you to take these letters and hold them for—well, safekeeping. Then, if you don't hear from me in three months time, I want you to open the letter addressed to you and mail the other one to my parents."

As Sarah had spoken, Brenda had turned sheet-white. "*If* I don't hear from you in three months time? What on earth is going on here, Sarah?"

Sarah sighed. "I have to go away, and I'm afraid— well, you may never see me again."

"My God!" Brenda gasped. Then she snapped her fingers. "It's that man, that Damien, isn't it, Sarah? He's the reason you're going away."

"Yes," Sarah admitted.

Brenda clenched her jaw and blinked rapidly. "I knew there was something funny going on here. The guy is never around, and now you're going away with him and never coming back?"

Sarah touched Brenda's arm. "The letters will explain everything, Brenda. Just remember that this is what I want."

But Brenda was shaking her head incredulously. "I can't believe I'm hearing this. You're saying that I'll never see you again? Will you please tell me what on earth is going on?"

"I can't," Sarah said miserably.

All of a sudden, Brenda's eyes grew enormous. "Don't tell me this Damien is in trouble with the law. Or is he—oh, my God!—he's not taking you behind the Iron Curtain, is he? He's not a communist or something?"

There, Sarah had to laugh at the irony. She would be disappearing behind a curtain—of sorts. To Brenda, she said earnestly, "No, Damien is not a criminal or a communist. All I can tell you, once more, is that this is the way I want things to be and that when you read the letters, you'll understand everything. Beyond that, just know that Damien has made me happier than I've ever been in my life." She stared at her friend beseechingly. "You wouldn't want to deny me that happiness, would you, Brenda?"

Brenda appeared miserably torn. "Well . . . no."

Sarah leaned even closer and spoke intently. "You must promise me that you'll do what I ask three months from now. And you must give me your solemn word that you won't look at either of these letters in the meantime."

"Sarah, are you sure this is what you want?"

Sarah thrust the letters into her friend's hand. "I've never been surer of anything in my life."

Chapter Thirty-One

The next day, Sarah drove back to Meridian and Miss Erica's house. She felt exhausted, drained from both the summer heat and her frustration at not being able to find any records proving that she and her baby had actually remained in the past with Damien.

Sarah did feel relieved that at least she was getting things set up so that she could remain permanently in the past with Damien, if she chose to do so. Yesterday, after some additional persuasion on Sarah's part, Brenda Birmingham had at last, reluctantly given her word that she would carry out Sarah's wishes and hold onto her two letters for the next three months. Brenda had promised that if she didn't hear from Sarah by then, she would open the letter addressed to herself and mail the other one to Sarah's parents. The two friends had then parted tearfully.

Now, after Sarah had her scheduled meeting with Jefferson Baldwin, all her affairs in the present would be settled. Yet Sarah would also be setting up an "out" clause with Baldwin; she planned to ask him, too, to wait three months before he acted on her power of attorney and placed the plantation up for sale.

Sarah had reasoned that surely in three months' time she would have made her decision regarding whether or not she and her child could stay permanently in the past with Damien. She prayed that things would work out the way she wanted, but if they didn't, she planned to return in time to keep Brenda and Mr. Baldwin from acting on her directives.

Back at Miss Erica's house, Sarah took a long nap. Her dreams were again haunted by the familiar, cryptic message, *Elissa . . . The three gifts . . . The answer is Elissa. . . .*

Sarah awakened late in the afternoon, feeling bemused as always by the dream, but also grateful that her nightmare of Brian had not returned in so long a time. Indeed, she knew now that she had finally laid her brother to rest when she went home to Atlanta. This realization filled her with a deep peace.

Sarah got dressed and fixed herself a glass of iced tea in the kitchen. As she passed through the den, she again stared at her painting of the old house with Damien's face so hauntingly superimposed there. Bittersweet tears filled her eyes. She needed to send the painting home to Atlanta, she decided. If she should depart the present permanently, she couldn't just leave the painting here; she wanted her folks to have it.

Sarah went to sit on the screened-in back porch,

393

staring out at the lovely, fluttering trees at the edge of Miss Erica's yard. What was she going to do? Her time here in the present was almost over now, and she still lacked the critical answers she needed. If only she had some sign to guide her! All she had was the strange dream, which still made no sense to her.

There was so many things she just didn't understand, such as the paradox of the window in time and the mystery of the cat, Casper, who had seemingly disappeared from both the past and the present.

While Casper might well be dead by now, Sarah still hadn't been able to figure out why the cat had possessed the uncanny ability to come and go in either century, when she couldn't. She remembered what Madame Tu had told her about not being grounded and how she must "believe." Yet she still didn't know how to make her belief strong enough to hold her in the past.

The only thing Sarah did know, out of all this confusion, was that she loved Damien and missed him terribly and yearned to be with him again. And another, very painful conclusion had dawned on her recently. Even if she never could become grounded in the past, perhaps her child *would* be grounded there; perhaps her child was meant to live there with its father. Damien had once called the baby his gift to her, selflessly saying he would never try to take the child away. But she must learn to be selfless, too. For this child, ultimately, wasn't just her possession; her baby would have its own destiny to fulfill, and it was her duty not to interfere but to help her child find out where he or she belonged.

Thus Sarah knew she must journey back to the past once more. She would pray that this time she *would* become grounded and that she could remain with Damien forever.

The next day, Sarah boxed up her painting of the old house, then drove into Meridian. After stopping off at the post office to mail the painting to her folks, she went to her appointment with Jefferson Baldwin. At his office, she found all the paperwork—including the final papers for settling Erica Davis's estate, her will, and the power of attorney—perfectly in order. Sarah signed everything and paid Baldwin his fee for the preparation of the additional documents. As she had previously decided, she asked Mr. Baldwin to wait for three months before he placed the plantation up for sale—in case she should change her mind in the interim, she told him. Baldwin agreed to abide by her wishes and not act for three months. Sarah thanked him for all his help and left, feeling greatly relieved that all her affairs in the present were in order now.

As Sarah drove out of town, she passed Madame Tu's cottage and spotted the negro woman out in the yard, pruning her roses. Sarah pulled over and called out a friendly hello.

Madame set down her pruning shears on the window ledge and walked over to Sarah's car. She wore her familiar, floppy hat, a flowered pullover blouse and double-knit slacks. She pushed back the brim of her hat, and her warm, chocolate-brown eyes met Sarah's. "Why, hello, honey. Good to see you again. I hear you back in town. You come in and have some tea wid Madame?"

Sarah gratefully accepted Madame's invitation, feeling warmed at the prospect of visiting with her friend and especially sharing her dilemma, once again, with this kindred spirit.

Moments later, when the two women were seated with cups of tea in Madame's dark, elegant dining room, the wise negro woman got straight to the point. "You been back again?"

At once, Sarah knew what Madame meant. "Yes. For seven months now."

Madame smiled as she looked Sarah over. "You have your baby soon?"

Sarah laughed. "Very soon."

"And you come back here for answers?"

Sarah heaved a great sigh. "Yes."

"But you not find any?"

Sarah shook her head in amazement at Madame's typical, uncanny insights. "No, not really. How is it you know these things?"

"Madame just know. You worried about the baby, child?"

"Yes." Sarah set down her tea, and her feelings poured forth in a rush. "Oh, Madame, I'm still so confused. I love Damien, but I still don't know where I really belong . . ." She paused, placing a hand possessively on her pulsing stomach. "Or where this child belongs."

"You still don't believe," Madame said simply.

Sarah's other hand clenched on the tabletop. "But I'm trying to. I'm trying so hard."

"You got to have faith, child."

"I know." She gestured her frustration. "But what if this baby is like me—not really grounded in the past?"

Madame thought about this a moment, then said, "Where the child born, that where it meant to live."

"But how can you know this?" Sarah asked in wonderment.

Madame shrugged. "I know."

"Then, should I try to have the baby back in the past?"

"That for you to decide, child."

"I don't know what to do. I'm more confused than ever."

Madame reached out and placed her wrinkled brown hand over Sarah's. "Then find a quiet place, child. Have a good long think."

Sarah laughed ruefully. "Oh, Madame, if thinking alone could have solved this riddle, I would have found the answer long ago. The truth is, I've thought about my problem until I've analyzed it to death. I need something concrete, some sign to show me the way."

Madame nodded. "Perhaps the sign still come, child."

"Perhaps so," Sarah said with bravado. Feeling the baby kick again, she sighed. "Look, thanks for your help and the tea, Madame. I guess I'd better be going."

"May I ask a favor, child?" Madame asked.

"Sure."

"I need a ride to the plantation. I see a friend there."

"A friend?"

Madame nodded. "She a white lady. She live near you—near the swamp. I used to work for her. Tomorrow her birthday. She be ninety-six."

"Ninety-six!" Sarah thought quickly, then snapped her fingers. "I know! Your friend must be the old woman I've seen from time to time near the swamp. I've called out to her, but she never answers."

Madame nodded. "Her hearing not good."

"What is this friend's name?"

"Her be Elissa."

"Elissa!" Sarah gasped.

Suddenly, a powerful chill washed over Sarah, and she knew in her soul that she'd finally been presented with the sign, the answer she so desperately needed. She clutched Madame's sleeve and spoke in a hoarse, impassioned voice. "Elissa! Oh, my God! For over a year now, I've had a dream where I keep hearing the words, 'The answer is Elissa.' Madame, you must help me. I must meet this woman."

Chapter Thirty-Two

The two women rode out to the plantation in tense silence. Sarah had the giddy, euphoric feeling of someone on the verge of a gigantic discovery. She knew she was about to find an answer, an answer straight out of the dream she'd had for so many months.

As Sarah turned her car onto the cutoff leading to Miss Erica's house, she asked Madame, "Where does this Elissa live?"

"She live in the swamp," Madame replied.

"In the swamp? But I've never seen a house or anything."

"She have a cottage there."

"How long has she lived there?"

Madame pondered this. "Ten years. Elissa, she come home to die."

The words made Sarah shiver. "How do we get to this cabin?"

"We walk from Miss Erica's house. It not far."

At Miss Erica's house, Sarah parked under the carport, and she and Madame headed off toward the swamp. The heat was oppressive, and Sarah stumbled slightly as they neared the first footbridge.

Madame caught Sarah's arm to steady her. "You all right?"

"I'm fine. I just stumbled over a root or something."

"You be careful; it not far," Madame said.

Once they had crossed the footbridge, Madame led Sarah directly into the forest, through a maze of tall cypress, tupelo and sycamore trees. Navigating was difficult in the tangle of greenery, but about 50 yards after they began their trek into the woods, a trail miraculously appeared. Sarah found to her relief that it was not as hot here, with the canopy of trees to shade their path.

At last they emerged in a clearing where a cedar cottage stood. Sarah stared at the small house in amazement; as many times as she had walked through these woods, she had never seen this bungalow before. The cottage was totally cut off from the world, picturesquely sitting at the edge of a narrow bayou covered with duckweed and giant water lilies. Like the old steamboat gothic house, the cabin was weathered, gray and timeless. It had a high, pitched tin roof, a flagstone chimney and a homey gallery spanning the front, complete with porch rockers and hanging baskets.

"This is where Elissa lives?" Sarah asked.

"Yes. Come, child."

With a building sense of wonder, Sarah followed Madame up the creaking gray steps. The front door of the cottage stood ajar; Madame didn't knock, motioning for Sarah to proceed inside ahead of her.

Sarah stepped inside and quickly caught her bearings. She stood in a large, homey room with planked floors and walls and crude, simple furnishings—a table and chairs, a single bed, a wardrobe. Tall windows lined the front and back walls, and the cabin was surprisingly comfortable in the brisk cross-breeze.

Soon Sarah's attention was seized by the familiar, white-haired woman, who sat in a rocking chair flanking the hearth. She wore a long gray dress which looked as if it had come from another century. Indeed, everything about the cabin appeared anachronistic, as if from another time. Even the smell of the room was aged—a mixture of weathered cedar, pomander balls and woodsmoke.

Then, as Sarah took a step closer to the woman, she gasped. For sitting in the woman's lap was Casper! He looked very much at home, gazing up at Sarah with his magnificent golden eyes.

My God, Sarah thought, so Casper had been with the old woman all this time. It seemed right, somehow. An eerie feeling gripped her—a feeling of discovery, of *déjà vu*.

Her heart pounding, Sarah stepped farther into the room. The old woman didn't seem to hear her or note her presence; she petted the cat, rocked slowly and hummed "Amazing Grace."

Sarah glanced at Madame, who gestured her onward. As Sarah moved even closer to the woman, she caught another sharp breath. For just beyond Elissa's rocker, on the wall next to the hearth, was a small wooden shelf.

On the shelf were three small gifts.

For a moment, time seemed to hang suspended as Sarah stared, mesmerized, at the three small boxes. The words of her dream, haunting and electrifying, echoed through her mind: *Elissa . . . The three gifts . . . The answer is Elissa. . . .*

All at once, Sarah staggered, and Madame rushed forward to grasp her arm. "You sit down now, Miss Sarah," she said sternly.

Like a sleepwalker, Sarah let Madame lead her to a chair across from Elissa's rocker. Madame went to the crude table, picked up a glass pitcher and poured Sarah a glass of water. She handed Sarah the filled glass and waited patiently as she drank. Only then did Madame turn to address the old woman. "Miss Elissa, you got company," she said in a loud, forceful voice.

The old woman at last glanced up at Sarah, and for a moment Sarah thought she spotted a spark of recognition in her dark eyes. Perhaps Elissa remembered seeing her near the swamp.

"Hello," Elissa said at last, in a cracked, aged voice.

"Hello," Sarah returned with a smile. She gazed at the old woman's wrinkled yet still lovely face, studying the deeply brown eyes which seemed filled with wisdom. "How are you doing today?"

The old woman didn't answer. She glanced downward and began petting the cat again and humming her hymn.

Sarah turned confusedly to Madame.

Madame moved to Sarah's side and took the empty glass from her hand. "Miss Elissa, she a little slow these days," she explained. "You just ask your questions, child, slow and patient-like. Okay?"

"Of course."

"Good. I wait on the porch, then. You and Miss Elissa talk."

Sarah nodded, watching Madame set down the glass and leave. Then she turned back to Elissa, who still seemed off in her own world, humming and petting the cat. Where should she begin? What should she ask this woman? She had no real idea what she was supposed to learn from Elissa.

Again, Sarah stared at the three gifts on the shelf beyond the woman. The tiny boxes were wrapped in white paper, now yellowed with age. Each box sported a different colored ribbon—one pink, one yellow, and one blue. Sarah somehow knew that these were the very gifts that had haunted her dreams for so long. But what did they mean?

As Sarah turned back to Elissa, she was astonished to see the old woman staring at her. "You like my gifts?" Elissa asked.

Sarah nodded eagerly. "Yes, I like your gifts very much. But they appear quite old."

"My mother gave them to me," Elissa said.

"Your mother?" Sarah repeated, feeling a chill streak down her spine.

"Yes. Right before she died."

Now Sarah's skin was beginning to tingle. "When was that?"

Elissa didn't answer Sarah's question directly. Instead, she rocked and murmured, "My mother knew she was dying. She gave me a box full of gifts. One to open each year on my birthday after she passed."

"Why, what a lovely idea," Sarah cried, touched by the notion.

"She was a good woman, my mother," Elissa went on.

"I'm sure she was. Tell me more about her," Sarah urged.

Elissa stared off at some point in space. "It was long ago."

"I know, but please, tell me whatever you remember."

Elissa was quiet a moment, rocking. Then she said, "She was pretty and kind. She loved me very much." She turned toward the wall and added, "She gave me these gifts."

Sarah sighed, realizing that the woman was quite tired and confused and that extracting any concrete answers from her would be difficult. She stared again at the gifts, biting her lip. "Do you have any idea what the gifts mean?"

Elissa seemed not to have heard her. "Only these three are left now," she murmured. "I'll open one tomorrow."

Sarah brightened. "That's right. Tomorrow's your birthday, isn't it?"

"I'll be ninety-six," Elissa said.

Suddenly, Sarah shivered violently as she realized that if she had had her baby in the past, in the year 1872, then this woman could be her very own daughter, now almost ninety-six years old! Sarah searched Elissa's features more closely. The woman was so old and wrinkled that it was near-impossible to detect a familial resemblance. Yet the woman's eyes—oh, God, why hadn't she seen at once that they were the vibrant, deep brown of Damien's?

With her heart in her voice, she asked Elissa, "What was your mother's name?"

Elissa stared at Sarah blankly for a moment.

Sarah leaned forward and spoke in a hoarse, desperate tone. "Please, you must tell me your mother's name."

"Fontaine," the woman murmured back. "I'm Elissa Fontaine."

"Oh, my God!" Sarah gasped.

Then, even as Sarah was reeling in shock, the old

woman asked, "Do you want to see my mother's grave?"

Moments later, the small group quietly, reverently, walked into the woods. Madame and Sarah walked on either side of Elissa, each holding one of the old woman's arms as she ambled along on her frail, faltering legs.

Shadows were growing deep as Elissa pointed ahead and said simply, "There."

Sarah stared ahead, seeing nothing but more trees and a tangle of brush, but Elissa continued slowly, steadily onward, leading the others through a small opening in a curtain of greenery.

Sarah gasped, for they now stood just inside a circle of trees, totally cut off from the rest of the world. In the center of the clean, swept grotto were two weathered headstones; in front of each sat a jar with dried flowers.

"My mother's grave," Elissa said, pointing. "My mother is buried here, my father there. I come here twice a week. I pray and read my Bible. I sweep the ground." A faraway, wistful quality lit her eyes. "I go to the other place, too, near the river."

Sarah stared at Elissa, electrified. "You mean, Vincy's grave? The place where Vincy and Lucy Fontaine are buried? You're the one who tends those graves, as well?"

Elissa stared at Sarah blankly as the wind whipped around her and the sun bathed her ancient face with an ethereal beauty.

"It's all right," Sarah said, feeling an intense welling of sympathy for Elissa. "Don't try to answer now."

Shivering with anticipation, Sarah turned and approached the headstones. She walked down the narrow path between the two graves. She glanced at the marker on her right; it was weathered and covered with lichen, and she could find no readable inscription. Then she glanced at the headstone on the left; its condition was only slightly better. The inscription was quite faded, but at last she made it out: "Damien Fontaine."

With a powerful shudder, Sarah sank to her knees, tears filling her eyes. "Oh, Damien," she whispered, her heart welling with love, wonder and exquisite sadness. She examined the stone carefully, but couldn't find a date of birth or death. Then she studied the marker on the right again. She ran her fingertip over the mottled surface, but could feel no lettering whatever. She turned to Elissa, who stood behind her now. "Can you tell me your mother's name?"

"Fontaine," was all Elissa said.

Sarah glanced at Madame, who merely shook her head.

"Can you tell me when your mother or father died?" Sarah asked Elissa anxiously.

Elissa didn't answer but hummed her hymn as she moved off to pluck a small weed from the foot of her father's grave.

Feeling intense confusion, Sarah rose and stared down at the graves. If only there were some sign, some way for her to know for sure! Damien was buried here, and Damien was surely Elissa's father. But who was the woman beside him? Even if Elissa had been raised by him in the past, had she remained as well? Or did someone else rest beside him here? Oh, why couldn't Elissa tell her more?

Then the wind whipped up again, and something very strange happened. Sarah sensed her own aura in the small cemetery. It was as if, all along, she had

had two souls—a soul of the past and a soul of the present—and now, at last, they had merged, becoming one forever.

Tears filled Sarah's eyes, and she was suddenly so choked with emotion and realization that she could barely breathe or swallow. With a feeling of absolute conviction, she turned and walked toward Elissa. "Oh, my love," she whispered.

Her daughter stood outlined in sunshine at the edge of the grotto.

Her daughter lay cushioned deep in her own belly, waiting to be born.

Sarah knew these things now.

With tears streaming down her face, Sarah embraced Elissa. Showers of light danced over their silhouettes as the breeze surged. Sarah realized that she held both the past and the future in her arms.

Chapter Thirty-Three

A few minutes later, the small party returned to Elissa's cabin. The old woman trembled as Sarah and Madame helped her into her rocking chair. Elissa's features were wan, her breathing shallow and raspy.

With alarm, Sarah turned to Madame. "Is she all right?"

Madame nodded. "Elissa just tired. We go now."

Sarah's heart sank. "But there's so much I need to know, so much I must ask her."

"I know, child," Madame said sympathetically. "But not today. Elissa too tired."

Sarah nodded resignedly. Casper, who had been sleeping on Elissa's bed, now crossed the room and hopped into her lap again. Elissa petted the cat and began to hum. Sarah watched in wonder.

Stepping closer to the old woman, Sarah smiled

down at her. "I'll come back tomorrow," she said in a clear, distinct voice.

Elissa nodded. Then she did something very strange. Reaching toward the wall, she picked up the three small gifts and extended them toward Sarah. "Here, you take these," she said.

While Sarah felt touched by Elissa's gesture, she was also confused. "But you're supposed to open one tomorrow on your birthday."

"You take these," Elissa repeated with agitation, her gnarled hand trembling on the boxes.

"Take them, child," Madame directed gravely.

"All right, then." Sarah took the three small gifts from Elissa and hugged her gently. "Thank you, Elissa. Thank you for everything."

"Good-bye," Elissa said.

"Good-bye," Sarah said.

Madame leaned over and said to Elissa, "I come back, later. You hear?"

"Yes," Elissa said.

Tears filled Sarah's eyes as she and Madame turned to leave. At the portal, Sarah pivoted to take one last glance at her daughter. Elissa was rocking with her eyes closed, again humming "Amazing Grace," with Casper sleeping peacefully in her lap.

With a low cry, Sarah turned and left with Madame. Halfway down the trail to the bridge, she felt her baby kicking in her stomach. She realized with alarm and awe that her child hadn't moved the entire time she had been with Elissa Fontaine.

"Tell me about Elissa," Sarah said.

It was ten minutes later, and Sarah and Madame Tu were seated in her kitchen drinking iced tea. Sarah had been relieved to find that Ebbie had

409

already left for the day when they had returned. On the table between the two of them were the three precious gifts that Elissa had given her.

"What you want to know?" Madame asked.

"Everything—anything you know about Elissa."

Madame frowned a moment. "I don't know much."

"Please, just tell me whatever you do know."

Madame nodded. "I think a long, long time ago, Elissa's family owned much land here."

"They owned this land," Sarah said.

"Maybe. Elissa sold it all many years ago, except for a few acres and her cabin."

Sarah leaned forward and spoke intently. "Why is it that no one in this area knows about Elissa Fontaine? Everyone I've asked has maintained that there are no Fontaines living here."

"That true," Madame said.

Sarah gestured her frustration. "But it can't be true, not if Elissa has lived here all her life."

"Elissa not live here. Only these last years."

"Then where . . . ?"

Madame scowled a moment. "I first met Elissa thirty years ago. She here on a visit. She hire me to keep her cottage while she gone."

"Gone where?"

"To Vicksburg. Elissa, she spend her life there."

"Vicksburg, Mississippi?"

"Yes. She ran a home for old Confederate soldiers. The last one, he die about ten years ago. Then Miss Elissa, she come home."

"Then why does no one in town know about her?"

Madame shrugged. "Elissa, she not go to town. Reuben Voisin, he fetch her groceries and take care of her business."

"Reuben," Sarah murmured. "Then if Elissa never goes to town, she must be a veritable recluse."

"*Oui*," Madame said. "Elissa, she tired. She come home to die. She sing and read her Bible now. Sometimes she go to church with Reuben and his wife."

"To a black church?" Sarah asked.

"Yes."

Sarah smiled to herself. If Elissa left her cottage only to attend church with Reuben, then this, too, would explain why no one in Meridian knew about her. Sarah was also intrigued by the thought that her daughter was the type of person who would be compassionate toward all people, that Elissa had not only cared for aged Confederate soldiers but had also attended a black church. Elissa had definitely embraced her parents' values, Sarah thought with pride.

"Elissa, she be happy," Madame was now saying. "Reuben, he look out for her. And I come see her several times each year—on Christmas, on her birthday."

"I'm glad," Sarah said with a sigh.

Madame finished her tea. "I go back to Elissa now."

Sarah touched Madame's sleeve. "May I come with you?"

Madame shook her head. "No, not today. Elissa, she too tired."

"She's my daughter," Sarah said simply.

"I know," Madame said. "She the child you carry now."

"If you knew, why didn't you tell me?"

Madame smiled. "I just now figure it out, child. And like I told you before, you got to find the answers yourself, Miss Sarah. You got to learn to believe."

Sarah nodded. "Do you think Elissa knows—I mean, about me?"

Madame frowned a moment. "She sense something, maybe. Why else she give you the gifts?"

"Indeed. But why would she give all three away the day before her birthday? It's as if she knows something." Sarah's hand tightened on her glass, and her eyes met Madame Tu's anxiously. "Oh, Madame, I'm worried about her."

"She be all right," Madame said. "Now, I go spend the night with her. I read to her from the Psalms. Miss Elissa, she like that."

"Good," Sarah said. "Thank you, Madame."

After Madame left, Sarah realized that she felt exhausted. She went into the bedroom, undressed and donned her nightgown and got into bed. As she snuggled into the bedding, a feeling of sublime peace washed over her. She had found her daughter, her beloved daughter Elissa.

Rubbing her stomach, she murmured wonderingly, "Sweet little life. Do you know you're going to be a girl child? Yes, you must know. Won't your daddy be proud!"

The thought of Damien made Sarah's eyes fill with bittersweet tears. She couldn't wait to get back to him and tell him all the marvelous, amazing things she had discovered.

For now that Sarah had found Elissa, she knew where her child belonged; her child belonged in the past. Her most critical question had been answered.

If only she could know where she belonged.

Toward dawn, Sarah stirred, awakened by a dull pain at the small of her back. She drifted back to sleep, only to have the pain recur 20 minutes later. She was stirring for the third time when she gasped at the sight of an anxious, dark face hovering over her.

"It Madame," Madame Tu said. "Time for you to get up, child. Time for you to go."

Sarah sat up, rubbing her eyes as Madame switched on the lamp on her nightstand. "What's wrong? Is it Elissa?"

Madame sat down on her bed and said gently, "Miss Elissa, she dying."

Sarah stared wild-eyed at Madame. "I must go to her."

Madame squeezed Sarah's hand. "No, child. Miss Elissa, she have a good, long life, and now she passing peaceable. But you can't be there when she dying, child."

Madame Tu's warning gave Sarah pause. "When I was with Elissa yesterday, my baby stopped moving in my stomach. It didn't move again until we left Elissa's cabin."

Madame nodded. "I know."

"Then my baby might not be safe if—"

"You can't be there when Elissa dying," Madame repeated. "The aura, it too strong."

"Then what must I do?" Sarah cried despairingly.

"You got to go back to the house, child. To the past."

"So my baby can be born there?"

"Yes. That where the baby be safe. That where it meant to be born and live."

"But where am I meant to live, Madame?" Sarah asked with an anguished gesture.

"Only you know, child."

"If only I could know for sure," Sarah sighed. "Yesterday in the cemetery, I thought I sensed my own aura, but I still can't be certain where I belong. There was no name on the marker."

413

"You go back to the house," Madame said. "You have the baby there."

"And then?"

Madame sighed. "Maybe you be grounded then, child." Sadly, she added, "Maybe not."

As she felt her stomach tighten, Sarah's alarmed eyes beseeched Madame's. "Oh, Madame! I—I think I'm in labor now."

"I know. You go back to the house now, child. It your only chance."

Madame helped Sarah dress in her old-fashioned gown. The negro woman volunteered to help Sarah journey to the old house, but Sarah refused, insisting that Madame leave at once to go care for Elissa. When Madame reluctantly agreed, the two women embraced and Madame left.

Sarah went to the kitchen and picked up the three gifts, placing them in the pockets of her long dress. By now, her contractions were coming 15 minutes apart, and they were beginning to hurt. She didn't even have time to consider leaving a note for Ebbie; she simply left the house.

Her heart was as heavy as her steps as she started down the path into the still-dusky forest. She longed to be with Elissa, but Madame would be there to ease the old woman's passing. As much as Sarah yearned to be with her daughter at her death, she knew that Elissa's birth must now take precedence. And as Madame had said, she wasn't even sure her baby would be safe if she stayed here while Elissa died.

Of course, Sarah was afraid to have her baby in the past, without modern medical help there if she should need it. She was going into labor three weeks early, as well. But she knew that she must have her child in the past; she knew that Elissa belonged there. As for where she belonged, she still wasn't sure. It could be that she would die later this same day, bearing this child. It could be that Damien would find someone else later on. It could be that after the child was born, she would be whisked back to the present forever.

And it could be that she and Damien would live to a ripe old age together. The possibilities were endless.

At last, Sarah left the woods and approached the timeworn spectre of the house. The sun was just rising, bathing the ghostly mansion with a fragile, ethereal beauty. Sarah could hear the birds singing behind her, like a celestial choir guiding her ascension. The air was sweet, dew-washed.

Climbing the steps, Sarah turned to look out at the twentieth century one last time. She waved a symbolic farewell and turned to embrace her destiny.

Sarah entered the old house, went into the parlor and sat down. She took several long, deep breaths to recover from the exertion of her walk. Once her heartbeat returned to normal, she stuffed a hand in her pocket, fingering one of the three small gifts Elissa had given her. Tears filled her eyes at the sweetness and wisdom of her daughter's gesture. Elissa had known, Sarah realized. She had known that she would leave this world today—and be born in another.

Sarah sensed that the three gifts were not gifts in the material sense, but essential essences of joy and hope and love. Hopefully, one day these would be the beginning of a cache of gifts she would leave as a legacy for her beloved daughter Elissa.

Sarah chanted her mantra and clutched the three gifts. She felt deeply relaxed and peaceful. Just before she drifted away, Casper came into the parlor and settled in her lap, purring against her belly.

Chapter Thirty-Four

"Sarah, thank God you're back!"

Sarah blinked to gain her bearings. The first thing she saw was Casper streaking out of her lap. The next thing she saw was Damien hovering over her, looking quite concerned. A surge of joy filled her heart as she realized that she was in the past again, in his beautiful parlor. "Oh, Damien, I made it back to you."

He knelt beside her, hugging her gently, and his wonderful essence filled her senses. A poignant expectation gleamed in his eyes. "Did you find your answers, darling? Are you here to stay?"

"I—I'm not sure," she said honestly. Then a contraction seized her and she tensed, her features whitening.

"What is it?" he asked worriedly.

"I'm in labor," she said breathlessly.

His eyes widened in shock. "Why didn't you say so at once, darling? Let me get you upstairs."

Gently, Damien picked Sarah up, carrying her out of the parlor and up the stairs. Soon, he was placing her on the large bed in their room. He began unbuttoning her frock. "Here, I'll get you comfortable, darling, then I'll go fetch the doctor."

"No!" Sarah said vehemently. She had read enough about past medical practices to know that prior to the twentieth century many women who died of childbirth did so due to infections caused by the physician's dirty instruments or hands. And she was not about to trust an 1870's country doctor to ascribe to the relatively new theories of Pasteur and Lister.

"You don't want a doctor?" Damien now asked incredulously.

She shook her head as another contraction seized her. She realized that she must have dozed for some time before she arrived here, for her contractions were now coming with alarming frequency. "Please, trust me, Damien. I'll be better off with just you and Baptista attending me."

The color drained from Damien's face. "You want me to help with the birth?"

Sarah half-smiled, realizing she had shocked him. Such a practice was unheard of in his century. "Yes, Damien, I want you to be with me. It's the only way I'll feel safe."

He smiled tenderly, stroking her brow. "Then of course I'll stay. But are you sure about the doctor?"

"Yes," she gasped. "Please, don't fetch him. Besides, there may not be time."

Damien could not doubt the veracity of her words as he watched another contraction grip her. "Very well, then, darling."

"Just make sure that anything that touches me is clean," Sarah added. "Promise me that."

"I promise."

"And you'll need to boil some twine for tying off the baby's cord."

"I will, darling."

As he continued to unbutton her frock, she thrust her hand into her pocket and added, "Here. I want you to take these."

Damien stared at the three small boxes Sarah was extending toward him. "What are they?"

"I'll explain later. Just put them in a safe place, will you?"

"Of course."

Damien dressed Sarah in her nightgown. Then he left to sterilize the twine and place the three gifts in his office safe downstairs. When he returned, he brought Baptista with him to help. They arranged clean linens beneath Sarah's hips. As Sarah's labor intensified, Damien was at her side every moment, his eyes filled with deep concern as he held her hand and helplessly watched her toss her head and moan. Baptista was very solicitous and compassionate, too, frequently wiping Sarah's brow and showing her how to grip the headboard when the contractions became excruciating. At least the room was relatively cool, since it was only midmorning.

Within an hour, Sarah knew that her baby would come into the world soon. Her pains were unbearable now, and they came with such frequency that she had little rest between contractions. Damien, too, seemed to know this. Baptista glanced at him askance when he insisted that they both wash their hands with lye soap, but she didn't protest, dutifully following him to the basin.

Soon, Sarah had the desire to push, and all modesty was forgotten as Damien and Baptista helped her bring her baby into the world. Sarah tried not to scream, but this resolve became impossible to cling to as the pain seemed to split her apart.

Damien remained remarkably self-possessed during the moments of birth. He kept whispering soothing words: "It's all right, darling . . . Don't be afraid to cry out. I'm here . . ." All the while, his eyes were filled with a terrible anxiety. Still, his steadfast presence and love made Sarah's ordeal bearable.

Then an earth-shattering pain gripped her, and she felt the baby forcing its way through the birth canal. She screamed and pushed with all her might. She felt the baby leave her, heard a plaintive wail that twisted her heart, then heard Damien talking to Baptista in hushed tones about tying off the cord. A moment later, she looked up to see Damien holding their child. He was in his shirtsleeves, his hair askew and his face glossed with sweat as he held the still-slippery infant. Yet his handsome features bore an expression of sublime joy, and his eyes were glazed with tears. Already, Elissa was whimpering in his arms. Never in her life had Sarah seen anything so sweet.

"It's a girl, darling," Damien said hoarsely to Sarah. "A perfect baby girl."

"I know," Sarah whispered back. "Her name's Elissa."

He glanced at her quizzically, but then the infant again seized his attention as she cried out and flailed with her little arms and legs. He took the baby to the daybed. Baptista, who had already cleaned up the afterbirth, helped Damien sponge Elissa off and diaper her. Then Damien wrapped a blanket about the baby and brought her to her mother.

"She's beautiful, darling," he said, settling the child in her arms. "She has your hair."

Sarah held the baby and stared down at her through tears of joy. Her child was pink and perfectly formed, with a crowning of wispy blond hair on her tiny head. "She'll have your eyes, Damien."

Again, a perplexed look crossed his gaze. "Darling, are you up to holding her? You look so weak."

"I'm all right," Sarah assured him. "Just tired."

"Do you want me to take her now?"

Sarah nodded. As he took the child, she whispered, "I found out that she belongs here. She's yours now, Damien."

Then Sarah fell into a deep, exhausted sleep.

By that evening, Sarah was feeling well enough to sit up and drink some chicken broth. Damien joined her, sitting on the edge of the bed. The baby had fallen asleep soon after she was born; even now, Elissa dozed in her cradle, a few feet away from the bed.

"How are you feeling, darling?" Damien asked Sarah as he took her emptied bowl and set it aside.

"Still a little weak, but much better." She glanced lovingly at the cradle. "I can't believe how she's sleeping."

Damien smiled. "I think she knows her mother needs a good rest." His smile widened into a grin of pride. "I'll wager she'll be up soon enough, wailing to be fed."

"I can't wait," Sarah replied, as the thought of nursing Elissa filled her with a primal joy.

"Darling, I've been wondering something," Damien said.

"Yes?"

"Why did you call her Elissa earlier? Why did you tell me she'll have my eyes?"

Sarah hesitated a moment. "I met her, Damien. I met her back in the twentieth century."

He looked stunned. "My God! Please, you must tell me everything you know."

"Then I think I'd best start at the beginning."

"Please do."

Sarah told Damien about her return to the present and her search for clues that she and the baby had remained in the past. She told him of finding Olympia's family Bible, and of how she'd learned that a contribution had been made to a Confederate war memorial "in the name of" Mr. and Mrs. Damien Fontaine. "But I found nothing that proved conclusively that I stayed here," Sarah said. "Then, a black woman I know in the present—Madame Tu—introduced me to our daughter."

Damien glanced at the cradle wonderingly, then back at Sarah. "Tell me all about our daughter. Our Elissa. Ah, Sarah, I do love that name. It suits her perfectly."

"I agree," she said with a smile.

Sarah told Damien how she had met Elissa, and everything she had learned about their daughter's life. He listened intently, occasionally asking a question, expressing great interest in Elissa's activities over the years. Sarah ended by saying sadly, "Elissa is dying on this very day back in the present, but as Madame Tu told me, she had a good, long life. Ninety-six years."

Damien shook his head in awe. "So our daughter is born and dies on the very same day. How difficult it must have been for you, to be near her when—"

Sarah nodded. "I wanted to go to Elissa today, to be with her while she was dying, but Madame Tu cautioned against it. She was afraid that the baby might not be safe if I stayed with Elissa while she died. Something about the auras being too strong."

Damien nodded. "In an uncanny sort of way, I think I understand." Eagerly, he went on, "But when you met our daughter, didn't she confirm that you were her mother, that you stayed here and spent the rest of your life with me?"

Sarah sighed. "I'm afraid she couldn't. Damien, she was very old and hard of hearing, and only lucid part of the time. However, she did take me to see her parents's graves."

Damien's eyebrows shot up. "Then you *did* find proof!"

Sarah shook her head sadly. "Unfortunately, no. Elissa did show me the two graves, but the markers were heavily eroded. All I could make out was your name on one of them. I couldn't make out my name or the dates either of us died."

Damien squeezed Sarah's hand and said passionately, "Still, I'm certain you're the one who will be buried beside me. I find any other explanation impossible to believe."

Sarah bit her lip. "I'll admit there was . . . something there, in the cemetery. I felt as if I sensed my own aura."

Damien snapped his fingers. "Then there's your proof. Surely you must know that you belong here —now and forever."

Sarah stared at him, her expression miserably torn. "Oh, Damien, I wish I did, but in some ways, I'm more confused than ever."

He embraced her and spoke hoarsely. "Sarah, you're meant to be here—with me and Elissa."

Yet Sarah could only pull away, fighting tears. "If I were, then I'd be grounded here, and as far as I know, I'm still not. My existence here is still tenuous."

Damien sighed, taking her face in his hands. "When will you believe that what we have is enough for me—for us?"

"You don't understand," she choked out. She glanced at the cradle with eyes brimming with love and anguish. "How can it ever be enough for her?"

Chapter Thirty-Five

During the next week, Sarah recuperated and enjoyed Elissa. The baby thrived on the milk Sarah's body supplied. Elissa was a good baby, sleeping for long periods and rarely fretting.

Casper had stayed around since he and Sarah had returned to the past this last time. Once again, the cat came and went from the house with impunity. He also showed a protective interest in the baby, which Sarah found fascinating, since she had found the cat actually living with Elissa back in the present.

Damien was busier now, since he had hired on a crew to clear the tangled fields. Next spring, Belle Fontaine would have its first planting since the war. But Damien still managed to spend every free moment with his wife and child.

When Damien was with Sarah, he often remarked on how Elissa resembled her. Sarah always smiled, for while Elissa's blond hair and fair skin were obviously inherited from her mother, Sarah knew that soon the baby's eyes would turn the mesmerizing deep brown of her father's.

On a warm afternoon a few days after Sarah delivered Elissa, Damien came in to join his wife in the bedroom. He carried with him the three gifts she had brought back from the twentieth century.

Just inside the doorway, Damien smiled as he viewed Sarah on the bed, nursing Elissa; Casper dozed nearby on the coverlet. Sarah looked radiant; her long blond hair gleamed as it caught the light, and her gaze was fixed devotedly on the child. Watching the baby drink nourishment at her mother's breast was a sight that never failed to move Damien. His heart rang with joy to know that the two people he loved the most in this world were sitting right before his eyes, and he intended to do everything in his power to see that he never lost either of them again.

"Hello, darling," he said in a voice hoarse with emotion.

Sarah glanced up and smiled. "Hello, Damien. Come, join us."

Eagerly, Damien crossed the room and sat down next to his wife on the bed. Kissing the baby's head, he placed the small boxes in Sarah's lap. He nodded toward them. "I've been meaning to ask you about these, but I wanted to wait until you were feeling better."

Sarah smiled at him through sudden tears. "Elissa gave them to me," she whispered.

At once, he appeared fascinated. "She did? Tell me all about it."

Sarah nodded. "I'll have to start with the dream."

"Dream? What dream?"

"You see, for almost a year now, I've had a recurring dream where I keep hearing the message, *Elissa . . . The three gifts . . . The answer is Elissa.*"

"How amazing!"

"It was. But for so long, I had no idea what the dream meant. Then, when I went back to the twentieth century this last time and Madame Tu told me she had a very old friend named Elissa, the pieces of the puzzle began to fall in place for me."

"Go on," he urged.

Sarah glanced down at the boxes. "When we went to Elissa's cabin and I met her, these three little boxes were on a shelf on her wall. I asked her about them, and she told me her mother had given them to her."

"Her mother!"

"Yes. Elissa said that when her mother knew she was dying, she put together a collection of tiny gifts—one for Elissa to open each year on her birthday after her mother was gone. She told me only these three are left now."

Damien had listened with an expression of wonderment, and now he glanced at their nursing child in awe. "Oh, Sarah! And Elissa gave you these last three?"

Sarah nodded. Emotion almost choked her as she continued, "After Elissa took me to see her parents' graves, she insisted that I take the three gifts home with me." Her eyes met Damien's, and tears spilled forth. "She knew, Damien. She knew that she wouldn't live to open another gift. That's why she gave them to me."

Damien's gaze gleamed with emotion. "She knew you were her mother."

"Yes, I think so."

"Oh, Sarah, that's the sweetest story I've ever

heard. And after receiving the gifts from Elissa, how can you doubt that you'll be staying here?"

Sarah sighed. "Elissa never identified me for certain as the woman who had raised her. For all I know, you may end up having to find someone else—"

"Don't be ridiculous."

"I'm not. I'm just being realistic. We both know that there's still no guarantee that I'll be able to hold onto my place here in this century."

An unhappy silence fell in the wake of her words. Damien hugged Sarah reassuringly and kissed her cheek. "Somehow, my darling, we must find a way."

"I hope we can, Damien." She stared lovingly at the baby and fingered one of the tiny gifts. "And I hope that one day, when I'm very old, I'll use these three as the beginning of a cache of gifts I'll leave Elissa."

"Of course you will, darling," Damien said feelingly. "Why else would Elissa have given the gifts to you? And until then, I'll keep them secure for you in my safe."

"Yes, that's a good idea." As Sarah gently shifted the baby to her other breast, she bit her lip. "Damien, there's something I've been meaning to ask your about . . ."

"Yes, darling?"

She stared into his eyes and asked softly, "Did you finish Vincy's memoirs while I was gone?"

"Yes, I did."

"Did you tell everything?"

He sighed, but she could see the relief in his eyes. "Yes, I did."

"Are you ready to let him go now?"

Damien gazed at Sarah and the child adoringly. "I think I did let Vincy go, at last, while you were gone.

You see, my love for you and our child has left room in my heart for nothing else."

Sarah's own heart filled with joy. "I know just what you mean. Please, tell me all about it—I mean, how you let him go."

He smiled tenderly. "One afternoon while you were gone, I went to Vincy's grave and laid down some flowers. My burden seemed to lift in that moment."

"Oh, Damien," Sarah cried, feeling an electric chill at his words, "I did the very same thing with Brian." At his quizzical glance, she explained, "My parents invited me home to Atlanta for a memorial service marking his birthday. I felt I had to go, so I flew home to be with them. Anyway, after the service, I went to Brian's grave and laid down some flowers. I think I made my peace with him in that moment."

Damien's eyes gleamed with sudden insight. "I wonder if we went on the same day."

She continued excitedly, "I'm sure we did. Brian's memorial service was June 3rd, and I went to his grave late that afternoon."

"My God, Sarah, that was the very time I went to the grotto and let Vincy go."

They stared at each other for a long emotional moment, feeling closer to each other than ever before. Then Damien stroked Sarah's cheek and asked, "And what of your family in Atlanta? Was it difficult seeing them again?"

Sarah shook her head. "I'm glad I went home. It brought me full circle in a lot of ways. I was able to feel some peace about leaving them."

"Did you tell them where you were bound?"

"No. But I left a letter for them with a friend. Brenda promised that if I don't return in three months she'll mail the letter to my parents."

"What's in the letter?"

Sarah sighed. "The truth."

He looked alarmed. "Do you think that was wise?"

"I felt I owed them that much."

"But surely they'd have a difficult time believing—"

"I don't think so. You see, while I was back in the present, I found six of Vincy's paintings that I had restored."

"You did?" he asked incredulously.

"Yes. They were housed in a museum in New Orleans. In my letter, I asked my parents to go see the restored paintings as proof that I had actually lived in the past."

"Do you think the paintings will convince them?" he asked skeptically.

"I think so," she said. "You see, the paintings were logged into the museum in 1920, and my name was entered as the person who had restored them in the 1870's. I do know my parents will have a hard time dismissing my signature on the back of each panel."

He whistled. "I'd say you've presented them with pretty ironclad evidence. And I'm really glad that Vincy's paintings and your marvelous work on them will be shared with posterity."

Sarah nodded. "I know. But what about Vincy's memoirs? They should be shared with the world, too." Eagerly, she added, "May I read them now that they're finished?"

He laughed dryly. "I thought you already had."

"I would love to read them again."

He nodded. "Very well, then."

She touched his arm. "Damien, will you think about having them published?"

He was silent for a moment, then sighed. "I will. Maybe one of these times when I go to New Orleans on business, I'll see if I can find a publisher."

"You should contact a Mr. Henry Clark. He's the one who will publish them."

"So you've told me," he said ruefully.

"But there's no rush," she added. "The memoirs won't be published until 1876."

He shook his head. "Then we'll not want to change the natural order of things, will we, my love?"

At his words, Sarah glowed with happiness. "Oh, Damien, I can tell that now you truly have let Vincy go. You can speak of him without pain."

"Thanks to you, darling," Damien whispered and kissed her.

After Damien left, Sarah smiled down at the baby sleeping so peacefully in her arms, stroking Elissa's head with its crowning of downy blond hair. She felt both joy and sadness over Damien's visit—joy because he was ready to embrace his world again, sadness because ultimately it was she who held him back.

"Oh, Elissa," Sarah whispered to the sleeping baby, "I love you and your father with all my heart. But how can I let either of you remain prisoners of that love?"

Within a few weeks, Sarah had almost completely recovered from childbirth, and Elissa continued to thrive. Sarah spent her time caring for the baby, being with Damien and rereading Vincy's memoirs.

Yet as her strength returned, Sarah also felt the old restlessness grip her at being trapped in the house. Every time she looked out the front windows of the house at the world forbidden to her, frustration gnawed at her. Whenever she watched Damien ride off to town alone, the separation tore at her heart. She knew that soon the two of them must address the issue of their future here. Her visit back to the present had convinced her that Elissa *would* be grounded here in this century, that her child was meant to live here with Damien. But in so many ways, Sarah remained an outsider.

Once Sarah had recovered most of her strength, Damien moved them across the hallway into Olympia's old suite. Olympia's adjoining sewing room was quickly converted into a nursery. Damien refused to allow Sarah to participate in any of the actual physical labor, but she did enjoy overseeing the layout and decorating of the rooms.

On another level, Sarah felt saddened by the change, since she saw the move as a very final statement on Damien's part, a confirmation that he would never again welcome Olympia Fontaine back to live in their house. Of course, they did need the larger suite now, but Sarah continued to feel daunted by the estrangement between Damien and Olympia, especially since she was the cause.

She asked Damien about this one night as they sat on the bed in their new room, with the baby dozing between them. "Damien, about your aunt . . ."

"Yes?"

"Won't you at least let her come for a visit and see the baby?"

Damien frowned. "Didn't you tell me that Aunt Olympia never listed our marriage or even our child's birth in her family Bible?"

"Yes," she admitted in a small voice.

He scowl deepened. "I'll give it some thought," was all he would say before he turned back to the almanac he had been reading.

Sarah's spirits sank then, and she was certain a reconciliation between Olympia and Damien was out of the question.

However, to Sarah's pleasant surprise, a few days later Damien went into town and fetched his aunt out for a visit with Sarah and the baby. The visit was formal and brief, held in the downstairs parlor. Olympia greeted Sarah coolly, but she did seem charmed by the child. She even presented Elissa with a silver rattle. Sarah was pleased that Damien was at least making an effort with his aunt. She also realized that it was probably best that Olympia not live with them and that they keep their relationship with her fairly detached. After all, both Sarah and Damien were aware now that Olympia would never truly accept their marriage.

As the days passed and Sarah's health returned in full measure, the house continued to feel more and more oppressive to her. Of course, she took her comfort from Elissa, but even as the baby's mother, she just felt so limited. Simple pastimes that other mothers took for granted—such as taking their babies for strolls in their carriages, or rocking them to sleep on the front porch—were frustratingly forbidden to her. Elissa still slept much of the time, and Damien was increasingly occupied with plantation duties, leaving her with much time on her hands.

One afternoon, she paced her room for over an hour, unable to think of any way to amuse herself. Elissa was napping later than usual, and Damien was downstairs working on his accounts. She didn't want to disturb either of them, but today the restlessness was gripping her with maddening intensity.

At last, Sarah rang for Baptista, asking her to sit with the baby. Then she went downstairs and knocked on Damien's office door.

"Come in," he called out.

As she walked in, he stood and came to her side, embracing her warmly. "Hello, darling. Are you feeling all right? You look rather preoccupied."

"I'm feeling fine," she said. "Damien, we must talk."

"Very well, dear." He led her to the two side chairs along one wall. "What's on your mind?"

She gestured her frustration. "Don't you know?"

"You're growing restless again in the house, aren't you?" he asked kindly. "Perhaps we can think of some way to make things a bit more lively. Don't you think it's about time we plan our *fête?*"

She lowered her eyes. "Damien, that's not it."

He lifted her chin with his fingers, forcing her to meet his troubled gaze. "What then, darling?"

Tears welled in her eyes. "You know, Damien. It's not enough, what we have."

He looked wounded. "Sarah, how can you say that?"

She stood and began to pace. "I don't want to hurt you, but you know it's true. It's not enough for Elissa, having all of us trapped in this house together. Elissa deserves a mother who can go out in the world with her. If it's not me, then I must go and you must find the one you spoke of—the one who will take away all your pain."

In an instant, Damien was beside her, taking her in his arms. "You're the one I spoke of, Sarah," he said in a breaking voice.

Gathering every reserve of strength, Sarah replied, "If I am, then my love is not meant to trap you here."

He backed away, his expression anguished. "What are you saying?"

She caught a deep, steadying breath. "I'm saying I must go out that door again tomorrow."

"No!" he cried, his eyes wild with fear.

Sarah was fighting tears now, but she refused to back down. Clenching her fists, she said, "Damien, it's the only way. I can't sentence you and Elissa to prison for the rest of your lives. If I can't be free, then I must free the two of you."

He gestured in entreaty. "Sarah, no. Say you won't do this crazy thing."

"I must," she said miserably.

He looked crestfallen. "There's nothing I can say or do to change your mind?"

She shook her head. "No, I'm afraid there's nothing."

He turned away and began to pace, his features agitated. "You know I could stop you—by force, if necessary."

"How could you make me more of a prisoner than I already am?"

He turned to her, and at once she regretted her words as she glimpsed the hurt in his eyes. "Is that how you feel? That my love has trapped you?"

"No, Damien," she said passionately. "Your love is the only freedom I've known here. It's my love that is imprisoning you—and Elissa—and that I can't bear."

He shook his head and whispered, "Do you realize that if you walk out that door, we may never see each other again?"

Sarah stepped forward eagerly. "There's another

possibility, Damien. Madame Tu said that if I had Elissa in the past, I might become grounded here."

"And you're willing to risk that?"

She sighed. "Oh, darling, think of it from a practical standpoint. I can't go to a church to see Elissa christened. I can't watch her at school or at play with her friends."

"I'll take care of those things, Sarah. It's enough that she has you here."

She hung her head and whispered brokenly, "It's not enough."

"Oh, Sarah." He drew closer, grasping her by the shoulders. "If you must go through with this, then I must add a condition."

"Yes?" Her anguished eyes met his.

"We must go through it together this time—you, me, and the baby."

"Damien, no—"

He pressed his fingers to her lips. "My only hope at this point is that if Elissa and I are with you, our love will be strong enough to hold you."

"But you or she could be hurt."

"No, darling. The barrier has never harmed you. We'll be safe."

Sarah felt miserably torn. "I wish you wouldn't ask this of me."

In a quiet but deadly serious voice, he replied, "Either Elissa and I come with you this time, or I swear, Sarah, I'll stop you. Somehow, I'll find a way."

"All right," Sarah said at last. "But you hold the baby when we go."

"So be it," Damien said. "But you hold my hand."

Late that night, as Sarah and Damien prepared for bed, a cloud of anxiety seemed to hang in the air

436

between them. When the last garment had been hung up, the last shoe put away, they stared at each other in anguish. Then, simultaneously, they rushed into each others' arms. They clung to each other like two drowning people, kissing feverishly.

"Darling, make love to me tonight," Sarah said breathlessly.

Damien looked down at her in joy, then concern drifted in. He stroked her hair tenderly. "Are you sure it's not too soon?"

"No. It's been over six weeks since Elissa was born. I'm healed now."

"Oh, darling." He drew her closer, caressing her back through her handkerchief linen gown. "I'm so happy I'll be able to hold you tonight. I just hope—"

He didn't have to finish his sentence. Both of them mentally added, *that it won't be our last time.*

While Sarah went to recline on the bed, Damien lit candles on the nightstands and blew out the lamps. Then he doffed his dressing gown and joined her. He feasted his eyes on her, drinking in her gorgeous long blond hair, her womanly figure, which was slightly fuller now and adorably enticing. He drew off her nightgown and ran his gaze over her shapely long legs, her lovely breasts and the enchanting cleft of her femininity. His heart caught in his throat at the thought of losing this woman who was his very life, his soul now. He worshipped her with both his heart and his eyes.

Even as Damien's heated perusal made Sarah break out in gooseflesh, she in turn feasted her eyes on his glorious nakedness, outlined by the flickering candles. His body was bronzed and magnificently muscled, his hair jet black and shining softly. His eyes were beautifully dark, brimming over with love, sadness and desire. She gazed over the chiseled planes of his face, memorizing each curve and contour. The thought that she might never again lie with him thus or know his sweet love was unbearable. And knowing that she was doing the right thing was little comfort to her now, as she faced the prospect of losing both him and Elissa.

With an inarticulate cry, Sarah pressed her body into his, clinging tightly to his neck. His warm, hard nakedness felt heavenly against her soft, pliant flesh, especially after their last separation and the long weeks of necessary abstinence. His male scent was the most potent aphrodisiac to her ravenous senses, making her pulses pound and her breathing grow rapid and shallow.

As their eyes locked with tumultuous emotion, Sarah knew that Damien shared her every thought and fear tonight. His kiss confirmed this, as his lips captured hers with rough, raw hunger. In this, as in everything, they were soul mates.

Sarah clung to Damien, loving the bold thrust of his tongue in her mouth, running her fingertips over the strong muscles of his back and glorying in the raspy sound of his breathing. He worshiped her body with his lips, kissing her face and neck, lingering lovingly over her breasts, so full with milk. She cried out at the unbearably erotic stimulation, thrusting herself forward to take his lips greedily.

As their desire intensified, Damien's fingers slipped boldly between her thighs, teasing and tormenting her, preparing her. Sarah writhed in ecstasy, reaching for his swollen manhood, stroking him provocatively.

Damien groaned in agonized pleasure. A moment later, he positioned himself above her, entering her slowly and exquisitely. Sarah cried out in rapture at the hard, splendid pressure, tossing her head on the pillow. He caught her chin in his hand and kissed her desperately, grinding his mouth into hers. She could feel the wetness of his tears on her cheek as his lips swallowed her moans.

Sarah was enraptured. She had almost forgotten the sweet agony of lovemaking—the wondrous piercing heat of him, how full and possessed he could make her feel, how in this magical dimension all was sharing, all was pleasure.

Damien tried his best to be gentle, yet Sarah's desire knew no bounds. She arched against him sensuously, taking him deeply into herself, as if she would demand to bear his imprint forever. His restraint broke, then, and he rolled over and brought her astride him. Sarah went wild as Damien grasped her breasts in his hands and surged high into her womanhood; the look in his eyes was so intense, so raw with hunger, that it took her breath away.

They rocked there with sweet desperation, devouring each other, each knowing that tomorrow time might tear them apart forever. Tonight, nothing could separate them. Together they transcended their own mystical barrier, whispering words of love, their eyes locked. Then Sarah cried out and Damien lurched upright, locking her deeply in his lap. Sarah felt herself melting, cleaving to him. Never had she felt so at one with him, so totally exposed to his love. The feeling was so intense that she clung to him, trembling and tearful.

A moment later, they fell across the mattress, both breathing hard, still entwined. Damien kissed Sarah's wet cheek and whispered vehemently, "You're mine, Sarah. Remember that always. Nothing—not even time—can destroy our love."

* * *

The next morning when they stirred, they both gazed in anguish at the first, rosy rays of the sun, just creeping across the rug. Each privately wondered if this dawn would be a beginning or an ending.

Damien caught Sarah close and whispered poignantly, "My love, please, don't leave me."

She stared up at him through her tears. "Damien, this is the hardest thing I've ever done. Please don't make it harder."

He kissed her quickly and possessively. "You could make it very simple. Just stay."

She gestured in pain and frustration. "Damien, please! I'm doing this for you and Elissa."

"Then why is it I feel no surge of gladness at your departure?" he asked with sudden bitterness.

Elissa's lusty cry from the nursery cut their argument short. Damien went to change the baby and brought her to her mother. He watched in silent torment as Sarah nursed Elissa.

Sarah's very heart was breaking as she held her baby close and felt her nourishing milk flow into Elissa's tiny, perfect body. She felt a deep, abiding bond with her child, a bond that might be ripped asunder this very day. Now, she feasted her eyes on her beautiful child, at Elissa's rosy skin and adorable features. She drank deeply of the baby's sweet scent, praying that this would not be the last time she held her child. Was she doing the right thing? Could she bear to leave this cherished child of her body, this beautiful manifestation of hers and Damien's love?

Still, in her heart, Sarah knew she had made the only choice. There would be no destiny, no freedom for any of them as long as her limitations kept them all trapped here in this house.

As Elissa finished nursing and fell asleep against

440

her mother's breast, Sarah leaned over and kissed her heavenly soft cheek. "Remember me, my darling Elissa," she whispered. "Remember that I'm your mother."

"Finished, dear?" Damien asked hoarsely.

Sarah looked up to see him, now dressed, standing by the bed. She nodded. "Will you hold her while I dress?"

"Of course." He took the baby gently. His eyes held a terrible anxiety. "I don't want us to argue this morning, Sarah. I just don't want to lose you."

"I know," she said as she rose. She glanced with wrenching anguish at the baby in his arms. Her voice broke as she added, "You'll get her a wet nurse—that is, if I don't . . ."

"Yes," he said raggedly. His gaze was haunted, pain-filled. "If you return to the present, won't you at least come back to visit us?"

She shook her head resignedly. "I can't."

"Sarah, please—"

"If I can't be with you, I must leave you free to pursue your own happiness."

"There is no happiness for me without you."

"Damien, don't say that. You must at least try for Elissa's sake."

He couldn't answer her. He continued to hold the baby tightly and watch her with tortured eyes as she dressed.

Once Sarah was ready, no further words were necessary. Her eyes said it all—how much she loved Damien and the baby, how much she hoped to be able to stay here with them. His eyes were filled with a yearning every bit as intense and desperate as her own. Sarah walked toward the door, and Damien followed her with the baby.

In the downstairs hallway, Sarah turned and

embraced them both one last time. Tears streamed down her cheeks as she kissed first the sleeping child, then Damien. "Say you understand, my darling," she whispered desperately to Damien. "Please say you understand."

"I do," he replied in a breaking voice. The pain in his eyes tore into her soul as he added, "I don't want you to do this, Sarah, but I do understand. I've found my freedom now, and I'm giving you yours, my love, whatever that means."

Sarah nodded, not trusting herself to say another word. She turned and continued on toward the door, her heart pounding harder with each step. She could feel the ominous barrier bombarding her as she drew ever closer to the front walls of the house. She didn't dare stop or look back at Damien, or she knew she would lose her nerve.

She was reaching for the doorknob when Damien's ragged voice stopped her. "Wait, Sarah. You must hold my hand."

She turned to him, and their eyes locked in a moment of infinite despair and love. He held the sleeping baby securely in one arm, while she grasped his free hand and felt his warm strength flowing into her fingers.

Sarah opened the door and inched forward into the portal. The energy was battering her now, but she didn't dare retreat. Taking a deep breath, she stepped out onto the porch.

For a moment, Sarah felt herself wavering between two ages, being tugged in two directions at once. *Believe*, she told herself, clinging desperately to Damien's hand. *Believe, and let Damien's love hold you.*

She heard him calling her name brokenly as the

442

powerful waves continued to batter her. She clung to him like a woman caught in a whirlpool and felt herself almost slip away.

Then suddenly, miraculously, it was over. All was stillness; all was peace. Sarah blinked to gain her senses. She stood with Damien and her child in the full brightness of dawn, sheltered on the porch, awash in the sweetest morning time had ever known.

Sarah looked about incredulously. The floorboards of the porch were stable beneath her feet. A tree fluttered nearby, bees buzzed at the sweet-smelling flowers, and somewhere close, a mourning dove was cooing, the dearest sound she had ever heard.

The window in time was gone forever. How she knew this, Sarah wasn't sure. But she *knew*.

She turned to Damien with her heart overflowing with joy and saw the tears of exultation in his own eyes. "Damien, I'm back! I'm truly back this time!"

"Oh, Sarah! Thank God!"

Damien embraced her gently, being mindful of the sleeping babe nestled between them. Their tears mingled as they kissed each other tenderly.

"Madame Tu was right," Sarah whispered. "Having Elissa here must have grounded me in the past. Oh, Damien, my darling, we *were* able to invert the hourglass. At last I'm here to stay."

Damien looked down at her with the triumphant eyes of a man who had just been born again. "I love you so much, Sarah. And though I had my doubts, somehow I knew that my love—and Elissa's—would be strong enough to hold you."

"Oh, Damien, I love you, too."

Elissa awakened then and smiled toothlessly up at

her parents. For the first time, Sarah saw the tiny brown flecks forming in the infant's beautiful eyes. "Oh, Damien, look! Already, Elissa has your eyes."

The three stood joyously huddled on the porch. The house was no longer their prison, but their haven. They looked to the horizon, to the bright dawning of their future together.

Dear Reader:

I can't believe how much has happened in my life and career since *A Tryst in Time* was first published in 1992. My question posed to readers then—"Should I write more time-travel romances?"—brought me thousands of enthusiastic fan letters urging me to continue writing this type of story. I can't begin to describe how heartwarming and touching so many of those letters were. And I'm proud to say I've now published eight time-travel novels in all—and Dorchester Publishing is reissuing *A Tryst in Time* for the second time with this volume!

During this same period, I've watched my daughters grow up and get married, and my first grandchild be born. My readers have shared all these triumphs with me, and have faithfully supported my career. Thank you all so much!

If you enjoyed *A Tryst in Time,* you shouldn't miss my *Embers of Time* (Love Spell; December 2000), a book that shares many of the same mystical and emotional qualities. And I've penned four other time-travel romances for Love Spell: *Bushwhacked Bride* (a Wink & A Kiss Romance); *Tempest in Time* (a Timeswept Romance); "The Confused Stork" (novella) in the *New Year's Babies* anthology; and "The Ghost of Christmas Past" (novella) in *A Time-Travel Christmas* anthology.

Two more of my releases are: *Lovers and Other Lunatics* (Love Spell; April 2000), my zany and adventurous contemporary romance set in Galveston, Texas; and my novella "Night and Day," in the *Strangers in the Night* anthology (Leisure Books; September 2000), a collection of nostalgic love stories set in the 1940s.

Hope you'll order all of my available titles from Love Spell and Leisure Books, or your local bookseller.

Thanks again for your support and encouragement. I welcome your feedback on all my projects. You can reach me via e-mail at eugenia@eugeniariley.com, visit my website at www.eugeniariley.com, or write to me at the address listed below (SASE appreciated for a reply; free bookmark and newsletter available):

Eugenia Riley

P.O. Box 840526
Houston, TX 77284-0526

Lovers and Other Lunatics — Eugenia Riley

Get Ready for . . . The Time of Your Life!

Teresa Phelps has heard of being crazy in love. But Charles Everett seems just plain mad. Her handsome kidnapper unnerves her with his charm and flabbergasts her with his accusations. He acts under the misguided belief that she holds the key to finding buried treasure. But all Tess feels she can unearth is one oddball after another.

While Charles' actions resemble those of a lunatic, his body arouses thoughts of a lover. And while Charles helps to fend off her dastardly and dangerous pursuers, Tess wonders if he has her best interests at heart—or is she just a pawn in his quest for riches? As the madcap misadventures ensue, Tess strives to dig up the truth. Who is the enigmatic Englishman? What is he after? And most important, in the hunt for hidden riches is the ultimate prize true love?

___52371-X $5.99 US/$6.99 CAN